Travels with
Dubinsky and Clive

David
Gurewich

Travels with
Dubinsky
and Clive

Viking

VIKING
Viking Penguin Inc., 40 West 23rd Street,
New York, New York 10010, U.S.A.
Penguin Books Ltd, Harmondsworth,
Middlesex, England
Penguin Books Australia Ltd, Ringwood,
Victoria, Australia
Penguin Books Canada Limited, 2801 John Street,
Markham, Ontario, Canada L3R 1B4
Penguin Books (N.Z.) Ltd, 182–190 Wairau Road,
Auckland 10, New Zealand

First published in 1987 by Viking Penguin Inc.
Published simultaneously in Canada

LIBRARY OF CONGRESS CATALOGING IN PUBLICATION DATA
Gurewich, David.
Travels with Dubinsky and Clive.
I. Title.
PS3557.U74T7   1987   813'.54   86-40498
ISBN 0-670-81621-3

Printed in the United States of America by
The Book Press, Brattleboro, Vermont
Set in Aster

To my son Ilya

Acknowledgments

The author wishes to express gratitude to his friends, especially Pat Mulcahy and Mike Johnson, as well as Donald, Gila, Irene, and Stephen, whose loyalty and superhuman patience made this book possible. Also the Yaddo colony, whose hospitality was indispensable.

Travels with
Dubinsky and Clive

One

The dream recurs regularly.

Dubinsky stands in front of a bleakly lit airline schedule, looking for his flight. Not only is the schedule hard to understand, but he is also unsure about his destination. It looks like Munich, but, according to the schedule, the only flight to Munich originates in Vladivostok on the fourteenth of the month, with the exception of December in leap years. In order to go to Vladivostok, he would have to fly to Novosibirsk (a flight every Monday), then change for a train (a three-day journey). . . . He realizes that the only Monday three days before the fourteenth falls on the seventh, which, according to the small print, is a vacation day for the airline. Besides, what if his destination is not Munich? What if it is Christchurch, New Zealand? The complexity of the modern world baffles him; he panics, realizing that he has only thirty seconds left before he will have to step down for the next person in line. He rushes to the ticket window and asks for a bus ticket to Reykjavik. "Sold out," the woman says. "Besides, you've got no pants on." He reaches below the waist. She's right. The militiaman is coming in his direction, about to arrest him for indecent exposure. Followed by whistles and sirens, he streaks to the end of the dark tunnel and opens the door; the driver asks for his ticket. Dubinsky shakes his head. The driver shuts the door, laughing. The bus pulls out. Dubinsky stands frozen in the dark of the tunnel, listening to the heavy steps of the approaching militiaman.

Dubinsky slept late again. The line had already formed outside the bathroom of his communal apartment.

Unwashed, unshaven, and constipated, he slipped out of the house into another January morning. Shivering in the wind, he crossed the paths of numerous black cats and walked under as many ladders on his five-block trek to the subway. Inside the train, swaying with the tightly packed mass of his fellow straphangers, he thought his usual early morning thoughts about the unfairness of life. His breath, unaided by toothpaste, stank, and his body, still covered by dried sticky cold sweat from the dream, did too; but so did those of his fellow passengers, so why worry?

In the bleak light of the same January morning, Dubinsky trundled on toward his place of employment, an impressive-looking pre-Revolutionary building with a sign that read INSTITUTE OF STUDIES OF AFRO-ASIAN PROLETARIAN MOVEMENTS.

Downstairs, he surrendered his coat to Aunt Dusya, the cloakroom attendant. Instead of hurrying off, she stared at him wordlessly.

He checked his fly. "Something wrong?"

"God bless you, child," said Aunt Dusya, her lips trembling.

As he climbed the stairs, wondering if Aunt Dusya had seen his dream, too, he bumped into Gribokhuyev from the Iran section and smiled politely. The brain-twisting differences between Majahedeen factions drove Grib to despair, and everyone knew that he had a secret urge to surrender his job (and his Party card with it). His wife had already left him, and his son was being expelled from school after school for continuous attempts to take faculty members hostage. Today, Grib's expression of horror was so profound as to stop Dubinsky in his tracks.

"What happened, Kolya?" Dubinsky asked. "Khomeini nuked Baghdad?"

"You haven't heard the news?"

"N-no."

Grib patted Dubinsky on the shoulder and hurried off. In the next few minutes, Dubinsky ran into more fellow researchers who shook his hand and slapped him on the back. Shrugging, he accepted their condolences and thanked them for their feelings. He felt ready for the worst, although he did not know what it was. He walked into his boss's office and shut the door quietly. Comrade Borzoi was slouched in the chair, and his head lay on the desk face down. Dubinsky tiptoed to the desk and quietly inspected it for traces of blood. He would not dare touch his boss's head. It would have been sacrilegious to touch the head of a legend who had personally supervised the training of Patrice Lumumba and survived two weeks in a Katanga jail. Dubinsky tiptoed back to the chair, sat down, and put his head in his hands, projecting profound gloom, still in the dark about its nature. A change of guard in the Kremlin? He searched for an answer. No, the subway was still running. The Moscow Dynamoes lost the ice hockey cup? But why pity him, who never cared?

Finally Borzoi rose, sighed, and came over to Dubinsky's chair; Dubinsky rose, too, instinctively, and was smothered in Borzoi's hug.

"Be brave, Oleg," Borzoi said. "It's a hard blow, but you have to take it like a man. Sit down."

Dubinsky followed the order.

"On no account must what you're about to hear leave this room," said Comrade Borzoi, every capillary in his purple nose straining to burst out.

"Of course," Dubinsky said in the manliest voice he could manage.

"It's Pizdo," Comrade Borzoi said. "Bad news, Oleg."

Dubinsky pushed his chin forward, thereby demonstrating his readiness to accept the bad news in a manly fashion.

"A coup d'état, Oleg. Concocted by the CIA, Mossad, and South African mercenaries. Streams of blood flow into the Zayebis-ka River. Schools have been set afire. Socialist co-ops, ransacked. The best minds of the country have lost their heads. And, Oleg,"—Comrade Borzoi laid his hand paternally on Dubinsky's shoulder—"this includes our friends and your classmates. Gabishev, Fogilev, Manankov, Sokolov, Hasanov. All dead. The reactionary chieftains on the CIA payroll have committed the unthinkable, Oleg. The bodies of our comrades. Their navels have been removed and dropped into the backyard of the Swiss Embassy in a brown paper bag. They are being sorted out now. Official interment on Monday. Twenty-one-gun salute." Comrade Borzoi picked up his otter hat from the rack, assumed the pose of Lenin at the Finland Station, and went into a chant: "Comrades, you're gone, but not forgotten. Your cause will live. Progressive Africa and especially the nation of Pizdo, with its uranium and pizdorvanium deposits and strategic Indian Ocean location, will revenge the sadistic deed, committed by corrupt imperialist lackeys. Progressive mankind—"

Dubinsky did not hear the rest of the speech. He stumbled out into the stuffy, smoky hallway, and, his eyes closed, proceeded to the bathroom. He threw up, and then splashed cold water on his face. His eyes were bulging out. He felt like a useless heap of scrap. He collapsed on the seat and groaned.

Gabishev, Fogilev, Manakov, Sokolov, Hasanov. Five years in the same study group. Never bosom buddies, still. . . . The farewell party. It was like yesterday. Sokolov's wedding ring they had sold to pay their way out of the drunk tank. Hasanov's father's car they had wrecked on the way from Manankov's parents' dacha. How happy they were to have been drafted and, after a three-month course, sent to Africa. What a laugh they had at the party over their papers: Sokolov, agriculture expert; Gabishev, paramedic; Hasanov, civil engineer. How much they had looked forward to their well-earned co-ops and Zhiguli sedans upon their return. Dubinsky would have benefited, too—he felt his face flush, and his body shrink in deep shame. How dare he regret all the new Levi's he would never wear and Deep Purple records he would never play. When all that was left of his class of '75 was five navels.

Trembling uncontrollably, Dubinsky broke down in tears, his nose running, his hands gripping the door handle (out of habit, since the door locks were broken). And one release was followed by the other, as his bowels shook and discharged themselves with a sound that completely drowned out his weeping. He was regular again.

As he washed his face, Grib walked in, a Camel dangling between his meaty lips. "So what are you going to do now?"

"Just . . . go on living, I guess," Dubinsky muttered, slowly retrieving his manliness.

"On what?" Grib inquired sarcastically.

Dubinsky's knees shook, and an invisible force stuck a blade in his stomach and turned it violently.

Back in the stall, thrashing about in the convulsions of diarrhea, he realized the true meaning of the sympathy in his colleagues' faces. The People's Republic of Pizdo had gone bust. And his Ph.D. dissertation, The Historical Role of the Communist Revolutionary Assembly of Pizdo in the Transition of the Pizdoan Society from Slavery to Communism, went bust with it. Down the drain.

Dubinsky's choice of a job, like most other college graduates', had been determined not so much by what he wanted to do (in lieu of promenading along the Champs-Elysées, he would settle for late-night dinners with wine and friends, reading in bed until noon, and attending film screenings in the afternoon), as by the direction in which his connections were concentrated. When a friend's friend lobbied Dubinsky's case at the Afro-Asian Proletarian Movement Institute, he considered himself lucky, for he was intelligent enough to realize that at an institution thus titled, he would be able to get away with doing as little as possible, and to use the remaining time to pursue paperbacks, rock records, and pretty girls. The job had lived up to his expectations, and now it was gone. He was out on his ass.

"Take the rest of the day off," said Borzoi thoughtfully. "I'm sure you have a lot to think about. It's really too bad about your thesis, Oleg. But you must understand how inappropriate it would be to defend it right now. I suppose you'll have to consider the possibility of retraining."

"In what?" Dubinsky moaned. "Pizdo has a weird language that goes back to Sanskrit. The brief Norwegian colonization has rendered its culture totally unique. Its social makeup is half Viking, half Samoan, with nascent proletariat—"

"I understand," Comrade Borzoi waved impatiently. None of this Samoan stuff could compensate for the lack of a cadre well-versed in the use of explosives. "Like I said, give it some thought. Nobody's throwing you out on the street."

"But I am the only expert on Pizdo alive," Dubinsky murmured. "Surely there must be something . . ."

"Comrade Dubinsky." Borzoi's voice hardened. "The situation has changed. There is no need for open research in Pizdo right now, and there won't be for some time. For the kind of research we're going to be concentrating on right now, one needs a clearance, Comrade Dubinsky."

"I thought after working here for all this time—"

"It's not up to me, Dubinsky. Now"—Borzoi lowered his voice, for such things were not discussed in the open—"if your name was, uh, *Petrov*—"

"I get it."

"I knew you would."

If my name were Petrov, I would be a Russian.

If I were a Russian, I would have a clearance.

If I had a clearance, I would have been sent to Pizdo.

If I had been sent to Pizdo, I would be dead by now.

And my navel would receive a twenty-one-gun salute on Monday.

As Dubinsky strolled down Yauza Boulevard toward the river, his mind went back to his job interview two years earlier. The personnel director had accepted his application with an air of gloom. As he was leaving the office, he overheard the official complain on the phone: "This is absolutely the last Point Five I'm taking. We're way over quota as it is!"

Point Five, in Soviet internal passports, indicates nationality. By now Dubinsky was old enough to realize that it was his Jewishness that upset the official and, had it not been for his friend's friend's lobbying, he never would have gotten the job. In retrospect, he wished he had reminded the fat retired KGB officer (all personnel directors are retired KGB officers) that the aged Grandpa Dubinsky had served in the Red Cavalry under Marshal Budyonny himself, and in a similar situation would not have thought twice about splitting the bastard's skull open wide enough to plant a cabbage in it. But Dubinsky was simply not a confrontational, door-slamming kind. He left quietly. And now? His mind wandered in several directions at once, none well defined. "Retrain"? As what? Neurosurgeon? No medical school will accept another Dubinsky. Stonecutter? With his physique he would be finished in a month. Computer programmer? Blah. Not only did he feel no special inclination toward a dazzling career in any of these fields, he also suspected that they would take up all of his time, leaving no space for his extracurricular endeavors.

We never care about what we have until we lose it—the more banal, the more true—he reflected sourly, dialing Nonna's number. Nonna would know what to do. She would open her arms, she would let him kiss her birthmark between her large breasts, she would let her hair loose, she would softly stroke his balls with her knee, and pinch him when she came.

"Where the hell are you?" she asked abruptly. "I tried to call you."

"Don't talk to me like that," Dubinsky murmured. "I'm suicidal, my life is finished . . . can we have lunch? At your place? I'm in desperate need of comfort, I haven't seen you for three weeks, I can't wait until tonight—"

"Actually, we do have to talk, Dubinsky," Nonna said in a voice that she generally used for telling her athletes that blueberry yogurt was not available. As an interpreter at the Sports Committee, she frequently accompanied groups of foreign athletes to various events out of town. "But not at my place. Come to the office."

On his way there, Dubinsky bought *Pravda* and scanned its foreign news section. Just as he had suspected, not a word on Pizdo. The general line was still in the development stage. It was tangent to so many factors: Do we want to include the CIA along with Zionist South African mercenaries, who were always fair game? Do we want to present the coup as a final blow to détente? Do we need to point an angry finger at Zaire? Somali? China? Do we have any links to the new government, and, on an outside chance that we do (and the Yanks don't), do we want to congratulate them on the revolutionary victory and express hopes for future cooperation in the name of progress, navels or no navels? And why did Nonna sound so remote? Does it ever rain? Or always pour?

He shivered under the combined effects of his thoughts and the chilly wet wind. The sky was overcast, and the wind-chill factor was rising. Must be the nuclear bomb-tests, he thought, and, desperately trying to find comfort in life, pictured the torrential rains of Pizdo: *better alive and cold than hot and dead.*

Nonna flitted out of the Sports Committee like an exotic bird out of a cage. When Dubinsky saw her, tall, dark, and vivacious, wearing a bright orange-and-white woolen hat with a matching scarf over her casually unbuttoned sheepskin coat, his heart sank. What have I done to displease her? What amends can I offer? He had already knelt in a puddle, begging forgiveness, when he had failed to procure tickets for the Elton John concert. His mouth grew dry as she turned her lips away. What was it this time? She could not possibly know about the upset with his thesis.

"You know me, Oleg," she said firmly. "I'm not one to beat around the bush." They were the only customers in a dismal-looking cafeteria with coffee and tea spills on the Formica tops. "And I don't want you to take any of this personally.

You're a very nice boy, and we've had a lot of fun together."

The cooks were screaming bloody murder at each other in the kitchen. A mop flew out and landed on the cash register. A yawning counter lady in a soiled white smock picked it up and went to the back to join the melee.

Grabbing the sides of the table, his stomach queasy again, Dubinsky waited for the blow to come.

"I'm going to get married," she said coolly. "He's a wonderful man, and not very bright on top of that."

"Who is he?" Dubinsky whispered in what he hoped sounded like a hiss. "I'll kill him. And you. And myself."

"You couldn't hurt a fly, my dear," she laughed. "That's why I feel perfectly safe sitting here and telling you this. Olezhka—"

He shuddered at her use of the diminutive form.

"—I really like you. But I have to think about my own life, too. What the hell, I'm not getting any younger. Have you ever thought about how much older I am than you are?"

"Please. A year should make so much difference that you go off and marry some clown."

"It's three years, Olezhka. I lied to you—a little. I'm twenty-seven, my dear. Time to pause and think about the future."

If she lied to him about her age, she must have lied—Dubinsky slapped the table. "Goddamn it, you're the one who's always avoided the subject. You're the one who was always afraid the fun would be gone—" Thank God she did. *Oof.* Three years older.

"Of course I did. Being married to a Ph.D. in Poli Sci, some fun."

Even more fun now that I won't have it.

"Oleg, let's behave like adults. I don't cherish the idea of working with all those weight-lifting mongoloids till retirement. I need a home, not a room in a communal apartment."

She crushed her butt slowly, and he watched her long red Lancome-polished nails, mesmerized. Nobody had classier nails. Nobody had classier hands. Nobody had a classier figure or classier fake designer clothes or a classier walk or a classier way of lighting a cigarette or a classier way of cutting people down to size or of complimenting them or of whispering things in his ear in everybody's view about the things they would be doing an hour later. Nobody.

Through the steam rising from the borscht and pelmeni in the back, he heard:

"—he only drives a tour bus, but he has his own house just outside Copenhagen, he showed me pictures, he adores me, I don't blame him, with a mug like his what could he count on—"

Nonna's going to Denmark, he realized, sensing a dull pain starting in the back of his head. Should he cry and whimper and tell her that she's been appointed by the Fates to deliver the final blow? Count on her sympathy—her charity—her generosity? Never. You're so far down, it doesn't make one bit of difference to you, a voice whispered. Kill the bitch, another said, or at least throw some hot coffee in her face. I'll miss, he said, and it would be her baby-blue angora sweater that would get the coffee. It's unfair to the angora sweater. *You couldn't hurt a fly.* He had politely closed the door when the personnel chief mentioned Point Five; nor did he slam it when Borzoi suggested "retraining"; and now, too, he is rising in slow motion from the table, collecting his cigarettes, and heading for the door at a cruising speed of ten feet per hour. In his mind's eye he sees her convulse in sobs behind his back, unable to contain her desire to live outside Copenhagen, unable to run out and call his name; in his eye's mind he knows she is relieved. And so he opens the tough, poorly oiled door, which gives a plaintive screech, and walks away. No slamming. The door is not to blame.

"See, you got it right there," said Znachar. "You never slammed the door on anybody in your life."

"I never saw any point in it," Dubinsky shrugged. "It's all just so much noise. And headache."

"It's a small price to pay for the release of your aggressions," Znachar persisted.

"Znachar is right," Vladimir nodded grimly. "Besides, humans need noise. It's a proven fact. Trainloads of hicks descend on our bustling metropolis daily from every corner of our Celestial Empire. Presumably, they are seeking canned goods and raincoats and vacuum cleaners, which, as our dissidents falsely claim, are unavailable thirty miles outside Moscow. But! A man lives not by bread alone, as the Jew said. And therefore, the reason they come here is to experience the rumbling trucks and jackhammers and streetcars and loud music—noise, gentlemen, and nothing else. *Vive le bruit!*" He raised his glass.

It was close to midnight, and a pleasant buzz hovered over the group. They knew one another so well that they could enjoy a brief silence and sneak a look at Dubinsky: "There but for the grace of God . . ." I won't get much sober advice here, he thought in despair.

Znachar broke the silence. "In the beginning, there was Oleg's childhood. Try to remember as much as you can. Especially the stuff you don't want to remember."

"I'm sorry to disappoint you," Dubinsky said tartly. "But it was perfectly ordinary."

Indeed.

Oleg Dubinsky was as normal a Soviet young man as they come. He was a good student at school, not at the top of his class, but comfortably close. Not a superachiever, not a bookworm—just your moderately intelligent, mildly skeptical young man, with pleasant features and curly hair. He played a lot of volleyball, although his spiking was never too vicious, and wrote a little poetry, which was bad enough to melt a few hearts.

"Totally unsatisfactory," Znachar frowned. "No sex dreams about your mother, no castration fears, no peeks at your parents screwing. Total repression. Volleyball is a profoundly non-Freudian activity."

"And the rest is even more ordinary," Dubinsky admitted. In college, his choice—like most other young men's and women's—was determined not so much by what he wanted to do (play more volleyball and neck until dawn on a park bench) as by his parents' set of acquaintances. It so happened that his grandfather, a Party member since 1917, had a friend on the faculty of the Modern Languages School. Dubinsky's English was decent, although slightly esoteric. Besides firmly knowing the difference between "straight leg" and "bell bottom," he knew about "Maxwell's Silver Hammer" and "counting the cars on the New Jersey Turnpike," although "eclipse of both sun and moon" befuddled him considerably. Apart from that, Modern Language School had a ring to it; it was cool; it was hip; it sounded like a place where people would know that Deep Purple is not just a color. Unfortunately, Grandfather's friend expired before Dubinsky completed his freshman year, and so, to his disappointment, he was assigned Pizdoan as the second language. He would have preferred Dutch (Amsterdam had a reputation as a cool place) or Italian (ah, Sophia Loren; oh, Ornella Muti). In comparison, Pizdoan sounded as boring as the steppe. But Dubinsky was growing up, and getting more pragmatic. By graduation time he was not mystified by the fact that names like Dubinsky or Znachar did not show on the lists of those recommended to work abroad. He realized there was something different about him and Znachar; he was just not quite sure what it was.

"The fatal realization of your Jewishness." Znachar sighed. "How true, how true. Witness the diabolical way the social issues intrude upon the already heavy personal complexes. Ah, the sublimation of it all."

"Well, Pizdo still brought me a good job," Dubinsky said defensively. "English speakers are a dime a dozen. All with Russian names, too. It was a good job, you bastards." He sniffled. "I want my job back."

"Now, now." Znachar patted him on the back. "Take this." He handed Dubinsky a pill. "As a scientist and a pharmacologist, I don't think you should take it, not with booze. As a clandestine disciple of Dr. Freud, I think you should give yourself a little slack. The hell with the rules." He looked them over, expecting approval. None came. "Maybe I have problems, too," he muttered, loosening his belt and letting his growing paunch heave freely.

Znachar had just defended his Ph.D. on the superiority of scientific Marxist-Leninist treatment of excessive perspiration over the capitalist exploitative sweatshop methods. Like every honest Soviet intellectual, he knew his thesis to be total crap which would guarantee him lifelong employment, a co-op, a car, and others of life's little comforts. In the underground, he was something of a star for his spirited defense of Freud from revisionists. He realized perfectly well, however, that his secret espousal of the idealistic science of psychoanalysis might lead to serious trouble, and spent a great deal of his time analyzing himself and trying to rid himself of this dangerous addiction. He hoped fervently to achieve a breakthrough before his colleagues discovered the disease.

Vladimir downed his glass and bit into lemon. "*Uccch.* Forget about your old job, Dubinsky. You're not getting it back. We have to think up something cozy for you," he concluded somewhat disingenuously, watching his friends follow the leader and down their glasses.

Vladimir himself felt plenty cozy. A senior researcher at the Ethnography Institute. The author of an illustrious Ph.D. dissertation on Marxism-Leninism as the Pivotal Force in Newly Emergent Ethnocultures of Northern Siberia. He had single-handedly put the Chichmek tribe on the map, somewhere just above the Arctic Circle. First he dressed his friends in deer hides; then he had a Mosfilm Studio makeup artist render their features vaguely Asiatic. Then he built an igloo on another friend's dacha. Then he handed them utensils he had borrowed from the Academy's Ethnographic Museum; and, finally, he took their pictures. He invented the Chichmek language and transcribed it into Russian and, inspired by "Strawberry Fields Forever," retaped Brezhnev's speeches—backwards. The result was presented as a sample of Chichmek dialogue. He had Dubinsky translate Pizdo myths to create Chichmek folklore. Then he craftily inserted references to Marx and Lenin and Big White Brothers with their hard-working iron reindeer into the newly born lore. Thus he created a modern classic, a staple of Soviet ethnography.

On his way to academic laurels he had obtained considerable funds for his field trips. Airline tickets were cashed in, hotel receipts were forged; only alcohol was used directly, for what he broad-mindedly considered medicinal purposes. The Chichmek bonanza kept Vladimir and his friends, from the Mosfilm makeup man to atonal composer Levant, commissioned to write Chichmek songs, in vodka, beer, and cognac (alcohol Vladimir consumed personally) all year round. Vladimir was a genius, just one of many alcoholic geniuses that Russia produces with such remarkable consistency.

The genius scratched his beard. "You could be it."

"I'm not sure," Dubinsky said gloomily. Yet another assault on my humanity, he thought.

"You could be the first genuine Chichmek," Vladimir declared triumphantly, downing another cognac. "To Chichmekia, this vagrant, decadent, golden fruit of my imagination."

"Plastic surgery." Slava nodded.

"Feasible." Vladimir nodded too, trying to drink out of the lemon and biting into his glass.

"I'll have to think about it," Dubinsky said uncertainly, although he was already too warm to think.

"What's there to think about?" Vladimir spat out a piece of glass. "I'm offering a life of methodical, round-the-clock leisure with unlimited liquor consumption."

"I'm not sure it's a good idea." Znachar frowned. "A massive psychological reorientation would be required. He would still need therapy first, to get over the shock. His psyche is too fragile to proceed without a thorough evaluation."

"Where am I going to get evaluated?" Dubinsky wondered.

Znachar coughed. "Well . . . actually . . . only *there*."

For a moment, they were silent again, as the walls of Dubinsky's room transformed themselves momentarily into Times Square and Ginza and the Spanish Steps. Good Soviet intelligentsia did not need an explanation of the meaning of "there." There was only *one* big "there," from Tierra del Fuego to

Reykjavik, from Monterrey to Taipei. Where man exploited
man and had so much fun doing it.

"Which brings us to an interesting possibility." Slava rose
from his armchair and walked over to the window. "Israel."

A hush fell over the room. Each had attended numerous
farewell parties, but the decision was still a matter of some
weight. Their lives rolled along on the tires of their sham
degrees and their connections with such smoothness . . . applying for a visa was an abrupt turn of the wheel: you could
very well find yourself over the cliff. Which, as they saw at
once, was Slava's point precisely: Dubinsky was already half-
way there.

Then they all shouted at once.

"You don't mean Israel *per se*, of course?" Znachar demanded a clarification.

"Why not?"

"That would be absurd," Vladimir declared, holding the
empty glass to his lips and waiting for the cognac to materialize. "Don't forget that both that brave little state, the darling of our dissident loudmouths, and this pig paradise, to
which we are beholden, were founded by the same crazy Russian Jew revolutionaries. History! History, my friend, lies not.
Unlike ethnography."

"Everybody lies," Znachar said thoughtfully. "But America
. . . Dubinsky, my boy, you're so *impractical.*"

"You'll perish without us," Vladimir confirmed, taking off
his pants and carefully folding them over a framed Bosch
lithograph on the wall. "And we'll perish without another
bottle! Slavka, you meretricious procurer! More frog shine!
Or anything!" He lay down on the floor, using a paperback
for a pillow.

"Nonsense," Slava chuckled, producing a small bottle of
Remy Martin. "How do you feel about it, Oleg?"

"Christ, I never thought about it," Dubinsky confessed. After
he had been denied a clearance for working abroad, he suc-
cessfully suppressed the idea of ever going west of Lvov. Or
thought he had.

"You do have an invitation, don't you?" Slava insisted,

pouring Remy straight from the bottle into Vladimir's mouth.

"I guess so," Dubinsky said. He was positively stricken by the visions that Slava's suggestion generated in his head: helicopters soared among skyscrapers, minarets loomed in the oases, and Nonna, in a long fur coat, was stepping out of a limo into the arms of a dozen uniformed doormen, with the Eiffel Tower in the background. . . .

"Everybody has an invitation," Znachar said gloomily. "Mine is from my grandfather-in-law in Samaria." He slid onto the floor, carefully holding on to his paunch, as if it were in any danger of slipping away. Both he and Vladimir were so used to the pure lab alcohol that French cognac made them drowsy.

Slava pulled Dubinsky by the ear. "Wake up. You're not in Vienna yet."

"I need a good Danish lawyer," Dubinsky muttered, as he rolled down the window of his car, parked in the shadow of the Eiffel Tower, and cocked his Beretta. "Because I'm gonna fill her cheating thieving heart . . . with lead so heavy . . . she'll sink like a stone . . . in the Loire . . . or in the Seine . . ."

"Forget about the bitch," Slava said amid the atonal snoring from the floor. "You have an invitation, and I think you should apply."

An invitation was a social passport, whether you meant to act on it or not, and was to be updated every six months at the Dutch Embassy; without it you were considered a conformist, whose trashing of the system was not to be taken seriously.

"I don't see any contradiction." Vladimir rose suddenly, as he was apt to do from time to time. "So you'll be a Chichmek in America. Instead of at my Institute." And he collapsed back on the floor.

Slava had less of a need for patrons than Znachar or Vladimir. He eschewed Party membership, which he could have gotten easily, with his true-blue Russian extraction and working-class roots; what's more, he dropped out of college. He claimed boredom; others said he had been clumsy when trying to bribe a professor. No matter. Few people in Moscow's demimonde did not know "Rothman," as Slava called himself. "The things I'm involved in, a Jew is better trusted," he'd say with a wink.

"Trust me, Dubinsky," Slava muttered, as they stumbled into the street. Znachar and Vladimir stayed back, untransportable. "Take it from a man who knows everything. I know that it pays to buy Spanish pesetas in Odessa and trade them for hash in Baku and trade hash for Volga spare parts in Gorky and trade spare parts for icons in Suzdal and icons for guldens in Leningrad . . ."

"I am not a peseta," Dubinsky protested. "I will not be traded for a spare car part."

As they stumbled over frozen snowdrifts on Tverskoy Boulevard, things were getting much clearer and at the same time somehow more confusing.

"And do I ever go to any of those places?" Slava insisted. "Did you ever see me sweat under ten Irish wool sweaters on top of each other, dragging a suitcase filled with Led Zeppelin LPs through the Kursk Station?"

"I'm not a railroad station whore," Dubinsky said proudly. "Where's that cognac?"

"I'm a consultant," Slava explained, handing Dubinsky the Remy Martin. "I tell people where to get what they want with the best resources they can find. There's not a deal in a major city of the Empire that I don't get a cut of. I know bartenders, I know hotel chambermaids, I know car mechanics. Cabbies bid for the right to chauffeur me around town. And I'll never get caught either, because I never *carry*. I know precisely which of my clients are KGB and which are just punks looking for a Sex Pistols LP. And they respect it. Now, Dubinsky, can you afford to ignore my advice?"

"I just don't understand why you're trying to get rid of me." Dubinsky sniffled between the swigs of cognac. "Are you acting on a special order to sweet-talk dumb Jews like myself out of the country?"

Slava tried to kick Dubinsky in the butt, slipped, and landed on his own behind. "Sonuvabitch," he berated Dubinsky, who was trying hard to help him to his feet, "I love you like a son, you're my vestal virgin . . ."

"I'm not a virgin," Dubinsky said curtly, dropping Slava back on the ground.

"And who fixed you up with that bitch?" groaned Slava, back in the snow. "The same person whom you're dooming to die of pneumonia at this very moment!"

"I want to know why you think I should go." Dubinsky lay down on the bench and stared up in the sky, seeking out stars between the trees' naked branches. The sky was clear, the wind was down, the night was quiet and intangible. It was still cold, but they hardly felt it.

"I think you should go because you're clean and pure and smart and—and you have no future here, damn it!" Slava yelled. "Got it, you asshole? Now help me up!"

Dubinsky slid off the bench into the snow and crawled over. "Now *you*'ll have to pick *me* up. What do you mean by 'clean and pure'?"

"You're a fucking idealist, that's why! And I like you and I don't want to see you become a piece of shit like the rest of us here!"

"I don't know if I can agree with that," Dubinsky murmured, loath to concur too fast, since "idealist" was not something people around him suffered gladly.

"What if I get turned down? What are the chances?"

"If you apply within a month, your chances are between fifty-nine and sixty-five percent," Slava said with sudden sobriety. "Which is considered excellent. Our benevolent rulers feel rather reconciliatory these days. They want arms reductions in certain areas, they want a few computer deals to come through—the congressmen responsible for the passage represent heavily Jewish districts—and, of course, the usual grain deals. The Yanks want those more than we do, but we want to cover all the bases."

Dubinsky fell silent, reflecting on the ease with which Slava

juggled "we" and "they." Slava's was certainly a very sophisticated variety of both doublespeak and doublethink. Slava
crawled over and hugged Dubinsky. "I'm saving your soul,
you bastard."

Dubinsky was rudely awakened by a kick in his side.
"You're gonna freeze to death, you fucking homo scum-
bags," the cop said.
Slava groaned, opened his eyes, and handed the cop a fifty-
ruble bill. "Fifty-four Gorky Street."
"Sure thing, comrade." The fifty disappeared into the cop's
pocket.
"What about my partner?"
"Twenty-five on delivery," Slava said. You don't haggle,
you don't get respect.

"It's wonderful how you handled them," said Dubinsky. They
were lying on the floor of the ancient elevator and listening
to the clanging of metal. They were not sure which way they
were going.
"A cop makes 130 rubles a month, Dubinsky. So there."
Neither of them could balance himself into a vertical state,
so Slava had to climb on Dubinsky's body to make it to the
keyhole. They fell in, laughing hysterically.
"You want to puke, Dubinsky?"
"Nah. I want to go to sleep."
They huddled against each other on Slava's gigantic sofa.
"Let's get married, Slava."
"I can't have children, Dubinsky."
"We'll adopt a Chichmek."
"You're going to be one yourself soon enough."

When Dubinsky opened his eyes, it was still dark. Slava was
snoring gently next to him. Both were still wearing their over-
coats.
Dubinsky struggled out of his coat—the buttons seemed too
difficult to undo, and, swaying under the weight that seemed

implanted in his head, he made his way to the bathroom. He opened the hot-water tap and sat down on the john.

Maybe Slava is right, he thought; maybe I should go; of course he's wrong about my idealism, I can be as tough and cynical as the next guy, I don't believe anything either side has to say, any ism is a piece of crap. In that, I'm like everybody else; in fact, I don't know anybody who believes in anything, period. Once we leave our cozy apartments or less-than-cozy basements, we set our minds in the LIE mode. Not a word we say outside each other's company can be called truth; it's getting to be so bad we have to make an effort to be truthful even to each other. And what have I gained from all this lying? My life is derailed, and if I turn into a Chichmek in Vladimir's lab, it will be no different from writing that Communism is a pivotal force in the development of Pizdo; and look where that got me.

"I'm a congenital liar," he said out loud to the array of brightly colored French shampoos on the shelf. "I liked my job because it enabled me to lead a life of lies."

Can I be that bad, he whispered.

Of course not, snickered Dylan from the poster on the door. It's, like, the system, man. It's not he or she or them that you belong to.

Slava is right, Dubinsky sighed, looking away, apprehensive about arguing with a poster. I have to go. If I stay, the bathroom is the only place where I'll be able to be honest. I have to give myself a chance. Besides, I'll see the world. There's nothing wrong with that.

He wiped himself carefully, stripped, and got into the tub, where he napped and had scattered thoughts about being honest in cool places like Haight-Ashbury, or Vondel Park in Amsterdam.

Two

Dubinsky's first hurdle was a written release from his parents, which necessitated a trip to Lipsk, three hours by train from Moscow. As he stepped aboard the grimy, sooty, sorry-looking conveyance, Dubinsky was overcome with mixed feelings. He had left the family bosom at seventeen and maintained minimal contact with his parents ever since. He never understood their old-fashioned ways nor ever sought to. It had never occurred to him to tell them of his life in Moscow. He knew in advance that had he chosen to answer their questions in detail and thus place himself under scrutiny, every act would have met with complete disapproval, so why bother? Especially now, after he had resolved to embark on a path of liberation from all the lies that enslaved him. There was one minor snag: in order to start down this Path of Truth, he had to tell another lie. It was particularly frustrating in view of the new vision that had opened to him in the bright light of the neon lamp in Slava's bathroom. On the other hand . . . his invitation was from a nonexistent uncle in Nazareth. His application was for a visa to Israel, while he was determined to go to Holland. So why not tell his parents something else?

Lies, lies, lies, he thought with disgust, swaying in the second-class car and inhaling the ripe odors of his fellow travelers' socks. Absolutely the last lie, he told himself. Once he stepped off the plane in Vienna, it was going to be different. He would lead a highly moral lifestyle and allow for no compromise.

By dusk he had reached Lipsk, where his parents had grown up and were now spending their golden years. Daytime in the old town was quiet, with an occasional milk truck rumbling by. The peace would be broken on the days of soccer games, when the fans, having consumed liters of vodka in celebration of victory or in the wake of defeat, would pour out into the streets smashing everything in sight. After dark the hoodlums from all over town converged upon the Angela Davis Culture and Recreation Park to settle turf disputes. Law-abiding citizens stayed indoors and watched the TV exploits of Soviet agents who tirelessly exposed the secret designs of American warmongers. The park, the geographical center of the Old Town, was an elaborate affair with fountains and statues of muscular female discus throwers. Originally named after Zhdanov, the Minister of Culture of yore, it was renamed subsequently after Khrushchev and then after Angela Davis. The local authorities were about to invite the courageous American Communist to the re-rededication ceremony, but Moscow vetoed the idea. Comrade Davis was certainly a tireless champion of human rights, but still an American.

The enormous German-built safety-pin factory was a strategically important installation, whose security could not be compromised. Dubinsky walked briskly to his parents' house from the station, ever mindful of the hoodlums. As he recalled the trivia from the town's past and present, he took a certain perverse pleasure in it. So dense and thick was the climate of lies, so complete the corruption, that assuming a high moral posture and picturing himself as a genuine truth-seeker required no effort whatsoever. As his eyes glided with the same pleasure over the old faded banners that confidently proclaimed the imminent victory of Communism in the entire world, his heart sang out with joy, "Lies and corruption, I fare thee well!" Indeed, the way he saw it, there were simply no complex moral issues to be resolved. An open-and-shut case for freedom of speech and expression.

He opened the rickety wooden gate and walked into the tiny courtyard of the hovel his parents rented. In the combination of lobby and storage room Dubinsky ran into his grandfather.

"Ah, the scribbler's here," Yefim Dubinsky croaked.

"That's me, all right." Dubinsky strained a grin.

They viewed each other for a moment, exchanging silent stares of pity.

To Oleg, Yefim Dubinsky was a living relic, the victim of zealously espoused Marxist theology, centuries-old ghetto mentality, and his own stubborn nature. Once upon a time, Yefim Dubinsky had rampaged across the steppes of the Ukraine in his Red Cavalry hat. By day he would chop off the Whites' heads; by night, seated with his friends and a jar of moonshine around the fire, he would dream of the future. After the victory on Russian soil was complete, he would cross the Atlantic on his mare Jeanne d'Arc and storm down Wall Street, chopping off the heads of the capitalists with their silk top hats. Then he would open the bank vaults, whither gold and diamonds would pour out into the hands of grateful American toilers. After the war, he had to postpone his plans, and applied his revolutionary fervor to leading the construction of the Belomor-Balt Canal, the first grand-scale industrial project realized completely through prison labor. The dream materialized in '37 after Yefim had been told he was a Belgian spy and sent to the Kolyma gold fields. His mind, pervaded by belief in the Party's infallibility, adapted itself superbly; he called his section "Wall Street" and still spared no effort for the cause. In '57, when he was handed back his old Party card in the local district office, he shed a quiet tear and attempted to re-enlist in the cavalry. It was this rejection and subsequent retirement that buried the dream and caused him to believe that his grandson was actually Isaac Babel, a Soviet writer who had portrayed an enthusiastic if not too rosy picture of the Red Cavalry, and was subsequently eliminated in the 1930s. As Babel, Dubinsky was responsible for most modern ills, from having passed nuclear secrets to the Americans in the 1940s, to the insufficiently patriotic quality of modern musical comedy. Old, hunched, and shrunken, Grandfather was the Party conscience of the household.

"I read the news," Yefim finally said, drilling Oleg with his mad coal-black eyes. "You betrayed the proletariat of Pizdo."

"Impossible." Oleg patted his grandfather lightly on the back, and proceeded to the living room.

"You traded them to the Rockefellers for fancy rags." Grandfather spat vehemently. The saliva landed on the package of herring, wrapped in yesterday's *Pravda*, squarely on the paper's logo.

"See?" Oleg pointed at the paper. "I'm going to take this to certain authorities first thing in the morning. They're going to take away your Party card again."

The old man shook violently and collapsed on the floor. His face went from white to blue.

"Oh, Christ." Oleg frowned. "Not again." He rushed to the medicine cabinet for the nitro and pushed a tablet under the old man's tongue. "I was just kidding, Grandpa. After dinner we'll go to the backyard and bury the paper. No one'll ever know."

"What happened?" His mother stood in the doorway, her arms akimbo.

"Hi, Mom." Oleg deposited his grandfather's body on the chair and turned to face his mother. "Grandpa's upset on account of Pizdo."

She shook her head uncertainly. "You must have said something. You just can't leave the old codger alone."

"Now why would I do a thing like that?" Oleg lovingly placed his arm around his mother's shoulders and led her to the living room. "You know I adore Grandpa. He's living history to me."

His father was contentedly watching the annual massacre of the foreign ice-hockey teams at the Moscow International Tournament.

"I'll tell you, Oleg, those Swedes might have two color TV sets each and whatnot, but their defense is still full of holes." He beamed at his son. "Mind my word, the West has nothing to teach us when it comes to hockey."

"They sure don't," Dubinsky agreed, looking at the close-ups of square-jawed faces, distorted in spasms of triumph. He felt encouraged. He had completely forgotten about the tournament. It was a definite stroke of luck. Soviet victory was guaranteed every time.

"You have a day off?" his mother inquired suspiciously. "Dropping in on us just like that, out of the blue . . . well, you know you can still count on a square meal here."

Dubinsky grinned, sprawling on the couch.

They were still fishing pieces of beef and potatoes and carrots out of the greasy stew when the conversation shifted to the family's black sheep, perhaps in the absence of any white ones.

"If you'd followed in my steps and picked communications, you would not have to shake in your boots every time a bunch of blackass apes want to sell out to Americans," Dubinsky Sr. said philosophically, sopping the remaining sauce off his plate with his bread. "Radio'll always be around. The sky's the limit. Look at all the TV satellites." Retired from his job in army communications, Dubinsky's father was perfectly content to teach physics at the local high school.

"I'm not shaking in my boots," Dubinsky said with dignity. "I'm going into a retraining program. I'm going to study the Yebun language and customs."

"Until the Yebuns decide to sell out to the CIA," his father grumbled. "I don't know what's wrong with you. I don't care if Grandpa's friend was on the faculty at the language school. You should've joined the army, and I would've gotten you a good job with the Signal Corps."

"Signal schmignal," Dubinsky's mother waved. "When I think of all that money we spent on cello lessons. Every time they show the Tchaikovsky Competition on TV, I cry my heart out. It's all that damn volleyball. And now Yebun. At least you're not digging ditches."

"He shtill might." Grandfather's jaws were working in low gear, which affected his speech. "The Pizhdo blood izh on Mishter Babel'zh handzh." He continued to mash his last potato with customary revolutionary fervor.

Nobody paid much attention to the old Bolshevik's prediction. Dubinsky helped his father clear the dishes, and, as his mother set the table for tea, he produced a neatly folded sheet of paper.

"Contrary to what you folks think of me," he said, hiding his hands to conceal the trembling, "the Pizdo fiasco has not damaged my brilliant career in the slightest. What's more, I've just gotten myself a two-week vacation permit for Bulgaria."

The activities came to a halt. Father Dubinsky dropped the dish into the sink. Mother Dubinsky spilled the tea. Grandfather Dubinsky belched, leaving his feelings open to interpretation. Dubinsky Jr. looked away as he spoke, afraid his eyes would betray him.

"So I need your signature on this." He unfolded the paper.

We, DUBINSKY Semyon Yefimovich and Polina Davidovna have no financial claims on our son DUBINSKY Oleg Semyonovich. We do not object to his departure abroad.

His father was the first to regain his composure. "Sure thing, son. If the Party trusts you . . ."

". . . I'll get the pen." His mother hurried off.

"I don't buy this." Dubinsky the Bolshevik shook his head, taking off his old-fashioned glasses, held together by a string. "Bulgaria ain't abroad. I remember it like it was yesterday. We liberated it from Marshal Pilsudski's capitalist rule in 1920."

"That was Poland, Dad." Father waved, trying out the dried-out ball point on the newspaper.

"... and Vitka the Cross-Eyed and myself personally hanged that Catholic priest, that opium trader to the masses, we hanged him by his balls on his *kostel*, church, that is—"

"Please, Father," Dubinsky's mother said squeamishly. "We don't want to hear this kind of talk at the table."

"Whatever it was, the Czech Soviet Socialist Republic is a part of the Union," said the old man stubbornly, spitting potatoes all over the cloth. "I lost half my platoon when we stormed Lvov."

"He's getting worse every day." Dubinsky Sr. grinned at Oleg apologetically.

"But you know how it is, son." Dubinsky's mother signed below her husband's signature. "His pension is as much as ours combined—"

Dubinsky watched the signing intently, restraining himself from leaping up in the air, from hugging and kissing his unsophisticated parents (who naively believed you needed parental permission to go to Bulgaria), from giving a finger to his senile maniac of a grandfather, from rushing out the door, from running all the way back to Moscow, to his typewriter, to add "*to Israel*" after "abroad."

"I wonder if they have any German radios for sale in Bulgaria," Dubinsky's father said wistfully. "How much money will you be allowed to exchange?"

"They have gorgeous mohair wool in Bulgaria." His mother's face assumed a beatific expression. "I could knit you such a warm scarf. And there'll still be enough wool left for a sweater, too."

"Suppose you're right," Grandfather Dubinsky said with a sudden hardness in his voice, "what will prevent Isaac here from defecting? From staying in Hungary? Ah?"

His parents chuckled.

"Nobody defects to Bulgaria, Gramps," his father said. "And why should Oleg defect?"

"He's a good boy," his mother confirmed. "Not some ballet dancer."

Thus, through what Dubinsky had hoped to be his last lie,

he made his first step toward freedom and at the same time won his parents' respect—for the first time in his life.

He politely declined their offer of a mattress on the floor and hurried through the poorly lit streets to the station in order to catch the last train to Moscow. He shivered in the chilly January wind; at the same time he thanked it for keeping the hoodlums off the streets.

The second-class was sold out, and he splurged on a first-class seat. Dropping his coat on the bunk, he crept past his sleeping fellow travelers out to the corridor for a smoke. It took him some time before he could light his cigarette—his hands were still shaking. Dragging hungrily, he tried to think of the hurdles still to be overcome; there were so many papers to be collected, especially the one from the job, the most important one. . . . The shaking would not stop. In fact, although the car was well-heated, his whole body was shivering. He returned to his compartment and threw his coat over his shoulders, yet he was still shivering. Perhaps a cold, he thought, pressing his forehead against the cool, wet window. What the hell, so I get in bed at home, hot tea with lemon, aspirins. . . . I got the paper, that's all that counts. Slava would be proud of me. Znachar would ask me how I feel about it, and I wouldn't know what to say.

"I am disappointed in you, Dubinsky," said Comrade Borzoi, looking at the two papers that Dubinsky had laid out in front of him.

One was a request to be dismissed from the Institute "of my own will"—as opposed to being fired—and the other was a request for a character reference "in connection with my emigration to Israel." An ostensibly absurd piece of paper— would any potential employer from Tel Aviv to Tulsa, Oklahoma, be interested in what Dubinsky's Soviet superiors had to say about him?—the personal reference was nevertheless the most important. It said, in effect, that Comrade Dubinsky was not a useful member of society and that his emigration would not cause the State any tears.

"I truly am," Borzoi repeated. "The first harsh blow of fate, and you're scurrying for shelter. When I hired you, I thought you were a *mensch*."

"My departure for Israel is motivated by a desire to be reunited with my uncle in Nazareth." Dubinsky recited the standard formula.

"Of course," Borzoi smirked. "I just thought you had what it takes. How do you think it makes me look?"

Dubinsky shrugged. Making Comrade Borzoi look good could hardly be high on his list of priorities.

"It makes me look like a schmuck," Borzoi continued. "It makes me look like I have not conducted enough ideological work with you. You're a black eye for me, Dubinsky."

"I did not mean it to be personal."

"It *is* personal, damn it!" Borzoi struck his fist on the desk. Dubinsky deftly caught a statuette of a Masai warrior that had dropped off the edge, and put it back in place.

"Thank you," said Borzoi dryly. "I suppose I could tell you I thought of you as a son, but I don't suppose it would matter now."

Dubinsky coughed, ostensibly to cover his feelings.

"And what about your dead friends? Do you realize how they'd look at you? Aren't you afraid they'll come haunting you at night? You've betrayed their memory, after all. You've pissed upon everything they held dear!"

Fully expecting another bolt of thunder, Dubinsky cupped his hands near the edge of the desk to catch the warrior. Knowing his classmates, he was sure that they would approve—even envy him a little. After all, he was going to pay discount prices for the things they would have gladly purchased at full price.

"What about your parents?" Borzoi demanded. "Your grandfather the Civil War hero? How do they feel about your decision?"

"They know a man with an iron will when they see one," Dubinsky said proudly.

"You're certainly getting an inflated opinion of yourself," said Borzoi, irritated. "Why do you expect us to let you go, anyway? Don't you think you know too much? You might be a catch for the CIA."

"I never signed for any kind of clearance in my life," Dubinsky said quietly, covering Borzoi's ten with an ace.

"Hmm." Borzoi was at a loss. "Well . . . I don't care." He signed both papers with a flourish. "But others might disagree with me, Dubinsky. I hope you're aware of it."

"I am, sir." Dubinsky rose, folding the paper. "And thank you very much, sir."

Borzoi waved him off in dismissal. "Go, go already. It's people like you . . . how do you think *they* look at someone like *me* after this?"

"I don't follow, sir," Dubinsky said, baffled. "I mean, you're not Jewish, are you?"

"I don't know it myself anymore," Borzoi said wearily. "Thank God, at this stage in my career it doesn't matter. Or at least I hope so. Go now." His voice came down to a whisper. "Good luck."

"Thank you, sir." Still stunned, Dubinsky left the room. Borzoi a Jew? Who could think . . .

"Varfolomey Yevstigneyevich is in a meeting right now," said the personnel chief's secretary with a mysterious air. "What do you want, anyway?"

Staring straight at her size Ds, Dubinsky handed her the papers. "Aha." She raised her eyes from the papers. "Come back at the end of the day. Five-ish."

At half past four Dubinsky returned, wary and apprehensive.

"Comrade Ovchar is gone for the day." She yawned. "A family emergency. Come back tomorrow."

"Will he be in in the morning?"

She shrugged.

They exchanged long, measured looks. You bastard, hers said, how dare you bother Comrade Ovchar with your Zionist schemes.

Bitch, said his.

"Thank you," he said.
"You're welcome," she answered.
It was a war; he knew it now.

"Of course it is," said Znachar. "What do you expect them to do, roll out a red carpet from your door to the airport? If they did, this city would empty overnight."
"With ninety percent begging to come back in a week." Vladimir nodded.
"Cheer up, Dubinsky," Slava said. "You're a fighter. You've got what it takes." And he explained what Dubinsky should do next. And Nonna was not at home.

Next morning at nine, Dubinsky was facing the personnel chief's door.
"He's in a meeting," the secretary said. "Come back around noon."
"I'm sending him my request for the reference by registered mail," said Dubinsky, following Slava's instructions. "If he doesn't respond . . ."
She pushed the intercom button. "He'll see you shortly."
Old, bald, and bespectacled, Comrade Ovchar leafed through Dubinsky's slim file and declared with ill-concealed satisfaction, "This will take time, Comrade. I will have to confer with Section One on this." Section One meant the official KGB representative.
Comrade Ovchar's office was decorated in 1930s fashion: oil semblances of the Founders and the Leaders, the oak desk, the inkset, the cabinets, the heavy, thick plush drapes that cascaded to the floor in semi-circles and filled the room with an air of gloom—all was oversized, all was designed to make it look like a place where, at the push of a button, the guard would materialize to take you away.
"I was never granted a clearance," Dubinsky said in a faint voice.
"Impossible," Comrade Ovchar shook his head. "Everybody's got a clearance."

"*I* don't."

This time Ovchar really plunged into the file. "An oversight," he murmured. "I'll have it cross-checked with the Section One files, I can't believe it . . ." Finally he looked up. "Come tomorrow. I'll have the decision ready by then."

From the Institute, Dubinsky, still in a combative mood, headed straight for the district VD clinic.

"I can't find your file," the nurse said. "What are your symptoms?"

"I don't have a file. Nor symptoms."

"So what do you want?"

"I told you. A certificate that I don't have a file."

"Why?"

"Israel."

The magic word brought the nurse to her feet. "Come back later. I have to really make sure you don't have a file."

Armed with his draft card, Dubinsky rushed to the induction center. Surrounded by posters that extolled the virtues of various branches of the national defense and their firm protection of the Soviet people from the saber-toothed imperialist invaders, he felt very insecure. They're going to have me strip, he thought, feeling waves of panic rise through his body; declare me fit, shear my hair, and pack me off to the boot camp. All within five minutes.

"Where's your draft notice?" asked the captain.

"I don't have one. I came to surrender my card. And get a receipt. I'm emigrating."

"You've never been drafted?" the captain asked distrustfully, looking through Dubinsky's file. "You're eligible for draft this spring, May the third. Present yourself here with your personal effects."

Dubinsky fainted.

When he came to, his head was soaked with water. The captain looked as if he was restraining himself from kicking Dubinsky in the balls.

"The army might make a man of you yet," he said, and then added in a whisper, "but I doubt it."

"I want to see your superior," Dubinsky muttered, scrambling to his feet.

"He's not here."

"His deputy."

"He won't talk to you."

"Ask him."

"He'll be back after lunch."

"So will I." Dubinsky staggered to the exit, with the captain glaring at his back.

"If you never had VD, then you don't have a file." Dr. Juliet Goldschmidt produced a gold-tipped Parker and signed Dubinsky's bill of health. "And that's that."

Dressed in an immaculate white robe, casually thrown over an expensive woolen suit, Dr. Goldschmidt exuded an air of confidence. For a moment Dubinsky wished he had an innocuous ailment, crabs or something, to have her treat him.

"Thank you so much, Doctor."

"You bet. And," she lowered her voice, "good luck."

"We'll have to review your case very carefully," said the major back at the induction center. "You're a lieutenant of reserve and are classified as 2022, Military Translator."

I am also Jewish, Dubinsky thought maliciously, which means you bastards can't draft me according to my specialty because you can't give me a clearance, and you can't draft me as a private, either. You can't draft me, period.

"I'll have to consult with my CO," the major said. "Come back tomorrow."

In the psychiatric clinic, Dubinsky got a second wind.

"You don't have a file on me because I've never been referred to you for treatment. So sign the form that I'm not crazy."

"Of course you're not," said the receptionist nurse, shaking her permed curls. "But I don't have the special form. Come back tomorrow."

"They all hate me," Dubinsky complained to Znachar.

"Of course they do," Znachar assured him. "According to them, you're headed for the land of Cadillacs and Coca-Cola, while they're forced to live out their lives of tedium, filled with the quest for Polish shoes and Bulgarian canned peaches."

"I don't know how long I can carry on like this," Dubinsky complained to Slava.

"You've got untapped resources in yourself you're not even aware of," Slava encouraged him.

"Yours is no special case," Vladimir said. "Everybody goes through the same shit. Besides," he added, "you're in the open now. There is no going back."

And Nonna was still not at home.

"Comrade Ovchar is out of town," said the secretary. "Come back tomorrow."

"I can't decide on these matters," said the major. "Only the colonel has enough authority to accept a draft card, and he's out of town. Stop by early next week."

"You're in luck," said the nurse at the psycho clinic. "I've got the form signed for you."

Dubinsky let out a faint smile. He was getting used to the pace of this war, to the fact that victories were borne out of small advances, and, so long as you didn't accept the defeats, you could cope with the delays. He went to the notary public and had copies of his birth certificate and college diploma notarized. The rules were strict: no Soviet official document was to cross the border. Next stop was the Office of Civil Acts Registration.

"I've never been married, and I want a statement to that effect."

"We don't issue such statements. We're only a district office. You have to go to the City Office."

"We don't store local files," said the City Office. "If you were getting married, wouldn't you go to the District Office? *They* would have the file."

"The office director is gone for the day," said the receptionist. "Come tomorrow. No one else would issue you a certificate that you're unmarried."

"Why?" Dubinsky was cold and tired and decided to make a pit stop anyway.

"Because you're going to Israel. One never knows . . ."

"Just between the two of us," the girl said, directing him to the bathroom, "I'm surprised. There are so many interesting and attractive young women who would love to marry you in order to leave on your visa. Would you be . . . interested?"

"I don't have a visa yet," he said.

"Don't get into this shit," Slava said. "Unless they are willing to contribute at least a five-carat diamond to your moving expenses."

"I'm getting out of breath," Dubinsky confided.

"The worst is yet to come," Slava said comfortingly.

"Your ability to draw a line between reality and fiction is deteriorating," said Znachar with concern. "Where are you going tomorrow?"

"The Domestic Pet State Association," Dubinsky said. "They'll certify I've never owned a parakeet."

"It's a thin line," Znachar admitted.

And Nonna was still not at home.

"Are you sure you never had a pet?" asked the serious young woman at the association. "You look like the kind who would enjoy keeping a hamster. If you had a pet, it might change your mind about leaving."

"I don't think so," said Dubinsky politely. It was only ten in the morning, and he had to save energy.

"Why don't you sit here for five minutes and think it over," she suggested. "We've got some lovely sparrows here. And the cage costs only fifteen rubles."

"I think I'd like the signed form right now."

She sighed and signed. "Maybe you'll get a pet *there*."

"I wouldn't rule it out," he said.

"You can start collecting the signatures now," said the secretary, handing Dubinsky his application with Comrade Ovchar's "No objections" on it. "The Triangle: Party Secretary, Komsomol Secretary, Union Secretary."

Dubinsky roared out into the corridor as if the application was a checkered flag. Swaying from the momentum, he hesitated for a minute, then, burning rubber, swung to the left, and roared on to the union office.

"Comrade Chihuahuashvili will be back after lunch."

Nonplussed, Dubinsky doubled back to the Komsomol, i.e., Young Communist League, office.

"Comrade Taxa is on a business trip. Won't be back until Monday."

Dubinsky tiptoed into the Party Secretary's office.

"Do you have an appointment?"

Dubinsky explained the situation.

"Comrade Volkodav will not be able to see you."

"I don't insist on seeing him," Dubinsky said wearily. "I just want him to sign the paper."

She returned promptly. "Comrade Volkodav is aware of your situation. Your personal case will be discussed at a Party meeting whenever a slot becomes available."

"When is that?"

She shrugged. "By the end of the month, perhaps."

Dubinsky accepted the signed proof of his single status with utmost indifference and stepped outside. The air was much warmer now, the snow was melting, the sky was a bright blue. The schoolchildren were merrily belting one another with their schoolbags. He headed for the Traffic Department.

"I've never owned a car, a motorbike, or a moped," he said. "I don't even have a license. Therefore I can't have any outstanding tickets."

"That's for us to decide," said the sergeant grimly. "How about jaywalking? Stop by in a couple of days."

They went to a closed-door screening of a French movie. Spiffily dressed adventurers with carnations in their lapels and guns tucked in their scanty underpants effortlessly foiled Interpol's every move, skipping with ease from country to country, constantly changing guises and identifications. He could not concentrate: his thoughts were on tomorrow's visit to the induction center. Afterwards, at Slava's place, his mind switched to the Party Secretary and his formidable reputation for screaming and bodily ejecting people from his office. He picked up a *Newsweek* and leafed through it absently. The Republic of Pizdo had brought in Albanian agricultural experts and applied for an IMF loan. He yawned.

When Vladimir inquired whether Dubinsky would like to read Updike's new book, which had come into his possession for two days only, Dubinsky did not react.

"It's called the Visa Syndrome," said Znachar with pity. "I'm afraid he's gone."

"It's too bad," said the Union Secretary Chihuahuashvili, a young Georgian with a bushy moustache, accepting Dubinsky's union card. "You always paid your dues on time. There has to be a formal expulsion at the meeting," he added, "but don't let it worry you. We can sentence you *in absentia*."

"Thanks." They shook hands behind the tightly shut door.

"Good luck," whispered the Georgian.

The visit to the library was a piece of cake, too. Dubinsky was an active borrower, and, faced with numerous entries, all stamped "Returned," the librarian signed the release without hesitation.

"The readership is *down*," she whispered confidentially, and added with sympathy, "What will a heavy reader like you do there? You'll have to *buy* books, that's expensive. I doubt there's anything free under capitalism."

"But think of the choice at the bookstore," Dubinsky countered.

"I don't think we want to draft you," the captain said. "But I won't release you now, either. What if someone else doesn't? Then we'd *have* to draft you. As a backup, you know."
   "And if everybody else releases me . . . ?"
   "Then no problem."

At the end of the day Dubinsky stopped by the photo studio to pick up his passport-size pictures. He was shocked at what he saw. His cheeks were hollow, his forehead looked like ruled paper, his eyes were dull and empty. He walked out to the street. He felt unusually hot in his sheepskin coat. Around him people were wearing light raincoats and sports jackets and sunglasses. The snow had all but melted. There was laughter and cheer in the air. A line for ice cream was forming on the corner. Blinking from the sunshine, he shed his overcoat, threw it over his arm, and went back to the Institute.

"Well, jeez, I've got to tell you, that's some news," said Taxa the Komsomol Secretary excitedly. Taxa was short and perky and quite a dresser. His specialty was economic cooperation between the Warsaw Pact countries, and he visited Eastern Europe regularly. Between the trips Taxa hibernated, and now could not pass up a chance to chew the fat with Dubinsky. When the time drew close to five, Dubinsky coughed and came to the point.
   "But there isn't really much I can do for you," Taxa said in a surprised voice. "I mean, I can save you the embarrassment at the meeting. I don't care much for that self-criticism bullshit myself. But, see, we cannot expel you. We can *recommend* that you be expelled. Only the District Committee can expel you, at their own meeting—I can cover that, too— and accept your Komsomol card. Okay?"
   Dubinsky inquired about the time frame involved.
   "A few weeks, I'd say." Taxa sighed. "Listen, do you think

it's easy for *me* to go anywhere? Hell, I went to ten different committees to go to East fucking Germany."

"The Party Bureau will be ready to place your case on the agenda of the meeting as soon as you straighten out your situation with the Komsomol," said the Party Secretary's secretary.

"I have no idea what you're talking about," said the woman at the post office.
"I want a release that I never . . . ?" Dubinsky mumbled and realized that he had no idea what he was asking for either. He scanned his list. Post office was not on it. How did he ever . . . ? And he had spent half an hour on the line, too. Perhaps the release from the psycho clinic had been premature.
"Well?" the woman asked impatiently.
"One stamped postcard, please."

Dubinsky took some comfort in his financial situation, which had not changed yet—so long as the paper chase went on, he was still drawing his salary. Yet the preparations for the lean times had to be made.
"Your best bet is teaching English to your fellow applicants," Vladimir said. "They're dying to learn it."
Friday night Dubinsky went to the synagogue to make inquiries. Inside were only the very religious old men who could go on praying to Yahweh the way they had for centuries and ignore the chief rabbi's pronunciamentos against Zionism and racism. But outside, members of the diplomatic corps, newly accredited correspondents, Congressional aides, human rights champs—everybody was polling the crowd, and the crowd did not care who was genuinely from Denver and who was just an undercover cop looking to set them up. The crowd was here for information, and the rest be damned. Including a dozen or so militiamen standing on both sides of the street and taking pictures openly. Altman moved from Miami to

New York, the climate in Florida was terrible. Bronstein's daughter went to San Francisco and married a millionaire, and now wouldn't see anybody from the old days. Cohen wrote from Manitoba—the climate was cool, the streets were clean, nobody minded you're Jewish. And, closer to home, Dantzin was X-rayed at the customs; Entkin's vases were smashed to pieces—perhaps the officer was in a foul mood. And, even further down Dubinsky's alley—Friedman had been turned down again, his grandmother had washed dishes in the Kremlin cafeteria before the war. Greenberg had received the visa— *mazel tov!*—but his wife didn't, no reason given, what can they do? Itkin's daughter in Delaware wrote to the senator on behalf of her father, the refusenik, do you think it'll work? Dubinsky's senses were operating at full capacity, he was absorbing every detail, he could sort it out later—right now he was hearing something he needed to hear, French movies and John Updike be damned. Although his inquiry about tutoring was met less than enthusiastically, for there were already enough American human rights activists in business, a couple of kind souls offered to ask around, and lack of immediate success did little to dampen his spirits. As he walked home through the clear March night, all forty blocks of the way, he felt euphoric. There were other people all around town, and in other towns, too, who, like him, wanted to embark upon the Path of Truth, illuminated by the neon lights of Times Square and the Champs-Elysées. He was not alone.

"Everything's cool," the Komsomol Secretary Taxa said cheerfully under the thunderous volume of the radio in his office. "According to the resolution we adopted, you're a moral cripple and an ideological monster. Congratulations!"

Dubinsky agreed that it was good news indeed.

"Now you go to the district committee." Taxa dictated the address. He had to say everything twice over the frenzied hollering on the radio. The Canadian team did not seem to have a prayer with five minutes left. They shook hands, and, as Dubinsky was about to leave, Taxa turned the volume even higher, and, amid the "Go Boys Go," Dubinsky lip-read "Good luck."

"Looks like you were a good pedestrian," said the sergeant approvingly. "Too bad you're leaving," he added in a customarily low voice. "We need good pedestrians."

In the district office, Dubinsky looked at the receptionist, he heard her voice, and a thick fog descended upon the stone canyons of Manhattan and the canals of Amsterdam.
"First Secretary is away."
"Second?"
"In a meeting."
"Third?"
"On vacation."
"Fourth?"
"I don't know."
"I'm not leaving."
They spent half an hour in this *drôle de guerre*, she typing a letter, he staring into space, trading looks that grew in intensity. Finally he started to pace the narrow lobby; she espied a short bespectacled man in an ill-fitting suit and a clip-on tie and summoned him to the rescue.
The man listened to Dubinsky, glanced at the card, and finally muttered, "I don't know anything about it, it's a serious matter, I'm not empowered, only the First Secretary . . . after lunch."

Dubinsky found a grocery store in one of the identical-looking gray-slab boxes of the new project, drank half a dozen glasses of tepid apple juice at the counter, read the Italian grammar textbook that he, in a burst of positive thinking (Italy was a layover country for Soviet emigration), had taken to carrying. *Io sono, tu sei, lui e . . .*
Reinforced with a stale open-faced cheese sandwich, he went back to the office.

"He's not here yet," the receptionist said without letting him open his mouth.

He sat down. Leafed through *Pravda*. The Communist Revolutionary Assembly of Pizdo were amassing forces in the mountains. Their chairman was visiting Moscow. Something stirred inside. *I could be getting shitfaced at a reception right now* . . . Too late, Dubinsky, the voice said. Get down to grammar now. *Noi siamo, voi siete, loro sono* . . .

First Secretary Traktorov, a square-shouldered monolith with a red banner pin in his lapel, fit to take on the whole Montreal Canadiens offense single-handedly, studied Dubinsky's card with a mixture of boredom and disgust. Then he opened the drawer and dropped it inside; he took a receipt form and signed it. Then he rose from his desk, indicating the end of the contact. Muttering thanks, Dubinsky retreated softly into the corridor.

He allowed himself a deep breath outside, then bought a one-copeck glass of carbonated water from a vending machine and threw it in his face, washing away the film of hatred that the two brief minutes in Comrade Traktorov's office had put on his face. Fuck you, Dubinsky whispered, hurrying to the subway, we're back in the game now.

"Obviously we cannot discuss your case on the eve of the great holiday of international proletarian solidarity," said the Party Secretary's secretary. "Come after the holidays."

Fuck your holidays, Dubinsky whispered.

As befitted decent Soviet intelligentsia, they left town on April 30.

"Every time I see these red flags on every corner, I feel like a hunted wolf," Vladimir said, mixing lab alcohol with tomato juice. They were sitting on the back porch of a ramshackle structure for which Vladimir's uncle paid an exorbitant rent and grandly called "dacha." "You know how they hunt wolves?" Vladimir went on. "They circle them with red flags and leave a gap in the circle. A wolf cannot run at a red flag, so he rushes into the gap. And that's where the hunters are: bang! bang! bang!"

"Speaking of which." Znachar chuckled. "We're expecting Natasha and Sveta and Nadya and Alyona. Especially the latter, for our soon-to-be-wandering Jew." Dubinsky grinned wanly. Nonna must be in Copenhagen now, stuffing her face with beer and cream and butter. Screwing everything in sight, too, according to well-known Scandinavian standards of depravity. He wandered away from the group, into the dark of the trees, away from Dylan questioning, "Will there be any comfort there, señor?" He prostrated himself on the grass and looked up into the sky. The stars looked back coldly and indifferently, but instead of feeling lonely and neglected, he felt strong, full of sap and the willingness to fight and die, if necessary. He smelled the grass, an infinitely strong and sophisticated and refined scent unreproducible in millions of Chanel bottles. He felt he could spare this moment of leisure, because tomorrow or three days later he would go right in and sock it to the bastards, he would outsit them, outwit them, outtalk them. He would get it.

"Where's our traitor-to-be?" Slava's voice cut through the girls' giggling.

"Taking in the great Russian nature," Znachar said, "something he'll be missing all his stupid life, however poor and free he will be." Dubinsky rejoined the group. Alyona, a slim, perky brunette with a quick mouth and laughing eyes, was almost as charming and sexy as Nonna. *That* bitch. He'd go to Texas, buy himself a shotgun, and kill her. Drop her right in the middle of the Tivoli Gardens.

"We cannot put your name on the agenda in the absence of the director of the Institute," said the Secretary's secretary. "Comrade Laika is attending an important human rights conference in Grenada."

"Grenada, Spain?"

"The island of Grenada. You haven't been keeping up with international events, Comrade."

▪ ▪ ▪

The rains of May came, quick and pounding. Dubinsky stayed indoors, glancing at the Italian grammar, listening to Simon and Garfunkel, dodging party invitations, masturbating over the alternate memories of Nonna and Alyona, and staring at the new spring leaves outside. Only Slava managed to break through.

"Listen, pal, watch out. I mean, you've got to keep your head together."

"I do. It's my version of samurai training. Buried in the pebbles with my head sticking out."

"Maybe I should bring you some sake tonight."

They warmed up the sake, Slava's commission for the sale of two fake icons to a Japanese businessman, under the baffled glances of Dubinsky's neighbors. "An ancient Jewish tradition," Slava was kind enough to explain.

He regaled Dubinsky with tales of Uzbek greed and Italian lust until they passed out to the voice of Janis Ian singing "Lovers' Lullaby." Visions of Mount Fuji and sword-wielding geishas faded slowly in Dubinsky's mind.

In the morning, a hung-over Dubinsky took the subway to the Institute, glaring at the fellow passengers as if they were rebellious *ronin*. He broke into the reception room fully prepared to chop the chairs and kick the desks.

"Your personal reference will be in the mail tomorrow," declared the Secretary's secretary in the slow, somnolent voice that would haunt Dubinsky to the end of his days.

Exhausted by his own militancy, he dropped on the couch. "Why tomorrow?"

"Because the messenger is already gone. She makes one trip to the post office a day."

"Why can't I deliver it myself?"

"Against the rules."

As if he'd peek into it. As if he gave a damn about what it said.

The post office took another week. Dubinsky went to a nearby project and joined an improvised volleyball game. Luxuriating in his anonymity, he fired off a series of impeccable Japanese-style serves. The base line lay in shambles. A pretty girl in a yellow summer dress laughed and clapped her hands. As if on cue, he dropped the next serve into the net.

Later in the afternoon, he called Alyona. They went to see an Italian comedy, they ate—and eventually got sauced—at the Adriatica Café, they necked under every lamppost, and, having safely arrived at his place, collapsed in each other's arms and slept till noon. As she brushed her teeth, Dubinsky, standing in the corridor of the suddenly empty—everybody was at work—communal apartment, dialed the precinct number. They had received it. The hours were ten to twelve, so come tomorrow. Dubinsky came up to the window and beamed at the garbage truck. Then he quickly dressed and, ignoring Alyona's offer of scrambled eggs, rushed to the induction center. The colonel had been checking with the precinct for two hours. And just as the minor civilian employees were sneaking out, one by one, to beat the rush-hour lines in the stores, just as cold sweat—what's-wrong-this-time—started forming on Dubinsky's back, the colonel's secretary handed him the receipt. He casually stuffed it in his back pocket. His obligations to the Soviet Army were over.

Next day at the militia precinct Dubinsky lingered downstairs, looking for the Visa and Registration Section in the wall directory. A captain passing by took in his unshaven jowls, his faded Levi's, his button-down shirt, and pointed to the stairs. "Room 22." Impressed by this insight, Dubinsky proceeded in that direction. The treatment in Room 22 was everything he had hoped for—cool and professional. The ample-bodied woman in a dark-blue suit filled out the checklist impassionately. Until she came to the last item.

"Where's the postcard?"

"W-what postcard?"

"A self-addressed stamped postcard. How do you expect us to notify you of the decision?"

In a flash of recognition Dubinsky reached into his back pocket. O miracle of miracles. It was crumpled and wrinkled and grayish from all the changes in the weather it had gone through. But there it was. He borrowed her ballpoint and wrote his address on the face of the card. He sat back, exhausted after a feat so monumental.

She handed him a scrap of paper with a phone number on it. "If you get nervous," she said with a glint in her eye, "you can start calling this number after about three months."

"Th-thank you."

Three

Filing for the visa was followed by an exhausting round of partying no one thought would ever end. They would get up in the afternoon, collect the empty bottles for deposit, and rush to the store to convert them into booze. It was the starting point for the day: after that, anything went.

One night, at 2:00 A.M., Slava decided to teach Dubinsky how to drive, something the latter could use in the West. The cabbie, mollified by half a liter of vodka, stepped aside. "You have to learn to drive under hard conditions," said Vladimir, blindfolding Dubinsky. "Holland needs its James Bonds." The car ended up in the fountain outside the Bolshoi Theater. Everybody was wet and happy. Znachar declared himself a prima donna of aquaballetic arts and requested political and moral asylum from a nearby group of Swedish tourists. Vladimir mistook the Marx monument for the Statue of Liberty and defined himself as a poor huddled Chichmek mass. Slava reclined in the back seat and dictated instructions on trading algae to the fish outside. Dubinsky, weightless and resigned, floated on the surface, telling Mission Control to piss off; he was not coming back to Earth, he was staying on the closest asteroid.

By the end of that tempestuous week, Znachar had sold the last retort from his lab, and Vladimir procured enough alcohol for trips to Chichmekia five years in advance. Slava traded his last pair of Polaroid sunglasses for a case of beer. He had also spent monumental amounts of cash keeping the foursome out of the drunk tank. Dubinsky lived in a happy pastel fog. The worries, the doubts, the frustrations of the last six months were washed away by the flood of Stolichnaya and Johnnie Walker and cheap red.

Vladimir went back to his paper on the dialectics of Chichmek morphology, and Znachar, to doctoring statistics on the superiority of seventeenth-century Russian herbal medicine over the Maoist-revisionist art of acupuncture. Slava resumed trading, for the summer market had always been bullish, both with hordes of Western tourists and with even more numerous hordes of locals on vacation, who wanted to look sharp and were willing to go to impossible lengths to achieve it. Therefore, Slava left for Sochi, the premier vacation spot on the Black Sea coast, where hotel managers vied for the privilege of supplying Comrade Rothman with the best suite available. Dubinsky came along. Summer in Moscow was a killer.

Slava conducted endless meetings with his southern business associates under a Martini-logoed umbrella in a secluded corner of the Intourist Beach, out of reach of the obedient native population. Homicidal-looking flunkeys silently refreshed the contents of a Japanese-made cooler, discreetly covered with a beach towel. Dubinsky would lie in the sun, chasing the last memories of the secretaries and Secretaries away, then go for a swim with a mask, delighting in the pink corals underwater; then he would go back to his blanket, to take in more sun and to devour the latest *Newsweek*. In Pizdo, the Communist Assembly, aided by the Cubans, took over, declared revolutionary nonalignment, and were now renegotiating a new IMF loan.

Sometimes Dubinsky would come to the conference umbrella for a Pepsi that Slava poured for him into a paper cup. "No need to be ostentatious, Dubinsky." Following Slava's instructions, Dubinsky stayed away from the Westerners, who made up the majority of the beach population. "It is watched too closely," Slava explained. "I get away with a lot, but there's no need to tease the Man."

Following a siesta, action would shift to one of Sochi's classier restaurants or to one of Slava's associates' villas. The crowd included dentists from Kiev and Customs officials from Riga, fruit dealers from Tbilisi and butchers from Odessa—all those with nominal 150-ruble-a-month salaries and 1,500-ruble—at least—incomes.

"Soak in some Socialist decadence," Slava said wryly, "before you hit the welfare rolls of the capitalist democracy. Have some shashlik and champagne before going on a hot-dog diet. And women, too, before you have to switch to paper napkins."

There was fucking everywhere—on oversized beds upstairs, against kitchen sinks, on the grass in the backyard, on marble steps leading to water. All those ample-busted and -buttocked blondes, hand-picked to please southern tastes, all those provincial actresses and *corps de ballet* hoofers, stewardesses and hairdressers—their blood was heated by too much sun by day and too much champagne by night, their buttocks spoiled by the lushness of the rugs, their palates by too much caviar and whitefish. For eleven months a year, they lived monotonous lives of waiting in lines for bread and cheese, but for one month they lived like characters in a French movie. Nothing was too much; no price was too high.

Dubinsky fell in love. Every night.

He first vowed chastity on his second night, after he espied the hairdresser Maya from the night before being mercilessly screwed doggy-style on the terrace by a Yerevan dentist. Two hours later, however, Dubinsky was happily copulating with the aggressive and spirited Rita from Kiev, who told him that she had been in Sochi for two weeks and he was her No. 29; she wouldn't rest until she got to fifty.

Dubinsky vented his frustrations to Slava the next morning.

"Good," Slava nodded. "A tested idealist is worth two untested ones."

"I'm not an idealist," Dubinsky snapped angrily. "I just don't like being No. 29."

"She's merely trying to make up for the rest of the year."

"I can't help it, I feel used."

"So don't fuck. I mean, don't fall in love."

But he did, the same night and the night after that. Until he met Katya, who studied design in Tallinn, and who told him that she loved him very much and would follow him wherever he went—preferably to Paris.

"Uh-uh." Slava shook his head. "No go."

"I think she's great," Dubinsky murmured. "She even laughs at my jokes."

Slava relented. "I'll make inquiries."

"She's already tried to marry a German and an Indonesian," he reported the next morning. "Watch out, Dubinsky, there'll be more of that." And, seeing his friend's expression fade, he slapped him on the knee. "We're going back soon anyway. There's time to play around and there's time to agonize about the future."

Back in Moscow, staring at the empty bookshelves and album racks, their contents already sold, Dubinsky felt his knees grow weak. He sat down on the floor and stayed there paralyzed, unable to rise and go to the phone in the corridor and dial the Visa and Registration number. He sat until it grew dark, and from the darkness there sprouted a black, invisible beast, radiating a power so overwhelming that he shivered and pressed his back against the wall, trying to dissolve, to disappear behind the wallpaper, to hide himself from the monster. He slept poorly, calling for Katya and apologizing to her for his mental cruelty, which she was free to cite as grounds for the dissolution of a marriage that never was.

The next morning he dialed the number.

"No decision rendered yet," said a female voice.

Thus started the autumn of Dubinsky's fears.

• • •

Still he sat inside his by now semi-monastic cell, listening to the steady pounding of the rain on the windowpane, watching an occasional leaf fall graciously and desperately in a trajectory unknown even to itself. In the middle of a card game, of a film, of a dinner with friends, his mind would wander again and again, inexorably drawn to the awful possibility: *rejection*. In vain did Znachar tell him that a rejection didn't mean shit, that in six months one could reapply, that it happened to many. In vain did Vladimir assure him that the Dubinsky-turn-Chichmek scheme could be activated on a day's notice. Slava only *tsk-tsk*ed and reminded him that it had been only four months . . . four and a half . . . five . . .

Had the authorities contacted his parents and found out about his lie? Had the Institute rescinded their decision, had they concluded that he did, in fact, know too much? Had the army decided that new conquests in the sands of Asia and the jungles of Africa were doomed without ex-Lieutenant-in-Reserve Dubinsky? Had the Traffic Bureau found that he had indeed once crossed the street at a red light? Could his never having had a hamster have affected the decision? Did he, at one time or another, drunk out of his gourd, say to someone that he was going to spearhead the émigré movement and lead a tank column at Red Square? Didn't everyone—at one time or another? And if he had, who would've informed on him? Nonna, to spite him? Znachar, to promote his own medical career? Vladimir, to ward off an inquiry into the Chichmek studies? Slava, to further his gains—or to pay his own way to the West? Hadn't Slava always been in some kind of contact with them? Hadn't everybody? They would've done it under pressure, wouldn't they? For everybody was vulnerable, no one he knew had his career and well-being protected by an iron-clad guarantee from State Security—no more than he had been with his Pizdo studies.

The questions pounded mercilessly in his head, ricocheting off the walls, filling the space with low, vibrating sounds, as though the whole room were a seashell, with his ear pressed to it, as though he were listening to the throbbing of blood in his own veins and arteries. Then he would stomp down Gorky Street, oblivious to the sudden gusts of rain, to the flickering of neon signs, to the pedestrians' perplexed stares. Occasionally he would stop for an espresso at the Mars Café, or at the Belgrade Hotel for a shot of cognac. He was afraid to go to the synagogue: if the odds were good, and he was the only one left behind, how would he feel then? Or, if the odds were bad, how would he cope without a hope?

For hope persisted: sometimes he simply felt good when a swig of cognac shot through his cold, wet insides after walking in the rain. He would warm up and eye women approvingly and say to himself, We'll drink a few at La Coupole yet. And sometimes he heard Slava whistling outside. "C'mon, Dubinsky, stop cracking your head apart. The cab's waiting." They would set off for the bar at the National Hotel ("Pussy is like everything else, Dubinsky; the best is for export"), where Slava would carefully select a couple of women whom he knew to be less dedicated than others to their KGB masters. In the morning, after the girls had left, Slava would grind the beans and say, inhaling the aromatic steam from the cup, "You're gonna get it, Dubinsky, mark my word." Before Dubinsky dismissed this as another empty encouragement, he would add, "They'll let you go because of your infinite insignificance. You're not a name. You're not a brilliant Jew computer whiz nor a human-rights ballbuster. You're of no use to them. Therefore, if anyone goes, it has to be you."

"That's just more hypothesizing," Dubinsky grumbled.

"There are no guarantees in this business," Slava admitted. "I wouldn't be surprised if I was arrested tomorrow and sentenced to death as a grand-scale black-market operator. It doesn't stop me from doing what I do."

"Why *do* you do it?" Dubinsky knew the answer, but, after a night of bodily delights, the least he could do was to tickle Slava's ego.

"Because I enjoy the game, Dubinsky."

Dubinsky could swear he heard Slava purr.

"Because I know the system with its million cracks like the back of my hand, and I enjoy filling the cracks. But I'm not foolhardy, Dubinsky. It's only a calculated risk I'm taking. Frankly, I'd be rather surprised if they did arrest me. But to get back to you—" He grasped Dubinsky's hand and held it in a firm vise. "If you lose—we'll think up something else."

They had played whist well into the night, and Dubinsky left the window open to get rid of the smoke. He woke up at dawn, shivering and sniffling. He shut the window and lay there, tossing and turning in the dissolving darkness, listening to his neighbors' morning fight in the line to the bathroom, and thinking about all the things he had done wrong in his life; somewhere, way back, he must have slighted or betrayed someone—unwittingly, of course—who had now decided to take revenge and prevent him from leaving. He slept fitfully for an hour or so and woke up with his nose stopped and his throat sore. Great, he thought, as he put on clothes to go to a pharmacy for aspirin. Perfect and altogether fitting. With New Year's Eve less than a week away, he was coming down with pneumonia. He traipsed down the corridor past his neighbor Mariya Timofeyevna, a pensioned salesclerk of pachydermous proportions, who used this opportunity to voice her wish that "certain people should go to Jewland where they properly belong." Mariya Timofeyevna had vested interests in Dubinsky's departure, which would enhance her living space. If it was up to her, I'd be out tomorrow, he thought, shutting the front door and registering with amazement a spot of white through the holes in his mailbox.

When he saw that the tiny scrap of paper was exactly what he had been waiting and hoping for so fervently, he sneezed. And again and again. He sneezed and coughed and sneezed and coughed, and then he grabbed the banister and started descending the stairs, sweating from fever and anticipation.

The back of the card indicated that he should submit certain documents before January 20. The card was dated December 21, Thursday. Today was the twenty-fifth. They ripped me off again, if only for five days, he thought with scorn, and his scorn transformed itself into hatred, and hatred into fury. He trundled on, huddling in the wind and soaking with sweat.

"Bullshit," he said to the secretary at the building management office after she informed him that the chief manager was sick. "I'm staying here until somebody signs the paper that I am surrendering my living space in good condition, that I don't owe any back rent nor electric nor phone bills—"

"I'll call the police," the secretary said, gazing with amazement at the maniac in a sheepskin coat, at his pale, bedraggled, stubble-covered face, at his shaking hands.

"And I'll tell them you tried to extract a bribe," Dubinsky hissed, leaning over to plant a few flu bacteria in her respiratory system. "I'll tell the manager's wife that you sleep with her husband. I'll tell the chief engineer that you inform on him to the KGB. I'll tell every fucking electrician and plumber and carpenter in this office how you inform to the militia on them selling the supplies on the side. I'll ruin your life," he gasped, "because the doctors told me this morning that I have one month left to live—"

She screamed. His knees grew weak. An arrest seemed imminent. He dropped on the floor and closed his eyes.

"What's the matter, Anna Dmitriyevna?" A low, well-modulated voice said. "Bodies lying around. Where is the cleaning woman?"

"This—this—" the secretary whispered. "Dying—Israel—"

"Go get a glass of water."

She must've left, Dubinsky thought, opening an eye. A tanned face, adorned with a thick handlebar moustache, stared at him.

"This is not an emergency room, young man," the man said with a studying expression on his face. "Come to my office."

Inside, the man nodded at the chair. "Drop that junk on the floor."

Dubinsky, instinctively obedient, transferred a pile of bulg-

ing files on the floor and sat down on the edge of the chair.
The man's Parker was already busily trotting along the lines
of a form. Dubinsky watched intently. He had an idea of what
was going on, and, if he was right, opening his mouth would
have been counterproductive.

The man signed the form with professional confidence and
turned it around. "Fill in your name and address."

As Dubinsky wrote, he read the signature: "V. Sharik, Chief
Engineer."

"Finished?" The man pulled the form back. "The execution
fee is three hundred rubles."

Dubinsky gasped. Not only because of the amount—he just
remembered . . . he had forgotten completely—he needed to
pay about a thousand rubles for the visa. True, the Dutch
Embassy, which represented Israel's interests in Moscow,
reimbursed the applicants, but you could not get inside the
Embassy without a visa! He needed a thousand for twenty-
four hours! Slava . . . And now three hundred more . . . He
licked his lips. "I don't have it on me."

"So go get it." Sharik lit a Winston with a debonair gesture.
"Can you imagine the number of things I can find wrong with
your room?"

Trying to locate Slava in the daytime was a futile enterprise,
Dubinsky knew. For a moment he stood in indecision outside
the office, then picked up a handful of snow and rubbed it
over his burning face. His heart was beating violently. He
opened his overcoat and wiped his face with his sweater. Then
he started walking slowly down the street.

Ten minutes later he stood inside a jewelry store, calmly
studying the engagement rings in glass cases. The clerk angrily closed the book she was reading. "Yes?"

"Tell the manager I'm a friend of Rothman's."

A large, fat man wearing a black blazer with an obscure
coat of arms sewn on the pocket, appeared and gave Dubinsky
an odd look.

"Yes?"

"I'm a friend of Slava Rothman's," Dubinsky repeated quietly, holding on to the counter. "He asked me to pick up some stuff for his sister's wedding."

"Oh, sure," the manager beamed. "For Slavochka—" He opened the door to the back of the store and followed Dubinsky inside, then shut it tightly. Dubinsky turned. A tall athletic man stood silently at the manager's side.

"I don't remember seeing you with Slava," the manager said, nodding to the bodyguard.

"I'm a personal friend of Slava's," Dubinsky said, weakly leaning against the wall and letting himself be frisked. "I'm not in the business."

The guard handed the manager the contents of Dubinsky's pockets and stood back.

"You're in the business of splitting." The manager handed him back his papers. "What can I do for you?"

"Thirteen hundred," Dubinsky said. "Till tomorrow."

The manager gave him a skeptical look. "The visa costs nine hundred. The ticket to Vienna, one fifty-seven."

"I've got fifty. The chief engineer at the building management is greedy."

"That's not greed," the manager said, peeling off the bills. "That's business, *boychik*. Your chief engineer is a smart man."

"I'll bring you a thousand fifty tomorrow," Dubinsky said. "After the embassy . . . wait a minute, you gave me fourteen hundred."

"You're allowed to exchange a hundred into dollars," said the man, eyeing Dubinsky with pity.

"I'll get you the balance in a couple of days." Blushing, Dubinsky put the money in his breast pocket. It looked like he was the only one ignorant of the rules of the game.

"I know you will," the man nodded, handing him a blank white envelope. "For your chief engineer. Learn to do business like a civilized man, *bubbele*."

By the time Dubinsky made it to the Visa and Registration Department, he could see it was too late. The waiting room was chock full of people—standing, sitting, pacing, smoking, talking. He headed back home, where he took four aspirins, drank three glasses of tea, and collapsed into bed.

It's all a joke, Slava says. If you take a good look at the card, you'll see it's a joke. Dubinsky studies the card. The address is in his handwriting, and the stamp looks authentic, too. Then he notices a tiny sketch of a smile in the corner. I don't believe this, Dubinsky gasps. The State can be anything, but funny—never. Maybe it's a different state, Slava says. You mean . . . you mean it is Israel that doesn't want me to leave? I guess so, Slava says. You must've told someone that you were really planning to go to Holland.

And that we cannot allow, says Sharik, the chief engineer. Shame on you, Dubinsky, growls Borzoi. As your uncle from Nazareth, says the jewelry store manager, I'll see to it that you are punished. Dubinsky begins to feel out of sorts: they're wearing nothing but towels, he's the only one in a sweater and an overcoat, and in the middle of a sauna, too!

I really have to go, he gasps, as they move closer. Slava! But Slava sits in the corner on the floor, handcuffed. I've just traded a whole batch of these, he says sadly, for half a dozen bottles of Crimean champagne.

In silence, they move closer and closer to him, he can almost sense their skin, through the white steam, he can hardly breathe. Please, please, he whispers, I need some space; but there's no mercy in their faces. I have nothing left to sweat with, he whispers, seeing his skin melt, seeing his bluish entrails leave his body and melt, too—leave me something! he tries to yell, with no sound coming out as a hand reaches for his heart and pulls at it; but the heart won't give in, it jerks back and forth. Please, please, Dubinsky sobs, take this—he searches for his penis, which has melted, too, all but for a bit of foreskin. Not the heart . . . he whispers.

I'm having a rotten time in the Kingdom of Denmark, Nonna says sadly, caressing his buttocks. And since I've just been told you're not coming, I'm throwing myself off the wall in Elsinore. And so will Maya, Alyona, and Katya. What can I do to save them, asks Dubinsky through the steam. Slava fondles his heart. Okay, Dubinsky whispers, if that's what it takes. He yanks at his heart, but it doesn't tear off; instead, it starts melting. What? Dubinsky yells. No good deed shall go unpunished, quotes Slava with a grin, and by a clever sleight-of-hand sheds his handcuffs. His face moves up at Dubinsky, closer and closer, until all Dubinsky can see is Slava's lips that say, Don't worry, Oleg, we'll replace your little heart we'll put something better inside I just got a great one with a microchip space-age technology comes in eighteen colors he comes closer and closer until Dubinsky disappears in him completely . . .

He woke up drenched in sweat and weaker than a baby. He started counting, meaning to get out of bed at one hundred, but then he realized he'd cheat and add another hundred, so he lifted himself on forty-five. He staggered to the kitchen, boiled a carton of milk, poured it over the instant, stirred in honey, then poured the concoction into a thermos. Armed with this plus aspirins, handkerchiefs, and a bottle of nose drops, he stepped outside.

There were already a few people outside the office, which was to open in an hour. They looked as though they had spent a whole night there, which was impossible, since the militia-man would have dispersed them. Dubinsky sat down on a stone ledge and lifted the collar of his overcoat all the way. He did not feel like kibitzing. After a while he closed his eyes, although he could not sleep because of the chill in the air. He sniffled and blew his nose to reinforce his determination.

The office opened, people kept arriving, soon the lobby was full; yet the door with the INSPECTOR sign on it was still shut. From the corner of his eye Dubinsky watched people silently huddle in groups, smoke, pace the lobby. Children played hopscotch on the tiled floor; a baby cried. Then the door opened, and the first applicant went in. Everybody started talking at once; there was a loud dispute about a place in line that almost turned into a fight, had it not been for the militiaman's presence. He eyed them indifferently; yet, as everybody knew, he would use the slightest hint at disorder as an excuse to throw them all out.

A man in a black coat and mud-covered shoes approached Dubinsky. "Are you by yourself? Would you be interested in taking a couple of rugs along? One for you, one for me?" Another offered to sell a share in his brother's car in Rome. Others offered dog-walking and apartment-cleaning services in Europe, phones of influential people in Miami and New York, and a share in a seat on the Haifa Commodities Exchange.

The only thing I really need is a warm bed, thought Dubinsky, and fresh clean sheets.

Finally the door opened: his turn had come.

The woman nodded at the chair and continued writing on the pad. Dubinsky placed the postcard on the desk, then added the certificate from the building management and the deposit receipt from the bank. She silently read his name off the card and dug into her file cabinet. He watched her out of the corner of his eye—she had a bony, avian face and horn-rimmed glasses; her complexion was sallow; from time to time she took drags on her *papirosa*, an old-fashioned hollow-filter cigarette. Rosa Klebb, Dubinsky thought with distaste; Old Guard all the way. His nose started overflowing again. He sniffled mechanically. She shot him a look. "Can't you blow your nose?"

Still holding his handkerchief to his nose, he noticed something that made his heart miss a beat. There it was, his visa. A slip of paper in a playful pink, with his picture on it.

She stared at the papers he had brought for a few minutes. He held his breath.

"What the hell is this?" She grabbed the paper from the building management. "Whose signature is it?"

"Chief engineer's."

"Did you forge it?"

Unable to speak, he shook his head.

"I don't like this." She looked him in the eye. "I think you forged it. What do you think? Do you think you can come in here and play games with me? As if I couldn't tell what came first, the seal or the signature!" She threw it in his face. "If you didn't forge it, then you can go back and have him sign it and *then* put a stamp on it!"

He sat in a stupor, listening to the beat of his heart, his eyes fixed upon the visa.

She misinterpreted his silence. "You don't want to go? Well then—"

She made as if she was about to tear up the visa.

He rose slowly. "I'll be back."

Outside, the crowd clamored. "What happened?" And, seeing his face:

"She should go out for lunch soon, she always gets like this about this time—"

He stepped out and flagged a cab.

Sharik motioned Dubinsky to come in. "I don't give refunds. What do you want?"

"A fresh one. The seal over the signature."

Sharik shrugged. "I don't know what good that will do." Yet he pulled out a blank form and filled it anew, completing it with a signature and a careful pressing of the seal. As he handed it to Dubinsky, his eyes lingered on Dubinsky's face. "Are you okay? You look sick."

"I *am* sick."

When he walked back into the lobby, he was told that the inspector had just left for lunch. Dubinsky nodded absently and pushed his way to the head of the line.

"You're not going in ahead of me, young man," a woman in a lamb coat declared.

"I am." Dubinsky lowered himself on the floor and ate three aspirins. "I've already been here." If he had known there was no rush, he would've stopped by his place to refill the thermos. And he was running out of handkerchiefs again.

"He *was* in the line," someone said. "I remember him."

"Yeah, that's the nut who is leaving with nothing but a shirt on his back."

"Shame on you," a woman said to the one in lamb. "The young man's sick!"

"Bastards, they would have us all die here!"

"Hush, the cop's listening."

"Leave the kid alone."

Someone offered him a chicken wing, and someone else gave him a cup of hot broth. The woman in lamb, blushing, offered him an initialed batiste handkerchief. Another one made a sour comment regarding Dubinsky's parents who let him go out sick, while yet another suggested he was most likely an orphan and as such used to deprivation. The crowd was getting agitated; factions were forming. One feared that Dubinsky had an infectious disease ("Please, it's only a cold," he whispered, but no one listened), and insisted on calling an ambulance. Someone else voiced a suspicion that Dubinsky was faking a fever and asked that a doctor be summoned to certify his condition. The women universally demanded that the orphan be left alone. The militiaman woke up and watched the scene with a wary eye, waiting for the pandemonium to break loose, so he could call for reinforcements and go back to sleep.

Dubinsky looked for a place to dispose of the chicken bones. He was actually feeling better, but wisely decided to keep it to himself. Finally, a doctor was found, although he insisted he was a neurosurgeon. Dubinsky opened his mouth and said "Aaah." The neurosurgeon touched Dubinsky's forehead and said he couldn't say anything without an X-ray.

At which point the Inspector marched through the lobby, and a hush fell on the crowd. Five minutes later, Dubinsky went in.

This time she was in a better mood; that is to say, she was humming a melody from the latest collective-farm musical and picking up crumbs of the cake off the plate in front of her. She swept off the paper he had brought and, without so much as a glance, clipped it to the rest.

"All right," she said. "Do you know what to do next? Austrian Embassy for a temporary visa—Dutch Embassy to get your money back—Aeroflot office for the air ticket—Foreign Exchange Bank—"

He nodded obediently.

"Let's see if I've got everything," she said cheerfully. "With you people and your little games, one has to pay attention." Still humming, she went through the papers again. And stopped. "What is this? When did you stop working?"

"January," Dubinsky whispered. And, remembering he had been on the payroll up to the day he received his reference, corrected himself:

"I mean, June."

She gave him another steady look, as her fingers did a quick drumbeat on his visa. Lying only two feet away.

"Your character reference is dated January."

So they had it all along.

"Would you like to tell me what you've been doing for a whole year? Have you ever heard of social parasitism?"

"It's a mistake," he uttered. "I worked—"

"Let's go," she said. He dragged his feet after her as they left the office. "Wait for me here." She headed toward the stairs. He leaned listlessly against the wall. The room swam.

"He's gonna die," someone said. "He's paler than a stiff." Someone else propped him up and handed him a nitroglycerine tablet. He shook his head mutely. The room expanded vertically, then horizontally. The militiaman reached for his holster. A siren sounded. Portraits descended from the walls and joined the crowd. "It's the end," said Brezhnev/Borzoi/ the rug smuggler. "I know," Dubinsky whispered. "I'm cold." "Rigor mortis," said Kosygin the neurosurgeon. "Here," said Nonna, handing him a bus ticket. "Next." He looked at his hand and his picture and the seal on the picture and the typed words around it. Dubinsky Oleg Semyonovich was free to leave the country for permanent residence in the State of Israel on the grounds of family reunion.

"Beware the Ides of March," said Slava. "I mean, you still have over ten hours before takeoff. Plus a delay, standard for

Aeroflot. Pick a deity and do a quick prayer. That nothing happens between now and then. *L'chaim.*"

They touched glasses, and the clink was lost in the megadecibel noise that filled the room. Slava's apartment overflowed with people. They sat on the floor, on the furniture, and on one another's knees; they slurped wine and Johnnie Walker; they stuffed themselves with ham from Denmark and *satzivi* from Aragvi; they laughed, they sang along with Bette Midler and made tentative passes at one another. It was New Year's Eve, the biggest Russian party of the year, untainted by the ideological overtones of the October Revolution or the First of May. And Dubinsky's flight to Vienna was ten hours and twenty minutes away.

"Something will probably happen," Dubinsky said casually. "But so what?" He remembered the Aeroflot office where they had demanded the proof he was not shipping any furniture. And his neighbors, who had camped outside his room, unable to wait until he cleared out. "It always ends well, doesn't it?"

He was floating in the air, in part because he had hardly eaten anything in the last two days, in part because Znachar had started him on a crash flu treatment, with pills and vitamin shots. He had also had Dubinsky inoculated against syphilis, yellow fever, and manic depression. Even if Dubinsky had not been stoned, he wouldn't've been able to sit anyway.

"What do I need the yellow fever shot for?"

"Here's a scenario: the plane is hijacked and taken to Madagascar or wherever they have yellow fever," Znachar explained. He was even more excited than Dubinsky. "This is all classified research," he added. "They only give these to astronauts and spies and Olympic athletes."

"Which one am I?"

"You're my friend. And I won't let you die." Znachar patted a very appetizing knee that protruded from the human mass on the couch, and suddenly emitted a sob. "I feel like I was the father of a bride," he whined. "You're leaving the bosom of the family, you cocksucker."

"Maybe I'm just growing up," said Dubinsky, who with

every minute understood less and less what he was doing.

Vladimir came over with a mayonnaise jar filled with bluish liquid. "That's alcohol distilled on blueberries," he explained. "Favorite Chichmek medicine for indigestion and growth pains." He took a swig and frowned. "It's all our fault in the long run. I wish you were staying. I'd make a perfect Chichmek out of you."

"He's going to learn that by himself," Slava said.

"That's right," Vladimir nodded. "For what is Chichmekia but a state of mind? Ah, but the pains thou shalt undergo, Dubinsky, as the Aeroflot jet takes you from being a Moscow connoisseur of fine wines and Penguin paperbacks to being just another Chichmek dishwasher in a Sheraton hotel. Ah, how your *toches* will hurt . . ."

The chimes on the Spassky Tower started sounding the farewell to the old year. "One . . . two . . . " the crowd counted.

Slava leaned to Oleg. "Countdown, Dubinsky. D hour minus ten."

"Ten . . . eleven . . . twelve!" The corks hit the ceiling, as the white foam overflowed the glasses, and the air filled with lip-smacking. Dubinsky, who was wearing the Slava-provided paper hat with "Outward Bound" written on it, got more than his share, as he was passed from arm to arm—*Good luck honey I'll pray for you Next year in Jerusalem*—until Nonna took him by the hand and led him to the bedroom.

They lay down on the bed among the fur coats and went for each other, disregarding another couple on the floor and people passing by within feet. She whispered and sobbed, while he caressed her back and kissed her on the lips, until it was all over. She sniffled and was gone, leaving him spent and wondering whether it was her or someone else, or whether it happened at all, or whether it was something he should be racking his brains about.

It was snowing like crazy when Dubinsky's friends dragged him out of the house.

"It's only half past three," he protested, pausing in the doorway.

"We have to take you to Red Square," Slava said firmly. "For the last look."

Dubinsky swallowed another one of Znachar's pills, shivered, and stepped out. He inhaled the air, clean and frosty, especially so after the smoke- and perfume-filled apartment. He treaded the snow, white and pure, a relief after vermouth puddles and sauce blotches on the floor. They walked down Gorky Street in silence, listening to the steady hum of the wind, exchanging grins and New Year greetings with occasional passers-by. They passed Mayakovsky, who waved them along, and Pushkin, who gave them a sad look and said nothing, and Count Yuri the Long-Armed, the city founder, who eyed them suspiciously.

"I'm gonna miss you, guys," Dubinsky said after a long inward struggle. "If it hadn't been for you . . ."

Znachar hushed him and passed around a flask with cognac. "To a better year for Dubinsky."

They drank. The snowfall was growing heavier by the minute, so that the last block before the Square took them a good ten minutes. Dubinsky kept sniffling. It was a night out of a fairy tale, white and blue, and the Nutcracker was to show on the crenellate Kremlin wall any minute.

Finally they made it to the Square and stood for a few minutes in front of the mausoleum in silence.

"Thanks for not shooting me," said Dubinsky to Lenin.

The guards kept staring into space.

A lonely Oriental was fiddling with his camera.

The clock struck four.

"So I *am* a fucking astronaut," Dubinsky said, referring to the well-publicized ritual whereby astronauts visit Red Square on the night before the launch.

They cut across old Chinatown and headed for Old Square.

"Of course you're an astronaut," said Slava, landing on the bench. "You're also a time traveler, and a champion of your own human rights, and a traitor to the Motherland. Take your pick." The flask was refilled and went around, as they talked and talked and talked: of the time Vladimir had come to school drunk and vomited in the back of the class; of the time

Znachar got clap in the bushes of Gorky Park; of the time Slava bribed the projectionist at Illusion Theater to show *La Dolce Vita* at midnight and they brought friends and booze and had a wild party until morning; of the time Dubinsky publicly French-kissed their old English History instructor at their alumni reunion.

Then they fell silent, because the past was in the past, and the future was only six hours away.

"I feel like shit," Znachar said. "I mean, here you are, just . . . breaking out, come what may, while we're gonna just fart away here till the day we die."

"I feel he's a fool," Vladimir said. "Leaving the only country in the world where you can get away with not doing shit and still do quite nicely for yourself. My God, Dubinsky, you've never worked with your hands. The only calluses you've ever had were from playing volleyball. What are you going to put on your résumé? Pizdo?"

"With proper ambition, something can be done even with that," Slava said lightly. "What was that stuff they mine there, Dubinsky? Uranium and what else?"

"I don't recall," Dubinsky said pointedly. As far as he was concerned, Pizdo was tainted and consigned to the past.

"Pizdorum, I think," Slava persisted. "Salvation springs out of unexpected places, Dubinsky. You want to be a saint, but you can't live on deferred payments."

"I don't feel like a saint," Dubinsky muttered. "Rather . . . I feel scared."

As they left the cab at Sheremetyevo International, Dubinsky tripped over the curb and would have fallen, had it not been for Vladimir's arm. Znachar fed him two more pills; Slava lightly slapped him on the cheek. "Stop shaking."

"I am a mess," Dubinsky admitted.

The snow kept falling. "Fucking KGB fixing the weather," Znachar muttered, helping Dubinsky with his only suitcase. "I hope they've cleared the damn runway."

They opened the last bottle of champagne—for the road—

inside the cafeteria. Dubinsky's mouth tingled, and his eyes grew teary.

"Godspeed, Dubinsky. Write."

As the glass door closed, Dubinsky cast a last-minute glance. Faces merged into one: Znachar's toothed grin, Vladimir's bushy beard, Slava's cool unsmiling eyes.

Good-bye.

It's all over, he whispered, looking at the airfield; a new and a wonderful life is about to start.

Four

They picked each other out of the crowd immediately. Both knew each other's looks: his, a stranger in a strange land; hers, a professional meeter, trained to put the likes of him at ease. She gave him a firm handshake, inquired about the flight, and steered him to the luggage claim area.

Dubinsky had rested on the plane, his stomach was fortified by a huge breakfast, and his heart was singing "Travelin' Band" by Creedence Clearwater Revival. He had been in the country for less than twenty-four hours, and he could not find a thing around him he did not like. The airport was a shining temple of glass and steel, surgically clean and light, with numerous signs, unambiguously indicating where one should look for departures, for arrivals, for bathrooms, for drinks, for banks, for pet storage rooms. The escalators slid silently up and down, the doors opened promptly ten feet in advance. Huge lit-up pictures of heretofore unbeholden beauty exhorted him to visit amusement parks and shopping centers he had never heard of. The ground personnel, in their smart uniforms, were cheerful and helpful. The enormity and the efficiency of the place were awesome. One could spend one's whole life here—sleeping, eating, reading, watching TV, shopping—and never be disturbed by the earthquakes and plagues and revolutions of the unpredictable life Outside.

They took the elevator to the roof garage upstairs. Dubinsky inhaled it all: the sun, the wind, the sky, the open space, the toy leviathans slowly turning on the ground, ready to take off for Montevideo and Butte, Montana. *I'm here*, he said; and then he closed his eyes for a second and pinched himself to make sure.

"Here we are, Mr. Dubinsky." Ms. Levine smilingly opened the trunk of the black gleaming Coupe de Ville. "You can put your suitcase in here."

He plunged speechlessly into the plush leather of the cushions, mesmerized by the myriad dials of the dashboard. *Is it amphibian?* flashed through his mind; *can it fly, too?*

"I'm so glad we're finally out of the airport, it is so dehumanizing . . ." Ms. Levine was bent on involving Dubinsky in a nonstop conversation; he was striving both to oblige her and to drink in the scenery.

According to Ms. Levine, the town of San Murray had a lot to offer an immigrant. It had a strong "clean" industrial base, several first-rank colleges, it had theaters—museums—shopping malls—waterfront—noble historical past—shining future—Ms. Levine was breathless. She need not have been, for Dubinsky already loved every minute of it. There was spaciousness and drive and freedom in the air; there was a feeling of Hail the Conquering Hero, Emperor Dubinsky rising on the Interstate into the Metropolis of San Murray. The downtown high-rises loomed in the distance, intricate webs of bridges soared over the proud waters below, the green expanses of the parks pleased the eye. The sun shone unobtrusively, lest it burn the illustrious guest. A light breeze blew, just enough to provide ventilation. A police helicopter hovered in the sky, X-raying the streets for possible assassins about to leap out of the bush and spray Ms. Levine's Cadillac with bullets, however unlikely the possibility that anyone would feel less hospitable toward Mr. Dubinsky. The tank-sized Cadillac engine purred obediently and contentedly. Dubinsky pushed the power window lever shut and smelled the rich odor of Safety and Dignity exuded by the soft leather. He released the lever and felt the Efficient Perfection and Automated Beauty outside promise him many blissful years in his new surroundings.

On their way to Dubinsky's new quarters, Ms. Levine invited him to have lunch at an establishment on Main Street. It was a diminutive red structure, a doll house, really: all the chairs and tables were shiny in bright yellow and red colors. Golden arches over the roof enhanced the fairy-tale appearance. What a lovely place, Dubinsky thought; so much attention is lavished upon the tots! Although he was a little perplexed as to why Ms. Levine had brought him here, and felt a bit silly in a place where they were likely to be served gingerbread or marzipan or whatever all those elves used for food, he bravely stepped up to the counter and copied Ms. Levine's order word for word.

"Do you like it here?" asked Ms. Levine, and, having been assured that he did, added, "This is an American institution, Oleg. Sad but true."

Dubinsky pleasantly smiled to commiserate with the sadness which he did not feel, and opened his cardboard box. "Oh," he said, rising, "they forgot to put in the forks."

Ms. Levine looked at him sympathetically. "You don't need a fork to eat this, Oleg." She took a bite out of her Big Mac and daintily touched her lips with a napkin.

"I see." Dubinsky attempted another smile. His heart was seized with panic. Cold sweat came through the pores on his forehead. Some elves, he thought. Ogres was more like it. He had never eaten anything that thick in his life without a fork and a knife. His heart thumped violently, for he understood only too well that this was it, this was the test to determine whether he belonged in this wondrous new reality. He nibbled on the edge of the bun; following Ms. Levine's example, he poured the potatoes out of the box. Then he tried to open the ketchup package. No dice. He followed the instructions. It would not give way. I understand the need for this tough packaging, he told himself, it's wonderful that they do it, otherwise it would fall apart before it reached the table, still. . . . Infuriated at his foreigner's ineptitude, he violently bit into the package. It popped and for a moment he was blinded. "Oops." Ms. Levine handed him a napkin.

As Dubinsky, wanly smiling, was rubbing the ketchup off his face, Ms. Levine held forth about the dehumanizing effect of modern packaging. Dubinsky forlornly dipped a fry into the ketchup, won at such a cost, and stared at what he termed an OgreBurger. The sandwich returned the stare indifferently. He looked around. People were biting into the goddamn things all over the place. A preschool cherub bit off a half of his MacJr. and reached for more. A prim bespectacled school-teacher, holding her pinkie aside, greedily clenched a Quarter Pounder between her dentures. A trucker swallowed two Big Macs without chewing and downed a strawberry shake in one gulp. I can do it, Dubinsky thought. I've been through worse, I ate chicken at the Metropol Restaurant in Moscow with nothing but a bent fork in front of fifty Frenchmen; I ate spaghetti alla marinara with nothing but a spoon in Venice; I'm not going to be stared down by a lousy piece of chopped meat stuffed in a bun. He opened his mouth wide, closed his eyes to concentrate, caught his breath—and his teeth connected through the watery tissue of the bun. The patty had fled the coop. It slid between his fingers back into the box and lay there smugly.

Dubinsky felt himself getting red in the face. Ms. Levine was staring intently into her coffee. Bullshit, he said to himself. It's three attempts, like in a high jump. If it doesn't disappear into my esophagus after two more tries, I'm taking a cab to the airport. The drummer beat a quick, nervous tattoo. Dubinsky carefully, slowly wiped his fingers with the napkin, picked up the patty, inserted it back into position, together with the lettuce and tomato and onions, and gave it a last final stare. The patty blinked. As Dubinsky took a few deep breaths, the drummer halted, and then he hit the cymbals, as Dubinsky's jaws pounded upon the miserable hamburger with the gaiety of a conqueror; like a borzoi, he plunged his teeth into the wolf's neck; and, stoically ignoring the pain that shot through his jaw, he fell on it again, merciless and vengeful. Only then did he sit back, now chewing slowly, enjoying the fruits of his victory, tears in his eyes both from joy and from the dull pain in his jaw.

The drummer—nay, a whole trumpet section—rose and did a collective bravura solo; the customers broke into "For He's a Jolly Good Fellow," clapping their hands; the schoolmarm blew him a kiss; the trucker came to slap Dubinsky on the back; a gray-haired, tired-looking man in a three-piece business suit introduced himself as the mayor and presented Dubinsky with a key to the city. The restaurant manager took pictures and gave Dubinsky a coupon book for many a Big Mac and a Coke. The celebration went on, and even Ms. Levine, teary-eyed, hugged him, gave him a full kiss on the lips, and, pressing her *zaftig* body against his, hotly whispered, "I'm so happy we picked you. We couldn't've made a better choice."

Dubinsky nodded gratefully. He tried to open his mouth and tell them how happy he was to have passed his initiation rites with such panache, but cringed with pain instead. The jaw was still hurting something awful.

Toward the end of the day Slava developed a splitting headache. At the end of the meeting with the manager of a toy factory from Kishinev he excused himself and went to the bathroom. He took out a French-made aspirin, poured water over it, and watched the bubbles bolt violently to the surface. He caught himself thinking that he had no idea why he was using the kind of aspirin that needed to be dissolved à la Alka-Seltzer. He also realized that even French aspirin was useless in his condition.

"I heard you're packing it in," the man said, as they shook hands, calling it a day.

Slava felt a cube of ice in his stomach. "People will always talk," he said casually. "Where did you hear that?"

"You started taking your *vigorish* in coins," the man said. "Don't tell me you're saving for a refrigerator."

Slava chuckled. "I'm building a vacation home in Tbilisi. The locals wouldn't take anything but gold coins."

"Far from Moscow, too." The man winked.

"What about yourself?" Slava asked, tactfully steering the manager to the door. "You ever think about it?"

"What am I going to do there?" The man chuckled. "I've got it made, knock on wood. You don't start from scratch in my age."

The schmuck is only fifty or so, Slava thought, closing the door. He makes sense, the pig. They all make sense, his clients. Why run away from a good thing? They have cars and co-ops and dachas, they spend summers on the Black Sea coast, their wives sport chinchillas and minks and pearl necklaces—what else could they ask for?

He lay down, poured himself a shot of Johnnie Walker. The throbbing pain would not go away. The manager had a whole section of a toy factory working exclusively for himself and his partner, who had found a way to save fifty percent on raw materials. The pig, Slava thought. Stealing from the State was one thing—if no one stole, the economic system would collapse overnight—but stealing from his own partner? They couldn't help it, he thought with disdain; the partner was stealing, too—he had come to Slava a month ago, seeking to convert a truckload of plush squirrels into Greek drachmas, for his wife, who was going on a cruise. Everyone stole. The pain still wouldn't go away. He took two sleeping pills, and soon he was snoring away. He dreamed of the clean, efficient-looking steel vaults of Zurich that would soon receive the fruit of the sweat of his brow. All the gold and diamonds in circulation on the Moscow-Odessa-Tbilisi triangle—he'd corner the market and buy everybody out for a song. And maybe he'd charter a Learjet to land somewhere in Karelia, pick up the load, and fly it straight to a branch of Credit Suisse.

• • •

Slava had never been idle, but the next two months saw a dramatic increase in his activities. He traded with a vengeance, converting his commissions into gold coins and diamonds and pearls and Swiss francs, just in case. And finally, it was time.

A week before his move to Tbilisi, the illustrious capital of the great free-spirited Soviet Socialist Republic of Georgia, Slava reluctantly met with Znachar and Vladimir. Since Dubinsky's departure, he had been steadily drifting apart from them, but to leave without a soul-to-soul talk was unthinkable.

"What if there's a change of guard in the estimable Government of Soviet Georgia?" Vladimir unscrewed the cap off a gallon container of lab alcohol. "Then you're stuck, pal."

"I don't think so. Shevardnadze has been in power for only a couple of years. He hasn't stolen enough yet. Besides, they have a long nose for those things in Tbilisi. And they wouldn't let me move in on their turf if I had not promised to leave."

"I don't know," Vladimir shook his head. "Are you sure they're not setting you up? You're a Russian, after all; master race. You'll be the one to take a fall if things get tough."

"You don't understand business," Slava said angrily. "Stick to your Chichmekland." As if the same thoughts did not keep him awake till morning. "Besides, if that was the case, Goga wouldn't get involved."

"You trust Goga," Znachar said, "because you have an Assyrian fixation."

"What's that?" Vladimir mixed the alcohol with lime juice and eyed the glass in the light. He felt overwhelmed with emotion. So tender, so transcendental was the yellowish color. I should've been an artist, he sighed, and decided to encourage an extensive use of the color in the new exhibition of Chichmek folk art that was to open in a month. The best hands on the Moscow underground art scene were toiling in their basements. As their patron, Vladimir felt, he could pretty much order not only the choice of subject, but one of colors as well. He felt proud and independent—a Medici of his time.

"I don't know what 'Assyrian fixation' means," Znachar confessed, "but it sure sounds great. I'd like to meet Goga," he said to Slava. "The complexes he must've accumulated in the five thousand years of Assyrian history must be mind-boggling. To say nothing of the polytheistic effect on his psyche."

"Goga isn't interested in a beak-nosed smelly old Jew like you," Slava said curtly as they drained their glasses. He opened a can of shiitake mushrooms for a chaser. "Goga is interested in blue-eyed, flaxen-haired fifteen-year-olds from the Moscow Boys' Choir."

"But what about science?" Znachar exclaimed. "What about progress?"

"No self-respecting Assyrian believes in progress," Slava said.

"It's all a mistake," Znachar summed it up, gloomily filling his mouth with sardines. "You have delusions of grandeur. The Mellons and the Du Ponts will eat you up. The Mob will bury you in cement. And the United Goldsteins of America will sell you to the Feds."

"First, the Georgians will sell you out," Vladimir insisted. "My ethnography-trained instincts don't lie to me."

"God, are the two of you full of shit." Slava downed his glass. He felt the alcohol distributing itself evenly through his body. Every artery, every vein, every capillary was being filled with the explosive cocktail. He rose and leaned against the wall. "You don't have the balls to leave, that's all there is to it."

There was a prolonged silence.

"What we have here," Znachar finally spoke, "is an externalized feeling of guilt about having expelled our friend Dubinsky into the cold of the imperialist jungle. Now you're trying to make up for it by following him. But it won't bring him back, Slava. He's gone, and your suicidal gesture won't bring him back."

"Indeed," Vladimir agreed. "Judging by his letters, Dubinsky is experiencing an eclipse of both sun and moon. His brains seem to have completely gone to mush."

"There's just no way things can be all that fantastic," Znachar added. "Mentally, Dubinsky never recovered from that Pizdo coup d'état. So by now he is simply externalizing his fantasies on paper. It's his refuge."

"Paper, a refugee's refuge," Vladimir echoed.

"That's not how I see it," Slava said, angry again. "But you assholes can go on kidding yourselves and making excuses for everything from egg prices to your own sluggishness till you go blue in the face."

They fell silent again. Slava ambled to the window. I'm not good at dealing with people except trading in stereos and pesetas, he thought, gazing at the lights of the Garden Ring outside. Instead of saving my friendships, I ruin them. But it's all their fault that they sit on their fat asses, unable to break out of their warm nests, forever content to be playing games with the State. I am not like that, he thought, turning to draw inspiration from Bernie Kornfeld's picture on his wall. But it was gone; he had traded it, he had thrown it in with his collection of Jimi Hendrix LPs, after telling the buyer that the man in the picture was Jerry Lee Lewis.

Captain Kabyzdokh emerged on Slava's doorstep on the eve of the departure. He had been drinking and appeared to be in a belligerent, albeit informal, mood. "You're not thinking of something stupid, are you, Vorontzov?"

"Like what?"

"Like hijacking a plane." The captain pointed at the empty apartment. "People who move use movers, Vorontzov. They don't sell their belongings down to the last chandelier."

"Comrade Captain, why should I take chandeliers to Tbilisi, the city of peerless glass blowers? Do you take your wife to Sochi on vacation?" He poured Kabyzdokh a Remy.

"I'm not taking my wife anywhere," Kabyzdokh said gloomily, after he downed a Remy and sucked on a wedge of lemon. "She's a pig. We go to a special-access restaurant, she orders a duck, she spends a whole evening picking the bones clean. She slurps on them, for Chrissake." He poured himself another Remy. "But why am I telling this to you, a black marketeer and quite possibly a traitor to the Motherland?"

Slava yawned. "Who are you going to tell this to, your colleagues? They'll sell you out."

"Hey, what happened to that Jew friend of yours?" Kabyzdokh's face lit up. "The underground analyst?"

"Please leave him alone," Slava said. "You approach him, he'll shit his pants."

"So what am I supposed to do?" Kabyzdokh whined. "What if I can't get it up any more?"

"Nothing," Slava said. "Your official psychiatrists will tell you to take cold showers, and underground analysts would be afraid to talk to you." He paused. "But I have a farewell present for you. A token of goodwill. Made in Belgium of powdered ivory tusks, mixed with the sperm of saber-toothed tigers—"

"If it doesn't work, Vorontzov, you're looking at five to seven for anti-Soviet propaganda," Kabyzdokh said in a suddenly sober voice.

"I'll throw in a color Hitachi, just to make sure it works," Slava coughed.

"You know how many times I saved your ass?" Kabyzdokh grabbed angrily the delicate neck of the cognac bottle. "You think a lousy Jap TV will make up for it?"

"You might also get it up again," Slava reminded tactfully.

"The hell with that," Kabyzdokh waved. "I'm better off just offing that bitch." He finished the Remy out of the bottle. "How come you never asked me why I saved your ass?" Without waiting for an answer he went on, "Because you're a Russian, and it warmed my heart to see you screw all those Jews at their own game."

"Anti-Semitism is a matter of personal choice," Slava said wearily.

"I'm not an anti-Semite," Kabyzdokh said. "Every time we arrest one of those dissident kikes, when I see their kids crying, all those little Moishes and Sarahs—do you think my heart doesn't bleed for the poor bastards?"

"I'm sure you bring them candy."

" 'Kiss-Kiss,' ruble-fifty a kilo," Kabyzdokh nodded. "How did you know?"

"People talk," Slava said evasively. "You have a reputation as Comrade Soft Touch, when it comes to crying babies. Every Goldstein in town coaches his little Moishe in crying, praying that you'll be the arresting officer."

"You're kidding." The captain's eyes grew moist. "See, Vorontzov, even kike dissidents . . . Tell me"—he grabbed the lapels of Slava's coat—"tell me—do you respect me?"

"Enormously." Slava turned away politely to avoid the stench. The combination of cheap red and Remy on the captain's breath was murder on Slava's olfactory glands.

"Then why would you spread the grease in Tbilisi rather than here?"

"They are better organized," Slava explained. "You people spend too much time arresting Jews and other poor fucks who happen to look too long at propaganda pictures outside the American Embassy. You lose sight of your primary activity."

"And what is our primary activity?" echoed Kabyzdokh, staring at the wall in a stupor.

"Why, collecting taxes from schmucks like me, of course," said Slava amicably. "For yourself and your family. How old is your boy now, thirteen?"

"You remember everything," said Kabyzdokh with admiration.

"I'll get him a pair of earphones. Sony," Slava said. "So that he doesn't bother you with decadent Western music."

Ms. Levine redeposited Dubinsky back at his quarters, assuming he needed rest after two long flights. "You must take things easy now," she said. "After all the suffering . . . and the jet lag, too. Do you like the furniture?"

He was stunned. There was a spacious living room that opened into an equally large dining room, a kitchen to its side. A door from the living room led to the bedroom. Three rooms. All to himself. "I could play soccer here," he murmured, then leapt across the room and performed a rather decent *jeté*, raising tiny columns of dust in the air.

Ms. Levine politely clapped her hands. She had heard that all Russians went to ballet school from the age of three, but to actually witness the experience. . . .

The phone rang. "Are you the head of the household, sir?" asked a melodic female voice.

The question took him aback. *Household.* Of course! Of course he was! "Yes," he said. *Household.* What a wonderful, sonorous word.

"What brand of dishwasher do you use?"

Dishwasher. "Hold on." He rushed to the kitchen, pulled at the knobs. The only thing in the entire kitchen that looked like it had something to do with washing dishes was a small, flat piece of rubber with sections for plates and silverware. But there was no brand name.

"I understand perfectly, sir," she chirped happily. "Could you ask your wife, perhaps?"

"No wife," he admitted. "Wife" was a requirement for a full-fledged household, he realized.

"Oh." She sounded stumped.

"Look," he said, startled by another realization, "you mean . . . *electric* dishwasher?"

"Why . . . yes."

"I'm sorry." He dropped on the floor. "I don't have one." *Dishwasher.* How premature his joys had been. What kind of household was it, without a dishwasher.

"Well," she persisted, "let me run a few names by you and see if you can recognize them: Whirlpool, Sears—"

He held the phone to his ear, stunned and depressed. Then he cut her short in mid-sentence. "Excuse me . . . I have to go now. I'm sorry. What's your name?"

"*My* name?" Now it was her turn to be startled. "Sheri."

"Thank you for your time, Sheri."

He picked himself up off the floor, and, because he had just told her he had to go, walked out the door. No lies, Dubinsky. Ignorance of dishwasher brands is no excuse.

His spirits picked up as he hit Main Street. There were not too many passers-by in this afternoon hour, but the stream of traffic was unending. He walked past another children's restaurant, with fried chicken imported from Kentucky; a Shell gas station; and then suddenly the sidewalk ended. The sprawl of the freeway lay ahead, and, above the cement and the concrete, there towered an enormous sign, HEAVEN HILLS MALLS. Dubinsky the explorer forgot all about his shame: how to get there? Crossing the freeway was out of the question: the cars zoomed by faster than Moscow fire trucks. Finally he found a footbridge that led to the parking lot, and soon he was inside a department store.

It was a dream—cool, subdued, elegant—with an unknown invisible band quietly playing "Blowin' in the Wind." He passed the escalators, gearing himself for the return to reality, but the fiction continued; he found himself in a large, covered courtyard, complete with fountains, trees, and shrubbery. It was a separate town all right; he was shocked to learn that he was on Munichstrasse. *Mädchen* in green embroidered uniforms flitted about with beer-laden trays. A mural behind the tables showed the Schwartzwald. The smell of fried sausage tickled his nostrils. He leaned against the column. I'm slipping, he thought. He turned back, for he had no desire to go to Bavaria, not just now—but the department store was gone, the welcoming letters J. C. Penney were nowhere to be seen. Instead, he was facing Chelsea Station, with a life-size cardboard Beefeater figure and an Underground logo. He turned in the opposite direction, which he deemed to be east, expecting to find Gorky Street and a line for eggs. Instead, there was Tijuana Plaza and the lively sounds of mariachis. Dubinsky's sense of geography lay in shambles.

He took an escalator upstairs and sighed with relief: he was back in the good old U.S., which he liked more and more by the minute. After a half-hour deliberation over the flavor, he bought a raspberry ice cream and sat down to reflect, carefully wrapping the paper napkin around the cone. With the floor so clean, a drop of ice cream would have amounted to blasphemy. And it was not just the floor and the walls that were so clean and shiny. Teenagers who crowded outside the record store; young women who streamed in and out of Jeans d'Arc boutique; aged couples in impeccably green coats and broad-checkered pants, who strolled importantly past the ice cream stand; tots who played in the sandbox—there were no blemishes on their faces, their geometrically straight teeth shone triumphantly, and all their limbs were in fine working order. In his mind's eye, he saw a marketplace in Kuybushev, thousands of people crowded in a space the size of an ice-hockey rink. The cheap, roughshod goods they haggled over and the mud they stomped with their boots. The drunks lying underfoot in the same mud and the cripples in rags begging alms. Had it ever happened? Was it on the same planet?

At first Dubinsky treated his little black-and-white TV indifferently. He had never owned a TV set. Among his Moscow friends it would have been an unmistakable sign of lack of taste and of utter conformism. And he was not interested in ice hockey or bumper harvests anyway. He was not sure it would be any different in America. He had always skipped descriptions of baseball games in American novels. But it was raining, and he had no desire to communicate with other émigrés. They did not share his enthusiasm about this country, and he felt that, in order to counter their arguments, he had to obtain more information. He did not expect entertainment from the little box; he was going to conduct a serious sociological survey. Therefore, he went to the store and bought a *TV Guide*.

From that point on, it was very hard for him to do anything else. Fortunately, the set was so small that he could haul it around the apartment without any trouble. Early on he dismissed the cartoons and thus was able to stay up late for old movies. He watched "The Price Is Right" over his scrambled eggs, "As The World Turns" over his Campbell's Cream of Mushroom, and "Charlie's Angels" over his Hungry Man Salisbury Steak. He watched Walter Cronkite while sitting on the john and Johnny Carson while reclining in the tub. The abundance and diversity of the TV world left him spellbound. The TV set was a mini-mall: it had everything; sociologists were shocked by the number of hours Americans spent watching TV. Dubinsky was stunned by the fact that people went to work, played softball, dined out, made love, and drove into the sunset, as if TV did not exist. Even on TV no one watched TV. Unlike other émigrés, TV told him what he wanted to hear: the United States was not only the land of plenty, but also the land of happiness. Look at the unabashed joy of game-show participants, even if they did not win a trip to Lake Tahoe and had to settle for a year's supply of Rice-a-Roni. Look at the luxurious apartments of simple working girls like Charlie's Angels. Look at the cars that Starsky and Hutch smashed with such nonchalance. Not only was the wealth overwhelming, it was also relatively unimportant; it was only the bad guys who were interested in becoming rich; the good guys always sought *happiness*—especially for others. Indeed, Dubinsky pondered, they walked along an unending Path of Truth; even the commercials confirmed his findings. Nobody was interested in a Buick or in a set of steak knives per se. Material objects served to bring all these smiling, beautiful people health and comfort and even more happiness (although from time to time he did have nagging thoughts about how much happiness one could stand). News, he watched more skeptically. In the international segments, congressmen made impassioned speeches about the need for friendly relations with Pizdo, disregarding the heavy influx of East German obstetricians into the country. Locally, a couple fell on hard times and had to move from a house to an apartment. So that was the local standard for misery, he thought.

The initially fuzzy picture, distorted by static, was clearing up, gaining focus, and becoming brighter by the hour.

. . .

Goga was waiting for Slava at Tbilisi International with a black Volga and a driver.

"Ay, *genatzvale* . . ." He opened his arms wide and stood up on his toes to buss Slava loudly on both cheeks. The sound was deafening. "*Vai, vai*—such long wait! Come to Goga's house, shashliks are on the spits, wine's in the goblets! *Vai*, what a feast we'll have for our dear guest!" Goga could speak perfectly good Russian when he wanted, but in full view of the crowd of Georgians he had a role to play.

As the car (borrowed, including the chauffeur, from the Georgian Ministry of Justice) rolled on to Goga's modest villa atop the bank of the Kura River, Goga chatted incessantly about the new grape harvest, about the almond crops, and especially about the new state prosecutor. Oh, Shota Georgiyevich was a man of such refined tastes! Oh, how he could tell the year and the winery just from a sniff of Gurjaani! Slava could see the reel-to-reel tape recorder running in full gear in the driver's head.

Afterwards, they sat on the terrace and watched the sun set over the mountains. A young boy in an ethnic costume brought chilled white wine, a hot loaf of *lavash* bread, a wheel of *suluguni* cheese, a dish full of tangerines, pomegranates, grapes. Slava blinked at the plethora of colors. Goga, who had changed into a heavy embroidered housecoat, broke off a piece of *suluguni* and started filling him in.

The whole thing would take from three weeks to a month, Goga said. Slava could file for a visa tomorrow. According to his papers, he was an orphan, which eliminated the need to deal with his father, an alcoholic lathe operator, who would never approve it. His official job was a janitor at the dairy run by Goga's brother-in-law. "I didn't think I'd have to file in person," Slava said. "I mean, I understand why you want me to be in Tbilisi rather than in Moscow just to be on the safe side—"

"My dear," Goga said, "it's just a precaution. A clerk receives your papers. She has to check your face against the pictures, for God's sake."

Slava nodded. He didn't trust the wily Assyrian, for whom

the laws of hospitality were meaningless; they could arrest Slava even at this villa, they could take him down to the local KGB and beat him senseless with rubber hoses and pour salt water in his nose and step on his balls . . . But there was a five-carat diamond that Goga wouldn't get until Slava cleared Customs. If he sacrificed Slava to Security, he wouldn't see anything. Trust was trust, and business was business.

"Tomorrow, after you file, you go to my surgeon," Goga said. "He'll do a good job. You won't even feel your diamonds."

Slava nodded again. "I'm sort of tired. After a long trip . . ."

"Sure." Goga patted him on the knee. "You want a girl? Just joined the local *corps de ballet*, straight out of ballet school . . ."

"I don't think so," Slava yawned. "Good night."

There was another way, of course, Slava thought, lying in the dark and watching the transparent curtains flutter in the breeze. He could have gone to any Westerner he had dealt with in the past, some computer analyst from California or oil-drill salesman from Oklahoma, and have the money deposited in the Chase Manhattan Bank. It would be so much nicer, arriving at JFK with an overnight bag, he thought.

But Slava trusted California computer engineers and Oklahoma oil-drill salesmen even less than he trusted Goga. At least Goga had a diamond at stake. With Americans, Slava had no leverage. All those drinking bouts in Moscow weren't worth shit, he knew that; back on the home turf, free of the constant fear of the KGB, the Yanks were capable of anything. They could turn around and trade him to the FBI and thus make it easier for them to obtain export licenses next time around. Or back to the KGB, to improve their own standing with their trading partners.

He turned on his side. Sleep was long in coming. Then he realized he was afraid. He was as afraid as Dubinsky had been. In the bottom of his heart, he had to admit he didn't really know the Americans. In theory, the same things that made everybody else tick applied to them, too: money, adventure, sex, winning at all costs. In practice . . . I can't worry about it now, he thought, taking a sleeping pill. I'll cross that bridge when I get to it. Maybe Dubinsky will provide some helpful insights.

There were no surprises at the Visa and Registration Office. Undoubtedly, the clerk, a heavy-set Georgian woman, had taken notice of a black Volga with the Ministry of Justice plates that parked boldly in front of the NO STANDING sign. Slava wore an ill-fitting Polish-made suit, borrowed, together with the Soviet-made Polyot watch, from Goga's gardener. There was no need to shock the woman with a Seiko, Goga advised. The precautions made Slava suspect that Goga's connections were perhaps not as powerful as the latter claimed. Yet the meeting went through without a hitch. Perhaps Goga did know better, after all, Slava thought, feeling his heart sink again. If, after all these years, I don't really know how the Georgian system works, how can I hope to conquer the American one?

"Sit tight, *genatzvale*," Goga reassured him. "Your papers are moving and so is the grease."

Slava did not inquire about the specifics: he was merely told to fork over so much gold and so many diamonds. He felt no resentment toward anyone involved. That was life; that was human nature. What he resented was the system that pretended that the opposite held true and thus imposed idiotic legal barriers wherever it could.

They went hunting for pheasants and partridges; they went fishing for rainbow trout in a mountain stream; they went to Borzhomi to take in the mineral baths.

"I like you, *genatzvale*," Goga said between the groans under the masseur's experienced hands. "For a Russian you're supersmart. But you were brought up by a Jewish family, right?"

"You know an awful fucking lot, Goga," Slava muttered, feeling exquisite pain radiating from every inch of his spine.

"It's my business to know things," Goga guffawed. "Anyway, you're an oddball. What's this thing about America? What can you have there that you can't have here? How many beds can you sleep in at once? How many women can you fuck with your cock at the same time? How much wine can you guzzle before your liver gives out? We'll go sailing tomorrow on my friend's boat—who needs your Bermuda Triangle, you can't get out of it anyway?" He laughed, pleased with his sense of humor.

"Perhaps having is not everything, Goga."

"Ah, so you're a young man, an idealist yet. *Mazel tov.* I envy you." Goga nodded approvingly. "You believe in God, too, maybe?"

"Not really."

"Hmm. Well, maybe you'll get there."

"Do you?" Slava asked with curiosity.

"No, of course not." Goga winked and nodded toward the masseur. "Assyrian faith is so much hassle, you know. Different gods for every occasion."

On the eve of Slava's departure for Moscow, Goga threw a farewell party in his courtyard. It was a relatively modest affair, twenty people or so, with singers and dancers from the local theater, and an emcee from a popular TV show.

Slava was hardly in a celebratory mood. He had had a bad night, with nightmares that featured men in silk top hats who tried to throw him off the Empire State Building. The gems Dr. Melman had implanted under his armpit added to his discomfort, but not so much physically; it was rather the very idea of an alien presence in his body. He picked indifferently at red Gurian cabbage and at *lobio*. The lamb tasted greasy and nauseating. He drank glass after glass of *Huanchkara*, but the wine only made him more disgusted. As the Georgian tradition prescribes, every round was preceded by a long flowery toast from the emcee. The toasts praised Slava's brains, force, courage, resourcefulness, and, above all, virility. The guests applauded. The local diva made eyes at him. He kept drinking, steadily losing track of things. The wine glasses sprouted tadpoles. The guests featured horns. The lamb was groaning on the spit. He went to the bathroom; the one indoors was too far, so he went straight for the bushes, as was the custom. Soon he was joined by a guest, a furniture-store manager, who insisted that Slava should call a certain Neiman in Maryland, who used to be the man's best customer.

"Neiman already bought himself a Cadillac," the man uttered between the groans. "That's why I like Jews. You're the Chosen People indeed. God blessed you with the greatest gift ever. You know what that is? The gift of how to make money. You know the Bible? You know about King Midas? He was the original Jew. Us Georgians, we like having fun too much, we're not serious enough when it comes to money. If the Russians weren't such drunks, to a man, we'd be no better off than the Azerbaijanis, those stinking Moslem pigs." He uttered another groan.

Slava was about to tell the man not to strain so hard, it was not good for his colon, when he discovered the lack of toilet paper.

"Ah, paper." The Georgian waved. "Here." He handed Slava a ten-ruble bill.

Slava fought an impulse to ask him whether he was serious, then thought better of it. You never knew with the Georgians; they were such a hot-blooded tribe.

Why not, Slava thought, wiping himself. I am in a country where a cleaning woman makes sixty rubles a month, why shouldn't a furniture-store manager wipe his ass with a ten-ruble bill? With Lenin's picture on it, too—had the official part-time dissident Yevtushenko gone through a similar experience? Is that what he meant when he exclaimed, "Take Lenin off the money?" in one of his patriotic odes?

When he returned, the feast was in full gear. The diva had just finished singing an aria from *Così Fan Tutte*, Goga informed him. Now the guests formed a circle, and the dancers launched into a *lezginka*, daggers between their teeth, their toes barely touching the ground. Slava felt dizzy from watching the swirling black shadows.

"You're not having any fun, *katzo*," Goga winked. "What's

the matter, you changed your mind about leaving? There's still time to reconsider, you know."

Slava shook his head. "I have a f-friend there," he stammered. "D-Dubinsky's his name."

"I heard of him." Goga nodded. "Isn't he the one who walked straight into Zalman's store and asked for a loan?"

Slava nodded.

"Zalman still tells the story. The punk scared the shit out of him."

"W-we're d-destined f-for b-big things," Slava said, feeling the diva's monumental breasts prodding him in the back. "We're g-gonna b-buy ourselves a sh-ship and s-sail into the s-sunset."

"That's great." Goga grinned. "I think Kirochka can take it from here, won't you, dear?"

"You've been a naughty boy," said Kira the Diva, pressing against him and enveloping him in a cloud of perfume. "You missed my aria. It was meant for you. But Kira is generous." She squeezed his buttocks. "She'll give you an encore you won't forget."

"You d-don't mind c-carrying me, d-do you?" Slava murmured, holding on to the wall.

She propped him up with her breasts, as her tongue went into his mouth like a bullet. "I'll love it," she gasped.

At ten o'clock sharp the next morning, Slava and Goga arrived at the Visa Office in Moscow in a Chaika limo and proceeded to the head of the line, disregarding the murmurs. One of Goga's flunkys had been there since six in the morning.

The official eyed Slava, a specimen of Aryan manhood, with resentment. "You—you're going to Israel, too?"

"Yes."

She hurled the visa in his face.

He calmly picked it up, thanked her, and was gone.

Ms. Levine called to invite Dubinsky to dinner. "Just a few friends, nothing special. I'll pick you up at six."

Dubinsky watched the scenery with fascination as the Cadillac wove its way smoothly along the tree-lined roads. He was a bit confused as to where they were: there were no houses to be seen, just rows of trimmed hedges, interrupted by gates.

Were they going to the Levines' dacha?

"It's called Cordeboy," she said. "It means 'Heart of the Woods' in French. Stanley wanted to call it Oak Grove, but I thought Cordeboy would be classier."

Dubinsky was impressed. Mr. Levine was a discoverer, entitled to call a new territory anything he pleased.

"*Developer*," Ms. Levine corrected him. "But you can tell him about this notion. He'll love it."

Was Vasco da Gama a developer, too? Dubinsky wondered, as a black iron gate opened magically, and they proceeded along the circular gravel driveway to the house.

"I copied the design from a lovely old castle in Scotland," said Ms. Levine with pride. "You can't imagine the resistance I had to overcome. Stanley is so conservative. As if a split-level cannot have towers."

Dubinsky agreed. Ms. Levine's "split-level," whatever the word meant, could definitely have anything, and it did: a fountain with stoned-looking cherubs, a gazebo in the distance, a swing, and a basketball ring on the wall.

"There's also a rock garden with a Buddha in the back. I built it between the tennis court and the pool," she chirped on. "Are you hungry, by any chance? I'm starving. We can go there later and meditate, if you want. Do you like to meditate? Do they have ashrams in Russia? You know, Zen is so important to me," she went on. "I'm taking this course in tae kwo doon—"

"Hi, there." The discoverer himself stood in the doorway, resplendent in his sweatshirt and purple suspenders, a martini nestled comfortably in his hand. "Oleg? Stanley Levine." They shook hands. "I'm a capitalist, and proud to be one. Just thought I'd make it clear to a Communist," he chuckled.

"Oh, Stanley, Oleg is not a Communist," Ms. Levine moaned. "I told you—he's a victim of religious persecution."

"Let me pour you a Stolly anyway. You want ice in it?"

Before Dubinsky could say a word, a thick glass, filled with vodka and tinkling ice cubes, was sitting in his hand. He eyed it with disgust. That was not a proper way to drink vodka. All he needed was a shotglass and a pickle. In Rome . . . like a true Roman, Dubinsky furtively emptied the glass into a flowerpot, quickly refilled it with Scotch, and set out to explore the living room. His cheeks were soon aflush with excitement, for by now he had no doubts about the proper mix of culture and wealth he was facing. The comfortable overstuffed couches and armchairs, positioned at odd angles to the coffee table and facing a fireplace, created an atmosphere of leisurely sophistication. The shelves held netsukes and matryoshkas and tin soldiers. There was a Japanese print of delicate white cranes and a large oil of the Wailing Wall. A Native Indian sculpture of a pensive-looking warrior stood in a niche between them, while the opposite wall was gleaming with hi-fi knobs and switches and meters. The bar held more booze than Dubinsky had ever seen in a private home, from Absolut to Pizdo coconut brandy.

And plants, plants everywhere—on the floor, on the walls, on the ceiling. A veritable hothouse, he thought; there was just one element missing, but he could not quite put his finger on it.

"Would you like some *crudités*?" Ms. Levine called from the kitchen. Dubinsky did not flinch. Whatever *crudités* were, in this house they were apt to be good. He stepped bravely into the kitchen, straight into the Kingdom of a Thousand Gadgets. Not only was he ignorant of their names, but in a thousand years he could not have guessed their function. Some of them were blinking their lights, and others were emitting groans. And yet it was no cartoon *à la Modern Times*, and he had no fear of being hit in the mouth by a malfunctioning corn-on-the-cob feeder. To the contrary, there were numerous homey touches—a charming pencil sketch of a girl in a miniskirt here, a gaily embroidered pot holder there, and even a Jewish religious calendar on the wall. In a word, it was a *household*.

Complete with a Maytag dishwasher. (Dubinsky leaned over to read the name.)

Ms. Levine was flitting merrily from the stove to the refrigerator to the table, humming something vaguely Wagnerian. She handed Dubinsky a plate with raw vegetables—"Help yourself"—and immersed herself in a cookbook. Of those there was a substantial number, he noted: from a slim booklet titled *Natural Noodles of Nepal* to a hefty volume of at least a thousand pages entitled *The American Hamburger*. Again, his heart was touched as he admired the wide range of possibilities open to one in this country. He also realized what was missing in the living room. There was not a single book there. Printed matter was represented by copies of *Reader's Digest*, *Life*, and *National Geographic* spread out on the coffee table. Of course, there had to be a library *somewhere* in the house, he thought. Walls and walls lined with pigskin-bound volumes, where Mr. Levine retired with his pipe and Courvoisier to plan new conquests of space.

The guests started arriving. Mr. Levinski wore a dark burgundy blazer and looked like a captain of industry, Dubinsky thought. His movements were precise and well-measured, whether delivering a handful of peanuts to his mouth or lightly patting his wife on her knee. Mrs. Levinski was a knockout, of course, with her blond mane straight out of "Charlie's Angels," and sporty pink pants that she filled to the limit.

"Russia must be an absolutely fascinating country," she declared immediately. "I have always, but always, wanted to go there. I saw *Dr. Zhivago* three times, and it's the best movie ever made. We could go to Greece for vacation and maybe go to Russia for a weekend. It can't be that far. Have you ever been to Greece, Oleg?"

Dubinsky coughingly admitted that he had not.

"Now, Judy is a world traveler." Mrs. Levinski nodded toward Ms. Levine, who had emerged from the kitchen. "Isn't Greece wonderful, Judy?"

"I loved it," Ms. Levine agreed.

"And all the *chachkes* you brought. Stanley takes her every-where," Mrs. Levinski confided loudly to Dubinsky.

Mr. Leventhal was a counterculture intellectual; Dubinsky could tell by his denim shirt and bushy salt-and-pepper beard. He lost no time in filling glasses with vodka. This time Dubinsky stood firm. "Just a finger, please."

"I thought Russians drank a lot of vodka," said Mrs. Leventhal playfully. She was short and dark-haired, also wearing denim, with all sorts of flora and fauna sewn onto it.

Dubinsky coughed and downed his glass. He had to chase it with a piece of cauliflower.

"You know, I'm sure you've been asked the question a thousand times . . . " Mrs. Leventhal started.

". . . how did you get out of Russia?" Mr. Leventhal finished for her. "You're so shy, honey."

"Well." Dubinsky cleared his throat. It was a serious question, and it deserved a serious answer.

"There must have been torture." Mrs. Leventhal's eyes shone.

"Nah, that's all *Reader's Digest* stories." Mr. Leventhal waved his hand.

"The Russians want peace—that's why they finally decided to respect human rights."

"Hah," said Mr. Levinski. "A lot they know about human rights. You should ask my grandfather how they respected his human rights in pogroms in Vilna."

"We're the only suckers in this human rights game." Mr. Levine voiced support.

"I still want to hear how it happened," said Mrs. Leventhal plaintively.

"Well," Dubinsky said, "at first there's an invitation—"

"Did you have to go to Israel?" asked Mrs. Leventhal.

"Do you know Igor—oh, what's his name, the young man we met last month—" Mrs. Levinski furrowed her brows. "Because he told me everybody had to pretend they were going to Israel. What *was* his name?"

"Alchinsky, I think," Ms. Levine said. "You must know him—he is from Moscow, too."

"I don't think so," Dubinsky said stiffly.

The bell rang in the kitchen.

"Let's go eat," said Mr. Levine. "I'm starved."

In the vicinity of the table Dubinsky grew edgy. Eating in the natives' presence brought back memories of the Big Mac. This was a social occasion, however, and he trembled in anticipation of rows of cutlery flanking the plates.

"It must be painful for you to talk about getting out," Mr. Leventhal said with a smile.

"Not at all," Dubinsky declared. "It's just a bit complicated, that's all. No pain. First you get an invitation from Israel—"

"So you must have relatives in Israel," Ms. Levine nodded.

"Not necessarily." Dubinsky's eyes fell on the cookbook on the side of the stove. It was French. At least I know where it came from, he thought. "You see, it's all a game. You pretend you have relatives in Israel, and the authorities pretend they believe you—"

"This is really complicated," Mrs. Levinski murmured. "Before I forget—Judy, this sauce is absolutely *de-lish*."

"Honey, it's so simple, you could whip it up in five minutes . . ."

Relieved, Dubinsky went back to his food. He had always been a quick eater, and before long he was the only one with a clean plate.

"Would you like more chicken?" Ms. Levine inquired.

Yes, but would it be polite? After all, perhaps the hostess planned to stretch the leftovers through the rest of the week, as they do in *households*. On the other hand—*no lies, Dubinsky.* "Yes please."

"What do they eat in Russia?" Ms. Levine heaped another helping on his plate. "I suppose it would be something very simple, very basic, but at the same time very natural and nutritious—I mean, look at all the athletes they have."

"Well . . . I don't know," Dubinsky muttered. What *do* they eat in Russia? It would have been easier to tell what they stand in lines for—chicken, eggs, franks. . . . "They eat whatever's available in the store—sometimes it's chicken, and sometimes . . . nothing."

They laughed. He looked up, alarmed: what was so funny?

"Of course you're talking about housewives," said Mrs. Leventhal reconciliatorily. "We have the same problem—planning seven different meals a week—"

"What if you don't want to cook?" Mr. Levine took over. "Can you just go to the store and grab yourself a can of borscht and frozen pirogis? Or do you go to a takeout place?"

"I'm sure they have fine public facilities," said Mr. Leventhal. "Don't the Soviets always insist on all things being communal?"

Dubinsky coughed and finished his wine. He vividly pictured the cafeteria on the first floor of his building: soup puddles drying on tables; a lonesome piece of gristle floating on the borscht plate; "cutlets" that fell apart before coming in contact with the fork, revealing a nine-to-one bread/meat ratio.

"No," he said firmly, picking the last exotic vegetable off his plate. "The public facilities stink. No takeouts. No canned borscht. No frozen pirogis."

They exchanged glances.

"Sounds like a hell of a place to stay away from," said Mr. Levinski contentedly, clipping his cigar. "I bet they don't have lox and bagels either."

"They don't." Whatever those are.

"So, what did you do in Russia?" asked Mrs. Leventhal over coffee.

Dubinsky explained, politely omitting the removed navels.

"I still don't understand how they let you out," Ms. Levine said. "They must be crazy."

"They certainly are," Dubinsky agreed again, pleased.

"You probably know State secrets, too."

"I don't think so," he said. "Most information for my research I copied out of *Newsweek*."

"You can buy *Newsweek*?"

"No, of course not."

"Such a strange country. No takeouts, no *Newsweek*—it must be such a relief for you to be here."

■ ■ ■

On the way back (the Leventhals graciously offered a ride) Mr. Leventhal asked what Dubinsky thought of America.

"I love it," Dubinsky said, delighting in his sincerity. This was what he always wanted—telling the truth and loving every minute of it. "It's clean, beautiful, comfortable. People are kind and warm and sympathetic—"

"This country has a million problems," Mr. Leventhal said thoughtfully. "There's poverty, illiteracy, racial discrimination . . ."

Dubinsky asked what Mr. Leventhal did for a living. He coughed and admitted he owned an ad agency.

"That's great," Dubinsky said. "I think the commercials on TV are so well made."

"That's Hollywood," said Mr. Leventhal. "I just buy time and space for Stanley and Murray."

"Have you given any thought to what you want to do in this country?" Mrs. Leventhal hastily changed the subject.

"Well . . . I suppose I would have to learn a trade," Dubinsky said. His stomach felt queasy; due to the cake, perhaps.

"You'll do fine," Mr. Leventhal said. "You have the right outlook."

"I'll think of something," Mrs. Leventhal said. "I have this friend at an employment agency."

There was just one matter left unattended, Slava thought. A small matter, a three-hour train ride. He knew he did not have to do it. Aunt Raya was not his real aunt, after all—but, perhaps, more. She was his communal-apartment neighbor, and when his father would disappear for days, she fed him chicken soup and gefilte fish and a sweet carrot concoction called *tzimes*, while her husband Yakov, who worked in a bookstore, helped him with his homework. Eventually, his father would come back, his face red and swollen, his shirt torn, his coat in hock, his eye decorated with a shiner. "Raissa Solomonovna, have some respect for a member of the dictatorship of proletariat. My soul's on fire. Three rubles till Friday."

He looked over his luggage, packed neatly. All set to go.

After a brief hesitation, he stepped out on the street and, shivering in the wind, hailed a cab. "Kazan Station," he told the driver, shoving a five-ruble note, twice the fare, into his hand.

Slava remembered his father, Vorontzov Sr., taking off his belt in the middle of an empty room (every item sold to quench his thirst), about to punish his eleven-year-old son for something that he in his befogged mind could not articulate. Slava fled before the belt was out. The same night his father was arrested for assaulting passers-by with a plastic toy sword and resisting the militiamen. He claimed he was the proletariat and therefore a dictator and was fully empowered to send the militiamen to the store for vodka, because they, by definition, were the people's—ergo, *his* servants. He got fifteen days for hooliganism.

"He's lucky Uncle Joe is dead," said Uncle Yakov. "He'd already be mining gold in Kolyma."

Aunt Raya sniffled and fed little Slava homemade chicken cutlets with onion and garlic. "He's a good man, your father. It's your mother's death that affected him so."

At the train station, he walked toward the ticket window, unseeingly stepping over the bodies of people scattered on the marble floor. There were never enough benches, there were never enough train seats, and people always had to wait for hours—for days. Instead of joining the line, he stepped directly to the VIP window.

"My secretary called." He pushed a small white envelope through the window. "One first-class to Vorograd."

The woman peeked into the envelope, saw the familiar red of ten-ruble bills. "I do believe we have a reservation."

He stepped outside, to the platform, away from the acrid smells of the waiting room and took a deep breath of brisk early-spring air. The train wasn't due for another hour. The restaurant was besieged, as usual. It didn't matter. He could wait. There were no other items on his checklist.

• • •

Slava remembered:

While his father was drying out for months in an anti-alcoholic center, he became a Rothman, for all intents and purposes. He spent days and nights in their room, he went shopping, he did the dishes, and he devoured *oladyas*, thick pancakes with sour cream, and French toast and chicken soup and everything Aunt Raya ladled out. Then Uncle Yakov moved to the hospital and was dead within a month. It was on the day of his funeral that Vorontzov Sr. returned from the sanatorium.

"Where are you going?" he asked Slava, who was putting on the Sunday suit that Aunt Raya had altered out of Uncle Yakov's for him.

"To the cemetery," Slava explained. "Uncle Yakov died."

"He is not your uncle!" Vorontzov Sr. hollered. "You're a Russian—Russian—Russian! Goddamn Jews have bought you! *Aaah!*" He raged around the room, but there was no furniture left to break. "Jew bastards!" He stormed down the hallway, kicking the doors and dragging the sobbing Slava all the way to the Rothmans' room. "Don't you dare subvert my progeny!" he yelled. "I'm the dictator of proletariat!"

The room was full of people in black, and an old man sat quietly in the corner and murmured words in a strange language. For a moment all grew quiet, their eyes fixed on Slava's father. Then Engineer Yermolayev grabbed Vorontzov Sr.'s wrists and conducted him to the front door, where he received a kick in his behind that sent him flying down the stairs. Engineer Yermolayev was a weight lifter who lived next door and had relied on Uncle Yakov for all the new sci-fi books that came out.

Slava sat in the corner, next to the old man who murmured in a funny language, and cried into the torn sleeve of his coat. He cried because he felt sorry for and ashamed of his idiot father; he cried because he knew he'd never see Uncle Yakov again; he cried because Aunt Raya was crying.

The old man interrupted his muttering to pat Slava on the head.

"Don't cry, *feigelah meine*. Don't cry. God will have mercy on your Uncle Yakov."

"I don't believe in God," Slava said angrily. "I'm a Young Pioneer. God is a capitalist throwback."

"Is that so?" the old man grinned. "Well, that's nice, too."

He paced the platform nervously, dodging the chaotic streams of passengers, rushing to and fro, laden with sacks and trunks and shopping bags. He lit one cigarette off another. At one point he stared uncomprehendingly at the umbrellas that had sprouted around him, and it occurred to him that it was raining, a fine quiet drizzle.

The boarding was announced. He walked slowly past the crowd outside the second- and third-class cars, turning away to avoid hearing the pleadings with conductors about incorrect tickets. There was no one at the entrance to the first-class. The plump blonde in the railroad uniform put his ticket in her cardboard file and stared at him openly.

"Traveling alone?"

He muttered affirmatively and pulled himself aboard.

"Party business, I bet," she said to his back, unwilling to give up.

Slava remembered:

There was a time when Aunt Raya tried to adopt him officially, which was, of course, futile, with his father still alive, although hardly ever at home. The Rothmans had one son, a fighter pilot, shot down on his first sortie in July '41. "He was like you," Aunt Raya sighed. "Fought every day—at school, in the yard." "It's too bad you can't adopt me," Slava sighed. "It doesn't matter," said Aunt Raya, sewing a button on his shirt. "It's only a piece of paper." So nimble were her hands, so quick. "You're like a son to me anyway."

Slava started paying attention to Aunt Raya's numerous visitors. A strapping youth at fifteen, he was a reliable bodyguard on the nights she had to work late; the streets were never safe. And sometimes he had to take a package to a certain address, and to pick up another one on his way back. Aunt Raya had no secrets from him.

"That's the world for you, Slavochka, and that's how people live."

He learned you had to be an idealist to live on your salary. He learned that the higher you looked in the hierarchy, the fewer idealists you found, hence more people there you could have business with. He learned to distrust rubles, which had been devalued in '61 and could be devalued again. He learned to value knowledge, but keep in mind that it was only a means to an end. So what was the end, Aunt Raya?

"Live in peace with yourself and your neighbors. Never go hungry or barefoot and always have enough to share with friends. And if you have to cut a corner here and there, don't worry about it. Let them catch you first. *They* made the rules; we're only trying to get by."

Aunt Raya was happy when he enrolled in the language school, and upset when he dropped out two years later.

"It doesn't make any sense to me, that school," he tried to explain. "Who needs all these homonyms and zeugmas and Party history? I've learned the language for my purposes, that's what counts."

"So what will you do now?"

"I'm in business, Aunt Raya. Remember those two hundred rubles you gave me when I went away? Well—I've already turned them into two thousand."

"I don't like it," she said sternly. "You have to graduate and become respectable, Slavochka. Uncle Yakov and myself never had any education, we never had a choice but to do things on the side. If you can get a decent job after college, Foreign Ministry or diplomatic corps, why do you need these people? They're criminals, Slavochka. We're just modest Soviet people." She started to cry. "It's all my fault; I shouldn't've gotten you involved in all those things."

"I owe you for showing me all those things," he said fervently. "We're all modest Soviet people, and the criminals are more Soviet than you or me—because that's what the system is all about—rip it off and get away with it." He tried to explain to her that the rough stuff was in the past, that he was setting up a high-class operation, that he was going to buy her a co-op, that there was no limit to what money could buy.

"It's all wrong." She kept shaking her head. "It's wrong—wrong—wrong. They'll catch you, and you'll spend the rest of your days in jail."

"They'll never catch me," he shouted, "which means it's not wrong—you told me that yourself! And who the hell are you to tell me what's wrong? Didn't you sell leftover cloth on the side? Didn't you buy the cakes of soap and sweaters and shawls that the girls from the factory smuggled past the guards? And resell it at a profit? And Uncle Yakov, didn't he charge double on the books that never made it from the warehouse to the store shelf?"

"Slavochka, you don't understand. Did we do it to buy a car? a co-op? We made barely enough to survive, maybe to buy a new pair of shoes once in a while—do you know how much Uncle Yakov's gravestone cost me?"

"What does a damn gravestone have to do with that?"

"And when you were sick, didn't I run out to the market to buy you chicken at five rubles a kilo from those farmers, those *khazerim* robbers?"

"That's it!" He banged his fist on the table. "That does it. Just like the Jews—nothing's for free! Whatever they do for you, sooner or later there'll be a bill to pay."

"There's no bill, Slavochka," she said quietly. "And we're not 'just like the Jews'—we *are* Jews. Dumb and ignorant Jews who never went to college. Who never had a chance."

"And now I have a chance, and you can go to hell!"

He slammed the door and he ran out into the yard.

As the last call aboard came on the loudspeaker, he realized he could not go through with it. He had sent her money, once or twice; it came back. She was even a patriot in her own way, Russia was everything to her; instead of reconciliation, more aggravation would follow. She was the past. I haven't had anybody for a long time, he said to himself; and I've done quite nicely, thank you very much. He scratched his armpit, as if to reassure himself. The rocks were securely in place. Dr. Melman had done a good job.

After a few whistles, the train came into motion. "Excuse me." He picked up the blond conductor, who was in the way, and gently set her aside.

"What are you doing?"

He muttered he forgot important papers, and jumped off. He ran a few steps together with the train, and stopped. His heart was still thumping in rhythm with the train wheels. He stood still for a moment, listening to the beat. Then he took a deep breath and turned back.

Aboard the express bus, Dubinsky nervously folded and unfolded the scrap of paper with the directions. His palms sweated uncontrollably, and his stomach was queasy. His adrenaline was pumping wildly in anticipation of his first job interview. This is it, he told himself, adjusting the knot of his Italian tie for the tenth time. Either he would get the job and enter the mainstream and become like everyone else, a happy, smiling owner of a popular-brand dishwasher—or he'd flunk it, he'd be doomed to be an outsider, standing by the side of the track and watching the shining bullet train of the American dream roar past.

"Your stop is next." The old black lady across the aisle laid down her Bible and beamed at him beatifically.

"Thank you very, very much." Dubinsky glued his nose to the window. A cluster of steel-and-glass towers loomed ahead. He blinked as the sun's rays reflected off the towers and blinded him. His heart beat wildly. Truly, it was the City of Tomorrow—with overpasses and roof garages and helipads. He remembered having seen it on the day of his arrival, as they drove from the airport, but it was like an illustration of the Communist Future in his high school social studies textbook, striking yet unreal. Now it was completely tangible; he could make out plates on cars and hats on women's heads. Now he was inside that Future—inside, but not a part of it; not yet. If his company was in one of those towers . . . if he got the job. . . .

"Electric Avenue," the driver announced.

Dubinsky bolted to the door and leaped out to the street. For a moment he stood on the sidewalk, unsure of what came next. He did not know where to look for a street name or a house number, he felt hopelessly provincial; he stood so close to the towers that he'd have to lean all the way back to see where their tops scraped the sky.

The revolving door admitted Dubinsky into the lobby. He stopped for a moment, to catch his breath and to let his heartbeat settle down. His heart was full of awe at the magnificence of this temple, of the straight, uncompromising, unaffected lines, of the generously open, brightly lit spaces. He impulsively reached to remove his hat, although he was not wearing one. There is nothing to fear, he told himself again. The people looked quite ordinary, mostly in business suits, some in jeans; no one was wearing a futuristic silver sackcloth or a pressure suit. Yet his eyes looked instinctively for hidden cameras. He realized that at this very moment the lines of his biography were running across the computer screen in the security room. *They already know I'm here, but so what.* He stepped bravely inside the elevator.

"Mrs. Levinter will be right with you. Would you fill out this form, please?" The receptionist smiled cheerfully and returned to her typewriter.

"Thank you so much."

"You're welcome." She smiled again.

Why does she smile at me? Am I important? Does she like me? Does she take me for the vice president's nephew? Hardly. They are just such incredibly nice people, the Americans.

Dubinsky lowered himself cautiously onto the plush couch and started filling out the form in quick, confident handwriting. His heart sank at the numerous spaces he was forced to leave blank: he belonged to no associations, he had no draft status he knew of, and his whole work experience was as Researcher of the Pizdo Proletariat. Thank God, it's just one page, he sighed, signing his name with a flourish.

"Thank you very much." The girl flashed another smile.

"Thank *you*," Dubinsky insisted, looking around and feeling his foreignness push him inexorably back onto the couch. I'll never get used to this cleanliness, he thought in despair. There was no room for dust, ashes, or apple cores in the office. The surfaces were so polished, they defied the laws of physics, they could be used in a lab; how could they generate friction against a moving object? Human hands are incapable of this cleanliness, he thought: a humming robot will roll in after five, furnished with vacuuming and dusting and apple-core–picking tentacles, and modeled after Siva or Vishnu, Dubinsky could not remember which. Perhaps even hum a Ravi Shankar selection. The furnishings were understated; all the lights were dimmed, except the one over the receptionist's desk. The functional Beauty of the Future . . . his clothes were shabby, he felt, with frayed cuffs and threadbare elbows; they were outmoded, they were too flashy, and simply inappropriate. He checked his fly; it was in place, but didn't his shoes need more polish? He felt his soles; no holes there, thank God, but the laces were half-torn. His mouth felt acrid: five minutes of brushing had been in vain. His whole body, every nook and cranny of it, was flooded with cold sweat, he could smell the stink he was exuding: the odor of uncleanliness and fear.

He picked up a copy of *Time*. Pizdo had been invaded by its neighbor, Zhopa. He could not read: the lines ran and stepped on each other's toes. He put it down and picked up a magazine called *Dental Design* instead. He was not particularly surprised to find the room around him reproduced in precise multicolored detail on the magazine page, down to the receptionist's Farrah Fawcett hairdo. "Bold and Soothing," the caption read.

"Mr. Dubinsky?"

He shot to his feet and was about to salute, such was the

military correctness in Mrs. Levinter's voice. But then she smiled and shook his hand, which he had taken time to dry on his coat, and his fears abated: here was another nice, warm, open-hearted American who would evaluate his prospects objectively. She would not hold his Jewishness against him, that went without saying. Nor would she bullshit him: if there was a misunderstanding, if they needed someone with a business degree and ten years of top-echelon managerial experience, she'd tell him right away. As for his body odor, he could promise to invest ten percent of his first paycheck in the appropriate lotions, the ones that made people on TV look proud and confident and downright euphoric. No? How about twenty percent? But would he have enough left over for a wonderful shiny polyester suit with double stitching?

He faced Mrs. Levinter again in her office, across the desk, against the background of the sky and faraway vistas. He perched on the edge of the chair to get a better view.

"Well." Mrs. Levinter put aside his application and smiled encouragingly. "You have no previous experience, your last job was in the Soviet Union—right?"

"Right."

"But you can type, your English is good . . ."

He kept nodding, afraid she'd stop and revert to the bad news.

"It's so amazing that people actually come out of Russia," she said suddenly. "How did you get out?"

He started explaining, deeming it to be the natural extension of his application; his signature at the bottom prevented him from embellishing his story or omitting important details.

"Well, it's pretty incredible," she said in the middle of the description of his visit to the pet agency. "How history repeats itself. I mean, my grandfather came on a boat, without a word of English . . ." She shook her head, a gesture Dubinsky found highly enigmatic. "Now, the crucial question—can you *file?*"

He nodded, immediately withdrawing his fingernails out of sight.

"Of course," she laughed. "There's a file on everybody in Russia, right?"

"I would imagine so," Dubinsky said tactfully.

"Well, then." She rose; he followed suit. "Welcome aboard."

Back in his hotel room in Moscow, Slava took the phone off the hook; then he took a double dose of sleeping pills and collapsed on the couch.

He woke up drowsy and weak. It was close to midnight. Ten hours before the plane. There was a note from Goga under the door. "*Gena tzvale*, we're celebrating at Aragvi. Grab a cab and join us."

He called the restaurant. "No party for me, Goga. I'll see you at nine at the hotel." He hung up without waiting for Goga's pleas. Then he called Znachar.

"I need Valium for tomorrow."

In an hour Znachar was at the door. "That's not nice," he started. "I thought we'd have a party, we're your buddies, after all."

"Thanks," Slava said, accepting the small box with the pills. "I'm sorry about the party. I just want to be alone."

"But we might never see you again," Znachar said in a low voice.

"I'm sorry," Slava repeated monotonously. "I just want to be left alone." He turned away and stared out the window.

"It's okay," Znachar said, his voice indicating to the contrary. "I understand. Good luck anyway. Say hello to Dubinsky. Don't leave him in the lurch, okay?"

"I won't. Thanks for the pills."

Znachar won't understand, Slava thought, gulping down the pills; Dubinsky might; but Dubinsky was in San Murray, light-years—or hours—away.

"Are you all right?" Goga asked, helping him out of the cab.

"A little shaky, that's all." He could not eat anything—not after swallowing that plastic-wrapped diamond the night before. It could put them off the track of the larger ones, he thought, feeling under his armpits.

"You don't have to worry about a thing," Goga whispered. "Everything is taken care of." He opened his palm, waiting to be paid.

"After the Customs," Slava said curtly.

"Oh. Sorry, I forgot."

Slava turned abruptly and looked in the Assyrian's eyes for a moment, and then he knew. Goga never "forgot."

Those double-dealing Assyrian eyes.

"In that case . . ."

Slava grinned and entered the terminal.

He was through the Customs in two minutes. The passport control upstairs took three minutes. He stepped inside the waiting lounge, looking for them. To approach him. To put a hand on his shoulder.

This way please.

Goga emerged from the VIP lounge, waving a borrowed Supreme Soviet Deputy ID. "Everything's cool, I told you."

"Give me a hug." Lying Assyrian hands around him. Expectant look in Goga's eyes, *Nu?*

"And a kiss." Goga's wet lips on his cheek. As Slava's hand drops a tiny black box in Goga's breast pocket. Goga feels the weight. The account is closed.

"God bless you, Slava," he whispers before disappearing.

Slava sits down and waits.

And then they come. Two, one in a black suit, the other in a brown one. He follows them silently into a sterile-looking room. "Strip." They stick their cold, greedy hands everywhere. He cringes as a gloved finger presses his sphincter. Nothing. They look at each other in indecision. They nod for him to follow them. He carries his Burberry and his tweeds and his shoes in a humble pile in his hands.

A dark room. A middle-aged woman in a white smock. We want all areas, says the brown suit. She nods; they leave. Please put your chin here, she says quietly; take a deep breath and hold it in until I— He grabs a plastic dish, he bends over

it, he sticks three fingers down his throat, he pushes triumphantly, his eyes bulging with effort—*come come you little
sucker come you're my insurance*—his mouth and his nose fill
up with saliva, with the sweet acridity of the fast—his whole
body shudders in one spasm after another, and a plastic-
wrapped five-carat work of art plops on the dish. You're bleeding, she says; in the pale light of the lamp her face is deadly
ashen and distorted in a grimace of horror as she gives him
a glass of water. There is indeed blood on the dish: he must've
bitten his tongue. Hold on to this beauty, he gasps in her ear,
inhaling the subtle scent of her neck, touching the blondish
curls ever so lightly with the tip of his tongue; I'll come back,
we'll get married, we'll have a house on the Mediterranean,
we'll have beautiful children, a boy and a girl (no ring on her
finger, he noticed).

"You have a fever," she says in a choked voice, and gives
him a washcloth.

A knock on the door. He slips on his pants. Are you done?
the voice asks. A couple more minutes, she says, as she lightly
moistens an X-ray picture to make it look as if it's just been
taken; as she mops up the dish and disposes of the bloody
washcloth. "We should be in business together," he whispers,
watching her tape the plastic bag with the diamond to her
armpit. Like a model Soviet citizen. The thugs confer some
more, they talk to their superior on the phone, but they don't
search him again. Too weak to stand straight, he leans against
the wall, panting for air, keeping his tongue in the back of his
mouth to hold back the bleeding. Finally the brown suit snaps
his fingers. Beat it, yid.

And Viacheslav "Rothman" Vorontzov, smiling wanly and
swallowing blood, proceeds to occupy seat 24A (smoking,
window) aboard the Aeroflot Flight 25 to Vienna.

Five

Dubinsky reclines in an armchair in an orderly well-appointed room, his slippered feet comfortably supported by a footstool. He is watching TV. On the enormous twenty-five-inch color screen, the hero, who bears an uncanny resemblance to Slava, is fleeing the evil mobsters. He jumps from roof to roof as the bullets graze the forest of antennas around him. Dubinsky's head drops on his chest, but he fights sleep: he roots for the Slava-like hero, and wants to find out the ending.

Finally, the hero is on the edge of the last building. With a yell, he releases his hold on the eaves and lands on the roof of a passing El train. Suddenly, the TV explodes and starts emitting a noxious blue smoke.

Dubinsky leaves the room reluctantly. Somehow he knows, although he is not one hundred percent sure, that it's *his* room, that it's *his* house, that there are more rooms in it. He looks for a smokeless one, but the fumes come from all directions: kitchen, basement, attic. He looks out of the window and sees both his coupe and his wife Linda's station wagon on fire. The orange tongues are reaching the gas tank, about to explode any minute. A woman bolts out of the bathroom, wearing a bathrobe, her hair in curlers.

"Don't just stand there!" she hollers. "Do something! Call the police, the ambulance, the fire department! What's the matter with you?" She starts sobbing. "It's our home, Oleg, we worked so hard for it."

"I don't remember working for it," he says. "And I'm not sure it's mine."

"*Ours*, Oleg, *ours*."

"We're married?" He's just stalling, he is aware of it; he's oddly relieved that the house is on fire. The furniture, the TV, the coupe—all gone, he's broke again. Leaving her wailing, he walks out the door, slippers and all, and starts walking down the road. An El train grinds to a stop, and through a graffiti-covered window he sees Slava leap off the roof onto the opposite platform. Slava picks up a phone, dials. Dubinsky picks up the phone on his platform.

"Did I wake you up?" Slava asked through the roar of the departing train.

"Not at all." Dubinsky opened his eyes. 8:15. The clock was silent. He must've forgotten to set the alarm again.

"You sound weird," Slava said. "You're not surprised to hear my voice?"

"What?" Dubinsky yelled, leaping out of bed, sending the phone to the floor with a crash. "Where the hell are you?"

"At Kennedy Airport. I landed an hour ago."

"Oh, my God, my God," Dubinsky wailed. "I'm so happy, Slavka, you bastard . . ."

"Listen," Slava said, as usual impatient with Dubinsky's emoting, "I was thinking of coming out to visit you for a few days."

"Great, great," Dubinsky whispered dreamily, afraid to believe he was not dreaming.

"Good," Slava said, his impatience rising. "I'll call you later to give you the flight number."

"Great, great . . ."

"I'll talk to you later," Slava said, exasperated. "You're sure you're okay?"

"Never—never been better."

"'Bye."

The line went dead.

"Aaah!" Dubinsky stormed through the room, extracting a shirt, a sock, a pair of pants out of the debris; he splashed water on his face, stuck a toothbrush in his pocket, and ran to the bus stop.

Aboard the bus this morning, instead of seething with anger at the sullen, indifferent expressions of the fellow members of the car-less underclass, dulled with earphones plugged in their ears, he loudly hummed the Beatles' "Birthday," and when he got tired of it, he addressed an elderly gray-haired black man across the aisle. "My best buddy just got out this morning. I'm real happy for him."

"That sure is good news," the man agreed. "What they lock him up fo'?"

Dubinsky paused. "For being smart."

"That's not smart," the guy said in a lecturing voice. "That's smart-ass." He rose to get off. "Tell him he better be cool now and not give any lip to his parole officer, you hear?"

But as Dubinsky walked into the office, his spirits sagged. He had another eight hours of dealing with files ahead of him. Looking at the grave, concentrated faces of his fellow workers. Listening to the impassioned arguments between the Burt Reynolds and Tom Selleck factions. Inhaling the noxious odors of plastic, exuded by the file covers. And being bored, bored, bored.

"I got a phone call today," he said to Maria Candelaria, the elderly bookkeeper, who was busy clipping the coupons out of today's San Murray *Sentinel Herald Dispatch*. "My best friend just got out of Russia."

"Well, congratulations," she said without looking up. "Are you going to talk to Mrs. Levinter about it? We might have another opening in the files. That Rodriguez boy is late again."

No sense of *solidaridad* there, he thought, and grinned, picturing Slava as a filing clerk. "You don't know my buddy,"
he said proudly. "One year from now he might buy this company."

"Then he's very stupid." She was stunned momentarily by
a full-color picture of a gorgeous St. Bernard licking his chops
at a can of dog food. "This company is going to the dogs. Do
you have a dog?"

"No," he said. "I was advised to get a hamster once, though."

"Too bad," she said. "This is really quite a bargain." She
clipped it anyway; at the very worst, she thought, she could
frame it and put it on her desk: the canine was so adorable.

Dubinsky retired to the bathroom to brush his teeth. He
took his time, hoping that one day his teeth would be as pearly
white as those of the natives, and loathing the moment he
would get back to the files. "I hate this," he said into the
mirror.

"Gotta brush," said his supervisor, JJ. "I bet you didn't
have Colgate in Russia, that's why you hate it so much. All
my grandparents had lousy teeth." JJ's grandparents had
changed the unpronounceable last name of Jonaskiavichus to
Jones; his parents, in a spasm of ethnic pride, christened him
Jonas; he encouraged people to call him JJ because it stressed
his easygoing nature and was good for sales. "Had a good
time last night, huh?" he asked over the noise of his urination.
Meaning, Why can't you brush at home?

Dubinsky nodded mutely; he was in no hurry to rinse his
mouth, since it would free it for talking to JJ.

He spent the rest of the morning torn between fits of frenzy
and protracted periods of coma. His mind, generally asleep
as he pushed the cards, humming the files' names, was now
afire: what was Slava going to do? Was he going to New York
to play the stocks? To Chicago, for the commodities? To L.A.,
for television? To Houston for oil? To San Murray—for what?
He vowed he would go to the library and read *Money Fortune
Barron's Forbes*, in order to file a comprehensive report on
the economy for Slava. His friend must be prepared.

At other moments, he froze in front of the cabinet, a file in his hand—what was he doing? where was he going? He had been asking himself these questions with increasing frequency for the last three months, but now that Slava was in the states, they became especially poignant. *What will Slava say when he sees me filing these dumb folders?*

Awakened from his stupor by a sharp look from JJ, he stepped up the tempo and, in the heat of the moment, pushed the files all the way through to the back, where they landed happily in the dusty darkness at the bottom of the cabinet. Ha ha. That's filing Russki-style for you.

At lunchtime Dubinsky brought his bagged ham-and-cheese to the fountain downstairs. He liked the fountain: it was clean and functional and mercifully devoid of Eroses and Psyches and other Greeks. Its bottom was uncluttered by ten-lira coins. It never broke down, not once, and murmured steadily through snow and rain. It was a triumph of American fountainship.

On his $150-a-week salary Dubinsky soon became resentful of the Electric Avenue prices. Of course it took Linda, who worked for another company in the building, to show him that there was nothing shameful about brown-bagging, that you could put your sandwich in a nice plastic bag and eat it out just as well. Linda had worked in offices for a long time and knew about practical things—helping him in a salad bar, for example, whenever they went out. She had briefly attended UCLA, where she majored in architecture, which knowledge she applied masterfully at the campus cafeterias with their ninety-nine-cent all-you-can-eat salad plates. Linda's salads were pure Bauhaus in their functional simplicity and their three-foot size. "You should be designing high-rises," Dubinsky said. "You're so funny," she said, blushing, although from time to time she did plan to go back to California and get state-certified as a salad stylist. Dubinsky liked Linda: she was cheerfully commonsensical, although, despite his initial attempts to the contrary, rather predictable in bed. Her last name was Lomá, which she routinely described as French, with the stress on the *a*, although once, after too many rum-

and-Cokes, she confessed it had been changed from Lohmann. Dubinsky found it exciting and liberating and considered changing his own name to Al Dubin.

"Don't you dare," she said. "You'll lose that inimitable East European flavor and become like everybody else."

"But that's exactly what I want."

And that's what *she* wanted, too, he thought in less generous moments, as he watched her emerge from the revolving doors. She had a cheerful, bouncy walk, mildly comical due to her shortness; her hand lay confidently atop her shoulder bag, and her long black curls flew every which way.

"Hi," she said, exaggeratedly out of breath. See how I rushed to meet you. She put her arms around his neck and gave him a kiss long enough for everyone around the fountain to take notice. Just to make sure they did, she lifted her left foot and bent it a little, the way she had seen a French actress do it in a movie. "I'm sorry I'm a little late," she said, unpacking her celery and carrot sticks. He politely looked away. Called *crudités* or by any other name, they made him sick. "This office is driving me crazy." She bit into a celery stalk with a crackle. "What are you eating? Looks yummy. This Polack slut Benediktowicz was late again this morning—can you imagine? She's in her third month—does this mean I have to type *everything*? I tell you, they really discriminate against you if you're single."

He chewed on his sandwich silently. Linda traditionally had the floor first (and second and third), and no coherent response from him was required.

She went on about Benediktowicz and their new salesman, Doug, whom she at first had thought to be gay, but who subsequently tried to pick her up, because she didn't have a wedding or engagement ring or anything, she explained.

Dubinsky finished his sandwich, rolled the plastic and the brown paper into a ball, and before Linda could remind him that plastic bags were perfectly reusable, he hit the trash can on a rebound.

"You're not listening," she said reproachfully.

"Of course I am."

She stretched her back, reassured.

"I got a phone call this morning," he started uncertainly. "A friend of mine—" He went on, somehow feeling that his account was far more ominous than it sounded.

"I think it's great." Her face fell. "What about your parents? Are they coming, too? I'd love to meet them."

He held a respectable pause. "No, they are not."

"Maybe we can visit them sometime." She forced a smile. "I'd love to visit Russia some day. Now, this friend of yours . . . is he going to stay with you?"

He sighed. "Yes, of course. Except for—" My God, it's unthinkable, he said to himself. Slava would freak out. Slava isn't the kind to open a coffee shop. And Dubinsky would have to quit his job, too—what would Slava think if he saw Dubinsky filing?

"Except for what?"

"For climate," he said quickly. "Slava is a real heavy-duty snow freak."

"We have winter," she said with a touch of hurt local patriotism.

"It's not snowy enough. He needs a *long* winter."

"Those Russians. All crazy."

Dubinsky was preoccupied through the rest of the afternoon, trying to stick Fernandez after Gurewich (according to the Russian alphabet) and thinking what to do about Slava. Of course he'd have to take a couple of days off . . . how about a week? Go with him to . . . Vegas? Dubinsky was not a gambler, but that's where everyone from the office went. Or perhaps he should come back with Slava to New York for a few days? He had spent a night in New York between Rome and San Murray. He didn't have a chance to see the Guggenheim or Rockefeller Center or the coffee house where Dylan had made his debut. Something is terribly wrong with all of this, he thought, staring at his reflection on the shiny black filing cabinet. I should be excited for Slava, not scared how I will appear to be a hick from San Murray.

• • •

Aboard the bus, he tried to read the *Newsweek* he had picked up at the reception desk. The Socialist government of Pizdo had succeeded in raising the literacy rate from two percent to ninety-two percent in just six months and reducing the infant mortality rate from ninety-two to two per thousand. Yet the CIA-backed bandits controlled the countryside and stubbornly kept burning schools and hospitals, routinely removing the navels of Bulgarian proctologists and Nicaraguan geometry teachers. Borzoi's pals had wised up to the attrition rate, he thought with respect. In the meantime, there were expressions of support from France and a development loan from Sweden. The CIA "no comment"-ed as usual, but the Congress was outraged anyway, and the Massachusetts delegation pressed hard for the recognition of the Socialist Republic of Pizdo and, not to be outdone by the Swedes, a $500-million development loan.

The monotony of the suicidal Western goodwill had failed to anger him long ago. He could not even concentrate. The hell with strategic pizdorvanium deposits, what am I going to do about Slava?

When he arrived home and looked over the barely furnished steppes of his apartment, his heart sank yet deeper. He had never gone shopping to add to the original agency-supplied furniture. He had not even tried to bring it up to the "household" level. He went out, roaming the streets aimlessly, feeling Slava's presence at his side grow by the minute. As his eyes slid over the graffiti-covered grim buildings, at the spilled garbage cans, at the rusting, scarred old cars packed bumper-to-bumper along the sidewalk, he murmured one apology after another, although he knew well that it was no worse than Lipsk, where his parents lived. And, more important, Slava was not even here. Yet. What a bleak road he, Dubinsky, was traveling. Some Highway of Truth. No wonder that Konstantin's building loomed at the end of it. That's right, he thought; all roads lead to the liquor store.

Konstantin, whom Dubinsky had met shortly after his arrival, was a sculptor who, back home, had created 1,026 likenesses of Lenin in stone, bronze, and marble, to say nothing of Marx and Engels and assorted Heroes of Labor. Now, in the absence of commissions to create the likenesses of Washington and Lincoln, he sold insurance. He asked Dubinsky how he liked America, and the latter gave him a full blast of the shining beautiful Truth, malls and all. Konstantin spat and called Dubinsky a victim of rampant materialism.

Actually, Dubinsky rather liked Konstantin. A loudmouth and a haranguer, he was at least not a complete moron. But in terms of socializing, that is, drinking, they were simply in different categories. A respectable welterweight by American classification, Dubinsky was a quasi-teetotaler by Russian standards.

He could tell that Konstantin was at home without climbing the steps. A battle was raging inside. The full, rich South Ukraine cadences splashed out into the courtyard; the image was pure Odessa, and the air was filled with the fragrance of blossoming lilacs.

"It's all your fault!" Konstantin raged. "It was your damn relatives, the mercantile hypocrites, who dragged me into this cesspool of a town!"

"You want me to bring up a child in Brooklyn?" his wife Oksana shot back. "She'll get maimed, knifed, raped, and kidnapped before the age of ten!"

Dubinsky sat down on the stairs and decided to have a cigarette before deciding whether he wanted to reveal his presence. His legs were in favor: he had walked for almost an hour, he had strayed from the bus route, he could use a lift. His stomach voted against: he needed food more than he needed a drink. But his heart, his soul were dying for one.

"If it wasn't for you, I would have my own gallery already!"

"A gallery! In American they need galleries like in Russia they need mud!"

"Yeah, and that's why I should've stayed in Italy! You're the one who wanted to come here!"

"You think Italians are such dummies, they need another unemployed sculptor, they'd give you a work permit?"

"I should've divorced you, bitch, and married Gabriela!"

"You promised—" she sobbed, "you promised never to say that name again! That's it—I'm leaving—I'm taking the baby and going back to Odessa—people won't let us starve—I'll live on bread and water—I'll camp outside the Embassy in Washington—"

"Don't you dare!" A slap, quick and resonant. "Don't you dare take my daughter back into the Bolshevik claws!"

The baby in question woke up and joined the chorus.

"See what you've done? Bastard, ingrate, philanderer!"

"Cunt—cunt—cunt!"

Konstantin stormed out to the terrace. "Got a match—what are you doing here, Dubinsky?"

Dubinsky tossed Konstantin his lighter.

"Enjoying *Scenes from a Marriage?*" asked Konstantin coolly. "Your fucking Bergman should only be here. But what would a stinking suicidal Swede know about the Russian soul?"

"I was just taking a walk."

"A walk? You're shitting me, Dubinsky, and you're not very good at it, I told you that before. Come on up—no, I'll come down."

"Who is it?" Oksana stuck her head out. "Oh, hi, Oleg. Come on up, I'll put on some tea."

"Thanks, I'll pass. Thanks a lot anyway."

Konstantin came downstairs. "I'll be right back, honey," he shouted. "Just drive Oleg home."

"But why can't he come upstairs? Konstantin, where's your sense of hospitality—"

"Stupid cunt," Konstantin commented quietly. "Let's get this show on the road, Dubinsky. There's a liquor store on Olive still open."

They shot out of the parking lot with the tires screeching.

"What's wrong, Dubinsky?" Konstantin asked quietly, lighting a new cigarette from the smoldering butt.

"Nothing. Just felt like having a drink."

"My kind of a guy!" Konstantin yelled, slapping the dash enthusiastically. "I knew you'd come around. Once a Russian, always a Russian!"

They bought a quart of the house-brand vodka ("Can't even

afford fucking Smirnoff anymore," Konstantin spat), then stopped at the supermarket for a six-pack, a jar of pickles, and a package of salami.

"A fucking feast, Dubinsky. A celebration of the indomitable Russian spirit!" Konstantin hollered joyously.

They headed for the Community Center for Senior Citizens.

"Russians despise bars, Dubinsky. We have to commune with nature!" Konstantin kicked the gate open, and they landed on the bench that had been given by a Mr. and Mrs. Levine, according to the plaque.

"That's my social worker," Dubinsky said.

"Oh, yeah? When's the last time you saw her?" Konstantin opened the bottle and poured vodka into the plastic cups he always kept in the car.

"Just before I got a job."

"So what do you sound so sad about?"

"I don't."

"She did her job, right? She got you off their payroll, didn't she? You're a success story, you're a feather in her cap! What do you want to be—her friend? Her lover? Her social equal? Ah"—Konstantin raised his cup—"may they all rot in hell, fucking hypocrites."

It was quiet inside the center, which was abandoned for the night. A car passed; a bird chirped in the trees. They talked in low voices, too, respecting the peace of the place; besides, for all they knew, they could be trespassing; even if it was a public place, it might be illegal to consume alcoholic beverages there; it certainly would be in Russia. But then in Russia, just about anything worth doing would be illegal anyway.

"Before I left, I went to Sochi with a friend for a week. Do you remember Plantain Boulevard at night, Dubinsky? The Promenade—the magnolias in bloom—the parading bitches on the sidewalk—the jazz pours out of the restaurants. . . . It all happened a thousand years ago, Dubinsky, provided it happened at all. To our memories, Dubinsky."

They drank, and Dubinsky talked of the good time he had had in Sochi. Konstantin nodded approvingly—he was familiar with the high life of black market operators, or at least pretended he was—but when Dubinsky mentioned Slava's call, he made a face.

"Your friend is a fool. All those underground millionaires rush to America to make a killing, only to get shorn by the Du Ponts and Mellons. He should've stayed on his own turf. Who the hell pulled him by the balls to leave? Mind my word, he's going to bite his nails a month after he gets here. He's going to bang his head against the wall the first time a bunch of spics rip off his cab in New York."

"I'm very close to him, Kostya. We're the best of pals. You can't imagine the things he's done for me. Including this, America."

"You should curse his soul forever!" Konstantin raised his voice. "You were in your own element, you were among your own people—what are you now? Lord of the Files!" He spat.

I should split his skull in two with this bottle, Dubinsky thought. But the bottle was still two-thirds full, and he postponed the act. "In the first place," he said, "Slava is a very smart guy, and I believe that filing was not what he had in mind for me when he urged me to leave. By farting away my life in the files, *I* failed *him*. It's not his fault that I lack the drive to advance myself." He sniffed lightly.

"And in the second place?"

"I don't remember," Dubinsky admitted, opening a beer.

"In the second place, Dubinsky, you're quitting your job and going to New York to rendezvous with your pal." Konstantin poured the vodka. "To Oleg Dubinsky, the voyager to the metropolis! Ah, Dubinsky." He shook his head. "You'll love the bright lights out there. . . . You left Moscow for New York, Dubinsky. Nobody leaves Moscow for San Murray."

"I'm getting drunk," Dubinsky stated soberly.

"Honesty is a poor substitute for the inability to hold liquor." Konstantin regarded the bottle in the moonlight. They were over the half mark. "*Festina lente,*" he muttered, pouring a round.

"I really should slow down," Dubinsky said.

"I should come to New York with you," Konstantin said.
"Why don't you?"

Konstantin shrugged. "You were there. You heard it all.
The albatross around my neck."

"What about Gauguin?"

"What about him?" Konstantin snapped. "You call New
York Samoa? Life is expensive there. Sculpting is an expensive pursuit, Dubinsky. And who the hell says I'm worth anything? I was once, Dubinsky, but that was a long time ago,
way before I broke my first hundred. I'm talking about Len-
ins," he explained. "That bald Tatar screwed up my career
for good." He poured more vodka. "If I could *really* sculpt him
the way I want, one of these days, in a ritual shawl, with
payssim and *tephillin* . . ."

Dubinsky just stretched out on the grass and wondered if
the sky looked any different in New York. From all he had
heard, New York was a vile, filthy, dangerous place. People
were stabbed in broad daylight for a quarter. You could not
enter the subway without wearing a gas mask, and you'd
better be inoculated against every disease known to mankind.
The rents were triple San Murray's. Every time a waiter put
a glass of water on your table, he'd charge you a dollar. Garbage lay unattended on the streets, and rats popped out of
the alleys and attacked babies in strollers.

Dubinsky realized he was turning more sentimental as the
sight of Slava marching into Gate 5 brought a lump in his
throat. Slava looked ten years older. He still looked gentlemanly in his Burberry, his carry-on was from Louis Vuitton
but oh the lines on his forehead, the fatigue in his eyes, the
shades of silver on his temples; the lump in Dubinsky's throat
grew as they embraced. Was that the way of the world? Was
Slava taking a beating, too? Was there a way out? Had they
both made a terrible, irreversible mistake?

Slava chuckled half-audibly as they walked to the luggage
carousel. "Growing a paunch, Dubinsky. No volleyball in
America?"

"It's all that junk food," Dubinsky muttered apologetically, thinking, And we haven't started on the subject of filing yet.

"It's not a world metropolis, San Murray," Dubinsky kept apologizing in the car. "But it's very . . . comfortable. Where did you go in Europe?"

"Here and there," Slava said. "Zurich, Frankfurt . . . Slow down, Dubinsky, this car was not made for seventy-five miles an hour." Linda's Pinto was, indeed, shaking violently. "I hope you're not showing off for my sake."

"It's not even mine." Dubinsky obediently eased on gas. "How did you manage to get out of Italy? Don't you need a passport to travel?"

"Passport is just another commodity, Dubinsky, available for an X amount of cash. We'll talk about it later. Step on the gas, you're clogging the traffic."

Indeed, Dubinsky thought, you can't drive thirty miles an hour in the fast lane. "So, as I said, San Murray is not such a bad place—"

"I think I'm getting the picture," Slava said, as his eyes scanned the malls on both sides of the freeway. "Abundance with a vengeance."

"Yep."

"It's still a puzzle, this picture," Slava said. "I'm trying to find Dubinsky in it."

"Well," Dubinsky swallowed nervously, veering toward the exit, "I have this job, which is sort of like a springboard . . ." He went on, and not until they entered his apartment and settled on the couch with beers in their hands did he realize that his whole speech was nothing but one long complaint. He also realized he was feeling much better.

"To your arrival." He lifted his Bud somewhat belatedly. "I hope you realize how much this means to me."

"Cuts both ways, Dubinsky," Slava said. "Listen, I'll take a quick nap, do you mind? You don't want me to fall asleep in the middle of dinner and embarrass you in front of your girlfriend, right?" And, before shutting the door behind him, he added, "You're worrying too much, Dubinsky. It's been only six months, what do you expect? Do you remember what you said at the farewell party? 'Somehow it always ends well, doesn't it?' So there. You're doing okay."

For a few moments Dubinsky sat immobilized, afraid to even flick his lighter. When the familiar snore came from the bedroom, he uttered a deep sigh of relief. He sprang to his feet, and he waltzed across the room; he felt a powerful, inexplicable sense of exhilaration sweeping him. At first it was ordinary relief, but now the seeds of something new and exciting were stirring in the air; Slava had not said one thing about his plans, but deep inside Dubinsky *knew*. Life was about to begin again.

On their way to Linda's Slava grilled Dubinsky on the subject of Mr. Levine. With every question, Dubinsky's mood sank. He had to admit that he didn't know the name of Levine's company; he didn't know how many partners he had, nor how they financed their development; he didn't even know what the prime rate was.

"He said he was proud to be a capitalist," Dubinsky mumbled.

"Why shouldn't he be," Slava grumbled.

"His best friends are a car dealer and an ad agency owner," Dubinsky went on without a clear idea why.

"You must've expected a rock'n'roll band."

"And he doesn't have a book in his house."

"It's going to be a long road for us, Dubinsky." Getting close to Mr. Levine on the basis of being a friend of Dubinsky's was a dubious prospect, Slava thought.

From the moment they entered Linda's apartment, she chattered incessantly, and Dubinsky was grateful. He knew Slava was a gentleman, but he was less sure of himself, and the impossibility of inserting a word in between Linda's questions about Russia and Slava's leaving and Dubinsky's parents was a saving grace. For double protection, he put away three glasses of jug Chablis in quick succession. Slava was taking Linda's inquisitiveness in good stride, grinning fully and responding to her questions by paying her a compliment a minute: on the tightly fitting bright orange jumpsuit she was wearing, on her taste in decorating her apartment (Dubinsky looked away), on her perfume (Dubinsky was not even sure it was legal under the chemical warfare treaty). My God, she suspects he's out to steal her away from me, Dubinsky thought, as she grew flustered and even more nervous, matching him glass for glass. He could not wait to leave. As he dejectedly strolled out into the street, he realized it was going to be one of *those* evenings; and nothing overtly scandalous had even taken place yet.

On their way to the restaurant Linda explained, with some determination, how although at first she thought that perhaps it might be more interesting for Slava to go to a typical American restaurant, now she agreed with Dubinsky that the place that he had originally suggested would be more interesting than your average steak-and-seafood joint.

Slava walked behind with a bemused air, but his eyes were restlessly scanning the mall, the J. C. Penney, the size of the parking lot, the direction in which the crowds were heading. He is at work, Dubinsky realized, and decided not to comment on Linda's explanation.

Ryga Lovka, an East African restaurant where they were heading, was located at the far outskirts of the mall, and it took them a good fifteen minutes to find it stuck between Shofix, a shoe-repair salon, and Blue Dahlia, a natural-flower-cum-mystery-bookstore.

"I told you we'd find it." Linda cheerfully pushed the door open.

I admire her frontier, can-do spirit, Dubinsky thought, examining absently the grease spots on the menu. I admire her sunny have-a-nice-day attitude that had persisted, on their last date, through a Buñuel double feature, while deep inside, he was sure, she would rather have gone to see *Kramer vs. Kramer*, to shed a tear or two into her popcorn (and the Old

Art Cinema, with its health-conscious audience, would not even serve butter with the popcorn). And now this Pizdo experience, while he knew she'd be much happier at Hamburger Hamlet any time.

But what was the point of it? he wondered. Why did she put up with it? Why did she agree so easily? Was it simply a courtesy, a desire to be nice and hospitable to a friend of Dubinsky's? He doubted that. And now this—poorly lit cavern with an Art Naif mural of Niagara (perhaps all waterfalls look alike), a forlorn-looking spear on the wall, and a short, squat, sad-looking idol in the corner. The latter looked like he was sick and tired of the Ryga Lovka offerings and would rather go out for a pizza. The only other customers in the place were two young men holding hands under the table. Dubinsky overheard them ordering "The Flaming Spear," the most expensive dish on the menu; the only description provided was that it was dedicated to the memory of Jomo Kenyatta. Linda cast a sharp look at the couple that left no doubt as to her feelings about people with alternative lifestyles. Dubinsky suggested they leave.

"Oh, no," she said, holding on to the menu with two fingers. "If you like it, then I like it, too." She quickly excused herself to go to the ladies' room.

Ah, but how easy it was to provoke a fight. *Don't you ever have your own opinion? Can't you clearly state what you want?*

"Maybe she was right," Dubinsky muttered, avoiding Slava's look. "Maybe we should've treated you to a bit of real true-blue Americana."

"It doesn't matter," Slava said. "This place is bound to be closed soon enough, might as well check it out."

Dubinsky explained that, according to the local paper, the restaurant had been started by a family who had escaped from Pizdo two years ago.

"So you wanted to come here to refresh your Pizdoan conjugations?"

"There are no conjugations in Pizdoan."

"Then it's an act of political contrition," Slava yawned. "With poor Linda suffering along."

"She's okay," Dubinsky said, still blankly staring at the menu. *Don't you agree?*

"She certainly is." Slava yawned even wider. "Excuse me. But she doesn't pull enough weight to rescue a confused Russian liberal."

Linda's return did rescue Dubinsky from an unpleasant necessity to ask Slava what he meant by that. But the sight of him, properly attired in an Italian suit, with his cufflinks protruding just the right inch, filled Dubinsky with sadness. Clearly, the Pizdo joint was a mistake. But would the three of them be more at ease at Le Café Irwing, San Murray's most outrageously overpriced French restaurant?

"I think the chicken sounds pretty safe," Linda sighed. "Maybe they'll go easy on the *jija* sauce."

"If you tell them, I'm sure they will," Dubinsky said gloomily. "Unless it's a matter of culinary pride for the chef, in which case they'll do a *juju* on you. Never mind, it's a bad pun," he added charitably.

They drank another toast to Slava's arrival to the land of the free.

"I really, really honestly hope that things will work out for you here." Linda opened her eyes wider to enhance the sincerity effect. "I'm sure you'll love it here as much as Oleg does." She shot him a support-seeking glance. Dubinsky nodded in resignation. "And I do hope, really, that maybe you'll like it here in San Murray well enough," she went on, reassured, "because it's really such a neat place, and there's plenty of jobs, too. I understand from what Oleg told me that you're such a great salesman, so you'd be great at door-to-door—"

Stop, goddamn it, Dubinsky almost cried out, sensing, even in the dark, a shadow coming over Slava's expression.

"I'm sure I will," Slava said quietly.

"Speaking of which," she said, "I have some good news for Oleg. I sort of wanted to wait till dessert, but then I said, what the hell."

She's actually trying to cheer me up, he thought, plunging deeper into melancholy.

"First"—she took a sip of her beer—"a woman at work is

selling her car. It's a Ford Fairlane, four doors—" She went into the car's description with such fervor that, had Dubinsky not known her, he could swear there was a commission involved.

"Great." he kept nodding. Sounded like a fabulous family car, damn it. No red 'vettes for this future pillar of society.

The waiter arrived felicitously in the middle of Linda's paeans to the transmission that was still under warranty. The waiter's swarthy East Indian features expressed yoga-like stoicism in the face of whatever the crazy white woman wanted to order.

"No chicken *blevo*," he said. "Our special is chicken *ponos*. Seven ninety-five. Is very good. Green sauce, not too spicy."

"That sounds nice." She sighed with stoicism to match his. "Is there a vegetable comes with that?"

"Many vegetable," he assured her. "What kind of dressing you want? We have Blue Cheese, Thousand Island, and Russian." Dubinsky cringed.

"Thousand Islands would be lovely," she said helplessly, exchanging looks with the idol, who was licking his fat lips at the sight of this nice, plump, schmaltz-bred offering.

The waiter turned his attention to Slava, who quietly opted for pork *rvota*, and then to Dubinsky, who settled for lamb *zapor*, with *toshno* sauce made with coconuts flown in daily. Blue Cheese. And another round of beers. The waiter closed his pad. "Excuse for asking, but what nationality are you from?"

"Holland." Dubinsky looked away.

"Why did you tell him that?" Linda hissed after the waiter was gone. "Do you think he's anti-Semitic?"

"Sort of," Dubinsky mumbled. "I'll explain later."

"That," Slava said, wiping his eyes, "was alone worth the price of admission, as you say in this country. You're a riot, Dubinsky."

"That Fairlane sounds real interesting," Dubinsky said. "Did you mention how many miles per gallon it gets on the streets?"

"Well, there's more," she said. "There's going to be a job

opening in our office, and I already talked to the supervisor about you, Oleg." The job was assistant bookkeeper, it paid $175 a week, and it had fabulous prospects. " 'Is he sharp?' she asks me," Linda went on, enjoying herself. "See, you have to be really sharp at this job, numbers and all. 'Is he sharp?' I said. 'Why, this guy,' meaning you, 'this guy played the whole Politburo for a sucker, he tricked them into letting him go to America. How's that for sharp?'"

"That describes it about right," Slava concurred.

" 'They got the same figures in Russia like everywhere else,' I said. So we laughed, and she said for you to come over Monday and fill out an application."

"That calls for a celebration," Slava said.

Dubinsky felt his stomach separate from his body and land on the floor. And even Slava did not hear the thud. What was the next rabbit in Linda's hat, he wondered. A furnished duplex in Cordeboy for one hundred dollars a month that they could move into right away?

The arrival of food interrupted momentarily the visions of Dubinsky's bright future. All three were hungry, and for the next ten minutes only the sounds of chewing were to be heard. Lamb *zapor* was one tough sheep, but Dubinsky was tougher, even with the treacherous knife as the Fifth Column. He wondered what culinary transgressions were concealed by the plethora of spices, but chose wisely not to share his misgivings with Linda, who, God knows, had her hands full with her own tough old bird. "How's your chicken?" he asked somewhat rhetorically.

"Fine," she nodded eagerly. Droplets of sweat formed on the bridge of her nose, both from the spices and the sheer physical effort of cutting. "I really like it."

"I can't tell you how much I appreciate your bringing me here," Slava said noncommittally, giving up on his *rvota*. "This is fun."

Linda eyed him uncertainly.

"Gives you a rare insight into the roots of Pizdoan social unrest," he said.

"I agree," Linda said quickly, afraid to lose the thread of the conversation. And she went on to say that who could think that the East Africans were such terrific cooks; that it was really a lot of food for the money; that she should bring her friend Karen here; and, last but not least, she wondered if she could get the recipe. Under the massive barrage of expression Dubinsky was forced to remark that his lamb was "quite interesting." Toward the end of the meal he could hardly feel anything at all, so badly was his palate desensitized; it was like the South Bronx on TV, alternatively set on fire and flooded from the fire trucks' hoses.

For dessert, the waiter threatened them with *mesivo* pie. Dubinsky shook his head, thus sparing Linda an attack of caloric anxiety by not asking if she wanted any. She gave his hand a grateful squeeze under the table.

"Delay would be deadly," Slava agreed, pulling out his wallet.

"The hell you do, Rothman." Dubinsky glared at him.

They drove to drop Slava off at Dubinsky's place. Dubinsky was relieved to see there was not a parking spot in sight. "Why don't you wait in the car, I'll be right back."

"Listen," he said as he handed Slava clean bedsheets, "this may not have been the greatest dining experience, but, you know—"

"I do, Dubinsky." Slava landed on the couch and lit a Dunhill. "I do know, only too well. Sit down. I have a favor to ask. You see, originally I was going to fly to Boise, Idaho, tomorrow morning, but something tells me that you might enjoy it more. Also, I want to get together with Mr. Levine tomorrow. See if we can do some business. What do you say to that? I'll pay all your expenses, naturally."

"Aw, forget that." Dubinsky waved impatiently. "What's a favor. Besides, I've never been to Idaho."

"I thought you'd like that," Slava said unsmilingly.

"What kind of business are you going to discuss with Levine?"

Slava paused, then said, "I detect a certain note of distrust in your voice, Dubinsky. Do you have a reputation with Mr. and Mrs. Levine that I might inadvertently destroy?"

Dubinsky managed a faint smile.

"I don't know what exactly kind of business," Slava admitted, "but I'm sure that at a certain point our interests may converge. Okay? Here's the ticket." He explained to Dubinsky what he was supposed to do.

"Sure," Dubinsky nodded, rising. He felt bad about keeping Linda waiting. "Well . . . feel at home. If you don't see something, keep looking. As for the refrigerator—"

"Sit down, Dubinsky. She can wait for another hour, as far as I can tell. Will be happy to, matter of fact. I want to ask you one question."

"Shoot."

"Do you know what you're doing here?"

"You mean, in San Murray?" Slava nodded. "Well . . . no. I'm not really sure—"

"No more questions, Dubinsky. Go give your girlfriend the bang of her life."

Dubinsky opened the door, but could not force himself to leave; not just yet. "What was the question all about?" he said quietly.

"I pushed you out here," Slava said just as quietly, "and, in a limited sense, you're my responsibility. I've heard pretty much what I thought I'd hear. Don't worry about a thing, Oleg. Go ahead and have fun. I'll take care of things."

After Dubinsky got back to the car, Linda was, much as Slava had predicted, too much relieved about his coming back, period, to be angry at him. On the way she chatted about how happy he would be, working at her office, how people were really nice and sympathetic, especially after she had told them of the hard life he had had in Russia. Assistant bookkeeper was a fast-track job that in a year or two could be easily parlayed into a full-charge bookkeeper position. And the experience would be absolutely invaluable if he finally decided to go for an MBA. Or he could make a great CPA. When you think of all the money accountants make, especially in April . . .

"I think I could use a drink," he interrupted her.

"I have wine at my place."

"Wine is not a drink."

She furrowed her brows. "Let me think for a moment. There aren't any really nice bars in my neighborhood."

"Let's go to a less-than-nice bar."

The less-than-nice bar was called Mulcahy's and featured disturbing amounts of green paint everywhere, including the King Boru pinball game and the waitresses' underpanties, which they displayed avidly when serving drinks. It took him four minutes to put away two Scotches and a pint of Guinness. Their waitress, a buxom redhead, kept chuckling at the lad's thirst and displaying her décolletage. Linda sat frozen in her chair, nursing a Miller Lite.

Something stirred within Dubinsky. Perhaps it was her silence that convinced him that she was at the end of her tether. He leaned over.

"You want to go home?"

"Yes, please." She took his hand and kissed it. "I hate to be such a party pooper, really . . ."

"You're certainly not." Her words brought about an overwhelming urge to stay.

In the car, she rested her head on his shoulder. "I really liked your friend, you know. He's so smooth, even . . . *soave.*"

"What's that again?"

"Well, you know . . . *urban.* Except for I don't really think he'll like it in San Murray," she went on, pressing her breasts against his shoulder. "I can see him in L.A., or some fancy place like that."

"Oh, yeah?" Dubinsky turned the corner abruptly, sending her across the seat. "Where do you see *me* then?" And I'll be goddamned if I help you out of this one, he thought viciously, roaring through a yellow light. Driving sobered him up the moment he laid his hands on the wheel. He had not yet driven enough to be blasé about the power he wielded over a thousand-pound contraption.

"I can see *you* anywhere," she finally said. "L.A. or New York or San Murray, you'd do great anyplace." And she beamed at him, expecting a return compliment.

"I hope Boise, Idaho, is included on your list of places for me to shine in." He told her of the next day's flight.

"I don't understand," she said. "Will there be more trips like this?"

"I don't know. Maybe," he said casually. He could not help seeing himself from the outside: what man doesn't look debonair while driving and a woman's head on his shoulder and a cigarette at the corner of his mouth and an elbow sticking outside with just one hand on the wheel free and easy here we go. . . . He stole a glance at himself in the rearview mirror; if he had one arm free, he would run a comb through his hair, too.

"What about the bookkeeping job?" she insisted. "You don't want it anymore?"

"I didn't say that." I don't even want to think about it at this time, he thought. This is the kind of dialogue that leads people to run into walls at ninety miles per hour. "One thing at a time, okay?"

"Okay." But the fear was now lodged firmly in her voice, and nothing he would say or do could remove it. "I talked to Mom on the phone last night," she said after a long pause, "and she asked me if you were coming over next weekend."

Oh, God. It was her father's birthday. He had completely forgotten.

"It's only a couple hours' drive. And they're so excited about meeting you, I told them all about you and how you got out of Russia. You'll really like them. I mean, some of their ways are really old-fashioned, like Daddy might ask you after dinner about your plans for the future, including you-know-what—"

"I-don't-know-what."

"Well, you know." She reached under his shirt and licked his earlobe. "Marriage . . . that kind of stuff. So if you don't want to talk to him about it, just ignore him."

He wheeled the car into her parking space and killed the

engine. Ignoring Linda's father, a former Golden Gloves con-
tender and a no-nonsense owner of numerous used-car lots
and junkyards, was going to be a cinch, Dubinsky could see
that.

Upstairs, they curled on the rug, they drank wine, she murmured, he nodded—until he removed her bra and sucked on
her nipples and rubbed himself against her and felt that nothing was happening. He was simply not interested. What he
really felt like doing was lying on his back and gazing at the
stars.

Murmuring that it was all right, really, it happened sometimes, he had had such an awful lot to drink, she took him in
her mouth but mostly in her hand. No use. He said he was
sorry. She hushed him and lay down next to him.

As he lay in bed, breathing in unison with the air condi-
tioner, he saw Nonna. She slipped in through the window and
approached the bed. I left Denmark, she said; I couldn't take
that cream-with-everything diet. I moved to Buffalo, so when
you called me, I hopped a plane, and here I am. She knelt
over him and lowered herself slowly over his body, leaving
only her crotch in the air; then she lowered it, too, brushing
his penis lightly over and over. He turned on his side, then
climbed atop the figure next to him, slid it in, and pumped.
She put her arms around him and breathed deeply. But it
was over before she could react fully. He stayed on top of her
for a few seconds, feeling even more bitter and empty than
before, feeling sorry for her, for himself, and the future that
was not to be. He opened his eyes. He was alone. A strip of
light came from the bathroom. Linda's sobs were heard inside.

"I'll be all right, really," she said when he came over. "But
it's so hard being with you. I'm doing everything for you—I
help you find a job—I help you find a car—I drive you around—
I helped you get a license—I'm taking you to see my parents.
. . . I make no secret of my feelings for you, I'm reaching out,
and you're not there. You—you—" A new outburst came out
of her, she dabbed at her already red nose with a wad of toilet

paper, but the tears kept running. "You never ask me about my job or how I feel about things or what I want to do or my plans for the future. . . . I'm just *there* for you, that's all. You never tell me how you feel about me, and it's very frustrating, because I really care for you, and I'd do anything for you—"

He picked her up easily and carried her to the bedroom.

"Don't you dare patronize me!" she yelled all of a sudden. "I'm not a little girl you can play daddy with and shut me up when you don't like what I have to say!"

She wrestled out of his arms and collapsed on the bed, burying her face in the pillow, her body quaking with the next wave of sobs.

"And now your hotshot friend shows up, and you're off and running! You can't come and go like this, Oleg. . . . I don't know anything about who we are to each other anymore . . . You just can't do this to me—"

He sat up, his back propped up by a pillow. His mouth felt rotten, but no worse than the rest of him as he watched her.

Tell her you love her, the voice said; tell her you want to marry her and never leave her; and then you can go to sleep—

I can't.

You don't have to mean it; millions of people say it every day without meaning it; what good is the truth when a human being suffers—

I can't.

So that's it, you don't want to tell a lie so that you could be a truth-teller, that you could feel superior to the rest of humanity, all those billions of liars—

I know. But I really can't. Can't can't can't.

Drop the apostrophe, the voice said, that's what your truth is really all about—*cant.*

He put his arms around her, he lay down next to her and pressed himself against her, and he whispered, "Linda, I really like you, I really do . . ." He went on like a broken record, until his mouth was completely parched and her sobs subsided and he heard her even, childlike sleepy breathing. Then he fell asleep, too, feeling like a seventy-year-old nun who had just burned the monastery with all the Sisters in Christ inside, but kept her virtue intact.

Dubinsky vomited his breakfast—omelet, sausage, and all—in the DC-10's bathroom. Then he returned to his seat and stared numbly at the cover of *U.S. News and World Report*. Two million Pizdoans were starving to death. Emergency food supplies were airlifted to the capital. The guerrillas offered free passage to food trucks, but the government wisely held on to the supplies until the guerrillas surrendered. He had been waving for a beer for a half an hour, and his wrist was hurting. The stewardess was a soulmate of Pizdoan rulers, there was no doubt about it. He was overcome by wave after wave of self-pity, self-loathing, and plain nausea. He did not give a shit about the whispering pines of the Beautiful Pacific Northwest, advertised in lush colors in the in-flight magazine. What the hell were they going to whisper to him, You blew it? He dozed off, but his sleep was heavy and oppressive:

He was back outside their, his and Linda's, burning house, wearing a worn housecoat and slippers, frozen to the spot, suffocating in the hot summer night. Linda was there, too, her hair in curlers, wailing over the lost washer and dryer. "Nothing doing," said the fireman; "too late." He removed his mask, under which he was Mr. Lohmann, Linda's father. "You Russki rat." He advanced toward Dubinsky, a tire iron in his hand. "You trashed the apple of my eye; you're gonna pay for this, Mr. Dissident." "Boy, you sure know how to mix up a metaphor," Dubinsky said jauntily, hoping to turn this into a joke. "I'll mix your ass now, boy." "Look, she's catching fire," Dubinsky yelled, dodging the swinging iron. And indeed there were tiny little snakes of fire dancing in Linda-Medusa's hair. Dubinsky, remembering what had happened to Atlas, quickly turned away. "Where's your buddy now?" The Gorgon hissed steam in his face. "Here," Slava said, holding the door of a black limo open. "We'll be landing in Seattle in fifteen minutes." His face was pale and dispassionate. "Wait," Dubinsky gasped, "please wait, those fucking Murray maniacs are gonna kill me." "Don't forget your hand luggage," Slava said. Dubinsky jerked away, slipped, and fell into a darkness that turned out to be the Sea-Tac International.

The Tater Airlines flight from Seattle was late, and he barely made it to the Miller Street branch of the Copper Bank of Idaho before closing time. Boise looked weird to him, clean and crummy at the same time. Suddenly he realized he was surrounded by exclusively white people. He was far away from San Murray. He felt like a stranger. Perhaps he should write a note to the teller: "I love you. Give me all you got in fives and tens. Have a nice day." He looked around. People were polite, but he suspected that gun laws were not too strict in Idaho. Even without attempting a robbery he could not help feeling like a criminal—a Russian spy, a Yankee peddler, a grubby Jew, who, to top it all, had no idea what he was doing.

Someone lightly touched him on the shoulder. He recoiled. A short girl in a leather jacket, her dirty-blond curls falling down her back, looked at him with concern.

"There's a teller available over there," she said. "Are you all right?"

"I'll wait for you," he said. "I'll tell you all about it."

"I don't have the time," she laughed. "I'm flying back to Seattle this afternoon."

"I'll fly with you," he said, hoping they were booked on the same flight. If not, he'd change it. It was America; anything was possible.

He stuffed the stamped deposit slip in his jeans pocket and leaned against the counter in the most raffish pose he could manage.

"You're crazy." She shook her head in disbelief, as they stepped outside. "Did anyone ever tell you you're crazy?"

"No," he said. "You're the first one."

His flight was leaving an hour before hers, and if he joined her, he wouldn't make the connection to San Murray. Fine, he said to himself; if that's the hand I've got, I might as well play it. "I'll take it," he said into the phone.

"We just happen to be on the same flight," he declared

triumphantly, stepping out of the phone booth. "A hell of a coincidence."

"Where do they grow nuts like you?" she laughed. "I mean, where's the accent from?"

"Staten Island," he said, "you know where the ferry goes, we're called the Staten Island Flemish, it's like Pennsylvania Dutch, only tougher, you know what I mean?"

"Staten Island Flemish," she echoed. "I'll be. On a Boise afternoon. Well . . . if you don't get picked up by an ambulance to take you back to the nuthouse, I guess we could share a cab to the airport. That bus gives me the creeps."

"Will be my pleasure," he assured her. "What shall I call you?"

"Jodie." She looked at him directly and unabashedly, a glint in her eye, stray locks of hair windblown on her forehead.

Aboard the plane, they were matching Bloody Marys one for one, and she was munching happily on his celery sticks. He was happily watching her munching on his celery sticks. A generous rosy glow, with a drop of Tabasco, enveloped the cabin.

She told him everything about her sick brother she had been visiting in Boise, and he, in a shameless exploitation act, told her he was all alone in this country.

"That's sad." She sighed and took another sip.

"It's unfortunate," he agreed.

"I don't like my family an awful lot," she said, "but I know they'll be there in a crunch."

"That helps," he agreed again, thinking how he had not heard from his parents since his arrival.

She went on to tell him about her father, who, like everybody in Seattle, worked for Boeing. "I better not tell you too much," she giggled, "you might be a spy."

He nodded absently, thinking, why should his parents write more regularly than he does.

She misinterpreted his expression. "I was only kidding." She touched his hand. "And if you're a spy, I don't care, either. Of course, I don't think you are." She paused. "I guess I'm getting drunk. I better slow down. I have to go to work to-morrow."

They felt the landing gear being released, and the thud brought the conversation to a stop. An uneasy silence settled in and persisted all through the landing. As he watched her get her lipstick and her compact, he thought: she's being met, and there's not a thing I can do about it. The plane wobbled and came to a stop. Dubinsky automatically rose, although he didn't have anything in the overhead storage. Then he saw her still seated, and sat back, too.

"I want to thank you for this flight," she said. "You really made it for me."

"Goes both ways," he whispered. "Listen, if this person—whoever's meeting you—am I right?" She nodded, watching his face intently. "If this person—just a hypothetical question, mind you—if he doesn't show up—"

"He'll be there," she said sadly. "I'm not sure it's such a good thing, but he'll be there." The crowd shifted uneasily toward the exit, bumping into the seats, the bags, and one another. "You really shouldn't wait for me." She forced a smile. "Thanks again. I'd give you a kiss, but I don't want to leave a smudge."

"A smudge is just a smudge," he hummed, still seated.

She laughed despite herself. "See, you made me laugh again. Please don't wait for me."

He leaned over and touched her cheek with his lips. It was warm and soft. He caught his breath and asked her for her phone number.

"I'm in the book," she said. "Jodie Gregg. Will you really call?"

"I don't joke around," he said.

"I noticed."

"You'll see." And he strode off through a semi-empty salon, looking as though he had a purpose, and not quite knowing what it was.

Inside the airport he went to phone Slava. From the distance, in the cold metallic neon light, he saw Jodie coming out of the gate, slowly, as if to be executed, he thought. A tall blond man, wearing jeans and a parka, stood motionless, as she approached him. Suddenly he moved as though to slap her, and she flinched. Then he put his arm around her, and they walked away. I can't believe this, Dubinsky thought; he didn't even pick up her bag—quite heavy, from the looks of it—or anything. Didn't even offer. Dubinsky picked up the phone book mechanically and looked her up. There were only two J. Greggs. No problem, he thought. It didn't occur to him for a moment that she might have lied. She simply couldn't.

As he dialed and talked to the operator, his eyes listlessly scanned the huge Departure schedule on the wall. And so, by the time he heard Slava say he was accepting the charges, he found it. United, Flight 78. "I need a return favor," he said, the phone slipping out of a suddenly sweaty palm. "Do you know how to pack?" He explained what to do with the keys, and gave Slava the number to call Dubinsky's office and break the news.

"Want me to call Linda?"

"No." I'll pay my own dues, he thought.

After a pause, Slava said, "Dubinsky, I just want you to know that you'll never regret this. I personally guarantee this."

"No need for that," Dubinsky muttered, barely listening; megavolts of energy were flowing through his body, and he knew exactly what he was doing and what he had yet to do.

"You're all right, Dubinsky. I've always known that. I'll see you tomorrow night in the Village."

Maintaining the momentum, Dubinsky called Linda. The machine answered. Dubinsky, the luckiest rat in the world, he thought, as he waited for the beep. "Baby, I have to go to New York," he said; "it's an emergency. I'll call you from there."

The next night he stood on the corner of Bleecker and Sixth. The sidewalks were overflowing with people; six equally bad street musicians representing every style tortured their respective instruments within hundred yards of each other, and one minority-owned enormous radio drowned out them all; the rats popped out of the alleys and the babies leaped out of their strollers and kicked the rats to death. The megavolts from the night before in Dubinsky's body raised themselves to the nth degree. He happily inhaled the air of exhaust and illegal substances. He felt at home, and when a panhandler approached him for change he cheerfully told the man to buzz off.

Six

Mr. Levine seemed properly amused: how, indeed, could a schmuck like Dubinsky have a slick successful cousin like that? Slava plunged into his pitch without delay. He felt hot, he felt on a roll, there was no time to lose. . . . He expressed his gratitude for Mr. and Mrs. Levine's charity toward Dubinsky, he expressed regret that he had not been around to help his long-lost cousin out . . . he had to take care of company business in Malaysia. His company, Intergalactic Trading, had interests all over the world, well, they were not Bechtel, you know, they never built anything by themselves, but financing construction projects was one of their major areas of interest, surely Mr. Levine knew his way around Europe, what, not really? what a shame, he should come and see it for himself, those countries had such *meshugge* tax laws, a person with ambition simply *had* to channel his hard-earned money elsewhere . . . and what exactly was Mr. Levine's line of business? Yes, he supposed he could reschedule his flight to San Francisco—if Mr. Levine thought it would be interesting. . . .

Standing on the twenty-fifth floor of an Electric Avenue highrise and poring over the blueprints he didn't understand worth a damn, Slava was agog with excitement. He felt immediate respect for Levine—hell, the man was planting money all over the place: an apartment complex in Texas, a condo conversion in California, and now a shopping mall in Kansas. . . . Slava's heart was beating wildly, his mind was overheating, as he tried to take in everything: the blueprints, the offering prospects, the plushness of the office. He felt swept away by the scale of events he had propelled himself into, he was hanging onto the railing, but his hands were strong, his muscles were firm, and the whole pit of Moscow Underground Shmattes Exchange stopped trading and was cheering him from miles away. The shopping mall was just the thing: it was huge and yet compact, it was what people wanted, the amortization costs were negligible, Sears was as good as in, and so were a couple more department stores, the neighborhood was growing, a cluster of hi-tech companies were moving in, the housing passed the $100,000 mark—now was the time.

Slava looked at his watch. Must not forget his San Francisco story. "Well, I must say it's certainly very interesting." He watched Levine's eyes intently—a glint of a scam going on smoothly? a mute sigh of relief? But Levine maintained the same amiable, relaxed expression he had had from the moment he ordered his Scotch and soda at lunch. You can be interested all you want, his eyes said, your money's welcome, but I'm not going to keel over if it's all a crock. Well . . . good enough, Slava concluded. Mustn't overreach. It's a crack in the door, shove in your foot and see how sturdy your shoes are.

"I figured Oleg would move to New York sooner or later," Levine said genially before they parted at the airport. "Say hello. From my wife, too. She wouldn't mind if he called her sometime." Slava wondered mechanically if there was something between Dubinsky and Mrs. Levine that he should have known before getting into this.

"They used to talk about arts, all that stuff," Levine added, as if to assuage Slava's doubts. "Nice kid, just a little too . . . impractical, I'd say. What company did you say he got that executive job with?"

"Oh, it's a trading company, nothing big. He just does translations for them." Slava grinned. "I know my cousin well enough to steer him away from the business end. Can you see Oleg in marketing?"

And they had a good, hearty laugh about this unlikely possibility.

"So you won't be coming back to New York for a while," Dubinsky said forlornly into the phone.

"Only a few days, Oleg," Slava said. "Don't make it sound like an eternity. I want to hang around, find out a bit more about that Levine character. I told him I'd be going to the Coast, so I can't show up right away. Don't worry, the wheels are turning. I already called Switzerland. I've got a pretty good feeling that this is just the kind of thing that Goldenburger might go for."

"Who's that?"

"My future partner." Dubinsky swallowed. *I thought I was your future partner.*

"I'll tell you the whole story when I get back. Don't waste time, Dub. I left you some money at the desk. This should be enough for a security deposit on a decent apartment."

"I have some money," Dubinsky said in a wounded voice. *Money money money.*

Dubinsky did not mind the microscopic size of his hotel room or its undisguised shabbiness; what mattered was that it was on the eighteenth floor, and he reveled in his acrophilia. The street outside was an electronic board game, with little yellow boxes progressing according to a programmed pattern. The air, however hot, oppressive, and humid, was the air of the heights, accessible only to the select crowd; high-rises did not dwarf him, but were his equals. In the morning he drank his coffee by his window sill, looking at the office building across the street and pitying all the Dubinskys and Rodriguezes who were scurrying around offices with file-laden trays.

The hotel had a fair-sized Russian contingent: elderly single men, fellow escapees from Dallas and Cincinnati and Detroit. Once they had been lawyers and warehouse managers, TV correspondents and economists—in short, people with "nontransferable" skills, as their caseworker would put it. In the evening they huddled in the lobby, smoking and reminiscing about the old days in Leningrad and Kiev. The night clerk, a dark swarthy man of uncertain age and vaguely Mediterranean origin, shooed them out periodically but without much enthusiasm; after all, they posed no danger to the legitimate tourists who stayed on the first four floors. They lived in cavernous dark rooms with a shower in the hall. They didn't mind; they'd perhaps been well off by the time they left Russia, but they had memories of growing up with no shower at all. And so they stood there, night after night, both drawn to and intimidated by the city that loomed outside the lobby. They ventured out in group sorties for a stroll along the brightly lit Fifth Avenue; the luxury and prosperity around left them intoxicated, drained, embittered. A newspaper editor in Mukachevo had had the clout, the status; he had ruled the waves of a little cesspool; he had dignity, occasionally bruised by the Party Secretary's references to his Jewishness; and he had dreams. Now he was welfare case #101-99-9999, Brooks Brothers did not take food stamps, and a former Greek or Turkish peasant, who had far better survival skills, yelled at him to git da hell outa da lobby.

Dubinsky passed the lobby without giving them a second look. They would not have given him the time of the day in Russia, and he was not going to dwell on the things that they and he could conceivably have in common. He was too busy.

But the apartment hunt was so frustrating. At best, he was generously allowed to leave an application, on which he, a proud traveler along the Path of Truth, shamelessly disclosed his lack of steady employment and bank references. Whatever was available was out of his financial range. He made forays into the outer boroughs. Brighton Beach was too far; Crown Heights was too depressing; the Bronx was scary; and what was the point of moving from San Murray to Flushing? The energy, the beat were not there. Walking along Steinway Boulevard in Astoria and listening to the wailing of bouzouki, he realized that, should he decide to move into the $175 apartment he'd just seen, he would immediately slide back into filing, which would be the end of him; and then what would Slava say? At the end, torn apart, he cashed Slava's check, added his own meager savings, and paid a deposit on a two-bedroom apartment on East Thirtieth Street. Plus six months in advance, in lieu of verifiable employment or a bank reference.

"No problem," said the landlord. Mr. Gegiyeh was a hefty olive-skinned man with a prominent belly, who inquired whether Dubinsky was as Jewish as his future roommate Mr. Rothman. Dubinsky, doing his best to stay out of the olfactory range of the man's enormous cigar, admitted as much.

"Me, I'm Lebanese," Mr. Gegiyeh said. "*Christian*. Death to Arafat!" He shook his cigar-holding fist in the air.

Dubinsky, feeling his breakfast rolling up his throat, forced a grin of sympathy. The man had, after all, practically taken him in—off the street, one might say. It was not a good time to think that the rent was not, properly speaking, a bargain. It was a good time to remove himself as far away from the chemical weapon in the man's hand as possible. And start off in search of work. To have something to show for the time he spent here before Slava came back.

He spent the daytime leaving his résumés in the hundred-odd translation agencies listed in the Yellow Pages. Soon his head was reeling from the multitude of tableaux that the city unveiled, and he realized that he was in a funk much deeper than he had heretofore experienced. The city had no mercy.

Most agencies were located in office buildings fit to be con-
demned. The elevator rides were trips into the unknown and
had to be booked through a travel agency on the ground floor,
whose walls shyly suggested steamship voyages to Ceylon and
French Equatorial Africa and charter buses to Niagara Falls.
At the end of the creaky goosebump ride he would face a sign
hanging aslant and pointing to a Rheingold Exclusive European Photo Studio. In the darkness of the hallway he would
espy the signs of an insurance office, a Cyprus export-import
company, and a temporary personnel agency; the translation company would be at the very end of the passage, with
the faded gold lettering on the door. The actual, working
door would be around the corner, and the entrance would be
gained after much ringing. Thereupon a woman's creaky voice
would inquire as to the visitor's identity, and only then would
he be admitted inside a dungeon no lighter than the hallway,
cluttered by dusty volumes and yellowed papers. There hasn't
been anything in Russian for a long time, she'd croak, there
wasn't anything now, and they weren't expecting anything
for a while; they had their steady translator, a Madame Bla-
vatski, a very fine old lady, a graduate of St. Petersburg's
Smolny Institute; they had had her for forty-five years and
never had reason to complain.

Other translation companies were housed in gleaming high-
rises, their reception rooms equipped with video terminals,
telexes, teletypes, and NYSE tickers. Dubinsky would wait
until a perky receptionist with a pair of headphones signed
for bulky passages, delivered by hand from Exxon, IBM,
and every law firm from Park Avenue to Wall Street. Russian? She'd furrow her carefully plucked eyebrows. We had
a Russian here once; he took two pages, and we never
saw him again. For French and other stuff we only use
people with native target languages. Sure, you can leave
your résumé. . . . Occasionally he would run into competition:
people who spoke Bulgarian with a Finnish accent, and vice
versa. But they exuded no intercontinental glamour: tired-
looking and oddly dressed, they stepped out of an Eric Ambler

novel. They were treated accordingly and paid at rates well below any federal minimum (which, of course, did not apply to the self-employed), as if they were illegals, which most of them surely were. The agencies, he found out after a couple of phone calls, routinely charged the client ten times what they paid the translator, who, it was tacitly understood, was always free to go back to Ecuador or Mauritius or wherever that funny accent, perfectly at home in Elmhurst, had originated; or wherever they issued those funny pieces of paper with all kinds of seals and stamps on them that encouraged their holders to think that they were as good as a graduate of the California State University at Fullerton.

The United Nations was an obvious target. But you had to be a citizen of a member country, which he was not—hadn't he paid five hundred rubles less than a year ago not to be one?— and the new country placed him on a five-year probation. In any case, he knew perfectly well that the colleagues of Borzoi's and Volkodav's were firmly in control of Personnel and would never hire a traitor like himself. I'm running out of options, he thought, panic-stricken; it's time to fall back and regroup. What else could he gainfully do? In his college days, most of his income had been derived from private lessons.

Dubinsky typed up ads and roamed the campuses: NYU, Columbia, Hunter, Baruch. He bought coffee in paper cups and lingered inside, reluctant to leave, long after the ads had been posted. The auditoriums and the libraries were large, spacious, well-lit. The students were young, boisterous, carefree, wearing the most casual of clothes, carrying soiled plastic bags and Frisbees. On the face of it, going to an American university seemed more fun than going to the Black Sea coast in Russia.

He reminisced about his old dormitory, with its crumbling paint and dark, unhospitable lobby; about the Language School, with its tiny airless rooms, with its atmosphere of nervous tension as the undergraduates jockeyed for position on the Komsomol Committee, looking over their shoulders at every word. He recalled his schoolmates' faces, gray and haggard after too much cramming in smoke-filled rooms. He thought that even he, a model of carelessness in his school years, had never looked as footloose and fancy-free as these kids. His mind told him that they were the same people placed in different circumstances, and his heart refused to believe it.

He returned to the apartment in a dark mood and spent the evening hours sitting in front of the window with a bottle of Early Times, staring at the rich panoply of lights that was midtown Manhattan. It was not unlike old Moscow days, except that he didn't have Slava's telescope, and that was for the better, too: if people on the forty-second floor were eating hamburger and watching "Happy Days" and playing gin rummy, he'd rather not know it; one did not need to go forty-two floors up in the sky to do those things. He preferred to think that every lit window concealed a global, epochal event: people were ironing out the last details on the $50 billion sale of Uruguay to Switzerland; planning a monarchist coup d'état in China; writing poems that would drive men to drink and women to tears.

Slava called to tell him that he was arriving the next day. "How are you doing? How's the apartment?"

"Okay," Dubinsky muttered.

"You don't sound too happy."

"It's the weather." *The sun is shining too brightly, Slava, showing me all too clearly what a jerk I am.*

"Well, we'll talk about it."

We may talk about it, but by the time we do, we're certainly going to *do* something about it, Dubinsky thought, pulling out the Help Wanted section of the *Times*. But even his fingers were shaking and stumbling off the buttons. Somehow he managed to dial three numbers and make an appointment for an interview. In Filing, what else?

The next day he woke up at six and spent two sleepless hours lying in bed and trying to read his future from the barely touched-up cracks in the ceiling. But he had never been adept in reading contour maps, and the crack he suspected to be the Line of Truth ran in uncertain zigzags and disappeared behind the curtain. Feeling empty and exhausted, his every limb aching, he forced himself under the shower. He made toast and coffee, then went to the bathroom and vomited. Already wise to Manhattan entomology, he wrapped up the toast to dispose of it outside and drank the coffee. Then he sat for another half an hour, staring at the empty cup. He put on a shirt, a tie, a coat, stumbled to the door, but had to come back. He spent another fifteen minutes in the bathroom and, as a result, was late.

I need it—I need it—I need it, he chanted to himself, sitting in the reception area and staring at the cover of *Town and Country* that featured the San Murray home of Mr. and Mrs. Levine. *I can't appear worthless in front of Slava again.*

"You're talking to yourself," the receptionist said. "Did you know that?"

It's a Russian mantra, you idiot, he wanted to say, but asked for a Kleenex instead. He had bought a pack downstairs, but it was already gone. Anti-perspirants work only for people applying for the jobs they want, he thought.

The interview was a disaster. He answered the questions listlessly and disinterestedly; in his mind's eye he saw himself running down the corridor with a tray full of files, being tripped, dropping the files on the floor and picking them up from under the feet of passing co-workers. The passing women had beautiful feet with slender, artistic ankles, but he could not see any higher, for he was too busy with the files. The woman interviewer was not hostile, and at the end she smiled and said they'd let him know, but he already knew the answer.

"What do you think?" Dubinsky asked nervously, nodding at the living room. He had spent the last of his money on the mattresses, but New Yorkers were a prodigal breed, and he was able to pick up various odds and ends off the street.

"Don't tell me you paid money for this." Slava wearily stretched on the floor. At least I scrubbed it, Dubinsky thought. "It will do, Oleg. We rented the place, we didn't buy it, after all."

"Are you going to buy one?"

"Not today, Dubinsky. Too tired. This country is so damn big. Russia is bigger, but you don't have to fly from Moscow to Vladivostok to do business." He uneasily picked himself up off the floor and proceeded to the bedroom. "Ms. Levine said hi."

"Great," Dubinsky said. "What about your mysterious Goldenburger?"

A deep, confident snore answered. Dubinsky stared out at the backed-up traffic on Lexington and thought that he should have washed windows, too—work was the best therapy. Znachar would smirk at that, he thought; but then Znachar never found himself sitting in a barely furnished room without a job or a party to go to, worrying over a Bud about such pedestrian stuff as rent or groceries or subway fares. Worrying about being arrested must feel more ennobling. It deserved a Remy Martin.

Monday morning Slava went to work. He carefully perused the bank leaflets and opened three different accounts. He filed an incorporation notice for the Intergalactic Trading Company, listing himself as president and Dubinsky as treasurer. He ordered boxes of business cards for both Dubinsky and himself, Clive Rothman.

"Clive means class," he explained to Dubinsky, "and class is what this operation is about. Americans are suckers for things British, and what could be more down-home than Rothman? It's an unbeatable combination, Dubinsky. I advise you to look into it seriously. Derek Dubinsky sounds pretty good to me."

Dubinsky promised he would think about it. He regarded the apartment with amazement. There was little furniture added—"What's the point of entertaining, if there's no room for a butler?" Slava said—but there were four phones with three lines, and there was a telex, an answering machine, and a stand on which, Slava said, a video terminal would be mounted, as soon as he picked the right one.

"You're buying a computer?"

"We're in the Information Age, Dubinsky. I want the market at my fingertips. I want my creativity released from the drudge of storing the information on how many drachmas a shipment of Bulgarian mohair wool is worth. It's a whole new ball game, Dubinsky."

"But who is going to operate it?"

"Why, you, of course."

Dubinsky shook his head. "Forget it. I still have problems screwing in electric bulbs."

Slava chuckled. "It has nothing to do with electric bulbs."

"I'm not going to be able to do it." Dubinsky stood firm.

"If you want to live in a cave, why did you leave Russia?" Slava was exasperated.

"Ask me another," Dubinsky snapped.

The phone rang. Slava didn't budge an inch. *"Nu?"*

"Nu what?"

"Get it." And Slava shoved his business card in Dubinsky's face.

"There's hundreds of people working here, Dubinsky."

"Oh." *Crazy-crazy-crazy.* He picked up the phone as if it weighed a ton. "Intergalactic Trading," he said with disgust, as the Truthmobile ran into a ditch, its wheels spinning helplessly.

A voice asked for Mr. Rothman in an inflection so Teutonic as to bring Dubinsky to his feet, but before he could deliver a decent *Heil*, Slava grabbed his wrist. "Put him on hold," he hissed, covering the speaker and pointing at the red Hold button.

I'm going to die. "Please hold." The manner in which Dubinsky complied left no doubt that the button was made of fecal matter and that he was heading for the bathroom to wash his hands.

"What shall I do with you?" Slava said quietly.

Take me out and shoot me, Dubinsky wanted to say, but the alarm in Slava's eyes was so genuine that he held back.

After a pause Slava said, "Please, Dubinsky, just this once— ask the man, as politely as you can, to identify himself."

He already knows it's for him, Dubinsky thought, releasing the Hold. "What's—I mean, may I ask who's calling?" Whence such obsequiousness, he wondered, as the voice introduced himself as Dr. Goldenburger's executive assistant and insisted that Mr. Rothman was needed on an important business matter. "Okay," said Dubinsky, bemoaning his life. "Hold on." He pressed the button again and handed Slava the phone. "Your once and future partner, Dr. Golden-fucking-burger." For some reason he recalled a large, loudly painted sign in a Moscow grocery: "Nothing is ever given us so cheaply and valued so highly as politeness." Flies shat on it, and people disregarded it, the way the Russians automatically disregard any sign or poster.

"You're forgiven," Slava said, tearing the phone out of the hands of his oh-so-unprofessional secretary-cum-treasurer. "Hundred percent. But in the future—oh, fuck this. Rothman speaking."

"Couldn't put it better myself," Dubinsky grumbled, heading for the bathroom. The Truth Trip was canceled, and where would he go to ask for a refund?

"Do you have a tie?" Slava called from the living room. Dubinsky looked inside his closet, as mournfully bare as the apartment. The tie was not in its usual place, draped over the coat. Did I dump it into the garbage in a post-interview spasm? he wondered. No, that would be equivalent to slamming the door. An Yves Saint Laurent, a gift from Linda, could not be blamed for the enmity between Dubinsky and Filing.

"Do you or don't you?" Slava kicked the door open.

"Why?" Dubinsky rose to face him, his hands involuntarily forming fists. "Are you installing a videotelephone?"

Slava shook his head. A delirious smile that smacked of a king-size drug addiction danced on his face. He came closer and put his hand on Dubinsky's shoulder. "I'm sorry I put you through this, Dub. A schlemiel like you should be broken in gently. Let's have an expensive French dinner and make up."

Dubinsky disengaged himself. "We're not in a quarrel, so there's nothing to make up about."

"Then we'll just celebrate."

"Goldenburger?"

Slava nodded. "It's nothing formal, Dub, good business rides on a handshake, not on a bunch of papers." His smile assumed a saner form, with his strong white teeth showing. "We're in, Dub! We're in business!"

"One thing you've got to hand to the frogs." Slava took a contented sip of Château Montrachet. "Whatever this shit's gonna taste like, it sure sounds good. '*Escalope Petit Cul*'— beats meatloaf any day."

Dubinsky waited. He realized he was off the Truth Road, but how far?

"I knew Goldenburger from way back," Slava said, enjoying the suspense. "And then I looked in on him in Europe."

Slava did not care much for Europe. Especially Italy, where people spent too much time drinking coffee in elegantly appointed bars. And no one rolled out a carpet for him personally. He realized that in Moscow Dr. Goldenburger may have been interested in icons of the Novgorod School, but there was nothing Slava could offer him in Zurich. They had drinks in a hotel bar with enormous chandeliers, where faultlessly shaven and clad gentlemen sipped vintage Scotch and spoke in calm, low voices; Slava was impressed, but, as Herr Doktor went on to speculate on Slava's new freedom to criticize the government, his hands grew weaker by the minute. He chose not to get insulted for being talked to as if he were a common dissident. There was nothing personal about it. He was as foreign to Herr Doktor's world as one can be; he *felt* out of place, and he *was* out of place. Not in a thousand years would the elegant, civilized drinking patrons accept him as a member of the club. They were—well, *gentlemen*. A hereditary plutocracy, to use a quasi-Marxist concept.

"They talk so slow, Dubinsky. They drink slow, they walk slow. You should ever try to cash a check in a bank in Switzerland—it's a rite, a ceremony." He shook his head. "These people are hopeless."

Dubinsky picked up an escargot. I'm getting to like this, he thought, gulping down his Montrachet. The bright lights and the dazzle of crisp white tablecloth and polished silver, to say nothing of snooty waiters, failed to impress him, especially since they tended to fade with each glass; but how in the name of God had he managed to spend twenty-eight years of his life without this *haute cuisine*, without these snails melting in his mouth, without this pungent sauce, without this wine that tasted like a bosomy brunette on a hot summer afternoon? How did anybody? Poor Slava, rejected by a bunch of cuckoo clocks—he must have been hurt badly, can he taste this luxury? His heart went out, reaching beyond his palate— "but wait. Why would Goldberg deal with you *now*?"

"Herr Doktor Goldenburger," Slava explained, refilling Dubinsky's glass himself, to the waiter's extreme annoyance, "knows from money. And the mall *is* a lot of money. Do you follow me, Dubinsky?"

"Anywhere, *mon général.*"

"Here." Slava picked up the glass of ice water. "Here is Goldenburger. Brimming with money like this glass with water. No place to put it. And here"—he drained his glass as if it were vodka, making Dubinsky flinch, and lifted it—"here is Levine, who needs the money for his mall. Now, how does this water get into this glass, Dubinsky?

"You pour it?" Ever since the college course called Scientific Communism, Dubinsky had been uncomfortable with the catechistic method of explanation.

"Right! And don't you deserve a fee for pouring it? A big, fat fee that will serve as seed money for more pouring?"

"And by God thou dost deserve it, sire!" Dubinsky cried out, plunging his old trusty saber into the *escalope* and disregarding the sputtering of the sauce on the linen.

"Because this is America, Dub!" Slava slapped the table,

turning the glass on its side. This time the waiter leaped to the rescue like a soccer goalie on a penalty kick. "Get us another bottle," Slava waved. "This is America, Dub, there's always another bottle, so long as you can afford it."

For *après-diner* they roamed the bars of West Broadway and Seventh Avenue South, and with a little help from a bunch of friends with cosmopolitan, mellifluous names like Courvoisier and Cointreau and Drambuie, Dubinsky slid painlessly from solid state to liquid to gas to plasma and now had no idea whatsoever what form of matter he represented. Everybody was so incredibly friendly and smiling, women flirted, and men slapped his back and wished him luck in his new land. It was just like San Murray all over again, but with a twist.

"It's not just because you keep buying them drinks, is it, Slava?"

"Nah." Slava leaned against a lamppost. "It doesn't matter, Dubinsky, believe me." Slava was in a world all his own, too, shared with no one but Chivas and Regal. "They're just a part of 'good time,' Dubinsky. In a bar, you buy friendship the same way you buy love in a whorehouse. It doesn't matter in the long run. Don't even think about it."

"Okay." And why would he think any kind of thought that would take him out of this blessed condition, a terra incognita to modern physics? He huddled with himself in the corner and took an inspired leak at the graffiti that demanded Peace for the People of Pizdo.

"You know what matters, Dubinsky?" Slava orated in the safety of the lamppost shadow. "This!" His hands soared in the direction of the World Trade Center. "This, Dubinsky, is beautiful. Look, I'm not a moron, Guggenheim is beautiful, too—but this is electricity, this is energy itself!"

"It's a hard-on."

"Aw, Dubinsky, it's not you, it's your cock talking. Shut up, I'll spring for a blow job later. Have you been to the Stock Exchange, Dubinsky? Wall Street in the rush hour? And Sixth Avenue? It's beautiful, Dub. And there's only one purpose to it all—making money. It's so clean, so unambiguous—wow!

That's the way to do it—no hiding in the doorways, no screening against stoolies, none of this goddamn grease to these shitass cops. There's pride in this, Dubinsky, there's . . . *dignity.*"

"And pomp and circumstance—like Switzerland," Dubinsky suggested, zipping up. He landed on a vacant doorstep and started flicking his Bic, trying to light up, but somehow kept missing.

"Yeah, man," a tall bearded type in army fatigues nodded approvingly. "Like, Switzerland is cool, man."

"Yes, Switzerland, too," Slava agreed, not noticing that a group of people was forming and paying attention à la Hyde Park. "But Switzerland is *closed.* America is *open,* pal!"

"Open?" A gaunt Latin spat. "When you people stop listening to fascist jive?"

Only then did Slava take notice of his soapbox position. He glanced at the motley crowd with unmistakable contempt and grabbed Dubinsky's shoulder. "Let's go."

"Hey, stop bugging the man!" a woman wearing an orange knit hat said sharply. "He can sleep wherever he wants. This is America, Jack, not your goddamn Switzerland."

Without opening his eyes, Dubinsky hummed approval. The crowd was clearly getting excited at the sight of a naive Swiss bourgeois trying to arrest a poor New York street person. The naive Swiss thought that he probably had more money in his left breast pocket than all of them put together have ever had. Given the context, it was an utterly idle thought. Wondering what in the world led him to it, he leaned over Dubinsky and drawled in Russian, "*Bah-by*, Dubinsky." *Women.*

"Where?" Dubinsky's eyes opened instantly.

"Just follow me." He flagged a cab, and, disregarding the crowd, whose mood was turning ugly, dragged Dubinsky in.

"He's getting kidnapped," said the lover of Switzerland.

"Just like Allende," the woman in an orange cap agreed. "This country is getting to be worse than Argentina."

The next morning, which was closer to noon, Dubinsky woke up with the cosmopolitan friends of the night before playing

pinball in his head. On his way to the bathroom, he saw Slava
buried in paper—*Fortune Barron's Money Wall Street Journal
Kiplinger. . . .* Totally unhealthy, he thought, and proceeded
on his way. But later, as he went over the metamorphoses of
the night before, sipping his first coffee of the day and peering
at Slava poring over the stock columns, his thoughts took a
different turn. Where did he fit in in that grandiose scheme
of Slava, Goldenburger, and Co.? He popped the question,
just like that. That's what mornings are for.

"Look at your business card." Slava set aside the paper.
Pork belly futures were exactly the moment that called for a
break. "What does it say? 'Treasurer,' right? Which means,
from time to time you'll have to take trips to Boise. Like
tomorrow. Also, haven't you put in about six months in filing?"

Dubinsky froze. He hadn't told Slava about the interview.

"You should be entitled to unemployment."

Dubinsky remained silent. The idea of being a public ward
made him think of the welfare office in San Murray where he
had once accompanied Konstantin's sister-in-law Lyuba, who
did not speak a word of English. There were two thousand
screaming, belching, crawling babies slapped and yelled at
by their mothers or anybody else who felt like it. Children of
more advanced ages were running around in circles, playing
leapfrog and practicing advanced stickup techniques. The
adults, especially the babyless ones, seemed to have been there
for a thousand years, and their expressions conveyed infinite
patience and readiness to spend another thousand years sitting on those hard, uncomfortable chairs. He told Lyuba he
was not feeling well, he needed some air, and he would wait
outside; she'd call him to come in when they called her. No,
the thought of public assistance had to be banished.

"Also," Slava went on, "although I expect something to
come in from Goldenburger within a few weeks—knock on
wood, in the meantime we need some pocket money. There's
nothing as ugly and obscene as a negative cash flow. So go
get a hack license. It shouldn't interfere with your unemployment benefits."

Dubinsky pondered. The cab was, on balance, not such a bad idea. Robert De Niro doing pushups in a dinky Brooklyn tenement. The Wild Side. Lou Reed. "And the colored girls went duh-duh-duh." The unemployment seemed less glamourous but could be regarded as a sacrifice.

The phone rang.

Dubinsky picked it up and froze, feeling Slava's eyes fixed on him. He cleared his throat and said, calmly and ever on guard against a trace of servility, "Intergalactic Trading."

A woman's voice, businesslike yet not unpleasant, inquired whether she could speak to Mr. Dubinsky the translator and tutor. Assured that she indeed could, she went on to say that her name was Michelle Morgan and that she was a graduate student in folk cultures and was interested in a certain article in the *Soviet Ethnography* journal. The agency rates were too high, she said, and she was not sure if she needed a complete translation in the first place, so. . . . Sure, he said; he'd be happy to take a look and give her an estimate.

"Did you hear that?" he yelled. "A bona fide translation job!"

"Nothing to bank on in the long run," Slava said skeptically. "Make sure you charge just below the agency rate. Meantime, don't forget about unemployment."

Dubinsky responded with the sweetest forgiving smile he could muster.

He walked inside and cringed in the throes of panic. The walls were gray, the air was gray, and the figures in the distance— it was a large office—projected undiluted gray misery. Taking a deep breath, he separated himself from the wall and advanced bravely. He joined the line to the Information desk and looked around. Something was strange. Unemployment looked different from welfare. There were no crawling, hollering babies, no slapping, yelling mothers. The people were dressed decently; some carried attaché cases and were reading the *Wall Street Journal*, while others, dressed more casually, pored over *Backstage* and *Variety*. It was no different from a line in a bank. In front of him, they discussed the latest

Godard; behind him, a woman was complaining that she had to come back from the Berkshires. He looked over at the section where people were seated, waiting to be called. An owlish-looking three-piece-suited man was doing a crossword puzzle, while a trim young black in an elegant leather coat was passionately praising Alvin Ailey's choreography to the girl next to him.

I had no idea, Dubinsky said to himself, receiving the forms. This is a club; where's the bar? He read the forms and decided he needed more time to read the booklet: the eligibility formulae were rather confusing. As he stepped out, a limo came to a stop; a woman in a fur coat got out and, clutching a yellow benefit book in her hand, rushed inside. I'll be back, Dubinsky vowed.

But, as he concentrated on the booklet, his hopes were blasted. It was right there, in black and white: he had left the job of his own volition, therefore he was not eligible. Only Kirill could help him now.

The appointment with Ms. Morgan was a good two hours away, and Dubinsky stopped by the old hotel to chat with Kirill and Apelsinov, the only two Russians he had befriended during his brief stay there. Kirill had the looks of a matinee idol (he had, in fact, been an actor), and the hole between his teeth was exactly the size of Lauren Hutton's, he declared proudly. His room was furnished with beguiling simplicity: a king-size bed and a chair; nothing else fit in.

Ben Apelsinov was short and slight, with wire-rimmed glasses on a perfectly ordinary face, and a seemingly unlimited supply of white pants. He was a poet and claimed a sizable underground following in Russia. He rather fashioned himself after young Mayakovsky, Dubinsky thought; he told endless stories about his attempts to *épater* potential rich sponsors. His hotel room featured a large portrait of Mao and a framed yellowed clipping from *Nedelya*, a Soviet weekly. Soon after his arrival Apelsinov had gotten into a nasty fight with a local émigré paper. He published an open letter in which he denounced the American Zionists, for having lured him to America and then denying him cab fares, and the military-industrial complex, which stubbornly blocked his attempts to get published. The letter was immediately seized upon by *Nedelya* as valid evidence that even a pervert and a pseudo-poet like Apelsinov was doomed to misery in the capitalist hell. In turn, the poet immediately seized upon the article as valid evidence that even a hypocritical publication like *Nedelya* could not go on denying his place in history forever.

The two friends survived on welfare and set their minds on finding an heiress, or any gainfully employed female. She would be completely overwhelmed by Kirill's looks and Apelsinov's talent (and their combined virility, it was understood) and would willingly place her body and her bank account at the friends' disposal.

"I've got it all figured out," Kirill proclaimed. "Fourteen million will make me happy. It's only seed money, of course."

They were drinking on his bed, under which Dubinsky had earlier noticed stacks and stacks of *Playboy* and *People*, sipping horrible white rum (Apelsinov's idea of artistic inebriation).

"All I want is a twelve-year-old Chinese girl," said the poet. "With a little boy's titties and the narrowest, tiniest peepee you can find. I would bathe her in warm cream and pour rose petals on her peepee."

Dubinsky decided wisely against invoking D. H. Lawrence's name aloud.

"You'll find some gorgeous midwestern girls, with thick, shiny, flaxen hair, and tender, perfectly rounded titties," the poet said. "And if they have friends who descend from infamous railroad barons, they can do penance at my altar. My God, Kirill, this bottle is *empty*."

"I can't believe we actually finished this fucking furniture polish," Kirill murmured out of the poet's earshot. Believing Apelsinov to be on good terms with the Muse, Kirill followed his line on booze and art. He was also trying to convince Ben to write a heroic epic monologue for himself, a vehicle certain to bring Broadway down on its arthritic knees.

"Are there any liquor stores open?" Apelsinov inquired.

"Ben, it's only eleven A.M.," Kirill said, borrowing two dollars from Dubinsky.

"I thought it was eleven P.M.," the poet said. "But then, it's always night in my soul."

He walked inside the coffee shop where the meeting was to take place and looked around. A couple of senior citizens were taking a coffee break from the OTB next door; another was staring into her coffee cup morosely, trying to remember the time when it had cost a nickel; an academic type was poring over the *Post's* Page Six, ashamedly covering it with the *Times* business section. The Muzak was playing a Bee Gees rendition of a Cole Porter tune; a poster in the corner featured a serious brown-haired woman in a tweed jacket playing with a pair of glasses. He could not see the name of the product. He leaned against the post; he was late; she had left; she found someone else to do the job; was life worth living?

"Mr. Dubinsky?" a voice called.

He turned as abruptly as Roger Moore in the pre-credit frames of a 007 movie. He pointed his gunless hand toward the woman on the poster and freeze-framed in his posture for the credits.

"I thought you were not coming," she said calmly.

"I'm sorry," he said. *I thought you were a poster.*

"Would you like to sit down?" she asked.

He nodded mutely. He had never seen anyone so beautiful so close. Her face was sheer textbook anatomy; not a feature was amiss or skewed; not a blemish marred the white, oh-so-lightly tanned skin—

"I don't know about Russia, Mr. Dubinsky," she said coolly, "but in this country it is not considered polite to stare at a person for a prolonged period of time. Unless, of course, you have something historically important to say. Do you?"

He shook his head. Then, pulling himself out of the trance, he proceeded uncertainly toward the table.

"Are you all right?" she asked, not unkindly.

He groaned quietly.

"You're shaking." She offered him her glass of water.

He drank the tepid liquid. "I'm on medication," he panted. "I have these terrible attacks of yellow fever from time to time. No." He stopped and shook his head. "It's a lie. I take no medication. It's just that I think you're so beautiful."

She coughed. "Thank you. This is the article—"

"I think I need a shot of something."

She shrugged. "There's a bar across the street."

"I'm really not like that at all," he said, after downing his Scotch. It felt like water. It could have been water. The bartender regarded them curiously and was capable of anything. They were the only patrons; there were no witnesses.

"You're a teetotaler the rest of the time."

"No, I mean I'm a very level-headed person. I'm a cold fish, really. Nothing throws me off balance. I've killed hyenas with my bare hands—I'm sorry, that's not true."

"I think perhaps we should postpone this meeting until you get cured of your . . . yellow fever, wasn't it?" She rose, stuffing the magazine back into her leather bag. She looked taller than he was.

"No, please." He grabbed the edge of the magazine. "I'll be right with you, it will take five minutes—" He kept murmuring, leafing through pages until he came across the bookmark. He froze. He was staring at his own writing.

About three years ago, Vladimir had commissioned him to translate an article on Aleutian lore from an American university review, whose name he could not remember. Then something happened, he could not remember either—God, it was like a million years ago—did Vladimir get a bonus, and did they fly to Tallinn to celebrate? In any case, they could barely meet the deadline; they had merely crossed out the Aleuts and written in the Chichmeks, throwing caution to the winds.

"Do you need a dictionary?" she asked.

He shook his head. What was he to do? Admit his shameful past? Miss Michelle Morgan was certainly a cool customer, she would seize upon an opportunity to denounce Vladimir to the international ethnographic community in order to promote her own work. Or should he just fake it—*again*, the voice asked—and translate it back into English? He sneaked a look at her. She was tapping on her cigarette impatiently, her full lips drawn tightly. Rich bitch, he thought angrily; she said she couldn't afford the agency rate. Those clothes cost as much as Vladimir made in a year, and there was a gold chain here and a diamond there and a stone in her ring, too. . . . But oh so strong and yet so delicate she looked. He clenched his teeth. I'm gonna lie, he said to himself. The voice was silent. Interesting, he thought. Apparently, some detours from the Truth Freeway were perfectly all right. "I'll do it," he said.

"How much will you charge?"

"I don't know," he said. "Nothing. It's really very easy—"

"I'm afraid that's completely out of the question," she said dryly.

"Five dollars?" he suggested.

"Mr. Dubinsky," she said, "you have certain ideas about this meeting that run contrary to mine. You're either a fraud or a sex maniac—"

"Why not both?" "Sex maniac" was a matter of opinion, but "fraud" went like a harpoon through his intestines. He felt like grabbing her by all those gold chains (two) and banging her head on the table until she passed out, then pouring ice water down her neck (oh those lovely stray hairs there), and doing it all over again, until his rage subsided.

"I'll read it to you off the page for—" He hesitated. "Buy me another Scotch, how's that?" In America, do as Russians do.

They were finished in half an hour. He was hammering out quick, precise sentences; she took notes in shorthand. He drained his third orange juice and gave her a dirty look, the remnant of his rage.

"That was quite amazing." She raised her head from her notes. "Just like that. I wish I could do the same with a foreign language. I'm sorry about what I said before. I truly am. But you *were* behaving quite oddly. In any case, there's a good deal in this article to think about. I guess I'll need some places to be translated on paper for quotes—I'd really like to know how much—"

"No," he said, looking away, for he was afraid to look into her quiet brown eyes and revert to his "odd" behavior.

"It's hard dealing with East Europeans." She hesitated. "Okay, I'll buy you a dinner. You pick the restaurant."

He swallowed and nodded, still looking away.

"Just don't get any ideas."

He rose abruptly, upsetting the empty glass, which she caught on the edge of the table. "Give me a call when you decide which passages you need." He walked out into the sunshine, proud, unvanquished, and in love.

Things were definitely going Slava's way. The transatlantic phone bills were staggering: Herr Doktor wanted to have a very clear picture of where his money was heading. Slava kept traveling to San Murray, to get as much documentation as he could, as well as some local color to lay on Herr Doktor, such as Levine's partners' first names and golf scores and car makes. San Murray was driving him bonkers, but "first pancake comes in a lump"; he kept quoting the old Russian saw to himself. After this one, it would be strictly handling papers in New York. For now, he had to impress both Levine and Herr Doktor with his meticulousness and indefatigability.

Most of this was completely arcane to Dubinsky, who was living a carefree, blissful existence on unemployment benefits, courtesy of New York State.

"It's gonna cost you five hundred," Kirill had said. "There's a guy I know who can carry you on his books for a couple of weeks. And then fire you."

After an initial shock, Dubinsky recovered. It was Slava's idea in the first place, so why shouldn't he come up with a loan?

"Look at it this way," Kirill said. "The unemployment runs

for thirty-nine weeks, that's almost three thou for you. You're still ahead."

Dubinsky nodded. Whatever it took to belong to that illustrious club.

"Cash only," Kirill warned. "And he doesn't want to know you. You give it to me, I give it to him."

I wonder how much your cut is.

Although Dubinsky obtained his unemployment benefits fraudulently, and lied every week about his alleged job hunt, the idea of getting paid—legally—for doing absolutely nothing was too irresistibly exciting to give it any further thought.

"That's what they told us in high school Communism would be like," he told Slava.

The latter nodded absently, poring over the Park Avenue real estate ads. The market was depressed, now was the time to buy. He couldn't wait for the commission to come through. "The unemployment benefits eat into the Federal Reserve," he said vaguely, "but they make sense in terms of maintaining the social order. No price is too steep to keep the society stable. That's the American way for you, Dubinsky. Buy the masses off before they trash the banks. Clever."

Dubinsky was disappointed. "I thought it was a part of the social contract."

At least that was how he preferred to think about it. The deviation from the Truth Freeway had not been painless: he broke into a cold sweat and almost fainted at the interview. But he was so happy to be signing for his check every Monday that he preferred to think of his route as a sort of feeder road that ran parallel to the Freeway and would eventually flow back into it.

Now his days were thoroughly relaxed and enjoyable. He took long walks in Central Park (he even managed to find a volleyball game a couple of times), he went to the Museum of Modern Art and an Ethiopian photo exhibit, he checked out stacks of books from the public library, he got a discount card for Bleecker Street and Carnegie Hall cinemas. The only element missing in this state of bliss was Michelle's silence.

Slava was not around often enough to tempt Dubinsky into a confession; he never even bothered asking what had come out of the job. Besides, there was something that held Dubinsky back from admitting to Slava his infatuation with the auburn-haired woman off the poster. She must have completed her thesis without the quotes. She must have seen through the scam and decided not to pursue it any further. Vladimir was under investigation, calling his friends about janitorial jobs. He, Dubinsky, had behaved like an idiot, and who could blame her for recoiling from his libidinous display?

He found himself frequenting the Soho loft where Kirill and Apelsinov had moved temporarily. According to Kirill, it belonged to a friend of a friend, who was conveniently traveling around the world. At first they stayed out late every night, but then Kirill discovered the loft owner's stash. They rolled fat, bulging joints and could not summon much energy to go out afterwards. Dubinsky joined them on occasion, but no Colombian was good enough to bear with Kirill's constant pondering about whether he wanted a Maserati or a Rolls once he bagged the heiress. Or with Apelsinov's incessant lamentations about his wife, who had left him for an American gallery owner. Ben was highly conscious of the historical role he was destined to play as a Russian poet. He talked often and with much gusto about putting the torch to Bloomingdale's or to the New York Stock Exchange, but in the meantime he would settle for a fellowship anywhere, from Oregon to Prince Edward Island. He also told numerous stories about his ramblings through the Times Square area, full of encounters with black pimps and dope dealers, all of whom tried to rip him off, but eventually recognized him as a soulmate, bought him drinks, and offered him dope and women. None of this sounded convincing to Dubinsky, and if it was true, where the hell were the dope and the women, and why did Ben have to borrow change for a token?

"You just don't understand Ben," Kirill said haughtily. "He's a poet. He loved and was loved in return and was ditched by a beautiful woman. What's amazing is that he's still alive.

You're a mortal, you can only dream of being loved and ditched by a beautiful woman."

Dubinsky did not respond; no provocation would draw Michelle's name out of him. His bitterness about her silence was compounded by the realization of his stupidity: who the hell did he think he was to turn down the money she had offered? An honestly earned buck? In order to perform an idiotic gesture. The thoughts of his inadequacy in dealing with the world drove him under the bed, where he pored over German porno magazines (of which their host had many), sneezing from the dust and jerking off in self-hatred.

It was almost as if he infected Slava with his melancholy. Slava's credit lines were wearing thin. He didn't worry about them; he worried about sudden lack of communication from Zurich. Herr Doktor had postponed his visit to San Murray twice; what was wrong? The obnoxious assistant quoted "previous engagements"; Slava's instincts kept telling him that something was wrong, wrong, wrong. In the anticipation of the visit, and the commission that went with it, he found he could hardly summon the energy to look for new leads. Two miserable roommates make a living hell out of an apartment. In order not to scare Dubinsky, who, as Slava knew, was given to panic only too easily, he wore a happy face, but he could not help sighing in relief when Dubinsky departed on his hadj to Boise.

Dubinsky gave up on trying to figure out the nature of his trips. All he knew was that (a) they created a diversion in an existence that was verging on the monotonous and (b) Slava needed him to go. But even so, he sensed Slava's impatience; in more logical moments he correctly attributed it to the silence from Zurich. But more and more often, he kept thinking that it was his own worthlessness and inability to help Slava out that caused the coolness.

Russia has not made an alcoholic out of me, but flying certainly will, Dubinsky thought with vicious satisfaction, cramming three Scotches into an hour-and-a-half flight from Boise to Seattle. He did not even have to ask for directions to the local oddity, a Moscow-clean mini-subway that operated between the terminals of Sea-Tac International. You have to be bombed twice as bad as I am to imagine you're flying to or from a destination more cosmic than Boise, he thought. The spotlessness of the train made his hands itch for a can of spray paint, as he realized that, perhaps, he had become too much of a New Yorker. Not till I open my mouth and spray the other person with my borscht accent, he thought, as he ascended on the escalator toward the American Airlines gates. But even before that he'd knock them dead with his distillery breath. Look, he said silently to the faces of passengers descending on another escalator a few feet away, don't let this throw you, okay? In Russia, a rare person did *not* have liquor on his breath around the airport. You had to keep yourself smashed to fly Aeroflot. It was an adventure, remember? you never knew whether you were going to get a ticket; if you got one, you could not be sure whether you were going to get a seat; if you got a seat, you never knew when you were actually taking off; and then, of course, you never knew if you were arriving. Although no air crash had, in his memory, ever been reported in the Soviet media, people always talked.

On the descending escalator, they smiled, laughed, arched their eyebrows—and all, to a man, woman, and child, were incessantly, contentedly chewing gum. And why shouldn't you? he addressed them; a flight with an American airline is safer than venturing on a freeway. No wonder he kept drinking; no wonder the time aboard he hated most was the gap between the boarding and the time the drinks were served. Don't you hate it, too? he addressed the descending passengers. A girl in a blue anorak knitted her eyebrows. Do I know you? he said silently. She smiled, and her smile almost made him sit down. "Boise," he said, trying to stop the escalator with a cold, unblinking stare.

"Jodie!" he yelled, reaching across the steel dividing them. She stared at him intently, as if trying to place him, and then shook her head. "Yes, yes, you are!" he yelled, running up the escalator. "Wait for me downstairs!"

Transforming himself into a mean little Ferrari and spitting out apologies, he swooshed at illegal speeds past standing fellow passengers. When he was no farther than twenty feet away from the top, the road was blocked by numerous khaki-colored bags and rolled coats. A whole U.S. Army infantry platoon was deployed solidly in the way of the excommunicated Young Communist Dubinsky. There was no point in jumping or even asking. The wall was as solid as the Berlin one. The escalator moved slowly and inexorably.

I'm all for peace, he swore, running down the other elevator, this arms race's gotta stop, complete demobilization, and what better place to start than airports? Just as he suspected, she was not there. All for nothing, he thought; there was not even anyone waiting for this funny Mickey Mouse train, which must have left a minute ago.

"I wonder if you have a catalogue of your libations," he said to Merrie the stewardess.

"Beg you pardon?"

He considered dropping it for a moment, clearly Merrie was not your Natty Bumppo to take you back to the Woods of Truth, but then what the hell. "I was merely wondering," he said, enunciating *verrry merrry* carefully, "if there was some sort of beverage in your otherwise most comprehensive selection that I haven't degustated yet."

My, what marvelous composition. He looked on with admiration, as she pulled the tray open. None of the down-home "Aint you had enough, Jack?" Hell, I can be cool, too. "Ah rekkin ah staht on da left," pointing at the microscopic bottle of whiskey sour. How kin people tawk lak dat, he wondered? Ain't their jaws gon hurt?

"If you don't mind my asking, sir," she looked at him quizzically, "where do you come from?"

"*Aye-labama?*" he grinned back.

"Hardly." She shook her head and was gone.

He steadily worked his way across the liquor compartment, leaving a vacuum in his wake, but he did not feel it made him any less crazy. At least not un-crazy enough to meet the criteria of blond girls with infectious smiles. And *waaay* insufficiently noncrazy to cause tall women with auburn hair and perfect jowls to return his calls. The road to noncraziness (by no means to be confused with sanity) was blocked by divisions and armies, by cruisers and submarines. He was not getting noncrazier—a bit sicker, perhaps. "To answer your question, ma'am," he assaulted the stern-looking woman in the next seat, "I'm not crazy. I'm merely a professional Chichmek. Or Pizdoan. It's all up to the beholder, you know what I mean?"

"I don't think I ever talked to you."

There was panic in her eyes. "Please don't be worried," he said; "I'm nauseatingly harmless. I'll never lose weirdness, Jodie won't compromise her standards, and"—he burped— "I wouldn't respect her if she did. And you can bet your, hmm, mortgage, that Miz Michelle Morgan has incinerated my phone number in a most fuel-conserving manner. Ergo—do you know where they keep the parachutes?"

"What parachutes?" She lowered her glasses back from the top of her head.

"Well, you know . . . what if we crash . . . don't they have parachutes for an emergency?"

"I wouldn't know," she said primly. "They do have floating cushions. Didn't you see the safety film? They showed it before the takeoff."

He recalled there had indeed been some noises between the Bloody Marys. "Anyway," he said, "I want you to know that, should anything like this happen, you can have my swimming pillow, or whatever you call it."

"What? I don't understand what you're talking about."

"I want you to have my floating seat, just to make sure you'll get out of the jam. Because I—" He stared at the blond curls on the back of the seat in front of him. "It doesn't matter whether I live or if I die. I fucked up that bad."

She stared at him, dumbfounded.

"Excuse me." His heart swelling with hope, he touched the owner of the blond curls on the shoulder.

"I'll certainly—" the woman started.

"Whaddaya want?" The man in the seat in front turned to face Dubinsky. He had a blond moustache and a large cruel jaw.

"You're not Jodie," Dubinsky said.

"Please disregard this young man," the woman said. "He's had far too much to drink, I'm afraid. I'll make sure the stewardess does not sell him any more liquor."

"Carrie Fucking Nation," Dubinsky said. "I'll tell the stewardess you pocketed the earphones. And you're not getting any of my floating parachute either."

As they approached La Guardia, Dubinsky steadied himself gradually. He knew his insides; the liquor consumption scale had been mapped and gauged years ago. The accidents occurred only when outside pressure was applied, as with Konstantin, or under extreme emotional stress, as in a post-Jodie state. Left to his own devices, he knew how to keep the buzz on without the valves blowing up. He had a wine split with his dinner, and a Drambuie afterwards. Carrie F. Nation was snoring peacefully. He considered pouring booze in her ear, but the bar carried no Sterno, and using Drambuie for the purpose would have been a waste.

He paused at the entrance to the building. The light was on; Slava was at home. What will he say? "Hey, how was the trip?" "Hey, all right." "Deposit okay?" "Yeah, here's the receipt." And what next? Slava's got an ambition, and it has nothing to do with what I want, he said, turning away and knowing precisely which way he was heading. His dashboard featured this new gadget, you see, a computerized map, he was on autopilot, he did not have to think where he was going, the chips did all the work, they knew that he needed air, and then more buzz, and more air, and after that God only knew what else.

Actually, it was Clive, not Slava, who had an ambition. Slava was different, *must* have been different, they had had friends like Znachar and Vladimir, they could talk things out with them, and they would understand, they always did. They knew that the world did not rest on the NYSE index, nor on Levine's malls; it rested, any sucker knows that, on three whales (or was it loaves and fishes): perfidy—lust—he couldn't remember the third one. The hell with it; lust and perfidy: two out of three ain't bad. How I'd love to see Michelle and tell her a thousand lies and embrace her haunches and kiss her between her cold breasts. And proceed according to instinct. Onward. Step by step. Thirtieth & Third. Bar one. Door. Hi. Scotch, please. Straight up. And a draft. Thank you. Thank you very much. It's the truth. I'll lie to you later, okay?

When he met a girl named Sandy in bar thirty-one or was it forty-nine, she was even drunker than he was and too upset about her boyfriend to care about Dubinsky's accent. He was intrigued, or at least pretended to be, by the contrast between the despair she was projecting intensely and the frivolous look of her drink, a pink umbrella over a purple concoction with unidentifiable globs floating in it. She appeared to be nicely built, and had a quick, energetic face, even with puffy cheeks and mascara running profusely. There was an opportunity to be a Good Samaritan and get laid at the same time, Dubinsky thought. *Demento:* lust and perfidy.

Within minutes he was swamped with information. Sandy's monologues were pure avant-garde, with flashbacks to a high school in Reseda, Cal., and flash forwards into her future in designing handbags for a fast-growing Maritime Provinces market. The present was alternately bleak, with her boyfriend Arnold too enamored with his mother, and bright, with Arnold to become a full partner any day now.

Dubinsky saw it all clearly now. After the second drink he placed his arm around her shoulders. "I think you're a remarkably together person." Liar, a voice boomed inside. *You got it.* Dubinsky downed a double bourbon to celebrate the victory over the voice.

"Really?" She dried her nose quickly. "You're very nice, too."

"I don't think you're getting a fair shake with Arnold."

"He doesn't care!" She sobbed more.

"You're the sexiest woman in the whole bar."

"That's real nice of you to say," she sniffled. "Arnold never says anything like this. Where are you from, anyway?"

"Holland." He quickly downed another glass.

She lived in a tiny studio between First and York. They undressed quickly, but then she decided she needed another drink and retired to the kitchen, her breasts flapping against her stomach. Dubinsky lay down, his eyes left open to keep the room from spinning.

She sat down on the edge of the bed, and, sipping from a tall glass filled with vodka, started telling him how she had found herself last year at the retailers' convention in Vancouver.

"I know exactly how you feel." He inserted two fingers inside her. She could not have been drier if she had used up a whole stick of anti-perspirant. He went to work, as she kept singing praises to Werner Erhard.

Est had been so good to her that Dubinsky had to change hands. Finally he went to work on her whole huge quivering body, disregarding the rediscovered Jungian relationship she had with Arnold's cat, Natasha.

His penis hurting, his head aching, his mouth dry, and his whole body about to keel over, Dubinsky vowed to find Arnold at any cost and force him to marry—Randy? Mandy? Sandy. . . . Drenched with sweat, pumping for release, he visualized Arnold, that bearded bespectacled scrawny little prick, who was at this very moment being ridden by his secretary, a gorgeous twenty-year-old redhead. He closed his eyes to concentrate and immediately had to open them again, sending the ball of nausea back to his stomach. The effort took its toll, as he grew soft. He pumped again and screamed with pain, as Sandy unexpectedly interrupted her harangue to push her stubby thumb up his ass. "Don't you love it?" she exhaled.

"P . . . p . . . please, no, no . . ." Dubinsky writhed in pain.

"Oh, this is so good!" Sandy groaned, and called on God, her mother, and someone named Jeff. Then she quivered and grew quiet.

He lay there, listening to the nonstop drumbeat of blood in his temples. He was limp, sore, exhausted, disgusted. He did not doubt for a moment that what he had just undergone was the punishment for having lied through his teeth an hour earlier, and the only thing he was curious about was whether the torture was over or there was more in store.

Deftly, without getting out from under him, Sandy lit a cigarette and launched into a lament about what a cold, callous bitch her shrink was. He rolled over and started counting sheep. On number seventy-seven she started sobbing again because her mother never loved her and wanted her to be a manicurist. Strangely, her sobs had a soporific effect on him, and he fell into a black pit, telling Slava that he was not an idealist.

When he woke up, a gray dawn was spreading across the room. Matching clouds of smoke hung in the air. He coughed.

"I don't know," Sandy said thoughtfully, "how I manage to keep my wits together with all the stuff that I go through." She lit another cigarette.

Dubinsky rolled out of bed and started putting on his clothes.

"Are you going to get some coffee?" she asked. "There's a Greek place open on the corner."

"I don't think so." He noticed his shirt being buttoned the wrong way; the hell with it, he decided.

"This is very unnerving," she said in a trembling voice. "I brought you here, we made love, it was wonderful, now it turns out you just wanted to use my body—"

The reference to her body, at which he tried hard not to look, made him miss his coatsleeve. "I really have to catch this plane," he muttered, "I'm managing this reggae band—"

"Do you realize how immature you are?" she cried out, driving herself into the first tears of the day.

"Yes," he said, stuffing his socks in his pockets and bolting out the door with his shoes on his bare feet.

Sitting at the counter of a coffee shop, he scribbled on a napkin:

> Ms. Sandy Le Vine
> 480 E. 82nd St.
> NY NY 10028

> *Bill for Services Rendered*

> Therapy .... 5 hours @$50 $250
> Less Intercourse .... $ 5   ($ 5)

> Total due $245

P.S. Hope this will ruin your day.

Dubinsky smelled disaster the moment he walked in. Slava was sitting in the living room, with his back to the door. He still had his three-piece suit and his shoes on. The phone was off the hook and lying on the desk. A bottle of Johnnie Walker rested on the floor and the ashtray that Dubinsky had washed before leaving was filled with butts. But it was Slava's huddled back and his head, face down, that said it all.

"I've been fucked, Dubinsky," he said without turning. *I know*, Dubinsky said to himself. He picked up a check that lay on the floor. It was made out to Mr. Clive Rothman, in the amount of one thousand dollars.

"An expensive fuck."

"Don't be an idiot, Dubinsky. The total investment of Doctor Goldenburger's group in the mall is—get ready—ten million. Half now and half later."

Having received the check, Slava did not quite understand its meaning. He called up Herr Doktor; the housekeeper asked him to call later. He called up Levine, his secretary answered. Slava asked casually if everything was okay. Oh, yes, sir, Mr. Rothman, she said cheerfully, and the wire from Switzerland came in, too, for the full amount. Which is . . . ? Five million, she whispered. He's such a nice man, Dr. Goldenburger. You met him? he asked. Oh, yes, he was here last month. I see, he said and asked to speak to Stanley. I don't know if I can reach him, she said, they're upstairs in the penthouse suite, celebrating. That's some cause for celebration, he said. Oh, yes, she agreed readily; we were afraid for a while, there were rumors Mr. Levine was going to have to cut down on expenses and fire people. But I guess we're okay now. Well, that's good to hear, he said. Have Mr. Levine call me whenever he can.

Then he called Switzerland again. Herr Doktor was not available, his personal secretary said stiffly; Herr Doktor was desert-sailing in Pizdo. I'd like to reach him there if I can. Out of the question, the secretary said. Herr Doktor is on vacation. And what is the problem, may I ask? There's a mistake with a check, Slava said; my name is Rothman, Transgalactic Trading Company in New York. There's no mistake, sir, the secretary said coldly, as if his infallibility had been questioned. I made out the check personally, following Herr Doktor's instructions. One thousand dollars? One thousand dollars? Do you realize, Slava asked, his voice breaking, that we're talking about a commission on a five-million-dollar investment? I'm afraid you should speak to Herr Doktor about this; good night, sir.

"I tend to agree," Dubinsky said sympathetically. "It does look like you've been screwed quite royally."

"You don't file contracts on stuff like this, Dubinsky. Or maybe you do. I don't know. I don't know anything anymore." He poured Scotch for the two of them. "My ass hurts something awful, Dubinsky, after this screwing. *L'chaim.*" They drank, and Slava continued.

"It's all supposed to ride on a handshake, do you understand? Maybe I'm wrong. I don't know."

"I think you're right. I think that's how it should be." Dubinsky, Harvard School of Business, Class of '75, came over and placed his hand on Slava's shoulder. "You'll rebound, man. You'll show 'em," he eulogized in a shaking voice. He had never seen Slava smitten so badly.

"The two fucks slapped me in the face, Dubinsky." Slava's sentences ran on feverishly, colliding, bouncing off each other like bumper cars in an amusement park. "They made a deal behind my back, Dubinsky. They muscled me out. I don't get it, Dubinsky, I don't get it at all, I mean—why? It doesn't make any business sense, I would find other places for Doktor and his cronies the tax evaders to put their money in, he knows that. . . . That Levine cocksucker, did you fuck his wife? you should've, you should've fucked her and left your sperm on their pillow . . . like they fucked me and slapped me in the face with a thousand-dollar check. . . . Why did they do that? Levine knows that I can find other people for next time, what did that Doktor offer him, a special high-yield numbered account in Zurich? Sonuvabitch Goldenburger, I mentioned eight percent, he didn't say a word, fucking cheese cuckoo clock, he didn't say a fucking word then—"

Dubinsky poured a round. *"L'chaim."* He felt awful. The Truth Syndrome Strikes Again. He had just lied to Sandy—shamelessly. When it didn't pay off, he thought it was the nadir. Little did he know.

"But you know what boggles my mind?" Slava ran on. "Why did they do that, what did they gain by that? Just to keep a lousy four hundred thousand?"

Sounds valid to me, Dubinsky thought.

"But there's so many clean ways to make money in this country, there's no need to screw anyone—oh, shit who am I kidding? It's the same shit all over—the same the same the same—"

He raised his face, and there was dampness in his eyes, or perhaps just a reflection of the Empire State's illuminated needle in the window.

"I didn't want it, Dubinsky. I swear on Aunt Raya's grave I didn't. All I wanted to do was continue doing the same stuff as in Russia, right? Only here it would be legal, but it just. . . . I don't know." He rose abruptly, still muttering, and paced the room. "Dubinsky, I don't want to be The Last Idealist. You know me, I practice what I preach. If that's the way they stacked this deck, shit, you don't pull out the stakes in the middle of the game. They can stop me from making money the clean way, but they can't stop me from making money." He grabbed the stacks of *Fortune* and *Money* issues and dumped them into a cardboard box. A few issues fell on the floor. "Lend me a hand, Dubinsky."

Dubinsky bent to pick up the magazines. "Stanley Levine, the Developer of the Year," a cover proclaimed.

"You know, I feel better now." Slava poured more Scotch. "I really do. I guess deep inside I've always resented making money the clean way. It's for Americans, Dubinsky. Think: those bastards, born, bred, and buttered here, they all went to their fucking prep schools, their business schools, even those with Moms and Dads and oil money and trust funds—they had a head start on us, all of them. What do they expect me to do, sell *shmattes* from a pushcart for fourteen hours a day in order to send my kids to college? Do you know what I'm saying, Dubinsky? If I'd been born in this country, I'd've retired by now. But I was not, and neither were you, and the only way for us to catch up is to take a shortcut. *Capito?*"

"*Capito.*" Dubinsky raised his glass. "To shortcuts. And," he added, stopping in midair, "I can't think of anything I can do to help . . ."

How about stopping drinking and getting a job, an inner voice said.

"But if *you* think of something, like white slavery or something—I'm your man."

Slava was silent for a moment, as if pondering Dubinsky's offer. "White slavery, huh?" He grinned gratefully. "I'll come up with something, Dubinsky, don't you fret. Just don't run out on me, okay?"

They drank and they hugged.

"Where the hell do you think I'm gonna run, you fool? Pizdo?"

"Why not? What's going on there now?"

Dubinsky snorted. On top of everything, all he needed was this reminder of his shameful past.

"Remember what I'm sure your mother told you," Slava said thoughtfully. "Whatever you know how to do, you won't have to carry it in the sack all your life. Think Pizdo, Dubinsky. There's gotta be an angle."

"I'd rather drive a cab." *Truth Taxi Co., Inc., that's me.*

Seven

Slava balked at paying for the medallion. It did not seem like a wise investment; the cab would be just a sideline, a temporary stopgap. Dubinsky, in turn, balked at the idea of buying a forged one; that, he felt, would be too far a detour from the feeder road abreast the Truth Freeway, straight to the crooked dirt roads of Lie County.

He rationalized it quite neatly, he thought; every such detour had been a disaster—remember Linda? Remember his involvement with Vladimir that, years later, caught up with him and separated him from the Woman of His Dream (*that bitch*).

All right, Slava said, and made a leasing arrangement with a Brighton Beach operator. He did not like doing business with Brighton Beach, they were too parochial for him, they had never expanded on the national scale like he had, they were still in Moldavanka and Peresyp', those quintessential Odessa neighborhoods immortalized by Babel. But business was business, and cabs were something they knew about. When

Dubinsky made a face, Slava remarked that if he did not like the idea, would he be interested in vending nuts off a cart? Dubinsky growled and said nothing. I should be sterner with the sucker, Slava thought tenderly; give him a few weeks of calm and rest between the Whitney and St. Mark's, he'll think all of life is like that.

From the moment Dubinsky got at the wheel of the cab, he knew the relationship was not to be an easy one. The Dodge's odometer reading left plenty of room for imagination: 111,666? 311,666? 911,666? Its problems were largely masochistic: it had to be torn out of neutral, its brakes needed to be floored a block ahead, and the left-hand signal required a heavy-weight punch to make it work. The latter was relatively un-important, though, since showing a turn signal in New York was a sign of weakness, something only one from Jersey would do. Dubinsky sighed, inserted a Vysotsky tape in the deck, and took off to the great Russian bard's angry accompaniment.

He had been relieved when the owner, a family man who had to be home for supper, offered him the night shift. Dubinsky doubted he could muster the *chutzpah* required for the rush-hour traffic.

He picked up his first fare in the Village. A woman waved, and he swerved to the right, elated at the effortlessness of finding a client, although he realized he might have been helped by the starting rain. He turned off the tape to make sure he heard the address right.

"Seventy-sixth and Riverside Drive, please."

He groaned. He did not even dare look up in the rearview mirror. He knew the voice: it had haunted him for weeks. He knew the eyes: calm, brown, they were everywhere he looked. He knew the thick auburn hair, casually spread down the tweed jacket she was still wearing. What an omen on the first night. Couldn't he have told it was her by the imperious manner in which she had flagged him? Hardly. That was the only way to hail a cab in New York.

"You didn't hear what I said," she said patiently, with only a hint of annoyance in her voice.

"I hoid ya." He made a desperate attempt to camouflage himself, and drove straight east.

"I hope you will not bother me with your speculations regarding the World Series or the Super Bowl or whatever they're currently playing," she said in the way of conversation.

Dubinsky growled, an appropriate response, he thought, turning the tape back on. "The lizard of indolence crawls through my bones," the bard sang.

As he approached the FDR Drive, it occurred to him that perhaps the West Side Highway was a better route. But showing hesitation or regret would have been unthinkable. Not if he was going to drive a cab in New York City.

They rode in silence; the rain was falling harder. The Dodge's suspension was no match for the potholes, and by the time they plunged into the tunnel, he felt he could have nails driven in his ass without feeling any pain. He could save himself the discomfort by slowing down, but he was afraid that if he had to spend five minutes more than necessary in the cab with her, he would be sorely tempted to run it into a wall, and the hell with the rest. "No longer does my heart freeze from the stab of love," the poet sang on. He raced westward on Seventy-second without any regard for the pace of traffic. He had to brake abruptly at Madison; there was a smothered shriek in the back seat.

"Sorry," he whispered. She remained silent. "I'm all transparent, like an open window," Vysotsky sang; "My heart stirs as if it were outside of me."

"What kind of music is it?" she asked.

"Is Bulgarian folk song," he said grimly. "Devoted to sheep slaughter festival."

"I should've known," she said.

They entered Central Park; he had never driven there before, there were forks in the road, he hung a left, a right; they were zooming at sixty miles an hour parallel to Central Park West. "I stay in bed; the noose looks farther that way," went the tape.

"I have a distinct feeling," she said, "that you're lost, Mr. Dubinsky. Please turn to your right." He obeyed. "And slow

down, you have an excellent chance of getting a ticket. Don't
hit the carriage, please; they're unaware of the broodings of
your Russian soul. That's a red—Pleeez! *Oof!* Whoever issued
you a license ought to be electrocuted."

"Get out." He turned off the tape. "I don't have to take this
xenophobic crap."

"First of all," she said, "you'll lose your license.
Second—"

"Second," he said, "I don't give a shit."

The rain was pouring in all seriousness now; the late-hour
dog-walkers and joggers raced toward the canopies, toward
their Books-of-the-Month, their "Tonight Show," their warm,
cozy beds. The light changed, there were impatient horns
behind him. He crossed Central Park West, pulled to the hydrant, and stopped. "You heard me."

"You really have an amazing ear for idiom," she said in a
slightly shaking voice. "You're an interesting ethnic specimen—"

"Miz Morgan, you're wasting my time." He turned in his
seat to face her, yet he could not bring himself to look her in
the eye; he knew that if he did that, his anger would evaporate
immediately, he would turn the ignition back on and not say
a word if she told him to drive her to Connecticut or Montreal
or Iceland.

"How's this," he said, "you Americanski go outski; I Russki
stay inski. You haff pay no dollar-cent. Free rideski, Americanski lady like, no?"

She held a pause. "All right," she said in a tired voice. "I
apologize for having not called you. I apologize for having
been rude and superior in the cab. But I'm really very, very
tired, and it's raining like crazy, and it's twenty more blocks,
and there are no cabs in sight, and I'll pay you a double
rate on the remaining mileage in recognition of your hurt
feelings—"

"Fuck you and your rate." He turned on the ignition. "You're
the pits, you know that? This is a pretty damn good country,
but you're just about the worst I've seen of it." He stopped

short, realizing he was sliding into anti-money rhetoric, moralizing, demagogical, and stupid, not unlike a Third World exchange student's soliloquy against American imperialism. Most important, it was completely different from what he really wanted to say, and whatever that was he knew he couldn't bring himself to say it. "Let's just keep quiet, okay?"

"Okay," she said in a small voice.

He pulled straight to the canopy of her building, and a ruddy-faced doorman in a Ruritanian uniform hurried outside with an umbrella.

"No tip," he said. "Please."

"Okay, okay." She rifled her handbag. "You Russian maniac. Do you still live in that horrible fleabag?"

"My whereabouts are of no concern to you, Ms. Morgan." At the last moment he stayed his foot, about to floor the gas— *no slamming Dubinsky;* the engine purred, propelling the Dodge a few yards toward the middle of the street, and died.

In the wake of the Goldenburger debacle, Slava felt oddly relieved and exhilarated. I'm sorry, Aunt Raya, he thought; but I was right and you were wrong. Now he realized that wild semi- and completely illegal schemes were whirling in his head since the day he arrived, but, one way or another, he had succeeded in blocking them. For God's sake, this was America. Whose business was Business. Who respected the integrity in a hardware store owner, but who positively adored a crook in a takeover tycoon and put him on the cover of all the weeklies.

"Dubinsky, is this 'pizdorvanium' related to your ersatz motherland of Pizdo?" Slava asked, without taking his eyes off the commodities listings.

"Uh-huh." Dubinsky spent the last thirty minutes with his nose against the window, despondently staring at the wet, rain-smudged street below. He had an absurd vision of Michelle, seized with guilt about her ethnocentric behavior the night before, burning to apologize and too ashamed to come straight up and knock on his door; Michelle, her eyes lowered, sneaking into the phone booth on the corner, dialing his number with her hands shaking and her nails breaking. . . .

"Dubinsky!" Slava yelled. "Where the fuck are you? One night driving a cab and you're a zombie! Where else do they mine this shit?"

The phone was silent. Dubinsky mechanically reached into his fourth-year lecture notes. "There are also mines in Patagonia and Burma, but Pizdo is the largest," he muttered, turning to face Slava. How could she break her nails, the pay phone on the corner was a push-button variety. . . .

"It trades at three-ten a ton," Slava murmured. "Kinda low. Went up from three-six last month. You need a shitload of money to cash in on that."

"There's not much use for it. From what I remember, they use it in microwave kitchenware and cathode-ray tubes. It's not exactly uranium, you know. But then again, their uranium profits went bust since the guerrillas blew up the mines."

"Still . . . ," Slava mused. "What's going on there, anyway? Is the regime in cahoots with Borzoi and Company, or are they into Citibank?"

"I haven't kept track recently," Dubinsky admitted. "Last I heard it was Borzoi, but they were flirting with Chase, too."

"What's the word on stability?"

"In Pizdo, it's never too high."

"I like it," Slava nodded.

Dubinsky's heart overflowed with admiration as he watched Slava punching the calculator, dialing numbers, making arrangements. I'll do anything, he pleaded silently. I'll carry your golf bag if you decide to have the wrap-up meeting in a country club; I'll pose as your chauffeur and your valet, I'll rub your back when you get tense and pretend we're a couple if your contact is gay . . . hold it, he checked himself, I'm taking this too far, but I can do the chauffeur bit real good.

"Dubinsky." Slava rubbed his temples. "This is too much. What's the matter with you? Are you sick or something?"

Dubinsky groaned. "Well, take an aspirin. I can't stand this. You've been staring at me like a dog for two hours. You're driving me nuts. Go to your room. Or better yet, go buy something for lunch—pastrami, tongue, roast beef . . ."

"Anything else, besides pastrami?"

"*What* else?"

"I don't know," Dubinsky shrugged. "Anything you want."

"Get the hell out of here."

When the phone rang, Dubinsky was barely out the door. Slava did not even have to look to know that it was the personal line. Just like Dubinsky, that demented Luddite, to neglect the convenience of the answering machine. He swore, picking up the receiver and barking Hello into it.

"Hello, may I speak to Oleg?" a woman's voice, arrogant and impatient, inquired.

One of these days, Slava thought, his creative peace will be guarded by a legion of Cerberus-like secretaries, gray-haired spinsters, worshiping their boss and prepared to smite an intruder who might distract Mr. Clive Rothman from making another billion. "He isn't here, you wanna call back?"

"Would you terribly mind taking a message?" the woman persisted.

A message? "No, why should I?" He mechanically reached for a pen. It was slowly dawning on him that she was talking down to him. "Who are you?" It also occurred to him, to his surprise, that he was not angry.

"My name is Michelle Morgan." She paused. "I apologize if I interrupted something. You don't sound as if you were in the habit of taking messages."

If he was standing up, he would have to sit down; as it was, he had to stand up. *How did she know?* "You're right, this is my first time. Only for Dubinsky's girlfriends . . ."

"What a preposterous suggestion," she said dryly. "I do not belong to Mr. Dubinsky's harem nor do I have any desire to. Whatever gave you the idea?"

"No," he said, "I can't picture you in anybody's harem. My

name is Clive, by the way. Clive Rothman. I am a friend of Oleg's."

"A fellow taxi driver?"

For a very brief moment Slava had a vision of an ocean-sized, knee-deep puddle outside the building where he grew up, and a narrow board spanning it. Dubinsky was standing on the board, daydreaming, oblivious to its dangerous creaking and wavering. Slava could say "Yes," leave him in this dubious safety, and wade across. "I have my own business," he said instead. "Of a financial nature."

"How mysterious." Her voice was not altogether mocking. "In that case, you must terribly resent an interruption, especially if it's caused by someone asking for your friend Dubinsky."

"The market won't collapse."

"I'm relieved. Anyway, would you please tell your friend that I called and he's welcome to call me at this number—do you have a pen?"

"I have everything." He wrote down the number.

"I owe Mr. Dubinsky a dinner. Don't ask me how it came about, the circumstances were rather unfortunate."

She had a cool, crisp intonation of someone who could not pronounce the word "please" or "sorry" except as a joke. How stupid it was of me to suspect that *this* could be Dubinsky's girlfriend, Slava wondered.

"Thank you for your patience," she said with a finality that signaled the end of conversation. "Again, my apologies for having interrupted your business."

"No problem," he whispered.

Still, she didn't hang up. "As a means of atonement—I'd like to invite you, too. Would your busy schedule allow for a dinner engagement? Tomorrow night?"

"It's fine with me," he swallowed, "but let me check with Oleg first—"

"I'm sure he'll find it convenient," she chuckled.

As she dictated the address, a key turned in the lock.

"Hold on," he said, pressing the Hold button. I don't know

if this is right, he wondered; could there be more going on here than Ms. Morgan would let on? And yet. If he didn't come along, there was a good chance he'd never hear her voice again. "I'm sorry, that was a call on the other line."

"Well, don't let me get in the way of your financial obligations. I'll see you tomorrow night . . . Clive."

Dubinsky called from the kitchen, but Slava was oblivious as he stared at the phone. Where could that schmuck have picked her up? Or, rather, where did *she* pick *him* up? *Unfortunate circumstances.* No, most of the time Fortune knows what she is doing—even if she overplots now and then.

"Do you understand how the stock market works, Dubinsky?"

"I guesh sho." Dubinsky put away another pastrami-and-tongue sandwich. Maybe he should get a job in a deli, he thought. Noshing on this stuff all day long. What a life. American automatic slicer reduced the physical part to nought. He peeked at Slava, whose face assumed a captain-of-industry expression, and decided against sharing this fantasy. "You buy low and sell high, what's there to know?"

"The trick is to know *what* is going to be high."

"That must be pretty complicated," Dubinsky sighed. "The multitude of socio-ethno-politico-cultural factors boggles my mind."

Slava shook his head. "This is a Vladimir-and-Znachar answer, Dubinsky. Sit tight, write a paper, cheat on your expenses. This country didn't get to where it is now with answers like that. *You* didn't get to where you are now with answers like that."

"I'm better at questions anyway," Dubinsky admitted, pouring the remaining Vouvray into his glass. "Like, Where *am* I now?" The joke was ignored. Dubinsky sighed. Slava had barely touched his wine, but he didn't comment. Food and wine have been known to interfere with bold, unorthodox capital planning. To say nothing of sex. Ah, but how it interfered.

"Earth to Dubinsky," Slava said. "Do you want me to go

on or would you rather go back to sleep? I didn't realize I was such a poor instructor."

"I didn't realize it was a lecture."

"Oleg, I just want you to understand a little bit of what I'm setting out to accomplish. You're a rational person, how else can I motivate you?"

"I don't know. Sex?"

Schmuck, schmuck, what a schmuck. Slava paused to touch his face lightly—was he blushing? "You had a call."

Dubinsky leapt to his feet. How many women in the world had his number? "Local or long-distance?" God, don't let it be Linda, he thought, biting on his finger out of shame.

"You do have a voracious appetite," Slava remarked, and told him about the call. He kept it straightforward, he didn't go into undercurrents or visions of boards spanning across the puddles; he did mention, ever-so-lightly, almost-on-second-thought, Michelle's emphatic denial of her girlfriend status. And his own having been invited. As an after-afterthought. "So tell me how you met this Michelle. And why is she so scared of being assaulted by you as to invite me along."

Dubinsky looked away. He knew it would be painful, and he even suspected that Slava would relish another proof of Dubinsky's inability to deal with the real world, yet he also knew he would feel better afterwards. He told him the whole story, from the coffee shop to Central Park West.

"You really told her to get out?" There was a glint in Slava's eye that Dubinsky interpreted as approval. He nodded.

"That's character, Dubinsky. Or hysteria. Depending on how you look at it."

They were silent for a moment. "Let me get this straight," Slava said. "You never got to fuck her, am I right?"

Dubinsky remained silent.

"Do you mind if I take a shot?"

Dubinsky swallowed hard. "Of course not."

"I see. You do mind. Well, what the hell." Slava yawned. "Forget it. Let's just go there, bring some good wine, chocolates, flowers—and have a good time."

"Wine *and* chocolates *and* flowers?"

"It's a little premature to stun her with diamonds, don't you think? You have to learn moderation, Dubinsky. Badly."

"She's a bitch! A cold, unfeeling, arrogant bitch! She'll probably apply for a grant to study us! We're all curious ethnic specimens to her!"

"And so is she, to us. It always cuts both ways, Dubinsky. Before I forgot—there's a trip to Boise in your future."

"*Si, padrón.*"

"I like your new attitude," Slava nodded, barely containing his joy. Everything, but everything, was falling in place so neatly. "But before that—like the day after tomorrow—we'll be flying to Washington, D.C. Nothing heavy, Dubinsky, just some chat in Pizdoan. Now, let me tell you something about commodities."

"And cabbages, and kings," Dubinsky nodded sadly.

"Cabbages? Maybe on the Russki commodities exchange; not here, Dub."

The dinner was fit to be written up in the *Times*. The vodka was chilled and placed in an ice bucket; the caviar came in a cut-crystal container with an ornament that matched the bucket. Everything came in sets at Michelle's house; everything matched. Dubinsky had four quick shots, disregarding Slava's sharp looks. What the hell, it went down so perfectly, chased with hearts of artichoke and creamy herring. Miss Morgan had her ethnography pat. He eyed ruefully the elaborate sculpture of pinkish-brown paté on the dish. He felt like an Ostrogoth as he cut into it with his knife. But it melted so promptly in his mouth he couldn't resist it. Slava took half a glass at a time. He was having the time of his life. This was Class with a C. The apartment was spacious, yet created an impression of intimacy in the minute details, in the almost invisible touches: a lithograph of an old New York over an antique cabinet, a Japanese ink scroll with delicately drawn cranes next to the window that opened on a breathtaking view of the State of New Jersey.

The hostess herself was the main showpiece, wearing a loose tan robe with a lightly understated ornament on its sleeves. The neck was cut low and bared an intricate antique-looking piece of jewelry. The long auburn hair, flowing freely, exuded a delicate whiff of a designer shampoo, and the pale yellowish diadem connected its color with that of her eyes. Slava looked into them and found what he wanted to find. There was respect, curiosity, challenge. There was also, at their very bottom, a four-poster with cool white sheets. He gave them another steady look; she did not look away; both smiled.

Through the dinner Dubinsky's consumption pattern remained steady: first he chased vodka with hors d'oeuvres, then he chased the twenty-dollar-a-bottle Trianon Montrachet with medallions of veal. He was as miserable as ever; he was grateful for booze and food because they occupied his mouth, which was about to burst out in sarcastic tirades, as well as his hands, which would happily grab the bottle and smash everything in sight. Perhaps not everything: just enough to ruin the sets. Then she would have to donate the rest to the Salvation Army.

He wished he could stuff the veal in his ears, too: the conversation had been unbearable from the moment they walked in. It was an unending flow of mutual compliments: Slava praised Michelle's taste in decorating; she admired his drive; he extolled her culinary skills, and she lauded his haberdashery. He plunged into a mildly ironical, lightly spiced description of his days in Europe; she told him of her father, a retired Canadian diplomat, and her numerous nannies and amahs who had taken care of her on the family's treks from Montevideo to Katmandu. I'm gonna be sick, Dubinsky said to himself; why don't they erect shrines to each other and burn incense in the middle of the room.

Dubinsky himself was re-introduced as the vice president of the company, and they had a happy, cheerful laugh at his cab-driving skills. "We're barely off the ground," Slava said modestly, explaining Dubinsky's presence at the wheel. They were also severely undercapitalized, the market was bearish, the Dow Jones was feverish, and their Swiss partners—Slava coughed and took a deep breath. *Drown in chocolate, they should.* But things were looking up, he went on, the new Administration was coming down strongly on the side of business, new prospects were opening up in the burgeoning Pizdo trade. . . .

"Ah, Pizdo." Michelle projected a faint semblance of a smile. "That arcane God-forsaken little acre on which our friend Oleg is such an inimitable expert."

"Fucking right," Dubinsky confirmed, picking his teeth with a dessert fork. "We sure gonna dump some manna on those fuckers' heads. Big White Brother gonna bring his little black cousins so much democracy they'll be taking Alka-Seltzer for years to come for relief. Once we unleash those free-market forces—lordy, the veldt will never be the same. Forty-five political parties, voting franchise for gay medicine men, *Penthouse* in every village's Seven-Eleven."

"Now you understand," Slava chuckled, "how hard I have to hold on to Oleg. The Under Secretary of State for Africa is on the phone every day. Matter of fact," he continued, "we're opening a branch in Mandah, Pizdo's capital, and Oleg will be leaving shortly to scout the location and hire the staff."

Fat fucking chance, Dubinsky thought, caressing his navel under the table.

"I'm sure Oleg will be an excellent manager." Michelle produced a charming smile.

"Yeah," Dubinsky nodded. "Whoever gives a better blow job will be the supervisor."

Slava coughed and retired to the kitchen for more wine. Dubinsky blushed. Did he really say that?

"I'm sorry to see that my initial impression of you had a grain of truth in it," she said. "And I was almost prepared to like you."

"I honestly have no idea why I said that." He stared into his napkin, unable to raise his eyes—again.

"I just hope that in the course of time I'll be able to see in you whatever makes you worthy of Clive's friendship."

Clive! Shit.

She brought in a cheese board. Slava finally returned with the wine. He told her that Brie was his favorite, unless this was Camembert. She asked him what cheeses they had in Russia. Dubinsky could not remember any. He chewed on his Roquefort mutely; he had nothing to contribute to this endless double panegyric. Almond ice cream with fresh raspberries improved his mood, however; he was almost prepared to bless them for richer or for poorer and drive his leased Dodge to a remote tropical island, where he would lead a virtuous eremitic existence, tilling the land and subsisting on all-natural foods. But then she brought in Remy and Courvoisier, he had four glasses one after another, his mind went back to sitting on the floor with Vladimir and Znachar and Slava (fuck Clive), and he moaned because it was all over, there was no going back, things would never be the same, he should stay in Boise and get himself a job in the mines, to die within a month in a front-page-rating mine explosion. He pictured vividly the women in mourning against the background of slag piles; none was waiting for him.

"Another espresso?" Michelle asked.

"Let me get my cigarettes." Slava headed for his coat.

"Sure, why not." Dubinsky pushed his cup forth. *Sonuvabitch, he already knows where the closet is and everything.*

"Please don't look so sad," Michelle said sympathetically. "Your expression makes me feel rather remorseful. I understand perfectly well how you feel, and I'm terribly sorry that you're not having a good time." She leaned forward to touch his hand. "I do hope we can be good friends. You're so talented, after all; it's your artistic sensitivity—"

"—that makes me such a jerk," he whispered, feeling the electricity that ran through his arm from the contact with her skin; and, to counter it, to get rid of his fear and his anger, he downed another Remy and said, "Why do you always construct such perfect sentences? Don't you ever feel like saying something incomplete or incoherent?"

She was taken aback for a moment, then smiled her trademark cool poster smile. "I save incoherence for proper moments, Oleg."

Which means that with me you'll always sound like a UN resolution, he thought.

They left about midnight amid more civilized puffery about what a perfect hostess she was and how (looking at Slava) she was always glad to see them and what a great fabulous splendid time had been had by all.

Outside, they walked on Broadway in silence. The cold air blew the liquor out of Dubinsky's head and moderated Slava's excitement. It was not until they reached Columbus Circle that Slava spoke.

"Can I do anything to help the situation, Dubinsky?"

"No."

As they approached the garish neon of Times Square, Dubinsky said, "I guess you're really hooked."

"Like never before," Slava nodded. "I need a woman like her, Dubinsky. Where the hell was she ten years ago? I would be ten times more successful now. We would have a home, we would entertain, we would have kids. I can talk to her, Dubinsky, I can share things with her, she understands me—"

Dubinsky was dumbfounded. And he thought they had been merely singing dithyrambs to each other. Had there been something he had missed?

"She's got class, Dubinsky, she's got style, she never says a wrong thing, she stands right, she walks right, she sits right, she—"

"Please," Dubinsky said. "Leave something for the imagination."

"Dubinsky." Slava stopped in front of a theater with brightly lit triple crosses all over its façade. "I'm not a back-stabbing bastard. If you feel that this is it, that if Michelle and I are together, we can't be friends anymore—just say a word. And I'll never call her again. I promise."

Blessing, everybody wants a blessing, Dubinsky thought in

despair. From their parents, their priests, their shrinks, their coaches, and now from Dubinsky. I can't deal with this, he thought, his despair expanding and enveloping him by the second; life is not a Truffaut movie. If Slava had said, If you don't like the idea of my fucking Michelle, you can go fuck yourself, I would respect him more; but with him standing there in front of a sign that reads SCANDINAVIAN STEWARD-ESSES ON MINNESOTA STRIP . . . I like him more for it, because I can't help liking him, because we've been together for so long. Despair spread beyond himself and crept upon a drunk who was propping the hydrant a few feet away. "It's all a CIA conspiracy," he muttered. "How about some change, mister?"

"*Nu?*" Slava asked, ignoring the plea.

Dubinsky sighed, feeling the despair leave him and settle on the drunk. "I'll get over this, Slava. If you just let me stay out of it for a while." He felt better as the last word left his mouth. Here it was, the cleansing effect of Truth, he thought with relief. The feeder road ended; he was back on the freeway again.

"Oh, good," Slava said. "Let's get going before I freeze my butt off. Besides, we've got to get up early tomorrow. Pizdo, Pizdo!" he sang.

Once You're a Jerk, You're Always a Jerk, that's what I should be singing, Dubinsky thought morosely.

"Can't you hear it calling, Dubinsky? Can't you see the palm trees and the azure-blue sea and the leisurely surf and the thatched huts and the happy, proud shiny people extracting pizdorvanium in the fragrant air of an open-strip mine? What color is pizdorvanium, Oleg?"

"Beats me." He felt like casting aside a manhole lid and plunging into some fragrant air himself. At least that milieu would correctly reflect his inner state. Whom was he kidding, jumping around with this "cleansing effect" like a deranged TV housewife in a detergent commercial? Unloved, forlorn, and light-years removed from the Truth Way.

"It's green, Dubinsky." Slava danced on. "As far as we're concerned, pizdorvanium is green and crinkly and smells like Chanel No. 5."

. . .

Aboard the shuttle, Dubinsky ordered a Bloody Mary.

"No," Slava said.

"Never mind," Dubinsky whispered to the stewardess.

After a while, he got up. "I can't wait for this airhead. I'll go get coffee myself." Actually he planned to buy a Scotch and pour it into his coffee.

Slava eyed him suspiciously and flagged a stewardess. "Please bring this gentleman a coffee *now*. He's having an attack of gastritis. He needs something hot right away."

"Certainly, sir. Cream and sugar?"

Dubinsky groaned and fifteen minutes later amended his tactic, claiming a need for a refill. The stewardess, flagged by Slava, rushed over promptly, flashing her robotic smile. In another fifteen minutes they landed. Once they touched the ground the thirst evaporated, but he resented Slava's unsolicited assistance in any case.

"I'm worried," Slava confided to Dubinsky in the cab.

"It's only an exploratory meeting, you don't have much to lose."

"I'm worried about you. Do you think you can play a secretary and speak only when you're spoken to?"

"A piece of cake." Dubinsky uttered a nervous laugh and went back to the sights. He found the capital a fine, stately city, although the idea of so many people concentrated in one place for the specific purpose of ruling America was vaguely disturbing to his libertarian mind.

"Are you daydreaming again?" Slava interrupted his musings. "Damn it, Dubinsky, if we pull this through, I'll hire you a guide to do nothing but stare at fucking monuments with. As if you haven't seen enough of Lenin's statues back in Russkiland. What's the name of the Soviet trade attaché in Pizdo?"

"Mochalov."

"Pizdo's minister of foreign trade?"

"P. Roy Do-kha."

"The year he graduated from Lumumba University?"

"Seventy-three."

"What's my name?"

"Afonin."

"What's your name?"

"Zykov."

Slava chuckled approvingly. "Good memory, Dubinsky. Now, remember—sit tight. This is not your cab; there's more than your lousy tip at stake if you let your mouth run loose."

For a luncheon with the senior counselor of the Pizdo Trade Mission, Mr. P. Rod Azh-ny Slava, had selected an Italian restaurant on a side street off Dupont Circle: classy and out of the way.

"Remember, Dubinsky," he said, as they settled at the table, "you can speak that Pizdo abracadabra only after I rub my nose. And don't show off with your knowledge of whorehouse slang. Keep it diplomatic."

"I don't know any Pizdo whorehouse slang. I'm pretty rusty as it is. Can I have a Scotch, please? I'm nervous."

"No, you can't. No Scotch. What's your name?"

"Zykov." Dubinsky sighed.

"What does Comrade Zykov drink?"

"Vodka." Dubinsky felt revolted at the thought. At noon. My God. Soviet officials were a tough act to follow. "If Zykov has been in the West for a while, wouldn't he be used to Scotch?"

"You've read too many thrillers, Dubinsky. Life is simpler. Shut up now. Looks like our crook is here."

Mr. Azh-ny maneuvered deftly between the tables with a beatific smile on his face, looking forward to the treat.

They were barely through the antipasto when Slava became convinced that they had their man. Mr. Azh-ny was a carbon copy of the officials Slava knew precisely how to deal with. From Vladivostok to Lusaka, the language of bribe, grease—*na lapu, bakshish, mordida*—was an international one.

Nevertheless, they chatted on merrily, recalling mutual acquaintances from Lumumba U. on the Lenin Hills, ah those nights at the Metropol Restaurant. . . . Was Minister Do-kha still fond of redheads? As for America, Mr. Azh-ny had been in the country for only six months and loved it as much as Dubinsky did. He was just as awed by the sprawl of the freeways and the glittering towers, but, oh, Pizdo was such a poor country, the embassy was run on a shoestring. . . . They were fortunate, Slava thought, that Mr. Azh-ny spoke English little better than Russian. Dubinsky's linguistic skills were going to come in handy.

Slava launched his pitch over the gelato. Everything was quite legal. At the Intergalactic they had just found out through their Silicon Valley contacts that pizdorvanium, an important source of hard currency for Pizdo, was going to become a hot new mineral in the production of microchips. And, of course, Exxon and IBM had no intention of paying a fair market price and thus promoting the cause of the Socialist revolution. Mr. Azh-ny's eyes shone with pride in the revolution. United Fruit, Slava continued, would rather see Pizdo children starve to death than pay an extra penny. Mr. Azh-ny nodded so sadly that Slava signaled for two more Gallianos and a vodka. Then he saw that Comrade Zykov was about to cry and changed the order to three Gallianos.

Now, Slava went on, our friends in Moscow have designed a plan to prevent the Rockefellers from committing another crime against humanity. But the plan must be held in total secrecy. Both Pizdo's Ministry of Foreign Trade and the embassy teemed with CIA informers. Mr. Azh-ny shook his head in proper indignation. Slava paused, letting him reconsider. Mr. Azh-ny promptly changed his expression into a pitying grimace: eh, human nature, comrades. . . . Couldn't agree more, Slava said. But that's why we need secrecy, in order to thwart AT&T's vile schemes. All you need to do—he cleared his throat and rubbed his nose, and Dubinsky stepped in—is announce that both ships of the Lumumba National Merchant Fleet of Pizdo, carrying shipments of pizdorvanium, have been hijacked and blown up with their precious cargo.

Mr. Azh-ny was impressed equally by the message and by Comrade Zykov's linguistic prowess. The Soviet comrades meant business. The Pizdo language, renowned for its direct-ness in conveying subtlety, was not easy for foreigners to master.

And Shell and General Electric would really have to shake

their booty, Slava concluded, rubbing his nose again and thus switching off the translation. There was no need to overdo it, he thought. The sonuvabitch might interpret it as condescension.

And the ships would be found? Mr. Azh-ny's eyes shone with delight.

Within three or four days, Slava said confidently. We understand that it's not going to be easy, Slava said. But it needs to be done three months from now, before the Silicon Valley announcement has been made. Mr. Azh-ny would need money, no? taking important transportation officials to dinner, leasing cars . . . perhaps making an offering to Najeeva, the spirit of business adventure. . . . Slava rubbed his nose. It's under the bark of the baobab (Pizdo had no word for tablecloth), Dubinsky said quietly; just under your plate. Azh-ny caressed the bump lovingly. It's but a token of good faith, Slava said. Come to New York next week, we'll talk about it in detail. Do you like New York? he asked. Very much fun, said Mr. Azh-ny, beaming.

On the way back Dubinsky was allowed a double Chivas to celebrate the success of Stage One. Sipping the balm, Dubinsky voiced his suspicions. "Pizdoans are not the most reliable breed, Slava. In fact, that's why they get along with the Russians so well—both have an unlimited capacity to botch things."

"Great. So they won't even have to stage the fuck-up with the ships. In all likelihood, it would be delayed anyway, and it's just a matter of our friend making a statement to the press."

"And that will send the pizdorvanium prices soaring?"

"Tenfold." Slava stretched comfortably. "What's your problem, Dubinsky? The Voice of Truth speaketh again?"

"I'd rather you didn't laugh at things like this," Dubinsky said. "As for Pizdo, I think it would be more foolproof if you sent a troup of ex-Legionnaires to *really* hijack the ship."

"*Oy*, Dubinsky, you've been reading all that junk again. It's feasible, but it takes more money and more time, the two commodities I have in short supply. And who says mercenaries are more reliable anyway? Not in recent history. Face the reality, Dubinsky: a well-placed bribe can accomplish much more than a battalion of your over-romanticized losers."

Dubinsky said nothing. He was ashamed to admit that the effectiveness of the operation was not among his considerations. He saw tan, leathery faces; muscular hands wielding Uzis; he heard the roar of helicopters and the whistling of bullets—all framed by the turquoise Indian Ocean with a dime-sized island with a lonely date palm in the background. The *osso buco* at lunch had been delicious, and so was the *gelato*, but oh so tame in comparison.

The next day Dubinsky woke up early, to catch the nine o'clock flight to Seattle. Even as he was brushing his teeth, avoiding, as usual, his morning face in the mirror, his stomach reflected an urge to get aboard and get bombed. I should do something about it, he thought—once this Pizdo thing blows over. It was Russkiland all over again—there is no reason to be sober if you're plodding through the mud of lies. Sobriety means a clarity of vision, and you don't need this unless you're traveling the Highway of Truth. He passed Slava's bedroom without giving a second look. Mr. Clive Rothman Cornfeld was soundly asleep as befitted an international crook of his magnitude. No pangs of conscience for the victims of Pizdo's annual famine there, Dubinsky thought sourly; I at least need Bloody Marys to handle them.

Two hours later he was happily on autopilot, using the omnipresent celery stalks for drumsticks and doing every solo John Bonham of Led Zeppelin had ever recorded.

Slava took a long look at himself in the full-size mirror at the Oyster Bay International Athletic Club. He had never been in the habit of admiring his long, muscular legs, his washboard stomach, his swimmer's chest; he had always taken them for granted, and was now mildly disappointed by the pockets of flab here and there. The strong chin, the prominent jaw, the unblinking look—still, even the face looked a bit tired. The skin tone was off. Ah, but the businessmen he had met looked like Olympic athletes. They worked out on enormous metal contraptions that kept a constant track of every breath they took. They arranged their conventions so they could soak in the sun; they used golf courses for intimate business meetings. (Fucking golf, he thought, resenting the idea that he would have to learn an idiot childish game like that.) But they kept themselves in shape, and their shape put them in good stead. Their bronzed skin, their muscle tone, their exuberant good health were not wasted; they were an important asset; they were good for *business*.

He barely endured the long-winded explanations from the Olympian instructor, whose body unpleasantly reminded Slava of the relief map of the Caucasus. Finally he strapped himself into the first Nautilus and pulled with a gasp. You'd better be worth it, he said to the coolly smiling Michelle in the mirror.

On his way from Boise to Seattle Dubinsky was disconsolate. Scotch failed to remove him far enough from reality; he was soaring just below the clouds, high enough not to feel the bumps yet still with an all-too-clear view of the ground. The thought of returning to Manhattan made him sick. Slava would already be cavorting with Michelle, leaving him either to seek out Kirill and Apelsinov and their dreams of Bugattis parked outside marble-floored villas—or to head uptown and run into another Sandy. How easy it was to get cornered in the Free World, he thought, riding the escalator at the Sea-Tac. There were no soldiers ahead of him this time—back to the shores of Tripoli, he surmised—but there were no dishwater blondes riding the opposite one, either, so what was the point of running? Trust your feet and don't get in their way: what a wise and enlightened Pizdoan adage it was. Never more appropriate than at the Avis counter. You don't have to try harder, miss, just a decrepit automatic will do fine. I'm uncomfortable with new cars, they make me think of Linda and the house, they're the gold watch, the apex of a career in Filing. The company American Express card—for an emergency, Slava said—had been burning his pocket long enough. *My life is an emergency.* Come on, Dubinsky, it's only forty bucks, including liability insurance.

Slava crawled under the shower, then on to the sauna. He lay down on the bench and closed his eyes, oblivious even to the fellow occupants' soft whispers of the imminent plunge in the prime rate.

Everything was going to be perfect, everything was going to be just right. A powerful surge of physical well-being was enveloping him, a feeling of oneness with his muscles, his lungs, his heart. He felt he was preparing for a wedding night, with Michelle as his Princess Charming.

For a moment he recalled his first time, preceded by a nasty, vicious fight behind the school building. It was pitch dark, and thus it was pointless to play by the rules; no one could see if you won fair or not. You had to hurt the other guy seriously; at least for long enough to claim the prize. The prize was the class flirt, the place was behind the soccer goal, the duration was a minute and a half. When it was over, he knew that this could not have been the reason he wanted to smash the guy's face. He never laid a hand on her again. She went back to the loser, whom she would abuse in front of the class, always with an eye on Slava. The lovesick boy accepted the torture; Slava watched, learning a lesson.

He was picky from the start; he never went through moments when you want it so bad you'd jump a chair. But if you spent a lot of time in the right restaurants with the right people, there were always plenty of girls who simply wanted to have a good time and who didn't expect you to call them the next day. They were always lacking in one department or another: blond bombshells who could barely read; two-hundred-pound teenage Ph.D.s; Politburo granddaughters who despised him, a *merchant;* quick-minded, fast-talking, shrewdly made-up manicurists, who saw him as their Big Break. None possessed a certain quality that cemented the beauty and the brain and put the polish on top. None had class.

Strength sought strength, Slava thought; he had no need for a little wifey to bring him slippers. He needed an equal, and such a woman would naturally be in a better position than anyone else to appreciate what he had to offer. Little girls could not help it if they had no class; it was something one was born with, the end product of long, careful breeding. Like Michelle.

He dressed with more care and attention than he had when meeting Levine or Goldenburger. Knotting his Sulka, he wondered if the bastards would have screwed him if he had originally met them in the company of Mrs. Michelle Clive Rothman. Goddamn Swiss cuckoo would drool all over his tuxedo and, dazzled by Mrs. Rothman, drop his gold-rimmed glasses on the floor. And by a pure accident Mr. Rothman would step on them and apologize and offer to pay the bill for a new pair.

As Dubinsky approached downtown, the dusk fell and the windows lit up in the high-rises. The view turned into a full-color picture in the *America Illustrated* magazine that some schmuck in Krasnoyarsk or Voronezh would buy for ten rubles under the counter, to tear the picture out and tack it to the wall and sit there on long winter evenings and stare at it and think of America, the land of glitter, the land of fortune, the land of filing jobs on Electric Avenue. The streets were emptying at frightening speed, as Dubinsky drove up and down the roller coaster of downtown Seattle, looking for a suitable bar. Finally he found one, but inside was a rude awakening. According to the local ordinance, this was a *tavern*, no hard liquor served. "Bars have to sell *food* to stay on the right side of the law?" he cried out in his anger and his shame. *Just like Russkiland.*

"'Fraid so, friend."

Friend? There are no friendships in this country, there's only networking, Dubinsky wanted to tell him, but held back and ordered a Guinness, which slid down very nicely, thank you,

you need some variety in life, another one like this and he wouldn't need dinner. He looked around. An awful lot of smiling was going on—unaided by booze, too, he speculated, although the locals surely wouldn't flinch at putting away a couple of six-packs on a rainy afternoon.

He dialed Jodie's number. Busy!!! *Wellll.* He lingered near the phone, dialed again—still busy. Murphy's watching, he thought, returning to the bar. Yeah, *Schadenfreude* and/or *Weltanschauung*, whatever those two meant, were out of place here; this was not a setting for a Woody Allen neurocomedy. Never mind, he thought, administering another Guinness to his problems. Murphy schmurphy, I've gotta be me. The me Clive wants me to develop. Why not, what astounding successes has the ex-me chalked up so far?

He dialed again. She picked it up this time. "Is this Miz Jodie Gregg?" And, interrupting her in the middle of a hesitant, drawn-out "Yes," he ran on like a bullet train, afraid to let her respond and hang up. "Uh, this is Officer Qwertyuiop Asdfghjkl with Boise, Idaho, Police Department. We received an uncivil complaint from a certain foreign-born gentleman whose name he would rather not reveal at present time concerning a vital organ of his he claims you damaged at the Copper National Bank at approximately fifteen-oh-oh and subsequently stepped on it without leaving a trace aboard the Tater Airlines jumbo jet—" But she was already chuckling, and so he stopped to catch his breath, because people seldom hang up in the middle of a chuckle.

"You shouldn't be doing this," she said. "Impersonating a police officer is against the law."

"Rich Americanski woman like Miz Gregg vill be hugely happy to make bail for poor refugee, no?"

"Don't make jokes like that," she said, and the sudden seriousness in her tone sounded as though it was borne out of experience, which did not make her "hugely happy." "Are you in Seattle?"

"Yes. Immediately drop whatever you are doing and meet me for a drink."

"If I see you being arrested, I'll leave," she said, already half in jest.

"Deal." And if she had suggested that he strip naked and climb the Space Needle, he'd consider it, too. Seriously.

Her hair was neatly cut, and she was wearing a loose, nicely tailored gray coat and a pair of matching slacks and she was not smiling. What's more, he could bet that her eyes were slightly puffed.

"You're one dangerous Russki," she said. "Picking up women in banks, following them on airplanes, then calling them impersonating police officers—what next? You've already told me you're counting on me for bail." But her eyes were laughing, and her smile was coming back through the wrinkles and the puffiness.

"I'm harmless," he said, soaring to the top of the Needle. "Have a drink, it's a long story."

"Let's start with Russia," she said. "You were kicked out because you were crazy, right?"

"You're right on the money," he said. "It's like in that book—if you're a real nut, they'll kick you out, like Castro did the Marielitos. But if you tell them that you want to leave, then they throw you into the nuthouse—because, from their point of view, you have to be crazy to want to leave."

"It's not quite like in that book," she said, smartly sidestepping the trap that he could swear he didn't mean to place there. "What are you doing in Seattle, really?"

"Spying," he said. "On myself, mostly. No one else has any reason to panic."

She looked him in the eye. He looked back. Are these violins for real, her eyes asked. I'm alone, his eyes answered; I'll be grateful for whatever you can spare.

"Maybe I should show you around," she said uneasily. "Although there's much more to see in the daytime."

"I don't mind."

They drove to her apartment on Capitol Hill. She had to feed her cat. Sitting in an ancient faded armchair that looked like something left on the sidewalk in his neighborhood, and watching her move around in a frisky, businesslike manner, Dubinsky suddenly felt bad.

"I think I'm really imposing on you. You don't have to show me anything."

She stopped in the middle of watering a fern. "You're not imposing."

"Well," he drawled, "you might have made different plans—"

She shrugged, looking away. "If you want to go—"

He looked around the apartment. It was modest, almost poor, you could tell that most items were from K-mart at best; a college student's apartment if it had not been so neat. The cat pit-a-patted over to him and rubbed against his leg.

"She likes you." Jodie smiled.

He rose and stepped toward her, feeling very shaky on his feet; then he put his arms around her. They stood like that for a few moments without kissing or petting or anything; he felt her heart beat against his stomach. Then she slid out of his arms, softly and silently.

They drove out to the nearest takeout and got a huge pizza. "With everything," he said. " 'Canadian ham and pineapple'?"

"Sounds horrible, doesn't it?" she laughed. "But it tastes great."

"You can have my pineapple," he said. "This is all too trendy for me."

She brought out the candles and beer glasses and laid out the red-checkered napkins. He sensed her fatigue and offered to help; she shook her head. "It's all ready." You're fussing too much over pizza and beer, he wanted to say, but then he saw the care with which she lined the knives and the forks alongside their plates and thought that perhaps she needed it more for herself than for show.

They were hungry and soon abandoned pretension and were eating pizza with their hands, stuffing their mouths shamelessly. The six-pack went fast, and they found they were unable to move themselves away from the table. And so they sat there in a content, somnolent silence, watching the wax dripping on the saucer.

"*Oh—leg*," she said. "It's a pretty name. What does it mean?"

"It means, 'He who rises like the sun and falls like the night.' "

"Oh, you're so full of it. You really are."

"I'm changing it. To *Oh-foot*."

She made a face. "Cute."

She remembered she had some wine left, and, amid moans and groans, they relocated to the couch. She felt small and warm in his arms; she did not respond to his kisses with much passion nor did she push him away. He realized then that his own passion was more due to what he had been conditioned to feel—dinner-wine-couch-girl—and that her languor oddly matched his own longing for peace. So he was perfectly content to let it go at that. Her sweater was soft and fluffy, and the curls over her neck cast odd, abstract shadows in the candlelight.

"You're nice," he said.

There was a strange hint of apprehension in her eyes. She straightened up, looking away. "Oleg, I don't want you to think I'm like that. I mean, that I pick up men in bank lines and bring them home two hundred miles away."

He assured her he thought nothing of the sort.

"I've just not been very happy recently," she said.

"I've never been more miserable," he said, "until you touched me in that line."

She swallowed hard. "You're making fun of me."

"I'm not, and it's true what I said."

But the moment was gone. She rose. "Let me get the sheets." And before he could protest: "I'll put you up on the couch."

"Okay," he said, and then, as they rolled it out, added: "We don't have to have sex, you know."

"Yeah, that's generous of you to tell me."

"I mean it."

"Look." She dropped the pillow case on the sheet. The linen had a warm feel to it, the faded floral design was barely distinct in the candlelight. "I just broke up with someone, okay? If you don't like this arrangement, maybe you should go to a hotel."

"I'm sorry."

"Good night."

"Good night." No kiss. A strange girl, Jodie; moody, open, closed . . . American? Strange, strange . . .

Dubinsky fell asleep, woke up again, tossed about for a couple of hours. It was happening too fast for him: one night, an orgy of masochism at Michelle's; next, a lunch in Washington, D.C., straight out of Frederick Forsyth; and tonight, a night with, or apart from, a strange girl three thousand miles away. His rhythms were changed; his mind was used to prolonged, sluggish periods—work-visa-San Murray-New York; it had trouble switching gears. Yet in another sense he was more relaxed than he had been only hours before. He felt no pressure, no strain, and the old threadbare sheets felt soothing to his skin. He woke up again at dawn, shivering in the cold. The blanket was thin, more of a coverlet. He hesitated, and then entered the bedroom. She opened her eyes, although he was sure he had not made a sound.

"It's cold out there," he said, climbing into bed with her. They took each other in their arms and lay there for what seemed like hours without changing position, smug and warm and cozy in the bleak gray light, in a silence now and then subtly punctuated by the raindrops falling outside. They kissed and caressed each other without saying a word and without trying to go any further. Finally he slid in, she was receptive, and he came soon, seeking release more than pleasure. She sighed and touched his hair lightly.

They were awakened by the alarm.

"Eight-thirty," she said. "I have a class." She worked as a T.A. at the community college, she had told him; English and English Lit.

As he dressed, he remembered that his flight was at nine-thirty. I won't make it, he thought; I'll have to reschedule.

"You don't have to leave." She looked into her coffee. "I'll be off in the afternoon, we can drive out to the lake. There's usually sun in the afternoon, Seattle is not as bad as they say—"

"I really have to go to New York," he said, feeling a weight in his chest.

"Okay." She nodded without looking at him.

The bedroom door was partly open, and he could see the rumpled sheets on the bed. "I don't want you to think I'm some kind of a rat," he said. "Here's my business card, and I'll write my home number, too—"

"Oh, God," she said. *"Business card."*

"I really enjoyed the time we spent together—"

"I said 'Okay,' didn't I?" She glared at him.

"Please don't be angry," he said in despair, searching for a way to make it—*What? Easier? Different?*

They rode in silence. He looked at the towers of the downtown, gray in the fog. He remembered Electric Avenue, eons ago. He felt nauseated, he felt scared—

"Here we are," she said, pulling up behind his car.

She remained at the wheel, waiting to make sure he could get started; her expression was stern, unchanged, oddly contrasting with the playful lock over her brow.

He turned the key and pressed the gas. The engine turned slowly, uncertainly, asking him "Do you really want to go?" "I guess it's okay," he said in a small voice. "Thanks for everything." He wanted her so desperately to leave the car, so that they could hug and re-create the moment just after the cat had rubbed against his leg. "I'll call you," he added. "I will."

"Have a good flight." And she tore away, sending up clouds of blue smoke that were visible only for a moment against the background of the bus shelter, and then evaporated into the fog and rain.

Now he remained at the wheel, even more nauseated and scared—

. . .

What if it was the real thing, Dubinsky? And you were such a blind jerk you didn't see it?

How well he understood Dubinsky, Slava thought, watching Michelle walk into the bar at the Plaza. Every step, every gesture this woman made was a work of art. The tilt of her head when talking to the maître d': just the right angle, attentive and superior. The walk: steady and confident, with just the right sway of hips, just the proper distance behind the maître d'. Slava rose to greet her and felt a tingling in his body as his lips touched her hand. They talked of this and that; she confided she was thinking of leaving graduate school; the degree was a piece of paper, and the natives that had looked so colorful and interesting through the limo's tinted windows appeared to be quite hopeless at close quarters. "The last illusion," she grinned. "They're all the same: Pizdoans, Aleuts, Chichmeks."

He suppressed a smile. No matter what, he would always have one up on her; today it was Dubinsky-Vladimir's scam, tomorrow it would be something else.

Her face became flushed after two martinis. She laughed at his understated jokes, purified of any bedroom/bathroom color; she chatted about her summer trip to Aruba. Then she stopped on a dime and said in the same playful voice: "It's smart of you to be paying attention to Aruba. You want to make a pile of money, don't you? The Caribbean is a good place to keep it."

"I know." He smiled, thinking of the sonuvabitch Vesco.

"Why do you want to make a lot of money?" she asked in a completely sober voice.

He saw a red bulb light up in her forehead: *Key Question!* "Do you want a long answer or a short one?" He played for time. He had answered the question many times, always with a wisecrack. He didn't know the answer. He wanted it; that was enough. Perhaps he should ask Dubinsky to phrase it for him one of these days.

She ignored his question. "Do you believe money is a cure for all ills?"

"No." Watch out, Rothman, watch out, it's thin ice. . . .

"Does everything have a price?"

"No. But once you've got everything that does, it makes it easier to concentrate on the rest of it."

She smiled. "I like you, Clive—or whatever you used to be. I don't really care, because I like what you are now. As far as I'm concerned, I might never be able to pronounce your former name, and you may have a police record ten miles long in Russkiland—I don't care. I like what you are now," she repeated and smiled again. "I think you're a very exciting man."

My God, she had tested him—the nerve, he thought admiringly. "We have a difference there," he said. "*I* care about your past because it's a part of you, and I'm interested in your present—but most of all I'm interested in your future." He paused again and fired a testing shot. "*Our* future."

Her eyes were calm, unperturbed; her gaze was straight, unblinking. He swallowed hard as he returned it. It was almost supernatural, had she studied hypnosis?

"Our future," she echoed finally.

He took a deep breath as his heart thrashed about in his chest, and he said in an unnaturally high voice, to mask the trembling, "Shall we go eat?"

"Are you hungry?" She put her hand on his. He felt his face turning red. He took her hand and did not let it go until they reached her bedroom.

They undressed slowly, prolonging the suspense. When they joined their bodies, he reflected, as he watched himself from the outside, that for the first time in his life he was breathing harder than the woman he was with. Her breath remained steady, her eyes half-closed, and a quiet, content smile lingered on her flawless features. He knew he was trying too hard, but he came quickly anyway. As he burst inside her, she arched her back slightly and uttered a groan. He was smart enough to know it was a fake, yet he was grateful to her for it: it was good and convincing and showed consideration on her part.

"Oh, Clive." She tousled his hair. "Clive, Clive—how did you come up with a dumb name like this? You should be Alexander, Mark, Nicholas . . . but 'Clive,' it won't pan out, you're such a boy—"

"It's Clive." Faked orgasm or not, he was determined to show her who was the boss.

"That's what I mean," she laughed. "You still confuse stubbornness with character, it's boyish and endearing, no matter what . . . I'm really happy we met, I'm glad I responded to that stupid ad on the campus—"

"Leave Dubinsky out of it."

"Loyalty," she nodded. "Another endearing quality. Okay with me. I suppose everybody needs his or her own Dubinsky."

They napped, they made love, they ate cold cuts and cheese, they washed it down with cold white wine, they made love again—it was getting better every time. And then they slept.

Slava woke up in the middle of the night and went to the bathroom. He stopped at the edge of the bed and looked at the stranger in it. Lit by moonlight, her face wore the same cold and imperious expression that she showed to the world. She had never really opened up, he thought; she told him how much she liked him, admired him, but what did *she* want? For a moment his mind was in the throes of doubt; ice needles were stuck in his back. Could it be a one-night stand for her? No, the setup had been too elaborate. Could she be somewhat frigid? That could change with time and care. Could she have an ulterior motive? What kind? She shifted to her side, and her face disappeared in the dark. He thought he'd never know her. But perhaps that was part and parcel of that class thing. And if it was, who was going to turn whom around? Stuck between him and a John Wesley Harding, which way would she turn?

I'm getting to be like Dubinsky, he thought with displeasure: doubts, doubts, doubts. Loyalty was one thing; excessive closeness, where Dubinsky's less desirable characteristics rubbed off on Slava, was another. She's here, he thought, lying down next to her, and that is all that matters. He felt a surge of pride and strength. That's what a good woman does to you, he thought. It was the women Dubinsky went with, the ball-busters, who sapped your strength; a woman like Michelle would enhance it. His last thought before he went to sleep was, All this pizdorvanium business is just for openers, oil is next. He could dream again.

The next week Azh-ny was feted at Windows on the World. It was a gala night, with Slava emanating so much energy that Dubinsky wondered if they could connect him to a generator and get the whole dinner on the house in exchange for the savings on the electricity bill. Michelle, in a Galanos gown that showed her neck, her back, and much else, caused lump after lump in Dubinsky's throat; he wanted to break the bottle of Mouton Rothschild on the sommelier's overbearing face; he wanted to stand near the window, with the Jersey lights in the background, and nurse his Drambuie—hurt, but still proud.

Azh-ny shone all over—his bluish skin glistened, his teeth dazzled, his eyes glinted. Dubinsky was strongly encouraged to engage him in conversation, but strictly prohibited to do so out of Slava's earshot. Dubinsky felt ambiguous about the diplomat; he felt that Azh-ny's greed was different from that of Slava's Georgian partners or Messrs. Levine and Golden-burger. He apparently took it all far less seriously; he might well blow all those thousands on entertaining his own friends in the Windows on the World manner, and the hell with the depletion allowance. It made him a more interesting case and at the same time a less reliable accomplice.

"What Soviet person like Comrade Zykov think of capitalist wealth like this?" he asked Dubinsky.

"Soviet person like me look at capitalist excess of caviar," Dubinsky said in his less-than-perfect Pizdo, "and he think very sadly of poor proletarians in Harlem." He was hip to those questions; in Moscow, he could field questions about dissidents, about Trotsky, about agriculture, and thousands of other unpleasant questions after a liter of vodka and a sleepless night without batting an eye.

"This is true," Azh-ny admitted. "No poor people in Russia, eh? I remember this liquor store near our dormitory in Southwest—"

"Is closed now," Dubinsky said curtly. "Everybody got rich, moved to Kalinin Avenue."

"Good." Azh-ny nodded. "Very happy to hear."

Dubinsky caught a suspicious glance from Slava and looked away. *Massa Clive, he think I so drunk I got our honored guest involved in Path of Truth symposium.* He was relieved when Michelle took Azh-ny to the dance floor.

"Take it easy, Dubinsky," Slava said. "I think we've got it under wraps."

I don't like any of this, Dubinsky thought. Slava-Clive was full of shit, P. Rod Azh-ny was full of shit, Michelle Morgan was full of shit. Plus unavailable.

"That's it," Slava said the next day. "I've just bought the options to purchase one thousand contracts of pizdorvanium ninety days from now. Which means that in three months we'll write our own ticket. What do you want out of life, Dubinsky? Sorry I never asked you before. A Learjet to fly to Rio? A co-op on Central Park West? Or is it still Miss Morgan and a modest but elegant studio in a St. Luke's Place brownstone?"

"I could be perfectly happy managing a bookstore," Dubinsky said sadly.

He had worked it all out as he walked home from the World Trade Center: Truth and Happiness were incompatible. Hence, he had to reconcile himself with a life of sadness and learn to rejoice in it. A bookstore, dark and quiet, would be a perfect milieu to be sad in.

"Sounds like an excellent tax shelter to me." Slava chuckled.

Eight

The aisle seats had been removed from the passenger cabin of the DC-10, converting it into a giant first-class. But even as it was, even though he was the only passenger in the salon, Dubinsky still couldn't get a drop of booze. It was water, water everywhere—Perrier Vichy Poland Seven-Up you name it. "Mr. Rothman's instructions," explained Merrie the stewardess with a sweet smile. "Would you like to have sex instead?"

"Is the position prescribed by Mr. Rothman, too?" Dubinsky grumbled, removing his coat. Hell, sex is sex.

She got into his lap, and she unbuttoned her blouse, revealing large breasts, heretofore hidden under the uniform. He was squashed, smothered, suffocated, and rock hard in a minute, but the seat was still excruciatingly narrow, and, after thrashing about for a minute, she had to reach upward and push a button, summoning herself for assistance. Then she reached behind the seat, and the armrest receded, creating twice the space. Dubinsky closed his eyes, thinking, If United did that, he could go on the wagon tomorrow. Suddenly she stopped squirming, he opened his eyes and was told to fasten his seatbelt. "I'm sorry," she said, the sweet smile never leaving her face, "we're about to land." She girded them both with a leather belt from a sex shop on Seventh Avenue, chatting about the temperature outside which, according to her, was one hundred degrees on every scale. Dumb slut, he thought, how could that be? But the plane was already static, and she was already up and beckoning him outside.

He immediately apologized to her in silence, for indeed within seconds he was drenched with sweat, and his nose was hit with a thousand pungent smells—clams? oysters? a certain familiar *je ne sais quoi*, sweet and sour at the same time, permeated the air of Pizdo and made his heart beat twice as fast.

There were no Customs, no welcoming committees—there were no people at all in the wooden shack that housed the Mandah International Airport. Straining his eyes in hellish darkness, he read a crudely spray-painted sign that instructed the guests to leave their valuables on the plane, for the Republic of Pizdo assumed no responsibility for them.

He stepped outside and stood under the leaky tarp cover, clutching his attaché case and waiting. The night was indecipherable. The trees that looked and felt like tangled hair were heaving in the wind, and the wind was groaning something in Pizdoan he could not quite figure out. A voice came on the loudspeaker. "Limo of the United States Ambassador Mr. Dubinsky, to the front, please. Limo of the United States Ambassador Mr. Dubinsky, to the front, please. Limo of the United States Ambass—" A sound of torn tape followed. I didn't want this job, Slava, Dubinsky groaned; why did you force this upon me, my navel smells trouble. . . . A Yellow Cab pulled up, and P. Rod Azh-ny, wearing a knit cap, stepped out. "Get in, my friend." He opened the door on the driver's side. "Well, I'm sort of like an ambassador now," Dubinsky murmured, climbing inside. There was no sense complaining about this reminder of his past. Not when Rod was busy load-

ing a rocket launcher next to him. "There's trouble in the
hills, Dubinsky," he said in perfect Russian. "Your boss's investment is in great danger. You have to prove your loyalty
to Transatlantic Trading Co—go!"

Dubinsky stepped on the gas and the Dodge leaped forward,
as the sky burst up in fireworks and the air grew thick with
whistling on both sides. "Name *this* tune," Rod cracked,
steadying the launcher against the back of his seat. The phone
rang.

"Can you get that, Rod?"

"I ain't your flunkey," Rod spat, pulling the trigger.

"You pointed in the wrong direction," Dubinsky thought,
as he was catapulted into the sky. It was unusually quiet. My
eardrums are gone, he thought sadly, but since nobody has
ever survived a blast like this, who cares about eardrums?
The stars were drawing closer, and the phone kept ringing.

"Good morning," said Michelle. "Would you like to have
lunch with me today?"

He received her voice in a purely cerebral way and, secretly
relieved, registered no tremors in his body. "Did we have a
date?" he asked. "Let me check my appointment book." Perhaps that was the way for him to communicate with her:
barely awake after four hours of sleep.

"Oh, you . . ." She laughed, and he felt, helplessly, his front-
line defenses collapsing, the barbed wire tangled up on the
ground, the massive anti-Michelle traps melting into the air.

"I'll make it easy on you," she said. "I'll make it two P.M. This
way you can go back to your dreams of fame and fortune."

"My dreams are of peace and quiet," he said.

"Only too true," she sighed before hanging up.

He crawled into the bathtub and spent the remaining hours
alternately napping and leafing through a collection of Chichmek folk tales that he had bought at the Russian bookstore.
There were a few new translations from English and French,
he noted sadly; Vladimir had found someone else for his "research"; everybody was expendable. They met at a First Avenue deli, unusually quiet in the off-peak hours.

"So others you invite to Le Cirque," he said.

She laughed. "Considering your propensity to inflict damage wherever you go, it might cost a small fortune to take you to Le Cirque. They use very expensive china and crystal, and what about the dry cleaner bills for their upholstery? Be reasonable, Oleg. Besides, I wanted you to be at ease."

"I may have once had an exalted opinion of you, but you certainly have a skewed one of me." My God, he thought, I'm already talking exactly like her.

"What shall we do with you, Dubinsky?"

His fork stopped in midair, and the cole slaw spilled on the Formica table top. For the first time since their arrival he summoned the strength to look her straight in the eye. "Banish me to Boise permanently, how's that? Out of sight, out of mind, as we say in Russkiland." Looking into her eyes he felt like crying. They regarded him calmly and sadly, and he felt an even deeper sadness filling his heart. I used to be crazy about her, he thought, but now it's worse—I *like* her.

"Who is 'we'—the People of the Unites States? The City of New York? And why is it incumbent upon 'you,' whoever 'you' are, to do something with me?" Poor Jodie doesn't have a chance, he thought, his heart melting as he watched Michelle lightly blow a stray hair from her brow.

"Clive and I are concerned about your well-being."

"Oh, my God." He abruptly left the table and was about to kneel in the aisle, when she rose and said in her normal cold voice, "I'm leaving. And sticking you with the bill."

"I'm sorry." He blushed. "I apologize."

"My God." She pushed away her lox and lit a cigarette. "Why the hell are you so difficult?"

"Do you think it's easy for me to sit here in the presence of a witness of my worst debacle in years?" He bit hungrily into his pastrami. Anger had always made him hungry.

"What debacle?" She waved. "You have no right to be such a pain in the ass. Now, if you had talent, if you were a famous poet or something, then, yes, of course, people write off many things when it comes to genius. But in the brief course of our acquaintance the only discernible traces of genius I have managed to ascertain—"

He groaned at her impeccable syntax.

"—are your supersensitive skin and your tendency to throw tantrums when people behave differently from the roles you have assigned them. And that, my dear schizoid Russki, does not fill the bill." She smiled at his lost expression.

Finally he broke the silence. "Can I finish your lox?"

She pushed the plate toward him. "I regard your appetite as a sign of recovery."

"You don't know me," he said, stuffing his mouth. "I've always had great appetite. In joy and in misery." He waved to the waiter. "Can I have more cream cheese, please? Anyway," he continued, "what do you people want from me? You wake me up after a sleepless night of intense soul-searching just to present me with a memorandum—your style is still inimitable, by the way—"

"Thank you." She nodded with a grin.

"—to the effect that I'm a jerk? That I have no gifts, no redeeming qualities, that I present an obstacle to the successful resolution of your cosmic *affaire du coeur*? Ask me if I care." He smeared the cream cheese on the bagel and piled up the lox on top of it.

"Dubinsky," she said solemnly, "I'm telling you for the second time—we care—"

"*I* don't."

"We love you, Dubinsky, and we feel for you. Especially Clive. You are the best friend he's ever had. How can you be so thoughtless? How many friends have you got?"

Dubinsky moaned again, gripping his head with his hands. "What the hell do you want me to do?"

"We want you to—" She half-, no, one-tenth smiled, a hint, a *soupçon* of a smile in the anticipation of victory, and that was her mistake. "We want you to go to a psychiatrist."

"Oh, no. Uh-uh. No couch for me." He hid his hands under the table to conceal the shaking. "I had this friend, Znachar by name—"

"Clive told me. But this will be a real professional, Dubinsky. An excellent therapist, her parents came from Vilna, she would understand perfectly what bothers you—the pains of adjustment, assimilation—"

"You want to know what bothers me? *You* bother me!" He reached for his fork to get more cole slaw, it fell on the floor— not a good day to eat cole slaw, he thought. "You just waved when I mentioned the debacle! Don't you understand? I never met anyone like you, so naturally I behaved like a fool . . ."

"I'm not perfect, Dubinsky, I'm an ordinary woman, believe me, and it took me many years and many painful experiences and many hours of analysis to come to terms with my natural characteristics and to accept the way they affect people, especially immature romantic fools like yourself—"

"Don't you dare call me an immature romantic! You've got a million flaws, I could catalogue them till morning—so what?" The coffee spilled onto the saucer and overflowed it, spilling onto the table. She applied her napkin without looking at him as he continued. "Do you know what it's like for me to be scorned by you?"

"I don't scorn you, Dubinsky, I honestly don't, I feel sorry for you—"

"Same fucking thing! And then you fall for Slava, I mean Clive!"

"What's so unusual about that?" She raised her voice. "Clive is a complete man—attractive, ambitious, affectionate, articulate—"

"He's got no B-qualities?"

"—boyish, of course, but that adds to his charm! Do you know how hard it is to find a man like that in this day and age in New York? And you," she shrugged helplessly, "you have your qualities, I'm sure, otherwise Clive wouldn't think of you so highly. You're a very nice young man," she concluded in a heavily forced voice.

"*Nice? Nice?*" I'm getting an advanced case of auto-echolalia, if such a thing exists, he thought. "I have my pride, goddamn it!" he yelled. "And you treat me like a joke!"

"You behave like a joke, what do you expect?"

"You bitch, you think life is a Truffaut movie"—*I already said that if only to myself*"—some *Jules fucking Jim?*"

"No, I don't!"

Beautiful when angry—how hard it is to holler at someone you worship.

He looked aside. The cooks and the waiters were going about their business as usual: no amount of yelling could elicit a reaction from them. Grist for tomorrow's mill. "Hey Sal remember that sexy broad and a scrawny schmuck had an accent like my grandpa, they had a fight? That was something, I tell you."

"Okay," he said wearily. "You're right, it was not such a great example. In the movie, at least, she slept with both."

"What?"

"Why not?"

"You're not suggesting—"

"I'll clear it with Clive—"

"Fuck you and Clive!" She raged out of the room, throwing crumpled bills at the waiter, who pocketed them nonchalantly, muttering thanks without offering change.

Outside, Dubinsky followed her for a few yards, his heart overwhelmed with adoration for the way her behind was swinging in anger. Then he caught up with her.

"I must have been propositioned ten thousand times in my life," she said, without looking at him, "but this is definitely *sui generis*. To translate it for you, Dubinsky—"

"—one of a kind. I've been told that about myself more times than you've been propositioned, believe me." He had rejoiced over having her lose her trademark composure, but now he felt sad and bitter again. They were right; his propensity for doing and saying dumb things was truly unlimited. "Michelle," he said softly. "I apologize for the *tzouris*. Can we stop for a moment. I'm not so young anymore."

She stopped, UN flags fluttering in the wind behind her back.

"I think we can be friends," he said in the same voice.

"Really." He took her by the shoulders and his heart stirred over the trusting way her body softened and clung to his touch. And they hugged and kissed each other on the cheeks, but then he kissed her on the lips, and the taste of her mouth connected with the stirring well below his heart, and he knew—without the smallest doubt—that what he had told her a minute ago was a complete, shameless lie.

Dubinsky stayed in his room for hours or maybe days. Windows were shut firmly, and a DO NOT DISTURB/DERANGEZ PAS/ NON DISTURBARE sign warded off unwanted solace. Sometimes he sat on his bed, and sometimes on the floor; sometimes he paced, or, rather, stumbled—all five steps' distance from the window to the door; and sometimes he just leaned against the window and stared at the streets outside, gray and baleful. At the start, it took him forty-five minutes sharp to arrive at the plane of the desired intoxication, and he had been cruising ever since. As dusk descended on the room, its walls stark and unadorned by Japanese prints or MOMA posters, he played his tapes: Dylan, Vysotzky, Simon and Garfunkel. Sipping and puffing, he stopped the tape only to talk—and he talked a blue streak: to himself, to Vladimir, to Znachar, to Nonna, even to Manankov and Sokolov, his ex-schoolmates, or, rather, their navels. But mostly he talked to Jodie, perhaps because no matter how often he called her, no one answered. He didn't know her, he knew that, but he also knew that it had been in her presence that, if only for a brief moment, he felt the ease and the lightness that he had not felt for a long time, not since Moscow and his room floor and Remy and Vladimir and Slava.

The windows were far from soundproof; on the contrary, they felt porous, even spongy, sucking in the city symphony of horns and sirens and boom boxes. He knew that life around him teemed with parties and affairs and scandals and deaths, but he didn't see anything. In Moscow, waiting for a visa, he had a purpose. He was powerless to do anything about it, but he knew that the problem would resolve itself, one way or another. He could look forward to America, where he would tread the Path of Truth; now it changed to the Freeway, somehow he took a wrong exit and got lost in the maze of side streets; lost so badly he didn't even know whether it made any sense to try to find his way back. As he had discovered on the plane from Seattle, it was irrelevant which route he traveled. The road came to an end, and it was useless to retrace his steps and try to find out who had steered him wrong. People lived their own lives, for better or for worse; some strove hard, like Slava; some coasted, like Vladimir or Konstantin, and if their paths crossed Dubinsky's, and he got bounced right and left, was it their fault that he was such a lightweight?

He realized that he could theorize till the Judgment Day, playing Cato and Cicero and Senate all at once, but no matter how he phrased or structured it, there was but one center to the labyrinth: something had happened to him; only a few months ago the world was his oyster, and now he felt spooned out of it and dropped on the floor. Besides Jodie, Slava was the only person who could pick him up, but he was also the last person Dubinsky wanted to talk to, for how could he say a word to Slava without lying? Without a shameful admission about Michelle? Do you have to be a devout Christian to feel bad about breaking certain commandments? Moses was a lawgiver, trying to cover as much ground as possible on the coveting score. Neighbors you can have a-plenty, but best friends?

He called Jodie from home, and he called her from the Ukrainian bars in the East Village, where he ventured late at night to watch the crazy mix of ugly-looking punks and drunken old East Europeans. But one night a gruffy male voice told him that Jodie was out and what was the message? Please don't hurt her, Dubinsky wanted to say, seeing in his mind's eye the lout who had met her at the airport.

Outside a bar on East Seventh, he shared a joint with a silent Hungarian, with whom he sometimes shot pool. Zoltan was not silent by nature, but he spoke ten words of English, and Dubinsky's Hungarian was nonexistent. This made Zoltan a perfect partner to share a joint with in the minispace between the bar and the street, disregarding the angry looks from the Gutzul, i.e., Western Ukrainian, bartender. The Gutzul had the face of a convict, and, as far as Dubinsky was concerned, had indeed executed hundreds of Jews-Communists-*Moskals* in the past.

"You like this?" Dubinsky pointed at the joint.

"Yes, yes," Zoltan muttered gratefully. "Is very good."

They fell silent. "Budapest," Dubinsky ventured.

"Ooh," Zoltan drawled dreamily. "Budapest very good, very beautiful town."

"New York?"

"New York." Zoltan swayed his head sideways, indicating uncertainty. "New York is good, too. Very good." As if Dubinsky was with the Immigration.

"Petefi?" Dubinsky decided to enliven the exchange by bringing up the name of a classical Hungarian poet. He wondered how the hell he knew things like that and why was his head at all times full of useless knowledge—had he spent his life in training for some ultimate game show?

"*Ach*, Petefi." Zoltan rolled up his eyes and launched into a recital.

Not a pretty language, Hungarian, Dubinsky thought. What the hell could Zoltan have been in Hungary? An attorney? A journalist? A Pizdo researcher? Most likely.

Zoltan finished reciting with a flourish and looked at Dubinsky expectantly.

"Very fine, Petefi," Dubinsky nodded. "Very beautiful."

"Yes, yes." Zoltan sighed. "He says, 'Freedom must,' oh, I don't know how it is in English . . ." He scratched his head mournfully. "Sorry. My English . . ."

"I know what he means," Dubinsky said.

"Petefi is the greatest," Zoltan said confidently.

"You bet," Dubinsky said. "Check this out: 'A poet's dead; a hostage of his honor/He fell, by gossip vilified/Lead in his chest and thirst for vengeance/And now wilted is his proud head . . .'" He could not remember the next line for the life of him.

Zoltan waited politely.

"That's it," Dubinsky said. Dammit, how could he forget, it was in the sixth grade, their teacher Nina Ilyinichna, a nice Jewish lady with a moustache and a consumptive complexion . . .

"Beautiful," Zoltan nodded. "Pushkin?"

"Close," Dubinsky said. "Lermontov." She once gave him a B and lectured him for an hour afterwards. . . . "Let's go get some beer," he said.

The bar clientele had changed that night—there were large groups of Poles and Czechs now, with a sprinkling of Hungarians; with a few exceptions, all were Dubinsky's age. Everything about them was exaggerated: their leather jackets, their cocky poses, the pitch of their voices. Freedom, he thought. They are enjoying Americanski freedom. From Dubinsky and Borzoi and Volkodav. They have created their own Bratislawa and Cracow. They don't know this country, they're determined to remain what they are, they pride themselves on deriding American barbarism, they want to break out of their ghettoes and move to California. There were a couple of young natives in the corner who looked like San Murray to him. Fascinated and awed by the cosmopolitan spirit of the place, they talked in low, subdued voices. It's your country, dummies, he sneered; you're the ones who should be talking loud.

He ordered in Russian. The bartender, an elderly Polish woman, brought him his beer, silently looking away. Aha, he thought, so she knows. Certain things you don't forget. He took his beer to the phone booth and called Seattle again.

This time it was her.

"This is Oleg," he said. "Remember? I changed my name to Ofoot." She laughed, a quiet easy laugh that seemed to have come from the very bottom of her being and made Dubinsky's hands tremble and spill the beer on his jeans.

"Sure I remember."

"What are you doing to me, I keep calling you, your cat told me you moved to Alaska, and now I spilled my beer—"

"Are you in New York?"

"I'm not sure, I think I'm in Miszkolz or Poznan, our tank brigade is leaving for a major offensive any minute now—"

"You haven't changed—"

"—please tell me you love me—"

"Oh, Oleg," she said in a broken voice, "you just don't understand anything, anything at all. Why should I tell you anything?"

"You never called me—"

"I'm trying to put my life in order—look, I can't talk to you right now, give me your number, I'll call you back—"

"You have my number!"

"I don't know where it is. Why did it have to be a business card. God. A cocktail napkin, a matchbook—*but a business card* . . ." The man's voice came on in the background, but Dubinsky could not make out the words. "Please don't call me again," she sniffled, "it was all a mistake, promise—I can't talk to you right now, I really can't—"

She hung up.

Well goddam. Fuck me with a Kalashnikov.

Dubinsky sat in the offensive yellow dusk of the booth, considering his meager options. Someone knocked on the door. He looked. It was a carousing brother Slav.

"*Psya krev!*" Dubinsky yelled. "*Kurva! Do prdela!*" He ran out of Polish/Czech obscenities and switched to Russian. "*Poshol na khui, mudak!*"

The man knocked again, his face turning red. "*Telefon*, please."

"*Ty kto takoy, blyad?*" Dubinsky barked, opening the door. "Do you know you're talking to Lieutenant Dubinsky, First Armored Corps? My tank is double-parked across the street! Hands up! Where's the underground printshop!"

The man, stunned, stepped aside. Dubinsky left the booth and leaned against the wall. His head swam, it soared over the thick clouds of smoke, bouncing off the peeling ceiling. "*Ya* MIG 25," he continued in Russian into his helmet microphone. "Maintaining a steady course *nach* Praga. Meeting no resistance from Czech revisionists whatsoever. Asking permission to normalize the strategic East Seventh Street location from hostile socialists with human faces. Over and out." And continued in his grandfather's croaking voice: "Permission granted, Lieutenant. Punish the human fuckfaces with the Sword of the Socialist Revolution. My cavalry's approaching the outskirts of Sofia. Belgrade will be ours in twenty-four hours. Over and out." He looked over the room. The silence was complete. The faces, carefree five minutes ago, eyed him with hatred. What have I done, he thought; no one, but no one has ever hated me in my entire life, I have been humiliated, dumped, ditched, walked on, but hated—never. That's progress, said Znachar, sipping his gin and tonic in the corner. People have strong feelings about you; that reflects favorably on your personality. They understood every word, said Borzoi, nodding. They've all been taught Russian at school. They can't help understanding it. They forgot who the boss is, said Volkodav, coming in from behind the Budweiser sign. You reminded them. You done good. And I am very happy to have issued you a certificate of good pedestrianship, said the militia sergeant with a straight face.

Suddenly a Pole/Czech broke out in laughter. *"Russki piany! Russki durak!"*

Catching every other word, Dubinsky grasped the meaning: Russian drunk, Russian fool . . .

Now they were all laughing, chuckling, giggling, guffawing: *"Davai, Russki! Yescho!"*—egging him on for more. *Oh what a show it was the former colonial governor making a drunken fool of himself go ahead Dubinsky one of them is already ordering a beer for you sing a Moscow Nights for them dance a kazachok*

Zoltan materialized out of the smoke, dragging along a friend, a brunette with long hair and striking Gypsy eyes and a laughing mouth—"Is my friend Oleg—he knows Petefi, Lermontov—this is my friend Maria—"

"Fuck Petefi!" Dubinsky roared, climbing on a chair and grabbing a pool cue for a baton. "Thundering with fire and glittering with steel," he started in a shaking voice, "The machines will rage into the march/When Comrade Stalin sends us into battle/And First Marshal will lead us . . ." His voice broke, but he picked it up again: "Thus go the Soviet tankists into battle/The sons of their great Motherland . . ."

The audience roared, stomped their feet, banged their bottles on the tables—but two older men, their faces distorted in fury, went for him—he tried to duck, he fell off the chair, they grabbed him by the jacket . . . *"Nie, nie, ne zdes,'"* hollered the bartender, pointing to the street. They dragged him across the floor, kicking and punching him alternately—as he smiled happily, finally someone slammed the door for him—and tossed him outside, on the steps between the garbage can and the railing. "The junkheap of history," he recalled the old *Pravda* cliché, reserved for imperialist warmongers. He felt his body for damages, they were minor: the left side hurt, the brow was split and oozing blood, but his head was clear, although his feet were welded securely to the railing—Jodie you bitch, he thought; what the hell do you mean, "mistake"? I made a mistake, not you, why do you usurp my prerogative to fuck up? And I dumped Linda for you and I suffered through Sandy for you and even settled for a Michelle-less existence, all in the anticipation of your asking me whether I was all right in that damn bank and your cat rubbing against my leg and us lying together at dawn, down to the last minute when you waited to make sure that my car started . . .

Some fucking mistake, he muttered, stumbling and falling and rising and falling again. Some fucking mistake. Thank you New York for being such a fucked-up place that no one cares if a guy can't keep his balance, it's all par for the course, I'm exercising my inviolable Constitutional right to fall into this very puddle and kneel in it and pray to a God unknown who at this very moment is having a nice breakfast of French toast with maple syrup on Alpha Centauri.

"Want a date?"

He looked up and saw a leprous, leonine face, eroded by disease, patches of skin hanging loosely, pale and deathlike in the light of the streetlamp. His eyes slid further down: there were masses of flesh, possibly mammaries, descending into a marsupial sac.

"Want a date?" the creature repeated in a whiny, adenoidal voice. Its torso ceased shortly before the ground and was connected to it by two pale, mud-covered, Ionic columns. The columnar knees were covered with scabs, and the toes were bleeding in shocking pink.

"E.T. call home," Dubinsky murmured. This was the real thing.

"Do you want to fuck?"

It fucks? Dubinsky was seized by a paroxysm of curiosity. What would be born of this coupling? A griffin, a centaur, a sphinx? Most likely a lizard, or a pachyderm-sized winged lemur. "Yes," he said ardently, and started taking off his shirt, fully prepared to donate his sperm to astrozoological science.

"You crazy?" She had trouble breathing. "You wanna be arrested? You got fifteen dollars for a hotel? C'mon, let me help you up."

"*Une geste humaine,*" he muttered, as he struggled to get up, helped by her paws, "*pleine de beauté au clair de lune . . .*"

"You German? Let's go."

But his feet weighed a ton each. "Leave me alone," he said. "Call for a priest, Lutheran or Shintoist, whichever comes first." He collapsed against a cast-iron fence and held on to it. There was static in his head; a thousand voices tried to break through, but the dial was jammed.

"You wanna fuck or what?" She scratched her head, presumably in hesitation, but then went on with evident pleasure.

"Let's get married," he moaned, "let's have a household, a dishwasher, Father Fyodor Mikhailovich will pronounce us man and wife, Jodie I swear I didn't mean to split your head with an ax I'm permanently insane—"

"Let's go to the parking lot." She put her arm around him and dragged him along the wet, glistening pavement.

He moaned apologies to Petefi; he pledged his body to *Solidarnosz*, and his unwritten, unmouthed, unconceived verses to the Czechoslovakian National Home for Socialist Unwed Mothers. At the same time E.T.'s mother propped him against the bumper of an Oldsmobile Cutlass '75, four doors, air-conditioning, unzipped his fly, and fished for its contents.

"Can't find it," she said. "You got a cock?"

"You ever read Camus?" He tried to change the subject.

"I found it." Her paws, rough and stubborn, went to work, and after some hesitation, it sprang to action, and then she stopped. "Give me the money. Ten bucks."

Miracle of miracles, Dubinsky thought, precisely eleven dollars. "One dollar tip may be made available for excellence in performance." He held a torn bill away from her. "Down with your drawers, strumpet!" he shouted, noticing that she kept pulling at it, in the hope that he would come prematurely.

She turned her back on him and held on to the rear door of a Chevy van, bringing up her rump and hoisting her dress. She was not wearing anything underneath. I'll never find it, he thought, regarding the curveless, plasmoid mountain of jelly in front of him. I might end up drilling her kneecap. My God, I never fucked—if fuck is the word—I never stuck it into anything like this.

She pulled him by the penis and inserted it. Dubinsky, seated on the bumper, watched with fascination the heaving of the mass in front of him. There was swishing of tires and honking of horns less than twenty feet away from them. The mass was uttering odd sounds, which he felt he should record and send to *Name That Tune.*

"You gon' come soon?" she inquired. "I'm freezin'."

"Yes, of course," he said with mechanical politeness, gave it a few weary pushes, and came quite satisfactorily.

"Okay." She straightened up, picking the dollar bill up from the ground. "See ya." And she was gone.

Dubinsky remained sitting on the Olds bumper, looking at the sky, completely dark—no Alpha Centauri or wherever E.T.'s mother had come from could be seen. The clock on the insurance company building on Union Square struck half past four. He was completely sober. He started zipping himself up—his penis, a stubby remnant of his libido, had already withdrawn itself into the warmth of his pants—but the fly got stuck. He inspected it and saw a condom, caught in the metal. He had been too far gone to notice her slip it on. A two-bit whore has got more common sense than Dubinsky, he told himself, starting on his way home.

Nine

Everything happened as Slava had predicted: in late August, as the city asphalt melted and the air grew heavy and blue and the hydrants spouted water at the happy underprivileged kids and the plaintive sounds of a saxophone flowed over Washington Square—the ships disappeared, the pizdorvanium prices went up, and Slava, doing a Cheshire Cat impression, purred *Sell* into the phone.

He was slightly disappointed, for the market proved to be more indifferent to pizdorvanium than he had hoped; still, even after subtracting the grease he had paid to Azh-ny, the profit was more than adequate.

With Michelle, he was positively triumphant. They were living an active social life: they went out to the right places and ate with the right people, who had graduated from the right prep/undergraduate/business schools and were wearing the right clothes from the right stores and working in the right investment houses on the Street. And what exactly were Mr. Rothman's credentials up to now? He came from Russia;

he was a reflection of this nutty Michelle's taste for the exotic.

"They're gonna lick my boots any day now."

"Of course they will," Michelle said, massaging his neck.

"They never had to deal with Georgians or Assyrians or toy store managers."

"Goodness no."

"They would've cringed and cracked and run for cover. They would've wetted their shorts."

She ran her tongue down his spine, making him shiver in the early heat of a Manhattan summer morning. "My dearest Clive, *of course* they're a bunch of little boys, *of course* you're twice the man any of them can ever hope to be, no matter how much *Esquire* they read or squash they play. Now, why do you have to pay so much attention to them? You're on your way; you know that, and I know that. Why can't you just stop being a petulant Dubinsky and be quiet and listen and maybe learn something?"

"I can and I do," he sighed. He didn't like her tone. Whose side was she on anyway? "But humility disagrees with me."

"As well it should." She put her arms around him, pressing her breasts against his back, and, with pleasure, felt his heartbeat quickening. "I wouldn't have it any other way."

"I feel on a roll," he said dreamily. "Let's go to Vegas, all three of us."

"If you want to be real tacky," she said, "Atlantic City is just the place. Personally, I'd rather give an end-of-summer party in the Hamptons."

"I've never been to Vegas," said Dubinsky, who would go anywhere to escape the muggy city.

"We are going to Vegas," Slava concluded. "Nights of wild abandon. It will be better than Sochi, Dubinsky."

Within five minutes aboard, Dubinsky hated Slava's guts. How dared he have exposed him, Dubinsky, to the indignities of the coach class when all this time there existed this Eden called first-class? But then the champagne arrived (the only civilized way to open the day, he concluded), and he relaxed. There was ample room for walking and stretching, there were no drunken football fans practicing their cheers, no stone-faced senior citizens playing gin across the aisle, no preadolescents crawling all over the floor. Most important, the booze was free, and started on its way into your hand the moment you lifted your empty glass.

"If Vladimir came to America," Slava said, "he would enjoy flying first-class more than cashing airline tickets."

"If Vladimir started flying first-class, the airlines would have to start charging for the booze."

They fell silent, momentarily immersed in the memories.

"It will be even better, Dubinsky." Slava finished his champagne and cleared the table for the soufflé. "You'll see."

"*Plus ça change* . . . ," Michelle drawled sarcastically from behind her *Times*, her lips still pursed in disdain for yet another editorial plea to keep the welfare rolls intact. She looked as elegant as ever in her Moldavian peasant blouse. She regarded Vegas as a gift to Dubinsky, and had persuaded Slava to fly to Puerto Vallarta afterwards, just the two of them. Dubinsky, a proud holder of a Green Card, was told he needed a travel document that he, naturally, had no time to get; he demurred without hard feelings. (Slava, of course, had all documents, from inoculation certificates for Pizdo to a dogsled driver's license for Greenland, ready at all times).

Since the hug in front of the UN, Michelle and Dubinsky had taken pains to avoid each other's eyes. This new stage in what he termed, in more generous moments, their "relationship," intrigued and scared him. He was more used to her now, and no longer dropped silverware at the sight of her; now that he had contributed to the success of Slava's venture, he considered the guilt account closed. The plans were under way for a spring wedding, and he had no desire to disrupt them. But the knowledge that under favorable circumstances there was a possibility of his going to bed with her still lingered, and God only knew what would come out of that. He might start dropping steaming pots and breaking off the doorknobs again.

Dubinsky looked around him; everybody was wearing a tie; everybody was going over the stock columns. He panicked. But loading up in his usual manner in front of Slava and especially Michelle for five hours. . . . Desperate situations required desperate remedies. Locating a joint in his wallet, he resolutely headed for the bathroom. It was occupied; for some reason, he relaxed, and proceeded to the coach-class cabin.

Slava was hanging out with Michelle's crowd nowadays. More than one martini was a sign of alcoholism to them; a toke taken outside a party was either a sign of being stuck in the sixties or a hint that at the other times the person was using a needle for his highs. Who knew what kind of tight-ass crap Slava could have contracted from those characters? We're floating apart, Dubinsky sadly thought, staring at himself in the mirror. In the gray hospital-like light, his face looked as much like an old addict's as that of a Rolling Stone. The plane rocked; he had to steady himself against the wall. Could he perhaps talk Slava into getting into the movie business and developing a remake of *Last Tango*, with the against-the-radiator scene shot in an airplane bathroom? They had done it in *Emmanuelle*, but it was in the first-class, with plenty of room. It lacked the cramped quarters, the urgency, the drama of the coach-class bathroom. . . . He realized he was procrastinating; he could not go back to his seat. Even physically— the plane rocked again, the seat-belt edict lit up, a loudspoken voice came through the humming, exhorting the passengers to return to their seats. But more so because he just could not stand the idea of four hours tête-à-tête with Slava and Michelle. I've boxed myself into a corner, he thought, as the plane wobbled, depositing him on the john. The door was knocked on, and an inquiry about his well-being was made. I better fake it, should they crash the door, he thought, dropping his pants to his ankles. The voice insisted on an update of his condition. A fat fucking lot you care, he said, suddenly gasping for air. This is it, he thought in despair, watching a trailer of his life playing in his mind; would the plane crash first or would he die of suffocation with self-pity, going straight into the *Guinness Book of World Records?*

The thought made him thirsty, pronto. There's no percentage in dying if you can have another beer, he concluded, putting out the joint. And then he screamed.

The banging on the door resumed. "I'M FINE!" he yelled, moaning under his breath and inspecting the damage. Ashes from his joint had fallen on his penis.

Dear Lord, there's a glitch in your system, Dubinsky said, exposing his woeful stub to the lukewarm water that was meant to be cold. Yes, I thought of *Last Tango*, and *Emmanuelle*, but I pulled down my pants as an alibi! Even with Michelle sitting a few feet away, I had absolutely no intention of jerking off! Dear Lord, if you're so confused about my motives—unless you are not, and I *did* intend to jerk off, but couldn't you make it more obvious next time? —how can you expect *me* to have any clarity about myself?

He stumbled back to his seat, still wincing from pain and staring at his feet. He was convinced that pinstripe suits were, to a man, Baptists and Hassidim and Catholics and Protestants of every denomination, who could see, only too clearly, the burning scarlet on his manhood.

It could have been midnight or it could have been noon; time stood still in the casino. Dubinsky was steadily falling off the chair, and the bartender made no effort to stop him, for he could not touch a guest until the latter's body actually connected with the floor. Dubinsky stood in the surf of the North Arctic Ocean, shivering in the air-conditioned chill, holding his ground under the crushing blows of the waves that came one after another in a geometric succession. He stood there like Jake "Raging Bull" La Motta, bruised and bloodied but still vertical. His head was a vacuum, and in it, thoughts were having a gang fight. They were not his thoughts, they were the lawless intruders, trespassing on his brain curves, treading on his gray matter, and stomping on it mercilessly. They were the misbegotten offspring of three lines of cocaine, several 'ludes, and unmeasured volumes of white wine and yellow whiskey whose name he could neither imagine nor pronounce. It was Vegas, and everything was available before you could think of it. The cocaine had been delivered to their suite, 'ludes had been purchased in the elevator, and he had a distinct memory of being offered a quickie on the golf course.

He had no idea what had brought him to the golf course; somewhere along the line he must have wanted to help Slava wrap up the final deal, the deal that would release Slava from his mad, insane, all-consuming quest for money and help him channel his energy into searching for ancient Sumerian palimpsests. The Final Deal would also provide Dubinsky with his walking papers out of this mad, insane, slavery-friendship and put him into the dank peaceful dusk of a *librairie* where he would sip Drambuie and Cointreau, and would be in the same exquisite buzzing state, but at least he would be definitely out of trouble and have a firm knowledge of his whereabouts in time and space.

The woman on the golf course was tall, delectable, and offensive.

"So gimme the money," she said.

"No cash," he said. "From now on it's strictly municipal bonds."

"I don't deal in those. You shoulda told me before you brought me here."

"I brought you here for the Final Deal."

"A hundred-dollar quickie is no big deal in this town. Buzz off, chump." And she walked away, cursing.

"Wait," he cried out, "I'd like to take a polygraph test, right now!" He followed her in a rowboat, running around in sandtraps, trying to restart the engine, which he must have transplanted from his leased Dodge. He looked for the Truth Fairway sign, but it was too dark. Yet he had no doubt that the shining edifice straight ahead was exactly that—The Tower of Truth.

He entered the lobby and placed his bet. "Ten dollars on Truth, please."

The ball stopped on black, the croupier raked the chips in; Dubinsky looked around: it was a hotel casino, and the freeway traffic was backed up for miles.

But somehow he had made it to the bar, and, if he was lucky, it was the bar of his hotel; whereas, if he was not, he could already be in Mexico and thus eligible for deportation *para los Federales.*

"*Muy bien,*" he said to the bartender. "*Dos olla mordidas* to go."

"Amaretto?" the man asked.

"*Amarcord.*" Dubinsky nodded. He vividly remembered the story of his life as it unfolded on the multiscreen panorama of the bottles behind the man's back. Bilo Mitzne, White Strong, his fourteenth birthday in Kiev (what was he doing in Kiev?). Kubanskaya, high school graduation day. Pertzovka, matriculation day. Kinzmarauli and Black & White, his first orgy. Walnut-flavored Bols, Nonna's favorite. Remy and Napoleon, evenings on the floor in Moscow. He had to find Slava and make sure it was Remy, because it could well have been Martin.

But Slava was busy, he found he had a gambler's streak, he kept doubling in blackjack, he threw pass after pass at the dice table, he, with proper seriousness, held on to the shoehorn in the baccarat pit. Dubinsky had no interest in gambling. Luck was a lady; he had given up on them.

Ah, Vegas the greatest con of all times. Dubinsky's lungs could not take the heat and the fumes outside. David Brenner he could watch on TV; the casino was all that was left. He could not stand it. He could not stand the blue-haired centenarian women who jumped on their stools when their hands went bust; the men with half-inch-high foreheads playing the slots with a concentration of an Einstein cracking relativity; the full-chested dime-store Fate, who was forlornly spinning the Wheel of Fortune. There were no takers; she had blond curls around a madonna face, bloated in the boredom of her depravity; she was chewing gum and from time to time popped a bubble, secretively covering this teenage transgression with her hand.

There was no telling what had brought Dubinsky to this place in the universe at this particular moment nor what had placed him in his current state of mind. Had it been Borzoi, Slava, or neurotic Sandy who never paid the bill that he forgot to send? Had it been the 'ludes, the cocaine, or the Scotch whose name he could not pronounce? Or had it been the kaleidoscope of the City of Evil; its towers, the kissing cousins of Electric Avenue; its lights that never went out; its air of unbridled greed and easy winnings and desperate losses? Vegas was one place that Dubinsky would rather read about than experience—still, what had it been? The bartender remained silent.

"You're the bartender," Dubinsky addressed him respectfully. "Tell me, what's wrong with this world?"

"Whatever it is," the man replied in the kind of esoteric tone found only in expensive self-help hardcovers, "whatever it is, it's right here."

"I don't like it," Dubinsky said. "I don't like it at all."

The man shrugged. "Who's forcing ya? It's a free country."

Freedom is too much for me, Dubinsky said to himself, carefully separating his *toches* from the barstool. I'm not a leader, I'm a member of the herd, even in the middle of all this freedom. I'm being cruelly, expensively enslaved by Mr. Clive Rothman and his conniving poster fiancée Michelle Morgan, the Pirate's Daughter.

"I'll go for a walk," he said to the bartender. "I need some air. Will you be open when I get back?"

"We're always open."

"That's good. What happens if I kill someone on the way."

"You'll go to jail."

"Well, find me a good lawyer while I'm gone." Dubinsky smiled pleasantly and waved; the man's face was tense as he was trying to photograph Dubinsky's features with the camera of his eyes.

I was only kidding, Dubinsky murmured; why should I kill anyone, no matter how stupid, greedy, and insignificant? I am a humanist, damn it. Otherwise I could not be thrown off my orbit constantly; I'm but a little asteroid traveling from one gravity field to another. In my universe one cannot slam doors; they all open automatically.

"Sir." He felt a hand on his shoulder. "Are you all right?"

Dubinsky suppressed a groan. The man had Volkodav's nose and Ovchar's ears. "I'm fine. Please remove your hand immediately. This is a public place, I am a guest of this hotel, and I have my rights."

"All right, son." The man was nonplussed. "Look at it my way: you are walking around, stumbling, talking to yourself."

"I have no intention of ever looking at anything your way." *Swallow back this spit, Dubinsky. Now.*

"You know, if you're lost or not feeling well, I'll be happy to help you back to your room. Just to help you stay out of trouble."

The man was a pro, he talked cool, he was not about to be put off by Dubinsky's righteous-citizen act. His job was to prevent trouble. Nip it in the bud. Before it blossomed and stank up the room. Before Dubinsky assaulted a guest. That fucking coke-dealing asshole of a bartender. Covering his ass in the hope of a payoff.

"I'm in perfectly good condition, officer. And if you do not immediately remove yourself from my vicinity, I will be forced to address proper authorities."

"Meaning you'll come to me, son."

"Meaning the Police Department of the City of Las Vegas."

"All right, son. Where are you from, by the way? Israel?"

"This is none of your f—" *Hold it right there Dubinsky don't let this cossack this* moussor *as we called them back home don't let this garbage trap you.* "Is it an interrogation?"

"No." The man squeezed a Jack Palance grin out of his broad, bored face. "You're on your own, son. But do take my advice and stay out of trouble."

Sobered up, Dubinsky looked around. A blue-haired hundred-fifty-year-old woman in a shocking-pink blouse and lime-green tights dropped her dentures on the table in amazement over her second ace. Dubinsky fled.

There was some unpronounceable whiskey left in the suite, he remembered, as he entered the elevator, shaking from head to foot. I'm not going to that bar, the posse is on the alert there; I need to feel the warm glass of the bottleneck between my lips— What hidden homoerotic tendency is this? he cringed, stabbed by a sudden inexplicable pang of homophobic hysteria. No—a very interesting half-exposed full breast came into view within a foot of him, and his nether sensor promptly registered an interest therein. As well as in a well-painted attractive face above the breast, right next to the health club schedule on the wall.

"Hi," moved the attraction's lips. "You a guest here?"

"I must be," he said uncertainly, recalling his past fears. "Which hotel is it?"

"The Gobi Inn." She nimbly switched her gum from cheek to cheek. "Wanna party? What's your room number?"

He frisked himself and came up with the key.

"Hmm, penthouse—I can squeeze you in in half an hour. 'Bye, cutie."

She blew him a kiss as she left the elevator. He rode on, maintaining a respectable erection.

He found the bottle on the table and embraced it with his lips. He took deep gulps, one after another, caressing its cool glass, its polished engraved label. Lochoglockomorra. Excellent. If I wasn't a Jew I would be a Mick. The only thing to be. If not Leopold Bloom, then Stephen Dedalus. Or Icarus. What's Icarus? Oh, yes, a make of a Hungarian bus. A huge one. Why not Petefi? Go get the shit beaten out of you again, Dubinsky. Go ahead. He stood near the window, watching the lights float uncertainly—now at him, now away from him. He read them—*Dubinsky Schmuck, Dubinsky Lost*. I didn't even gamble, he said; just the ten bucks on Truth. . . . And you've lost. You had a thousand options and you picked all the wrong ones. You scored big while rowing on Clive's trireme; what's next? Whatever Clive comes up with next? Then you fly to Rio, another penthouse suite, Christ with a cross, the Sugar Loaf, do you know enough Portuguese to read, *Dubinsky loco? Dubinsky perso?*

"Clive?" Michelle's voice came from the upstairs bedroom.

"No, goddamnit!" Dubinsky hollered, sending the bottle crashing against the wall. "I'm not your fucking superman Clive! That's Dubinsky el Schmucko!"

"Oleg." She came down the stairs. "What's wrong? Did you lose all your money?"

He shook his head. He had to sit down on the floor. The sight of her neon-illuminated loose brown hair made him hide his head in his hands.

"What's wrong?" She came up to him, placed her hand on his hair.

He shook all over, tightening his grip on his temples, peering into the darkness of the rug in front of him.

"Are you crying?" She ran her hand through his hair. "Are you sick?"

"Yeah, I'm sick all right."

"You're just being your usual self, only more so."

He rose to his knees and reached under her nightgown, he ran his hands along her hips and he pressed his lips to her belly. She was bed-warm, her skin was sheer silk, smooth curves, freshly paved, no bumps, no cracks. He dove under the cloth, kissed her on the upper thigh.

"Don't Oleg . . . Clive will be here soon . . ."

How many of them had said no and meant yes but he always thought they had meant no and bit his lips afterwards but he had no doubts this time, as he felt her legs shake and buckle.

He licked her and licked her, and his tongue would not stop as he ran it up and down and in and out, slurping and feeling loose hairs in his mouth. He was self-absorbed, finally his mouth was causing no trouble, finally it was good for something . . . all the sundaes in the world, all the chocolate truffles strawberry cheesecakes banana splits charlotte russe could not beat this poignant sourness . . . her knees kept buckling

and quaking, she moaned or was it the hum of the wind outside or was it the blood in his vessels, were her legs seashells?
was he inside of her? as her hands came down on his throat
and pressed it . . . hold it, he gasped, that's more than I
bargained for. . . . His neck was killing him and her hands
were choking him, what is it, even when it is so good, something has to go wrong, oh but she had to be weird, she was
too perfect in every other way . . . I'm gonna die, he thought,
biting her on the clitoris. She shook, loosening her hold, and
he withdrew; panting, he collapsed on the rug. He watched
her kneel in front of the window and press her head to the
glass. "You almost killed me, you bitch." She tried to say
something, but her breath was too short for her to articulate.

The knock came on the door. She shrieked.

"Don't be silly, Clive has a key." He came to the door. "Yes?"

"It's Cheri," she sang.

"I can't party tonight," he said, "there's been an accident
here. We're expecting the sheriff any minute."

"Oh, shit." And she was heard no more.

He staggered to the bathroom, drank a glass of water, and
brought one for Michelle. She sat on the floor now, with her
back to the window. She drank it in one gulp, and he brought
her another one. Then he sat down next to her; his face was
still wet with her. She reached for his hand and kissed it. "It
was lovely."

"You should go to a shrink," he said. "This choking
thing—"

"Shut up, Dubinsky. Or go back to your whore. Just don't
spoil this moment. I have a problem . . . we can talk about it
later—show some generosity, for Chrissake. This is so perfect."

Generosity? From him? Toward her? "Yeah, sure," he murmured. If only the door were a little closer, if only his legs
were a little steadier, God, how he would slam it. *Con forza.*
Con tutta la forza. Off the fucking hinges it would go, shat-
tering the room up to 5.9 on the Richter scale.

Well, that's it, he said to her silently. I don't love you any-

more, Michelle. This obsession had always had overtones of
danger for me, but now I can see how this could be fatal.
Crazy I may be; suicidal, never. Her hand ran down his stomach, reached into his pants. In the heat of the moment he had
forgotten all about it. And, as she closed her lips around it,
the key turned in the lock.

"What are you guys doing, sitting in the dark?" Slava turned
on the lights. Dubinsky squinted. Slava's face was a relief
map, with wrinkles rising and falling all over it.

Slava gave them a curious look. The picture was somewhat
odd, the two of them sitting on the floor, leaning against the
window; Dubinsky fully dressed, Michelle in her nightgown.
Slava sniffed. "Dubinsky, did you spill that Irish whiskey?"

"Some."

"Asshole."

"Did you lose a lot?"

"Some." *Eighteen thousand, how's that, you jerks.* He wanted
to make a wisecrack about how they might as well have sex
while they were on the floor, but he was too tired. Tired and
upset. Money was nothing. He had had more faith in his luck,
that's all. Now he knew better. His luck did not hold. His
mouth was too dry for speeches.

"Good night." He climbed the stairs to the bedroom.

They sat immobile for a few minutes. Then she said, "Good
night, Oleg," and kissed him, gently and moistly, below his
ear. "You're a darling," she whispered. He put his hand on
her breast—small, full, and taut—and gave it a tentative
squeeze. "Not now," she whispered. "Later." And she left him,
her feet climbing the stairs silently, an apparition illuminated
by the same flickering neon lights.

Dubinsky sat there for a while. His head was clear and
empty again. Then he crawled to his bedroom, which must
have taken him awhile, too, for by the time he started the
climb into his bed the sun, strikingly orange, was rising between the buildings. Wishing he were less tired in order to
enjoy the spectacle, he crawled forth to the window and pulled
the heavy drapes shut. Then he crawled back into bed, and

almost immediately, in the emptiness of his head, there emerged a dot of a thought, and, as he was falling asleep, it grew and expanded; and for a split moment before he did fall asleep he knew what it was: *the first thing I'm going to do tomorrow is to leave this place.*

He had spent too much time getting out of bed, too much time standing in the shower that left him with his skin wet and his ears humming. He had spent too much time composing his good-bye note (he settled on "See ya in the Apple," terse and cheerful); too much time buying aspirin and waiting for his orange juice and coffee in the coffee shop downstairs. And now he was in the airport, and the next flight to New York was not due for another three hours. The bar, for a baffling reason, was closed. He glanced at the schedule; there was a flight to Seattle leaving in twenty minutes. He came up to the counter and produced the company American Express card. They should call it Freedom Card, he thought. He'd rather die than leave home without it. Do they have credit cards in Rusha? he asked himself in a solid American voice. No, sir, he replied. And they sure are a bunch of miserable sonuvabitches on that account.

As he proceeded to the gate, his mouth could feel the cool, fresh salvation of a forthcoming Bloody Mary. Who am I kidding, he rebuked himself rudely. I'm going to see Jodie, whether she wants it or not. And, just in case her salmon fisherman is there, I should pick up a gun, too. A nice, heavy Smith & Wesson. This is America—when is the last time you killed for a woman, Mr. Dubinsky? Are you afraid to die? Are you still in love with your best friend and employer's fiancée, Miss Michelle Morgan? Who tried to choke you to death for an unfathomable reason and would perhaps bite off your manhood afterwards? *Be generous, Dubinsky.*

The stewardess, peeling off the promotion junk, opened his ticket and asked him how he was doing today. He asked her (being perfectly within his ethnic tradition) if they served drinks before the takeoff.

. . .

As he drove north on I-5, he noticed with surprise that the Seattle sky was an unexpected cerulean blue, with the sun still gaining yards in the last quarter. He rolled down the windows of his Hertz T-bird, turned on the local hard-rock station. "Gonna break your legs/Gonna pluck your eyes," the band crooned. "And that's number five with a bullet," said the deejay with a disarming cheerfulness. That's not where the bullet should be, he thought, changing the station; the punk lyrics made him feel old, tired, longing for the barricades of yesteryear.

He glanced at the giant warehouses on the left, kept an eye out for the downtown signs, thought of the meaning of life. The three BMs he'd had on the plane put him into a lax, melancholy mood: there was nothing to be gained from this side trip, regardless of its outcome. And he had decided not to call in advance. Nothing would be gained from that either. All right, so he wouldn't find her—the house had an edge bigger than in roulette, so he'd check into a Holiday Inn, buy a local paper, go to a bar, listen to some music. And if, against all odds, he hit the right number and found her—well, he'd be very calm, there'd be no long-distance emoting, they would go out for a beer, if her lumberjack was not at home. If he was, well—back to Schedule A.

According to the map, Capitol Hill lay to the east of the freeway. He took the exit and drove on, racking his brain—was it right or left here? And the next one? And the one after that?"

After half an hour he gave up. It was completely dark now, and even with adequate street lighting the task was a hopeless one. He pulled in front of a coffee shop, walked in, and after a brief hesitation approached the pay phone.

She answered promptly.

"Just thought I'd stop by," he said.

"Oh, that's sweet of you." She paused. "Where exactly are you?"

He named the coffee shop.

"But that's only two blocks away." She fell silent again.

All those silences. He felt he was in the middle of a Bergman movie.

"If you already made plans . . . don't you have fifteen minutes for a cup of coffee? Please?"

"Okay," she said. "I'll be right over."

"You'll have no trouble recognizing me," he said. "I'm the guy on the white horse, although my armor could use a wax job."

"How about some body work? No dents?"

"I don't know if I can afford the rates."

"I'll see you, crazy Russki."

He saw her walk in and pause near the cigarette machine. He waved; she waved back and walked toward him. She was small, compact, normal, uncontrived. Men did not follow her ass with whistles, although it was nice and taut, which was not apparent in fashionable shapeless pants. She did not have the desperate bounce of Linda or the perfect swing of Nonna or Michelle. She walked with a somewhat absent air, immersed in her own thoughts; only a table away from him she looked up and greeted him with a shy smile. With Nonna, he would interpret this as a deliberate act of teasing; with Michelle, only twenty-four hours ago, he would've been crestfallen; with Jodie, he was touched. She was her own person, who lived—or tried to—her own life.

"Anything else you want?" he asked after she ordered her coffee.

She shook her head and apologized for not inviting him over. "It's a real mess. I stumble over things."

Recalling her apartment, he translated "the mess" as a dirty glass in the sink. He apologized for doing what she asked him not to and calling her. She apologized for having been rude on the phone.

"How about we stop apologizing?" he said. "How have you been?"

"Not too good," she said.

"Your boyfriend is in town? I thought it was salmon season now. Or is he a lumberjack?"

"It's not funny," she said. "Doug's not all that macho, he just talks that way. And he's not a lumberjack. He grows marijuana."

"He what?"

"Don't yell, please. It's pretty nerve-racking with the Feds snooping all the time. He already got one sentence, suspended."

"But you're holding on to him?"

She paused. "I'm trying not to. It's hard to say good-bye after five years. But it's even harder to stay. He's totally psychotic. He throws ugly scenes, he shoots at the cat . . ."

As she synopsized the soap opera of her life, he studied her expression, anticipating a teary conclusion. But Jodie's voice had no moisture in it. There was a matter-of-factness and "that's the way it is" between the lines. She was not trying to involve him in it as an ally or as a mentor. He did not feel obliged to interject her soliloquy with "I see's." He had a feeling of watching a well-edited slice-of-life documentary, a close-up of the face talking about her life. He was free to walk out of the theater or to stay.

"He tells me he's going to pour sugar into my car engine if I don't let him come back. And then he taunts me, 'Then you can go to the Feds and have me locked up.' As if I couldn't've done it a thousand times by now."

You've got to be a bastard, he thought, recalling his original impulse to get a gun. Bastards like Doug get nice girls like Jodie every time. Bastards like Dubinsky get nice girls like Linda every time. Maybe he should try to fix Doug up with Linda—or Sandy, never mind the bill . . .

She grew silent. "How's work?" he asked sullenly, realizing—again—the impracticality of his designs.

"Work helps." She paused and looked him in the eye. She had a warm look, her lips were curved only slightly, it was the mildest interest imaginable. "You know, you don't strike me as the happiest man alive," she said finally. "Are you still vice president?"

"If I'm a vice president," he said, "your friend Doug is God-father Corleone." He explained his flights to her. He told her about Slava, censoring himself on Michelle. He felt he did not have to explain too much; he felt she already knew most of the background, instinctively, emotionally; she was a long-lost sister (". . . but I lost the ring . . ."), with whom he had gone to bed, with pleasure, and would do so again . . . the incestuous nature of Mad Monk Dubinsky, he thought, round-ing the story of the mall investment. "But it's all right now," he added vaguely. "The new one worked out all right. We just went to Vegas to celebrate."

She smiled absently. "Doug used to go there, too."

"Fond memories, huh?"

She shook her head. "Doug is out. I'm even breaking in a new lock tomorrow."

"I wish I could help," he said, "but I'm lousy with tools."

"You're silly." She smiled. "What is a nice boy like you doing in the middle of a fast-buck scheme?"

"He's my friend," he said. "Lovers come and go; friends stay."

They fell silent for a moment. Then their eyes met, furtively, and locked in the air. He took her hand. "Is my time up?" he asked, begging her to save him from having to spell it out.

"Yes," she said. "Did you make a hotel reservation?"

He considered a lie, then shook his head.

"You have to stop relying on your charm, Dubinsky." She smiled again as she rose from the table.

"I can find a hotel, Jodie. Really. This is not Novosibirsk."

She took him by the arm as they walked out. "It's all right. I feel bad about the night you called. And all the stuff I said about your business card. I should've known right away you were a fake."

"Including the Russianness."

"I don't care if you're a Gypsy."

He opened the car door and paused. "I like you, Jodie."

She nodded. "Me, too. I think we can be good friends."

I still don't know what that means, coming from her, he thought, following her to her place—all two blocks of the way.

He made love to her with a tenderness and gentleness he did not know he had in him; he kissed every inch of her body, firm and trim yet soft under his mouth; he licked her and he soaked in her juices; when he finally entered her, he lay there for a moment, reluctant to move, because every move would bring him closer to the end. She responded to him, her body moved easily, anticipating deftly his every move; small, barely audible moans came from her, but her eyes were closed, and he did not mind, he knew the truth, and was only afraid she would mention Doug's name. But she did not, and when, after what seemed like hours, he finally came, burying his face in the sweet-tasting sweat of her neck, he clenched his fists in impotent fury, because he wanted it to go on forever.

In the morning they were silent, but it was a silence without hostility; each simply knew what the other one thought, and a spoken word would destroy the moment. Dubinsky felt the ambience was ideal: how many situations had he wrecked with his mouth?

As she rose to wash the cups, he rose, too; he placed his hands on her shoulders, very gently—no marks, no bruises, and his lips touched the curls on her warm neck. His hands intercepted the cup. "I'll do it."

"Okay." She lit a cigarette and said, "You're a nice, nice man, Oleg. But what you do—it doesn't make sense."

"Don't worry, I washed dishes before I became vice president."

"I'm talking about your scams, silly. You're just not the kind of person—"

"Are you kidding?" He almost dropped a cup. "*I* don't belong in the fast lane? *I* don't belong with Learjets and weekend trips to Paris and Rio?" *Jesus this is the second time we've been together, she already tells me how to live.*

"You don't belong in Leavenworth," she said. "I haven't

known you as long as Clive has, but I know enough about life, and I care enough about you, and I just wish you did something else with your life," she ended in a breaking voice. "You know, I look at Doug, I look at you, I don't want to live anymore. So maybe we shouldn't see each other again. Otherwise, I feel like I'm going to be some kind of a gun moll all my life. Can't you do something else?" She put her arms around his hips, sticking her nose into the small of his back.

He felt warm and tender. And excited. "*What* else?"

"I don't know. Teaching?" she said shyly.

Teaching had a stigma in Russia: losers taught; winners did things. "Look, my diploma is just a piece of paper in this country—"

She shrugged. "You told me it was Russian Ivy League."

"So?"

"So maybe a community college might hire you part-time, while you get some credits at the university. You want to send me a copy of your diploma? I'll look into it." And at the last moment she added, "If you want me to."

He nodded. The seeds were falling on fertile ground, but *teaching*? Don't you go into a skid if you brake too abruptly? "I'll have to move to Seattle, right?"

"No, you can just keep on commuting. Nobody's dragging you here, unless you think it's—Dubinsky, why are you such a fool?" She paused, waiting for her anger to pass. Anger makes things too obvious. "All I'm saying is that if you do move, you're welcome to stay here. Until you find a place of your own."

She is talking about it as if it had all been decided, he thought on his way to the airport. I forgot to slam the door, and I'm not even sure I should have.

On the plane he started, as usual, with two BMs, no time to waste, but when the long-awaited buzz arrived, he registered with surprise that he no longer welcomed it. He had serious decisions to make and it was interfering with his decision-making process. The buzz was encouraging him to go back to

Vegas, to join Slava and Michelle, to go to Acapulco, the hell
with the papers, somehow he'd get in and out. He fought back:
he had no wine with his lunch, and three black coffees after
it. Every word Jodie'd said made sense to him now. Teaching
was not such a bad idea, come to think of it; there was little
money in it, but did he really need to stay in penthouse suites
in Vegas? But how different was Seattle from San Murray?
Did he need New York that badly? Had he left Moscow for
Seattle? No, he just left . . . and Jodie . . . she left some bruises
on his ego, but let's be objective now, Dubinsky: how much
of an ego can you afford?

As they approached New York, he decided that he'd done
enough thinking for one day, and had a double Scotch after
dinner. He walked through the terminal in a jaunty, unhurried
manner; no one waited for him on East Thirtieth Street; no
one would make a scene about having to warm up the dinner.
And then he saw the papers.

PIZDO DEFECTOR REVEALS COMMODITIES SCAM
ARRESTS IN VEGAS AND D.C.

Unable to say a word, barely able to remain on his feet,
Dubinsky fished in his pocket for change. He carried the paper
to a bar where, with the help of another Scotch, he tried to
make sense of it. The truth could not be any simpler, he learned,
fighting his way through the pages filled with bikinied bodies
who'd just won two thousand dollars in a lottery, with the
soap opera stars' divorces, and with dishwasher ads. According to a recent Pizdo defector, Mr. P. Rod Azh-ny had liked
Slava's idea so much that he lined up several fronts to buy
pizdorvanium contracts for himself. Both the SEC and the
Republic of Pizdo were hot on Azh-ny's trail, and the FBI
spokesman expressed no doubt that good old P. Rod, stripped
of his diplomatic immunity, would be apprehended soon. Several of his cohorts had been detained in Las Vegas and Washington, D.C. Among them: Mr. Clive Rothman, 30, a recent
Soviet émigré—

Dubinsky's every pore was clogged, his every vent sealed. An enormous black mass filled his lungs; he could not breathe. He grabbed the bar's railing, as the bottles on the shelves played musical chairs—now it was Beefeater, now it was Cuervo Gold without a place to rest on, now it was Dubinsky, Specially Blended and Distilled in Russkiland under the Supervision of the State Committee of Communist Crooks by Special Appointment to the Politburo . . . He stared at the rest of the article unseeingly, and bits and pieces of hack nonsense floated in front of his eyes: the KGB connection, the Taviani Brothers who controlled the Gobi Inn; Qaddafi, Mossad, the CIA, the Teamsters, the Omega Seven.

"You okay?" asked the bartender. Dubinsky nodded mutely. "You want a refill, you gotta order now, we're closing."

"You ever been arrested?" Dubinsky asked. "You ever been through a lie detector?"

"What's that to you, pal?" The bartender looked at him unpleasantly.

"Nothing." He climbed off the chair and walked away.

Jail, jail, jail: they would be able to run freight trains through his ass by the time he was eligible for parole. Or would it be deportation? And he might have already ruined his chances for a job by selling Vladimir down the river. Had Michelle ever done anything with the article?

He dialed their own number on East Thirtieth Street first. A male voice said hello. Dubinsky hung up. He took off his windbreaker, his cotton shirt from Barney's; his T-shirt was soaked through in the middle of the air-conditioned terminal. He went to the men's room, took off the T-shirt, stuffed it into his shoulder bag. Threw cold water on his face. Put on his cotton shirt from Barney's. Walked out and dialed Michelle's number. It rang three times. He waited. An unfamiliar female voice answered. He asked for Michelle. She's out of town, the woman said. Tell her it's Oleg, he said; I'll wait.

"Dubinsky," Michelle said, "where the hell are you?"

"Miami." He had read enough thrillers.

"Don't come back, Oleg," she said, and in his heart he was

saddened again, for there was pain and bitterness in her voice. She doesn't deserve it, he thought; it's all crazy Slava's greed. "Good luck," she said. "Read the papers."

"Will you be all right?" he asked. "They're not gonna arrest you?"

"No," she said. "Oleg, hang up, it's enough time for them to trace the call, please run, you dumb crazy Russki jerk—"

"I love you," he lied, before hanging up. He could not think of anyone who would not feel even a tiny bit better when told that simple line. He leaned against a column and took a deep breath. He was ready. He had finally mastered the telling of a lie—which, he realized now, had been his objective all along— *not* to tell all the truth and nothing but the truth—*not* to lie through his teeth at every turn: no, from now on he would be telling the truth *and* the lies, but he'd do it of his own free will and he'd know the difference.

He glanced at the video. There was a flight to Seattle, the last one for the day departing in fifteen minutes. Omens, my life is nothing but omens, he thought lyrically, turning into O. J. Simpson and flying over the crowds and the counters toward Ticketing.

Ten

The phone rang. "Hello," Dubinsky said. There was silence. "You'll have to try again, I can't hear you."

He was sitting at his desk, grading papers. Unlike other instructors, he did not complain about the chore: how could he, the little jerks had to learn how to *write*, where else would they learn it, on TV? Their language was thick with "you know"'s and "like"'s, and in his class they were not getting away with it. Jamie Alvarez, his best student, told him once, giggling, that she was ribbed at home for speaking English with an East European accent.

"It is better to speak with an accent," he said in his increasingly self-congratulatory manner, "than express yourself in the like-you-know-far-out manner. I would strongly recommend, however, that you attend Mr. Castro's class once in a while. He speaks Spanish with wonderful Castilian inflections. Your Latin heritage—"

"Yeah, yeah," she waved, "*la raza*, ethnic pride, I know all that stuff—"

"Many well-educated and even better motivated people put in a lot of time and effort to inculcate our national consciousness with 'all that stuff,' " he said sternly. "Wouldn't you like to read Gabriel García Márquez in the original some day?"

"Who's he?"

Dubinsky removed his glasses in frustration. He did not need them that much, but he felt they reinforced the academic image that he occasionally found difficult to maintain otherwise.

"I gotta go, Mr. Dubinsky. *'Byyye!'*" She rushed off, her long, tanned legs leaping in the air.

"Vaya con Dios, hija mia," he said solemnly.

Now, back home, as he was going over Miss Alvarez's uphill struggles with tenses, he thought that perhaps one course of English as a second language plus one course of Russian were not enough to qualify him as a full-fledged member of academia. But he loved it anyway. Students stayed over during breaks, trading jokes, bombarding him with questions, unloading their worries. He was less popular with the faculty, most of whom lived in constant fear of unemployment. He did not, he knew he would take it philosophically, he considered what he had a fluke, and with his two courses he could hardly regard himself as their peer. So what, he thought; it was a start. Someone knocked on the door. Dubinsky shrugged— Jodie was in Boise, who else?—and peered into the Magic Eye. Then he flung the door open. "You bastard."

"What a welcome," Slava said.

It was just like old times. Sitting on the floor with Johnnie Walker between them and "Highway 61 Revisited" on the stereo.

"You done good, Dub," Slava nodded. "Moscow in Seattle, who could think."

"*Two* rooms. And no more sharing a kitchen and a bathroom with fifteen people."

"Can't have everything. But the ambience, pure Gorky Street. I could walk out of here straight into the Mayakovsky monument."

"It's a home."

"Not a household?"

Dubinsky sighed. "I guess we'll be moving together. Soon."

"Who's undecided?"

"Both." He paused. "We have a great time together, I care about her a lot, I don't know what I'd do without her—what do you call it, love?"

"Comfortably close," Slava said.

"I didn't really know Michelle, did I?"

"You didn't know her at all. But neither did I. It didn't turn out quite the way I thought. We don't see each other anymore."

"I'm sorry."

Slava shrugged. "Life, Dubinsky. Nothing but."

He looks so much older, Dubinsky thought. Forty, at least. All his hair has silver endings. Should I nod and say, You paid the price? and he'd nod again and say, Life, Dubinsky? We know each other too well for that.

"Michelle is a fine girl," Slava said bitterly, "but the class showed—she had no stomach for life with a convicted felon."

"But you were never—"

"What do you think I am?" Slava grinned. "It's suspended, but it's a sentence. I'll get rid of the record in a couple of years, my attorney's working on it, but it was all too much for her. I must say, she did it with class, too—I had been right about her all along, I just didn't understand the full meaning of the word. She found a lawyer, she arranged for the bail . . . she came through, Dubinsky. It was later, we went to this bar—Hanratty's, I think—and she said to me, 'Clive, it won't work.' " He paused and took a deep breath. "I thought I didn't hear her right—it's a noisy place, I guess that's why she'd picked it. But she was right, we don't belong together."

It is still painful for him, Dubinsky thought, and he felt Slava's pain together with him.

"Don't *you* look sad," Slava said. "The field is open. Give her a call. She remembered you with affection. I guess you guys patched it up at the end."

"Yeah." An unpleasant but necessary lie by omission.

"So . . . ?"

"Aw, who are you kidding? If the two of you couldn't make a go of it . . ."

"She did warn you to stay away at the end, though."

"*You* saved my ass at the end."

"It was nothing, Dubinsky. Don't even think about it. I told them you knew nothing about it, but they were not particularly interested in you anyway."

Slava stood up and paced the room. "Pretty town, Seattle, isn't it?" he said after a pause. "Except for the weather."

"It's not that bad. And I like it. Fits my mood."

"That's not good, Dubinsky. We must do something about your mood. Send you to some tropical climate. What do you make at your school?"

Dubinsky coughed and named the figure.

"What?" Slava stopped. "Is that what they pay their educators? No wonder the country is teeming with illiterates. God, it's no better than Russkiland."

"I'm not tenured," Dubinsky said defensively. "I'm part-time. I'm just starting—what do you expect?"

"There's only so much of a range between the bottom and the top levels in a given field." Slava grew angry. "You're wasting yourself again, Dubinsky. Goddamnit, you're just hopeless. Moscow—San Murray—Seattle—"

"Thanks a lot." Dubinsky rose to his feet. "I'm gonna put fresh sheets on the bed."

They had a brief argument about their respective sleeping places, but their hearts were not in it. Dubinsky lay down on the couch and closed his eyes. Goddamnit, I still don't know shit, he thought. Here I was, pretty content, getting along, if not exactly ahead; true, there's little money in it, perhaps even less prospect than I had told Slava, but I enjoy it, I really do—

"Dubinsky," Slava called from the bedroom.

"*Nu?*"

"You're flying to Rangoon tomorrow. Stay overnight and come back."

Dubinsky lay in silence, clutching his heart, telling it, No visa for you, no grand-aunt in Rangoon, you know too much, you're not going anywhere—

"Silence generally denotes 'yes,' " Slava said. "Good night."

After a few minutes or hours, Dubinsky got up, and, to jam this subversive station, this Ginger Baker solo that his heart was sending, he reached for Johnnie Walker and finished it out of the bottle. He took a deep breath and pressed his forehead against the window glass. The Rangoon night was hot and clammy, even hotter than the Pizdoan one. Police pedicabs were all over the place, looking for hashish-smuggling part-time community college instructors of Russian extraction. And Jodie said, "If I see you being arrested, I'll leave." Well, here I stand, just like in a Hollywood movie: hands flapping in the air like some moronic bird's wings, an attaché case lying open at my feet, and twenty-nine Uzis pointed at my vital organs. "I won't be your gun moll," Jodie said. Gun? he screamed, as Rangoon's finest started disturbing his heretofore peaceful anal passage with their arsenal. Who *did* you want to be? A *friend*? I've got a friend! Then how come it's your ass being poked, not his? she said, climbing aboard the 747.

You never told me you loved me, he called in despair. I should've, I know, she said, handing her boarding pass to the stewardess. Well say it now! She turned to face him, an expression of infinite pity mixed with curiosity on her face, and her lips moved; but the roar of the engine drowned the sound, and lip-reading was not Dubinsky's forte.

In the morning, the sky was overcast as usual, and drops of rain fell uncertainly on the window pane. The air was not conducive to talking, and their silence over coffee felt appropriate.

Dubinsky morosely stared into his cup, trying to prophesize, but Melitta No. 4 filter did a good job, the liquid was smooth, not a speck floating in it. If there were any dregs, they would be in Spanish anyway, he thought. If I want to read my future, I should buy Jamaican. His mood could not have been any darker. His job was a joke, the city was a backwater, and the woman who had lured him—he was convinced of that by now—into this neck of the rain forest was playing some damn games with him. Why couldn't she plain tell him she loved him?

"How the hell am I going to get to Rangoon? I don't have a visa or a passport."

"You told me you have a refugee travel document to go to Canada, right? You can get a visa at the Rangoon Airport."

Dubinsky paused. "Can you take all this junk back to New York? A suitcase, a garment bag, and a cardboard box?" He realized that in merely two years he had tripled his possessions. Where will *that* stop.

"Sure." Schmuck, Slava thought; still afraid Jodie might change his mind for him.

"I just don't want any tears," Dubinsky lied. He was sure there wouldn't be any—not in his presence, anyway. She was too tough. Nor was she one to use it as emotional blackmail. Too straight for it. "What's in Rangoon, anyway?" He started interlaying his records with flannel shirts to make sure they didn't break; he did not want to waste time by going out and getting protective cardboard.

"Just a package. Perfectly safe. Outrageously legal. I'd just rather send it with someone I can trust. You're my friend, Dubinsky. Without you, I'm nowhere, I'll have to trust one of those Levines . . ."

As Dubinsky was moving the contents of his desk into the suitcase, he saw the glossy pictures of Jodie and himself on a rafting trip they'd taken down the Snohomish River a month ago. Here they were, in bright orange life vests, laughing hysterically over their soaked cigarettes. . . . He swallowed hard as he felt his chest contract. Good-bye, innocent pacific happiness in the slow lane. Back to the risks of the fast lane. "Back to the subject of Rangoon," he said. "No drugs?"

"No drugs."

"Because I'm not good at crossing borders."

Slava chuckled. "You're a natural. You just don't know it."

Right, Dubinsky thought, customs officials are officials, no different from Volkodav, they can spot a schmuck a mile away. The only person who had ever thought him capable of mischief was the security man at the Gobi Inn, of whom Dubinsky now thought warmly. Should drop him a postcard from Rangoon. "The 'son' made it to his room but is back in trouble now." Unless the bastard had been shot by some drunken cowboy.

On the way to the airport the sun peered in through the clouds, further depressing Dubinsky. Slava filled him in on the goings-on in New York. Konstantin, San Murray long behind him, had been in a group show and was broadly panned from right to left. Kirill had met with Slava and immediately spun a dozen fabulous-sounding schemes. "Long on PR, short on practicality," Slava chuckled. "Who wants to enroll in a Gulag Therapy Center program, to be locked up for days on bread and water? They only talk about it." Apelsinov had published a book about his Times Square adventures and mentioned Dubinsky in it.

"Really," Dubinsky said dryly. "I can imagine."

"Don't feel sad," Slava said. "I mean, I understand how you had fun in Seattle, and Jodie seems like a nice type—she took you in, no questions asked . . . hell, maybe she'll want to join you in New York."

"No, she won't," Dubinsky whispered, staring straight ahead.

"A good woman is hard to find, Dubinsky."

"You're telling me."

"I'm telling you something I've learned since I saw you last. A good woman—"

"Please shut up."

They rode in silence. Slava followed the signs to the Sea-Tac Airport. "We're almost there."

"Listen," Dubinsky said suddenly, "how come you never asked me to join you in your operations back in Russkiland?"

"It wasn't your scene, Dubinsky. You've seen all that trash I had to deal with. It's different here. Think Rangoon, Dubinsky, think Hong Kong, think Rio—what a life! This time we're going straight to the top."

Rangoon, Dubinsky thought obediently. Just outside the Golden Triangle. Top of the World, Ma. You don't belong in Leavenworth, Jodie said. He glanced at Slava and noticed a hundred new wrinkles. Is he carrying nitro in his breast pocket, too?

"It won't work, Slava," he whispered.

"What did you say?" Slava parked outside the rental agency and headed for the office without waiting for the answer.

For a moment Dubinsky watched Slava drumming his fingers on the desk, saying something to the clerk, making her laugh. I can't, Dubinsky said, I simply can't. He came up to the pay phone, punched Operator, and asked for a number in Boise. She answered on the second ring.

"When are you coming back?" he said, in the way of greeting.

"Tonight, as planned. What's wrong, Oleg? Are you all right?"

He was silent. She did not need to spell it out. Her voice just told him all he needed to know.

"Talk to me, goddamnit!" she yelled. "ARE YOU ALL RIGHT?"

"Jodie," he said, "Jodie—" He turned to face Slava, who was waiting for him so patiently, and who now turned away, so gentlemanly, God forbid he should overhear a word or constrain his friend with his presence.

"Jodie," Dubinsky repeated, taking a breath deep enough to suck the whole Sea-Tac International into his lungs, "how come you never told me you loved me?"

"What?" She was silent. "Oleg, where are you? No, don't tell me. I don't want to know." Now, he could tell, she was struggling hard not to blow up, no wonder, people don't call you with questions like this at 10:00 A.M.

"Dubinsky. I don't play with words. I told Doug I loved him, it only made things worse. How come *you* never told me you loved me? Never mind, it's not important—Dubinsky, are you okay? You're not defecting back to your damn Russkiland, you lousy sonuvabitch?"

"I'm okay," he said, "you don't have to—"

"Of course I love you," she said. "And if I don't see you tonight—"

"I'll see you tonight," he said, raising his voice just loud enough to bring it within Slava's earshot. Just so he wouldn't have to say it first.

They stood in silence, facing the parking lot, disregarding the shuttle bus driver's announcements to get aboard.

"So Jodie does tell you what to do," Slava said in a sober, Sergeant Friday voice.

Dubinsky shook his head. "She doesn't even know you're here."

"So what is it? Are you having a relapse with that Truth business?"

Dubinsky sighed. Love won't convince him. Truth-seeking won't convince him. Ethical joys of teaching, forget it. The clean, unambiguous beauty of Mount Olympus on a clear day— what a laugh. *You're losing a friend at the speed of light, Dubinsky.* "Remember I asked you how come you never got me involved back in Russkiland? You were right then—not now. I can't go again through that night at La Guardia when I saw the paper about your arrest. I'd like to go to Hong Kong and Rio, but I'd rather do it differently. I'm not prepared to pay the price, okay? There—I'm a coward, Slava!" he yelled.

"Calm down," Slava said quietly. "My hearing is quite good. You're not a coward, and you're right. If you're afraid, don't do it. Ride this funny bus with me to the terminal, would you?"

Dubinsky practically flew aboard. His feet were as light as his heart, and his heart was lighter than a feather and clearer than the mountain air.

"One of these days you'll change your mind, Dubinsky—"

"Will you keep the door open?"

Slava nodded. I'll keep my door open, too, Dubinsky wanted to say, and you might need mine before I need yours—but how can I tell you this now? And does it matter who's using whose door first so long as both are open?

Slava looked away. "We need friends, Dubinsky. I tell you, if you kept it up with your pouting, I would've dumped Michelle. Lovers come and go—"

"—friends stay."

The bus arrived at the terminal, and they got out. Then they hugged and stood on the sidewalk for a while. "You've got to go," Dubinsky said. There was something about that hug he did not like.

"Yeah. Come visit sometime," Slava said in a small voice, still looking away, and started on his way; the doors slid open.

I don't know what it is, Dubinsky thought; why didn't this hug feel the way it would have a few years ago? Are we older and weaker? Are we more American, and thus more likely to think that only certain types of people do this sort of thing in public? Or are we all of the above plus no longer Dub and Slava but Dubinsky and Clive? His heart contracted, and he was about to go, not quite knowing where, when Slava called out, "Dubinsky, how the hell are you going to get home with all this?" He indicated the luggage on the sidewalk.

Dubinsky shrugged. How could he think of transportation at a moment like this? "There's an express bus, I think."

Slava sighed and, shaking his head reprovingly, handed him a twenty. "Take a cab. I dragged you out here, after all."

And he was gone, a suddenly smaller, huddled, shrunken figure, dissolving into the glass and the steel of the Electric Airlines terminal.

Slava was right—again, Dubinsky thought, waving at the fading image. I do need a cab. I have to make the class on time.